THE OLD WEST AT ITS WILDEST

It was a world where redskins and bluecoats fought battles that would decide the fate of the American frontier. Katherine Coltrane's own battle to survive took her from an Indian camp to the red-light districts of roaring mining towns, from dealing in men's desires to beating them at their own business games, from robbing stage coaches to running the biggest ranch in the Wyoming territory. Her friends and foes, lovers and partners included prospectors, outlaws, shootists, generals, politicians, railroad barons, black cowboys, and mountain men. She was a woman like no other in a time like no other, living and loving lawlessly and dangerously—in an enthralling novel by one of the most powerful storytellers to capture the Old West and bring to vivid life the people who made it great.

THE SEEKERS

"Fans of historical westerns will appreciate the author's mastery of settings and events and his avoidance of the cliches that plague this genre."

—*Publishers Weekly*

THE SEEKERS

Paul A. Hawkins

A SIGNET BOOK

SIGNET
Published by the Penguin Group
Penguin Books USA Inc., 375 Hudson Street,
New York, New York 10014, U.S.A.
Penguin Books Ltd, 27 Wrights Lane,
London W8 5TZ, England
Penguin Books Australia Ltd, Ringwood,
Victoria, Australia
Penguin Books Canada Ltd, 10 Alcorn Avenue,
Toronto, Ontario, Canada M4V B32
Penguin Books (N.Z.) Ltd, 182–190 Wairau Road,
Auckland 10, New Zealand

Penguin Books Ltd, Registered Offices:
Harmondsworth, Middlesex, England
First published by Signet,
an imprint of Dutton Signet,
a division of Penguin Books USA Inc.

First Printing, July, 1994
10 9 8 7 6 5 4 3 2 1

 REGISTERED TRADEMARK—MARCA REGISTRADA

Printed in the United States of America

Faith!
To Peggy Walsh
and Frank Moreni,
colleagues always

BOOK ONE

Foreword

Excerpts from a September 1904 interview with the writer-editor Henry Burlingame of Harper's Weekly.

Now, the notion that life on the frontier was a romantic, rewarding experience is balderdash. I have to call it "frontier" for wont of a better word. It was a misnomer. It was only a frontier to invaders who put their stakes down in a land that had been settled by a native civilization hundreds of years before we ever arrived. Whatever, during the period that I worked out there, there wasn't a more dangerous and unpredictable countryside that I can imagine. And I shall say the same about many of the men and women I met while on assignment. They, too, were often a dangerous and unpredictable lot. Survival. That's what it always came down to, survival. Women? Yes, a few women, several I chanced to meet in my tenure of fifteen years. Jane Canarray was one. Notorious, indeed, a regular harridan. She had her own set of rules. Calamity personified. But even so, this woman had a heart for humanity. The other one you mentioned, Katherine Coltrane. Well, she was one of the most complex human beings I ever met. A beautiful woman, too, make no mistake about that, and some say as nefarious as Calamity Jane. There are dozens of stories about Katherine Coltrane, but she and Jane were as different as night and day. There were only two things these women had in common. At one time, they were both mule skinners, and they were both soiled doves. Jane, penniless, ended up in a pine box in Deadwood. Kate Coltrane? She was a miraculous survivor.

Prologue

"Judas Priest, hold 'er up, Charlie!" George Lathrop screamed. "They've got a piece of artillery!"

Charles Towson, yelling "whoa, whoa," began rearing back on the reins of the four-horse team at the same time Lathrop was elevating his shotgun. Directly in front of the stage not more than forty yards up the rutted road in a narrow gully were two men standing beside a small cannon, an eight-pound howitzer. One held a burning torch, the other a white flag and a rifle.

"What the hell!" cried Lathrop. His eyes were bulging.

"Put that goddamned turkey-buster down, George," Towson shouted at his partner. He pulled back again on the reins, the stage stalled in the middle of the road, and the heads of several passengers poked out between the canvas shrouds covering the windows. "Put that gun down, George, the son of a bitch is ready to torch the thing. For crisesakes, he's got it leveled right down on us!"

From one of the windows of the Cheyenne–Deadwood coach, an alarmed passenger asked, "What's going on?"

George Lathrop, leaping clear of his seat yelled, "Everybody out ... get the hell out of there. Some fool's getting ready to blow this rig to kingdom come! Never saw anything like this in all my born days!"

One passenger, grasping his hat, stepped out of the coach, momentarily stared up the road at the bizarre scene, and suddenly screamed, "Look out!" He dived headlong into a tumble of rocks at the roadside.

Simultaneously, a rider, his face hidden by a big, blue bandanna, rode out from the cottonwoods on the other side of the coach brandishing a Winchester. He shouted up to a stunned Charles Towson, "Everybody just sit ... hold it still. They're not going to touch off that howitzer unless you put up a fuss about this . . ."

"No fuss, mister, no fuss," Towson said. "No, sir, we ain't moving."

"Throw the box down," the rider called to Towson. And, pointing the Winchester at George Lathrop, he ordered, "Get rid of that shotgun." Lathrop, carefully setting the gun aside, stepped away with his hands in the air. Towson, fumbling around under his high seat, finally heaved the box clear, saying, "You got it, young feller . . . there she is."

The masked bandit's laugh was light, boyish. Then, back to Charles Towson: "One more, mister, come on. Toss the other one down, now . . . the real one. Hurry up, before my partners down there get impatient."

Rummaging about under the seat once more, Towson sighed. "Yassir . . . yassir . . . other one, got it right here, I do." And with a little grunt of despair, he chucked it from the wagon.

"Well-done, men, well-done." With a flourish of his rifle, the rider said, "All right, everyone aboard, now . . . move out, and hold on to your seats . . . he's going to set that thing off soon as you get clear."

"Holy shit!" Charles Towson gave the reins a mighty flick, and the horses moved briskly ahead, swerving around the cannon placement below. Not more than thirty yards down the road, both Towson and Lathrop, horrified, glanced back over their shoulders. The two men by the small cannon had already whirled it about, and moments later, a tremendous boom rent the late afternoon air; a black ball went zooming over the wagon; the four horses bolted, and the northbound stage went bouncing crazily down the road and disappeared in a cloud of dust around a distant bend.

A short time later, the howitzer, its muzzle still spewing black smoke, was standing alone; its two attendants had melted away in the adjacent cottonwoods; there was a long, shrill shout. "Yahooo!" There was a clatter of hooves from the rimrock in back of the cottonwoods, then, silence, nothing more but a few startled magpies crying out, flitting through the shadowy trees looking for sanctuary.

In the rolling hills several miles above the Chugwater stage station, up alongside the banks of Sybille Creek, Buford Reasons caved in the side of the metal-rimmed box with the flat end of his ax. The lock shattered, and Alva

Tompkins thew open the fractured lid. A few letters, a packet, some loose coins. Buford Reasons wiped the sweat from his brow, cursed, "Shit!" and began hacking away at the second box. Ultimately, it flew apart. Alva Tompkins gleefully shouted, "Lord 'a mighty. O sweet charity!" Grinning broadly between his whiskers, he plunged his hands into the box, withdrew several packets of neatly packaged scrip. "Brand-new!" he exclaimed, shoving one of the bundles under the nose of Buford. "Smell it! Smell this stuff. Sure 'nuff, it ain't smelling like hen hockey, is it?"

"Must be a fortune, here." Buford Reasons beamed. He, too, reached down into the box, plucked out a small bundle, and tossed it to the third member of the trio. "Goddamned right, you were, Kate. Two boxes, just like you said, one a fake. Look at this . . . enough to set a man crazy in the heat."

"Or a sweet split-tail like you, Katie!" screamed Alva Tompkins. "Enough for a king's ransom . . . enough to buy yourself a herd of critters."

Katherine Coltrane, her blue bandanna hanging loosely from her neck, a faded drover's hat tilted back over her upswept mass of brown hair, wafted the money under her nose. Lovely new greenbacks. Yes, what a delicate fragrance, almost as sweet as prairie roses. Yes, what a wonderful bouquet of posies she and her two partners had plucked from the roadside dust, never to reach the greedy hands of the Deadwood squatters. She smiled. Her lovable old coots had such little use for money. Oh, but she had use of it, she certainly did.

After hiding the two boxes and stuffing the money into a gunny sack, the three rode away, taking a wide circuitous route, covering their tracks in the hardpan, riding back and forth through tumbles of sage, juniper, and buffalo grass, ultimately hitting the trail up to the pine-flocked homesteads on Bluegrass Creek.

Chapter One

Katherine Coltrane

May, 1876. Fort Fetterman, Wyoming Territory.

They entered the fort late in the afternoon, a troop of twenty-four mounted soldiers, two supply wagons to the rear with seven Indian women and two old men perched on top. Amid the furor of General George Crook's preparations for his campaign to the north against the Lakota and Cheyenne, the small party attracted nothing more than a few curious looks.

The captives riding on the two wagons were from one of Crazy Horse's bands. One, a white woman, had been missing for five years. Except for Katherine Coltrane's tall stature and greenish-blue eyes, she appeared to be just as much Indian as any of the other unhappy, blanket-draped women with her. The Indian captives were taken to a large tent shelter for food and additional blankets and clothing. Katherine Coltrane was taken to the headquarters building where she sat on a chair outside Colonel Benjamin Bradford's office.

Inside Colonel Bradford's office, Lieutenant Thomas Clybourn made his report. Lieutenant Clybourn's troopers captured the small Sioux group on the Little Powder River. In an unexpected encounter with one of Crazy Horse's bands, most of the Indians escaped across the river after pinning down the troopers with a barrage of rifle fire from willows on the opposite shore. Two of Clybourn's men had sustained superficial wounds before the Indians retreated and disappeared in the dusk down the river. Lieutenant Clybourn had been unable to estimate how many were in the moving village, probably no more than a hundred, but the braves who had opened fire were equipped with repeating rifles, and he thought any pursuit on the following morning was ill-advised. The famed Indian scout, Porter Webb, and a

Miniconjou breed, Joseph Brings Yellow, volunteered to follow the band to ascertain the natives' intentions, but other signs and distant sightings already had indicated an exodus of many Indians toward the valleys to the north.

"They definitely aren't moving back toward the reservations," Clybourn said. "The Coltrane woman says the tribes are gathering somewhere to the north for their annual ceremonies ... Sun Dance ... Sacred Arrow renewal rites, things like that. She didn't say much more. In fact, she's pretty upset about this whole affair."

"Upset?" Colonel Bradford said. He drummed his fingers on the desk. "Well, who in the hell isn't upset around here, Mister Clybourn? Katherine Coltrane, is it? Once a freighting family. Parents passed on. Good people ..."

"You know her, sir?"

"Personally, no," said Colonel Bradford. "I am surprised she's alive. A train her older brother was leading was attacked back in seventy-one or seventy-two below Laramie. Looted, burned by renegade Oglala. There were no survivors ... not until, now."

"She's distressed," Clybourn said. "Half-stunned, like maybe in a state of shock. For a while I had a hard time of it talking to her. Shall I bring her in?"

Colonel Bradford shook his head. "No, Lieutenant. It's bad enough sometimes trying to understand a sane woman out in this infernal land, much less one in distress. No, I'll wait until tomorrow. Until she gets her new bearings; gets herself adjusted to being a white woman again."

"That may take some doing, sir. She just seems to be staring around but not seeing much of anything. You want me to put her with the rest of those women ... those two old codgers, bed her down in that squad tent for the night?"

Colonel Bradford replied, "She's a white woman, isn't she?"

"Yes, sir, and even in that Indian garb, a quite attractive one, too."

"Well, take her down to Slaymaker's boardinghouse," Bradford said. "Put her up there for the night, and tell Manny the army's paying for it. See if you can get anything more out of her. I'll talk to Miss Coltrane tomorrow morning, find out what she wants to do, where we can send her. Back down to Cheyenne, I suppose. That's where the Coltranes based their freighters."

"Yes, sir," answered Lieutenant Clybourn. "But begging your pardon, sir, I don't think that's where she'll be wanting to go."

"And why not? She can't stay here."

Lieutenant Clybourn paused at the door and saluted. "She wants to go back to the Powder River country, sir. During the fracas, she got separated from her family. Her Indian family, that is. She says her mother-in-law is a sister to Crazy Horse. Her mother-in-law has her daughter, a four-year-old, and she wants the little girl back. Says she knows what the bluecoats do to women and children when they raid villages."

Lieutenant Clybourn and Sergeant Marvel Hansen escorted Katherine Coltrane down to Manny Slaymaker's boardinghouse, a small hotel consisting of eight rooms and dining facilities. Manny and his wife, Mary, were already doing a booming business, housing several officers and four members of the press who had come to follow General Crook's campaign into the northern valleys; they quartered Katherine in the one remaining room, a small cubicle to the back of the building, nothing fancy, a cot, commode, table and chair, and a tiny mirror. The lone window faced north toward the North Platte River, away from the confusions of the overcrowded fort.

Katherine's attention remained on the room briefly. "I understand everyone's concern," she said haltingly, "but it would have been just as well if I had been left with the others. Some of them don't understand any of this. They're afraid."

"Afraid? Afraid of what?" asked Clybourn, standing at the tiny doorway. "They have nothing to fear. They're being taken care of . . . fed. Even sleeping rolls being put in for them . . . good food, coffee."

"You don't understand," Katherine Coltrane said. "They've heard the stories. They've talked with others, some of the Cheyenne who were attacked in their village."

Clybourn knew of the attack on Two Moons's and Little Wolf's peaceful hunting village on the Powder. Colonel Joseph Reynolds had believed the camp to be that of Tashunka-Witko, Crazy Horse, the elusive Sioux chief who had consistently shunned the reservation, making the unceded lands his home for more than eight years. The mistake was compounded when the Cheyenne, recapturing their entire pony herd from Reynold's command, escaped to the north and took refuge for the rest of the winter and spring with Crazy Horse's people. General Crook, humiliated and incensed, had Colonel Reynolds court-martialed. And, now, it was no secret—General Crook was obsessed with capturing or destroying Crazy Horse, his Oglala people, and, indeed, the whole Indian nation. Lieutenant Clybourn said, "That was a terrible blunder, Miss Coltrane, a big mistake ..."

Katherine Coltrane smiled bitterly, "They're always mistakes, aren't they? Sand Creek ... Washita. I want my daughter back. Don't you understand? I want Julia back before she becomes another tragic mistake in the whole bungled affair. She's all I have now."

Clybourn nodded. "Yes ... yes, I understand, and maybe it will all work out. Once everyone is back on the reservations, we can help you get it sorted out, and find your daughter."

"No, Mister Clybourn," Katherine said, "none of you seem to understand. The government has broken the treaty again, ordering these people back. They're not going back peacefully. It's already been decided. Mato-Nazin told me himself. There's going to be another big war, just like with Red Cloud and Dull Knife. Many people are going to die."

"Mato-Nazin?"

"Standing Bear ... the father of my daughter, Blue Star ... Julia. I call her Julia. They call her Wicapi Hinto, Blue Star. Crazy Horse is my uncle-in-law. He tells everything to the family. He says, 'We are going to fight the white man, again.' Now, everyone is saying it. Good Lord, Mister Clybourn, this is what few seem to understand."

"I understand their plight," confessed Lieutenant Clybourn. "I do."

"And, mine?"

"Yes, of course, Miss Coltrane, I'll do what I can for you, I promise."

"I want Julia back," Katherine Coltrane said determinedly. "Get me a horse, and I'll ride up there, myself."

Clybourn shook his head and gave Sergeant Hansen a pathetic look.

Marvel Hansen, a veteran soldier, shrugged and said, "That's impossible, Miss Coltrane. Against orders, for one thing, and another, it's a foolish act of desperation. You'd likely perish before you ever got up there."

"Would you have me perish down here, instead?"

"The army will see to your well-being," Clybourn said.

"Fundless ... without family. Good heavens, I'm destitute!"

"Your place in Cheyenne. We'll get you back there," assured Clybourn. "By the end of the summer, we can check the reservation, work out a thorough search through Fort Robinson, the agents there."

Katherine, sitting on the edge of the small bed, stared disconsolately down at the plank floor. "Cheyenne? ... our house?" she asked. "Lord, if the neighbors haven't looked out for it, it's probably full of pack rats, by now. Five years? My brother's dead. So am I, as far as everyone knows. Our wagons are gone, all except the Kern freights we left behind, and I suppose they're useless from neglect."

Mary Slaymaker arrived and pushed through the small doorway. She was carrying a big kettle of hot water, towels and clothing draped over her other arm and shoulder. "Let the woman get herself washed up right proper," she said to Lieutenant Clybourn.

"Yes," nodded Clybourn, stepping aside.

Sergeant Hansen said to Katherine, "You speak Siouan, Miss Coltrane?"

"Yes ... enough, I suppose."

"Well, if you want, I'll go down later with you, and you can talk to your friends at the big tent and explain everything is going to be all right. We'll be taking them to Fort Robinson tomorrow sometime. Back to their own kind on the reservation at Pine Ridge."

Tears suddenly rolled down Katherine's tanned cheeks. "How can I possibly explain that? Their families ... children ... are all up north where my own family is. They know what's going on around here. They know all about preparations for war."

"This is all so inconceivable, so strange," mused Clybourn. "Yes, your daughter, I understand, but that you should feel this way after what they did ... to you, your brother. If you'll pardon me, it's damned confusing, Miss Coltrane. But you should feel relief being here."

"Mister Clybourn, do you know what it's like to wait year after year for someone to come and get you? Do you realize how it feels to be forsaken by your own people? . . . abandoned? At first, it was just surviving. But when I was with child, I knew I had to do more than survive. I had to live. So, you see, I adapted. Oh, I knew this day was coming . . . sooner or later, I knew it was coming. I just wasn't quite prepared for it. Not for losing my child this way. Not for losing Julia."

"I'm sorry," said Clybourn. "I'd better go like Misses Slaymaker says. I'll be back later if you need me, or if you want Sergeant Hansen to go with you down to . . . your friends, I'll be back in about hour. I'll escort you down to supper, Miss Coltrane."

Katherine looked at what Slaymaker had brought. Then at the large pitcher of water standing on the commode, and beside it in a small dish, lay a bar of yellow-colored soap in a big tin wash pan. Katherine sniffed at the soap; she hadn't seen a bar of white man's soap in ages; it had a tint of lye to it; she would smell like medicine but it was a clean odor. She carefully inspected the clothes Mary Slaymaker had brought, a long cotton skirt, two blouses, one frilly at the top, ruffles, full at the front to disguise her bosom without brassiere, long sleeves to hide her tanned and well-muscled arms, a pair of black stockings wrapped around a tortoise comb, white underpants, too, bloomers, everything used, everything appropriate, and everything clean. This was charity. Mary Slaymaker was a kind woman.

Katherine removed her moccasins, draped her buckskin skirt over the back of the chair, and slipped out of her faded calico blouse. The tears in her eyes mingled with the warm water as she poured it over her head, let it course down the length of her body, down her middle, down her legs onto her feet. It puddled in the tin basin, her toes were dirty, and with a large cloth, she methodically began washing, a foot and a leg at a time, finally pouring the last of the water once again over her head, then gouging away at the crevices inside her ears. This was her bath, an impromptu bath, but she felt clean enough to slip into her white bloomers. She then sat on the chair near the window, and began combing out her long curtain of dark brown hair. It was still damp when she parted it in the middle and pulled it tightly behind her head and fastened it with her strip of leather. Katherine thought the frilly blouse was much too prissy; she chose the simple, pale blue one; it had white, pearl-like buttons on the sleeves that matched three buttons on the small collar. Twisting her Lakota blue and white beads into a smaller loop, she hung these around her neck. Finally, staring at herself in the small mirror, she smiled for the first time in days, only the barest trace of a smile; she approved of her looks; she was a pretty woman, and only because of this had the glimmer of a smile shown. Without Julia, her new freedom meant nothing.

As he had promised, Lieutenant Clybourn returned in about an hour. When she opened the door, Katherine Coltrane immediately saw the look of surprise on his face and knew that her appearance pleased him. She, in turn, was relieved that he had come back because, except for a few words with Sergeant Hansen, this young man was the only white man with whom she had spoken at any great length during the three days since her capture on the Little Powder. She liked him; he was understanding, and at least he was trying to be helpful, whether out of pity for her or just in the line of his assigned duty. And, if he were surprised to see her as a white woman, she was likewise surprised when he handed her a box. He smiled at her under his black mustache, a mustache well-trimmed, one that curved up under his ruddy cheeks.

Presenting her the box, he said, "You look nice, Miss Coltrane . . . the beads and all, not much like a squaw, I should say." Nodding at the box, he added, "I hope those fit. Only two pair of them at the sutlers, and I took the biggest . . . not that you have big feet, mind you, but the other pair was pretty damn small."

That brought the second smile of the day from Katherine Coltrane. "I'm not a small woman," she replied. "I do have big feet," and upon opening the box, she discovered a white shawl and under it a pair of very shiny brown shoes with pointed toes and buttons up the sides. "My gracious, Mister Clybourn . . . this is very gallant." Her glistening greenish eyes looked up at him. "Out of your salary, or does the army pay for these?"

"I have good credit at the mercantile," he said. "Please don't cry. It's my pleasure, a welcoming back gesture."

Katherine Coltrane began pulling off her moccasins, exposing the black stockings that Mary Slaymaker had given her. She crossed her legs and extended a slender foot, and like a knight, Lieutenant Clybourn graciously knelt beside her, saying, "Here, please permit me." He fitted the shoe to her foot, shoved gently, and watched admiringly as she pressed it to the floor, jiggled it several times, and finally exclaimed, "It fits!"

When they had finished with the second shoe, Katherine Coltrane stood. She was a tall, slender woman; the high heels made her even taller, and her smile of appreciation was almost at a level with that of Lieutenant Clybourn's. He placed the white woolen shawl around her shoulders. She shook her long hair over it in the back as he escorted her out the door. "Don't be nervous," he said with a grin. "No one should be nervous about eating cornbread and stew."

"How do you know the bill of fare?"

"I stopped and asked," he returned. "I thought you might like chicken and dumplings for your first meal ... something like that. It's stew, boardinghouse stew."

"No one but my brother ever took me to supper."

"I'm honored to be the first, Miss Coltrane."

"I am nervous, you know ... they'll look at me, wonder all kinds of things ... whisper."

"You shall ignore them, be attentive to me. I'll tell you my life story. It will captivate you, Miss Coltrane, and if anyone whispers about you, it will be because you're a very attractive woman. Just pretend they desire your company."

"Ridiculous, Lieutenant! A woman who has consorted with Indians for five years? ... an unwed mother? Such a notion!" Such a notion, indeed. Except for her daughter Julia, five years of her young life had been wasted on the prairie, and at twenty-six, she felt twice that age.

There were four men at the middle of the table. Pausing in their conversation to nod politely, they quietly went back to the glasses of wine and talk without casting another glance her way. Writers, Thomas Clybourn told her, reporters from the East out on war assignments. No other women were present; none of General Crook's command had brought their wives with them. Crook anticipated this campaign would be a short one, and departure for the unceded lands to the north was imminent. Clybourn thought that by midsummer, Katherine Coltrane would find her daughter on the reservation below the Black Hills. Katherine Coltrane wanted to believe Clybourn but she had lived with the Lakota; she knew the Indian mind and sense of purpose, and she was much less optimistic.

Mary Slaymaker soon came; she had white plates, utensils; she came back a second time with a platter of hot cornbread and a steaming bowl of stew; there was coffee, bread pudding, and a small pitcher of condensed milk.

Thomas Clybourn told Katherine Coltrane his life story, about his home in Columbus, Ohio, his parents, his graduation from West Point, his short tenure at Fort Buford, a transfer to Fort Laramie, and now, his temporary assignment at Fort Fetterman. He was twenty-five years old; he was an engineer, loved the army, and intended to make it his career.

Through the tangled web of her thoughts and mixed emotions, she listened, and by the time supper was over, Katherine Coltrane felt like his mother. Two glasses of Burgundy wine arrived; the four men at the middle of the table stood and raised their glasses in a toast, and a stout man, coatless but with a bulging vest and a gold watch chain dangling from it, spoke for them. He said, "To your return, Miss Coltrane, and the very best of luck to you."

This writer tarried, and after the other three had left, he came over to Katherine Coltrane and introduced himself. His name was Henry Burlingame. He was on assignment for *Harper's Weekly,* and was interested in hearing about her life with the Sioux, if she was so inclined to discuss it. Katherine Coltrane thanked him, but no, she had no inclination whatsoever to discuss it. It was much too personal, too bizarre, too grievous to her scarred soul. How could she possibly describe something like this, her capture, the inner struggles, the eventual capitulation, how she had survived? Biting her lip, Katherine Coltrane shook her head; Henry Burlingame graciously bowed and left.

By dusk, some of the tension, the fretful anxiety of the present and the unpredictable future had dissipated, and Katherine, draped with a blanket and once again wearing her Sioux moccasins, walked back to the fort with Thomas Clybourn. She would talk with her Lakota friends, but in their present pitiful plight, wearing her new shoes and her pretty white shawl was more than she could bear. She had been one of them for these past few years, and she abhorred the thought of sitting among them newly adorned as a white woman. It bordered on humiliation, something she had once felt herself when some of these same women had attempted to befriend her, to teach her the customs and rituals of an alien society, one she detested, didn't understand, and one of which she wanted no part. Smiling wanly, Katherine looked at Lieutenant Clybourn. Did he understand? Could he understand that despite the animosities he had questioned her about, that despite her afflictions, the pain in her heart, she still had some empathy for these people? That, unlike the white man's government, she considered them her friends, not her enemies, and they were being wrongfully persecuted. Without prejudice, did he perceive? He nodded; he perceived. He knew all about the historic clash of cultures; they were as ancient and scarred as the jagged peaks to the west, now stark black against the dying sun.

The entry of the big squad tent was open, and the flaps to each side raised; a lone soldier was standing near the front, and he saluted at Lieutenant Clybourn's appearance. The guard's presence was customary, not for precaution, for these few women and two old men had no thoughts of escape. They had no place to go, had no provisions, no weapons, and they were without their most prized possession, horses. They were pitifully alone, but they had been well fed, and were now sitting toward the back of the tent attentively listening to one of the old men who, cross-legged and staring into a tiny fire of smoldering juniper and sage twigs, was chanting lowly, his hands extended, palms upward. Katherine Coltrane entered and sat near the opening of the tent at the front.

Thomas Clybourn, sensing something spiritual in the fragrant aroma of juniper and sage, was hesitant to follow, dared not intrude, so he stood behind her in the shadows. But curious, he whispered down to her, "A ceremony? . . . some kind of a ritual? Can you understand it?"

Katherine whispered back, "Maza Blaska . . . Flat Iron. He's an old holy man, once a warrior. No, not a ritual . . . not in an unholy place like this." She listened for a while, then whispered again, "He's telling them stories . . . stories in song. He says east is the white man's country . . . west is where he belongs. His old friends are now dead, and he soon may be with them . . . but . . . but he's not afraid. In this new place . . . this white man's lodge, they should not be afraid either, for Wakan-Tanka has given the women the Blue Elk to watch over them . . . the Blue Elk is out there watching over all the females. If they have faith . . . if they have faith and listen, they will hear the song, the inner song, the song from within, and . . . it will give them peace."

"Putting them at ease, is he?" asked Clybourn. "This is what you came to do, isn't it?"

"Realistically," she returned. "I'll tell them no harm will come to them, not reassure them spiritually. Only men like Flat Iron can do such things. Standing Bear . . . the man I had, says Flat Iron has had many visions in his time." Pressing a finger to her lips, she went, "Shh, listen . . . he knows you're here."

"He never paid any attention to me on the train down. Three days, and he barely noticed me."

"Old men like this one miss nothing, Mister Clybourn . . . nothing."

"Who is this Blue Elk who's watching over the females?"

"A spirit elk given big medicine by the Great Spirit."

"Interesting," mused Clybourn. "If one is a true believer, this has promising possibilities. A ray of hope, I should think. This blue elk spirit thing will look out after your daughter until you find her."

"I don't know what to believe anymore," she whispered back. "Now, he's singing about battle . . . the Oglala, he says, are powerful . . . never defeated in battle . . . *'ai ya he ye, ai ya he ye, okcize iyotan micilagon, miye sni se, ityotiyewakiye-lo'* . . . he was once mighty in battle . . . honored. Now, he is old and wretched. He says he was never afraid to die young . . . to die in battle when one is young is honorable." Katherine turned and whispered up to the lieutenant. "For your benefit, Mister Clybourn . . . or General Crook's, he's letting you know in a roundabout way, you're going to lose if you battle the Oglala. You won't die with a toothache, like Flat Iron."

Chapter Two

Porter Longstreet Webb

Toward noon on her second day at Fort Fetterman, Katherine Coltrane waved good-bye to her Oglala sisters and the two old men. They were all blanket-shrouded, seated in the back of an empty freight wagon, and amid all the bustle and noisy activity of the fort, Katherine touched her breast and cried out to them, *"Heya, waon welo, waon welo."* This was the best she could do, to tell them her heart was with them. Had she embraced and talked with each of them, the weeping and wailing would have been unbearable, the sadness and despair only compounded. *Mistaput neotukit, hechetu welo, hechetu welo.* Go away, now, hurry, go away, it is finished. Oh, how she wanted it finished, but she knew it wasn't.

And now she would wait another day or two, at the suggestion of Lieutenant Thomas Clybourn and the approval of Colonel Bradford, until the scout, Porter Webb, the man known as White Hawk to the Lakota, returned and disclosed the location of the Sioux. That meant a possibility, however dangerous, of freeing Julia before the disaster of war once again fell over the northern valleys. There was one hope, Clybourn valiantly tried to assure her—when the tribes discovered they were being converged upon by armies from several directions, when they learned their situation was strategically and numerically impossible, hopefully, they would return to the reservations peacefully and strike a new treaty.

The one man who could go and talk with the Lakota was Porter Longstreet Webb, a man who had smoked with the tribe many times during the past ten years, and was now a friendly enemy of sorts. It was Porter Webb who had told the Lakota during the Moon of the Strong Cold that the white man's government had broken its word, abrogating the right of the Indians to use the unceded territory, and that General Crook was planning to attack them during the time of the Hungry Moon. All of this had come to pass. The man called White Hawk was not a liar.

All of this was well and good, opined Katherine Coltrane, but she thought such conjecture at this point in time, that of making peace, was wishful thinking—if, indeed, this was the true thinking of General Crook, and she doubted it was. There *was* one thing she did believe. Porter Webb was about the only hope she had to get Julia out of an Oglala village. Standing Bear would certainly have something to say about it, though, and there was White Bone, too, Julia's doting grandmother. And if Crazy Horse got involved, the issue was as good as dead; his word in the clan was absolute law, and he hated the greedy world of the white man and what the *wasichu* were doing to his people.

Katherine Coltrane had only seen Porter Webb twice in her life, once a short time after she had come west when she and her brother, William, had freighted two loads of supplies into a small territorial community called Hawk Springs. One of the wagon loads had been ordered and paid for by Porter Webb, a tall, angular man who was breeding horses on a developing spread near Hawk Springs. The handsome young Sioux breed, Joseph Brings Yellow, was also with him at the time, and Joseph had done most of the talking. The second time, after she was "rescued" and had lost Julia, she was sobbing; he had given her a violent shake. "Get a hold of yourself, woman! Well, well, this is a fine kettle of fish . . . a white woman."

He hadn't remembered meeting her before, didn't even know who she was, and he spent most of his time squatted down beside old Flat Iron, smoking and talking, then after a chat with Lieutenant Clybourn, had packed on a few extra rations and had ridden to the north with Joseph Brings Yellow. At least Joseph had remembered her and had taken some time to talk; he knew her predicament, knew all about Julia, and she supposed he had said something about her problems and who she was to this somewhat arrogant Porter Webb.

Clybourn denied that Porter Webb was uncaring. He had known Webb for a year, and had ridden on several patrols with him. He was just a quiet man with problems of his own—but what kind of problems, Clybourn didn't explain. It was rumored that Webb had once lived with the Miniconjou when he was a young man, only a rumor, because he never talked about it and neither did his constant companion, Joseph Brings Yellow. Lately, Porter Webb had been serving as an emissary between Colonel Bradford's command and the Indians because Bradford seemed to have some empathy for the harassed Sioux and Cheyenne. Thomas Clybourn said Webb thoroughly disliked both General Crook and his superior, General Philip Sheridan, both of whom he claimed understood nothing whatsoever about the dangerously inflammatory situation on the frontier.

The third time Katherine would meet Porter Longstreet Webb was in the quarters of Colonel Bradford where, at the colonel's invitation, not his command, she had come to have tea and shortcake. Once again, she had been escorted by Clybourn, and along with another colonel, Jason Armitage from Crook's command, they sat at a small table especially arranged for the occasion. To Katherine's surprise, there was real silverware, china cups and saucers, and the table was covered with a white linen cloth. Despite Lieutenant Clybourn's usual reassurance, she was nervous and uncomfortable, yet the conversation was polite, and she thought by prearrangement, purposefully avoided the personal aspects of her life with her Lakota captors. The officers, particularly Colonel Armitage, were more interested in Tashunka-Witko, Crazy Horse, his recent travels, his contacts with other tribes, who his visitors were, movements of the so-called hostiles, and their probable destination. Was Crazy Horse the leader, the organizer of the recent exodus of the villages northward? Did she believe this gathering was truly for the purpose of the annual spring rituals, or were the tribes preparing for battle campaigns? Had she see any other tribes from the Lakota nation, the Sans Arc, Miniconjou, Hunkpapa, Brule, or Yanktonai? And how about the Cheyenne and the Arapaho?

She knew many of the answers. She knew the Indians were meeting at several locations beyond the Rosebud country, places where they could congregate peacefully and celebrate the Sun dance, and prior to her capture, she had heard little talk of battle, only Crazy Horse's assertion that his people and the Cheyenne would fight again if they were provoked by General Crook. And, at least at that time, the Oglala knew nothing of the army's plan of convergence upon the northern valleys. However, they knew all about General Crook's presence at Fort Fetterman, but apparently weren't too alarmed or concerned about it. After all, she said, a small winter village of Cheyenne and a few Sioux had thwarted him during the Moon of the Ice Going Away. True, Crook's men had destroyed the village and stolen most of the Indian's pony herd, but in turn, the Cheyenne and some Oglala led by Chief Low Dog recaptured the herd in the middle of the night and drove off all of Crook's cattle and many of his horses. Crazy Horse didn't seem to be in the least frightened by General Crook's ability to wage a battle. Tashunka-Witko was now in command of over a thousand warriors, most of them equipped with rifles, and many of these weapons were captured repeaters.

"There was a council earlier this spring with some Cheyenne chiefs representing Dull Knife and Two Moons," Katherine said. "He made this abundantly clear. If Crook moves north again, he'll send him back to the Geese Going River like a whipped dog."

Staring over his cup, Colonel Armitage, Crook's capable adjutant, asked, "And do you believe this, Miss Coltrane, after seeing what General Crook has assembled here?"

Without blinking an eye, she answered, "I'm no authority on war, Mister Armitage. I do know how the army has fought in the past. If your general thinks he's going to catch Tashunka-Witko asleep in his lodge, he's mistaken. It simply won't happen. And if he has to fight, it won't be on your terms. Tashunka-Witko prides himself on his military knowledge. He's been observing your tactics ever since his people ran General Conner out of the country ten years ago. He was at the Battle of the Hundred Slain. He knows all about the Wagon Box and Hay Field fights. He saw General Carrington leave Kearney, saw the forts along the Bozeman burn. He's been watching you people for years. Gracious, I've lived in his presence for five years. One thing I learned, he's a man of his word."

Lieutenant Clybourn stirred nervously in his seat and raised his brow at Katherine. She was talking like an Indian, a rather proud Indian, not a repatriated white woman.

Colonel Armitage obviously shared the young lieutenant's reaction. Setting his cup aside, he said, "You admire this man, I see. You like him."

With a little blush, Katherine said, "Personally, no. I just know him. He's my uncle by marriage. If I admire him, it's because of his allegiance to his people, his honesty. This has nothing to do with my personal likes or dislikes of him, or how his people treated me. After all, I was in bondage. For God's sake, I'm still in bondage ... my daughter's up there, and if she's harmed in any way, I'll never forgive you people—" Frustrated, embarrassed, she suddenly broke off.

"Yes, of course," Colonel Armitage said nervously. "We're going to try and work this out most prudently and cautiously, Miss Coltrane. I understand your feelings, and I'm sorry if I offended you. These aren't the best of times for any of us."

Shortly after this an officer briefly appeared and announced that Porter Webb had returned. In he came, all six-feet-plus of him, lanky, booted, dressed in a dirty, red pullover shirt, a Colt pistol on one hip and a long skinning knife on the other. His hair was shaggy, his mustache drooping, he badly needed a shave, and after shaking hands with Colonel Bradford and Lieutenant Clybourn, Porter looked at Colonel Jason Armitage. He shook his head sadly.

"Hello, Bird Dog. Your boss has no idea what he's in for." Porter plucked two cakes from the platter on the table, then momentarily stared at Katherine Coltrane. "Well, well, well," he said, munching, "our little fish got herself out of the kettle ... Miss Coltrane, isn't it? By God, you look a lot better for all the wear and tear. Right pretty."

"Thank you," she returned coolly. "I don't feel much better. What happened to my people ... were any of them wounded? Do you know?"

"No, for a fact, I don't know. Couldn't get that close, but I know where they are ... or were four or five days ago ... Little Goose Creek. Joined up with another village, a big one, and from what I could see, and some talking with a few friendly Miniconjou bucks on the way back, I'll allow it was your uncle's Oglala band, Crazy Horse."

Katherine Coltrane felt herself flinch. Her "uncle." Well, indeed, Joseph Brings Yellow had told Porter Webb her story; the man knew about Standing Bear and Julia, but he hadn't gotten close enough to see a thing, not even a travois carrying the wounded, if there had been any. She was in a daze again, but through the mist she heard Webb continuing. What he had discovered only confirmed most of what she already knew and had told the three officers, except for one startling development ... the appearance of Sitting Bull.

"... All moving north toward the Greasy Grass," she

heard Webb saying. "The old shaman, Tatanka Iyotake of Teton, is sitting up there at the headwaters of the Tongue, yes sir, Sitting Bull, himself. From what I hear, he hasn't moved north yet, but he will. They're planning a big festival. Dull Knife and several thousand Cheyenne are already on the Rosebud. Joseph and I saw four more tribes moving in from the east on the other side of the Powder . . . agency people, I suspect, mostly Lakota from Standing Rock, and by now, they all must be camped on the Rosebud somewhere, not too far from the Greasy Grass." He stopped and looked at Colonel Armitage. He chuckled once. "They know all about your boss, old Three Stars, know that he's camped here preparing something. Some news has come down the Yellowstone, too. They know old lard-ass Gibbon marched down the river to that cantonment at the mouth of the Powder to meet Terry's command. What I suspect, though, is that Terry and Gibbon are ready to move south and no one, not even the Crow, knows there's nine or ten thousand Sioux, Cheyenne, and Arapaho gathering below them . . ."

"Ten thousand!" exclaimed Colonel Armitage. "Ye Gods, Porter, how do you come by that kind of a figure?" Clybourn and Colonel Benjamin Bradford were also startled.

"Joseph," Porter Webb replied calmly. "He talked with several bucks passing through. I made a few friendly contacts, and a couple of nights ago we started toting it up. Hell's bells, Sitting Bull has three thousand or more in that camp on the Tongue, maybe more. We sure as hell weren't going up there to take a personal look. Damn lucky to pick our way back through all that mess without getting in an argument ourselves. Did a bit of riding at night in the foothills until yesterday . . . slept in the morning, and did some glassing around in the afternoons, but we sure as hell kept our heads down most of the time. Yes, ten thousand, and you can figure three thousand or more of them can fight, but they're not looking to fight. I reckon they think there's no one around stupid enough to take them on." He grinned at Colonel Armitage. " 'Less it would be old Three Stars."

Armitage smiled back. "He wouldn't appreciate your assessment."

"That's why I'm working for Colonel Ben, here, Bird Dog. I'll be damned if the general can tell one Indian from another, and before this is over, I'll allow some of his blue bellies will be shooting at his own Shoshoni and Crow scouts. Oh, you can tell him all of this. I don't give a shit."

"You said they weren't looking for a fight."

"They aren't," retorted Porter Webb. "Now, look here, Jason, you don't mean to tell me your generals are prepared to move into that country to talk, do you? Word from the Miniconjou is that Terry has the Seventh Cavalry along with him ... moved out from Fort Lincoln. If this is true, it means Colonel Custer is in the party, and he never was one much for talking, was he? No more than that asshole boss you have."

Colonel Benjamin Bradford chuckled. "If what you say is true about Sitting Bull and Dull Knife's presence, General Crook might want to get up there first and do some talking."

Before Katherine Coltrane could suppress herself, she said, "Or get his ass whipped, again."

Porter Webb grunted disdainfully. "Do some talking! I reckon it's a bit late for this, Ben, you know that. The commissioner and the politicians already did the talking didn't they? Ordering those people back in the middle of winter. Hell, they knew that was an impossibility." He looked across the table at Armitage who was staring glumly into his cup, swirling the residue of tea leaves. "'Sides that, your boss killed those chances two months ago, sending Reynolds up there to do his dirty work."

Colonel Armitage shrugged. "Reynolds was only following orders."

"Eagerly," countered Porter Webb.

"What if he did agree to try and make some kind of peace?"

"I doubt Crook would even consider it," returned Webb. "And how in the hell could he get word up to General Terry? Besides that, not all of those Indians are going to want to be herded back, especially Crazy Horse and some of his Oglala, too damned dishonorable." Casting a sidelong glance at Katherine Coltrane, Webb added, "Why should he want to move out of the valleys, eh? He's been doing just fine where he is the last six or seven years ... doesn't have any hankering to that chuckaway reservation shit, does he?"

Katherine Coltrane merely shrugged. Certainly, what Porter Webb said was true—Tashunka-Witko's followers had been at peace. They scorned reservation life, only went near the lands when they had an occasion to do some bartering at the reservation trading posts. In fact, Katherine hadn't seen one white person in her five years in the upper valleys.

Colonel Armitage said to Porter Webb, "You could talk with the chiefs ... take one last shot at it. It's not entirely impossible, is it?"

"Oh, no, not on your life, Bird Dog, not even if Crook wanted to try it. I've been up there twice now, earning my pay, and my tour of duty is about over. I still have friends up there, and I'm not about to wear out my welcome ... such as it is. No, sir, I'm not going back. I have a lot of work ahead of me this summer down below, chores long neglected. I've shot my wad. I'm going home."

Katherine suddenly saw her glimmer of hope grow dim, the great, esteemed and trusted Porter Webb, one of the few men around with entrée into the northern valleys, was pulling stakes.

Port Webb must have detected some of her concern. He said to her in a surprisingly unusual tone of softness, "Don't fret, Miss Coltrane, about that little girl of yours. They're making a village up there bigger than Cheyenne City, and I'll allow no soldier is going to get into it, not without getting crucified like the good Lord, himself."

Later in the day, the news came down to Manny Slaymaker's boardinghouse, by the way of the writer, Henry Burlingame, who encountered Katherine, Mary Slaymaker, and Sergeant Marvel Hansen sitting on the porch having coffee. General Crook was moving his army of cavalry and infantry totaling twenty companies the next day. The activity down below the fort that Katherine had been observing all afternoon was the arrival of civilian packers and teamsters, several dozen wagons and big freighters that were to bring up the rear of the contingent. Burlingame opined that war was inevitable; he and his four writer cohorts had been assigned to one of the wagons. He was in a hurry to send out one last dispatch on the midnight stage detailing all of the battle preparations. Not too long after Burlingame had hurried away, Lieutenant Clybourn, Webb, and Joseph Brings Yellow arrived. Clybourn had come to relieve Sergeant Hansen of his escort duties, and at the same time inform him that they had been temporarily reassigned again—this time the two of them were going to head up an advance patrol with three guides, Frank Grouard, Louis Richards, and

Baptiste Pourier. Sergeant Marvel Hansen took the news calmly; this was the army, and he did as he was ordered. However, Lieutenant Clybourn delivered the news less than nonchalantly; this wasn't what he had expected; this wasn't his anticipated return to Fort Laramie for some long overdue rest and relaxation. His disappointment showed, not only in his face but in his words and Katherine noticed this. Ever since her repatriation, this young man had been her closest friend, and she had believed that he was to be one of the officers escorting her back to Laramie within the next several days. Not so.

"I'm sorry," Katherine said. "I'm sorry they picked you."

"Not exactly the duty I'd presumed," answered Clybourn. "Quite the contrary."

"I'll miss your company," Katherine said. "You and Colonel Bradford have been very kind."

Webb found a seat on the long bench, his companion, Joseph Brings Yellow, sat on the steps and leaned up against one of the porch posts. He spoke adequate English, but he looked up at Katherine Coltrane, smiled, and said to her in Siouan, "You do not have to miss his companionship Tall Woman." (Tall Woman was the name the Oglala had given her.) "If you wish to face danger, there is a way."

Katherine understood his words but not the meaning, and, momentarily puzzled, she stared down at him, then looked across the bench at Webb, who also gave her a small smile. "He's right," Webb said. "Since you're so all-fired concerned about getting back up there, we came up with an idea . . . just an idea, mind you, because I sure as hell don't know what good it'll do you, a long shot at best. Has its drawbacks . . . can get you up there, all right, but what happens then, God only knows. You might be right back where you started . . . captured, again. Depends on who comes out on top of this thing, and I'm not too optimistic about the army's chances."

Staring at each of the men curiously, she said, "I'll do anything to get Julia back . . . so . . . so, what is the idea?"

Lieutenant Clybourn shook his head doubtfully and said, "I don't think it's exactly legal . . . yet, there's no explicit orders against it . . . at least, I know of none."

Webb said, "Be one of those mule skinners, Miss Coltrane. Get you back at the reins again . . . help drive one of those freighters in the supply train."

"Good heavens, are you serious!" exclaimed Katherine. "Why, why, I'd be spotted before the wagon pulled out of the fort! The men—"

Lieutenant Clybourn sighed. "They won't object. They won't say anything about it. Fact is, knowing how some of those fellows are, they'll probably be your worst problem—"

"They will want to mount you," Joseph Brings Yellow spoke up bluntly in Siouan. "White men have no honor. They mount anything with two legs."

"Oh, Lord!" moaned Katherine.

Porter Webb chuckled. "Said you'd do anything to get Julia back, didn't you?" But before Katherine could reply, he held up his hands saying, "Now, hold on . . . wait a minute, Miss Kate, there's another woman in the party, and I'll allow if you stick close to her, you'll be having no problems."

"Another woman?"

"Yep," said Webb. "Came in driving one of those outfits this afternoon . . . Jane Canarray . . ."

"Oh, my goodness," whispered Mary Slaymaker. "That woman!"

"No look like woman. No talk like woman," said Joseph Brings Yellow in English.

"Well, hell yes, I agree," Webb said. "She's a regular harridan sometimes . . . abides no nonsense from anyone, 'less she wants some nonsense. From Quinlan's outfit, and he's short a couple of skinners . . . one down with the jaundice, another outright quit."

Katherine asked, "You talked with this Quinlan?" She looked at the men.

"Not I," Lieutenant Clybourn said, nodding at Porter. "He did."

Webb shrugged and said, "Only in passing. I know him; Jane, too. When I saw her I just got the idea if you wanted to get back into that country, maybe you could handle one of those teams, too. I didn't say anything to Quinlan about it, but I reckon he knew your brother before you people got ambushed. He's been around these parts for five or six years now. Pete Quinlan. Get yourself out of that dress and into some pants, boots, and a big old hat, and he'd likely give you a chance. Probably a dollar a day and grub . . . get yourself a stake to get started on when you get back to Cheyenne. Just a notion."

Clybourn put in, "A damn foolish one, and dangerous, to boot."

"I'm not in any position to be choosy, am I?" she asked. "I'm a piece of charity, even the clothes I'm wearing. Certainly I can handle mules."

"You're no Jane Canarray," retorted Thomas Clybourn. "Calamity Jane . . ."

Webb smiled. "She's a tough bird, Jane is. She doesn't like to be called Calamity, either. Martha Jane . . . Jane, but not Calamity. Might just knock you on your hind end, Thomas, you go calling her that to her face."

"I know, I know. That's exactly what I mean. Damnit, Porter, she's no lady . . . she . . . she, well, she hung out all last winter down at John Owen's place on the Six-Mile with the rest of those doves, that infernal hog ranch."

Katherine sighed wearily. "Well, no one is going to call me a lady either, not after what I've been through. I'm tainted merchandise, too, am I not? 'Spoiled,' as the Oglala would say. This Jane person, at least she got paid for the soiling. All I got was pregnant . . . my baby, and now I've lost her." She got up from the bench and said to Porter Webb, "Come on, Mister Webb, show me this Pete Quinlan. I want to have a talk with him."

Webb replied doubtfully, "Not looking like that, you don't, Miss Coltrane. If you're dead set on this, you better let me make the proposition, and if he agrees, I'll sign you on as K. Coltrane. Find you some clothing more suitable for all of this, this craziness."

" 'Craziness.' It's your idea, isn't it?"

"His idea, all right," Clybourn answered. "Wild as a goose."

"Just a notion," Webb said. "Only trying to be some help . . . get the burr out of your britches."

"A job is a job," huffed Katherine. "I can't sit around the North Platte all summer picking chokecherries and digging turnips like an old woman, waiting for some word to come in. I just can't do that."

Clybourn sighed, "It wouldn't be all that bad. If you want to stay at Fort Laramie for a month or so, I'm certain Colonel Bradford can give you a recommendation for some position around the post . . . at the store . . . the mercantile, something to tide you over. You shouldn't be too hasty about this you know. Where we're going isn't the most pleasant—"

"My Lord, I've been living up there for five years!" Katherine interrupted. "I know what it's like." But her face came to a sudden flush; she felt flustered, foolish, ashamed that she had cut him short. Bless him, Thomas Clybourn was concerned about her welfare; everyone seemed to be genuinely concerned. "I'm sorry. My well-being. I understand."

There was an uncomfortable silence between them. Webb was staring down between his knees at the plank flooring. Joseph was idly cleaning the stem of his pipe. Clybourn had turned away, hands on the porch rail, contemplating the distant compound. Mary Slaymaker had gone, and Sergeant Hansen was walking back to the fort.

Finally Webb quietly said, "Aw, shit, Miss Kate, none of this is worth a bean. If you want, you can come on down to Hawk Springs with Joseph and me ... take a ride back up to Fort Robinson this fall, locate Crazy Horse, see if anything worthwhile turns up, and try to work out something. I think all of this is nothing but an empty bucket with a big hole in it ... that's what I think."

Momentary silence again. Clybourn was the first to break it. "That's not a bad idea Porter has. It's something you should consider. You'd be safe, you know, out of harm's way."

Katherine was startled at Webb's suggestion, yet she was pleasantly surprised, too. She glanced back at Clybourn with a guilty look. His head was cocked slightly, his brow furrowed. It was sort of a "didn't I tell you" look. Momentarily torn by indecision, she nudged the point of her shoe against Joseph Brings Yellow, a young man who had lived in two worlds, both white and red. To him she said in Siouan, "Ho, brother, what say you?"

Tapping the residue from his pipe, Joseph was hesitant, contemplating. "Who am I to hear the inner song, the song that binds mother and child? It is true. Old men say this ... only a woman with a heavy heart hears this song. I must believe you will hear no songs down here, nor will your heart have songs to sing."

Katherine stared at the somber men, each extending a hand of friendship, each sharing her own frustration in a deplorable situation, yet not entirely a fruitless one, the practicality of it—a job, and one that would take her within reach of Julia. After a moment, she said to young Joseph. *"Heya, wagnikte. Pila miyah, hechetu welo, miya kola."*

Lieutenant Clybourn glanced questioningly at Webb. Porter got up from the bench, gave Katherine's head a gentle tousle, and said to Clybourn, "Come on, Thomas, let's go find old man Quinlan. Miss Kate's decided ... it's over. She's going back north."

As the two men walked up the lane toward the conglomeration of wagons, Katherine spoke to Joseph in Siouan. "Neither of them looks happy. Do men hear songs? Don't they understand that I have to try? Don't they realize I'll have no peace?"

Joseph Brings Yellow said quietly, "My friend, White Hawk ... Porter, understands. He always looks unhappy. This is his way. Sometimes, he is a silent man. Sometimes, he says nothing for one sun, but he understands. He has learned to listen, and in his time, he has heard many songs."

"A strange man," Katherine mused. "I know you admire him greatly. How long have you lived with him?"

"Since I was very young," replied Joseph. "Since my mother died of the big cramps. I went south to Hawk Springs to help him with his ponies. He has many ponies. I never went back to the Miniconjou, only to visit. I have been many winters with White Hawk."

Katherine nodded. This young, intelligent Lakota breed was no more than eighteen or nineteen; he had left his people when only a boy to live with Porter Webb, a man perhaps fifteen years his senior. Porter's age she could only guess from that tan, weathered, leathery look, the fine crowfeet lines at the corner of his pale blue eyes. Not a young man, not old either. Just the aging frontier look so common out here. Her brother William had looked to be thirty; he was only twenty-five the day he was shot. Katherine asked, "Did Porter live with your people? I have heard such a story."

"Yes, the story is true," nodded Joseph Brings Yellow. "He lived with the Miniconjou long ago for almost two winters. He is honored by the Miniconjou. He is a good pony thief. He has fought many enemies. Some, he killed. When a man steals his ponies, he steals them back, and sometimes he takes more."

Katherine sat on the stoop beside Joseph. Porter Webb and Thomas Clybourn had disappeared somewhere in the jumble of freighters at the edge of the fort. Observing the confusion, she said, "You say Porter has killed men, stolen horses, and yet he detests the idea of this war. How do you explain this?"

"I cannot speak for White Hawk."

"No, but what do you think? What guides him?"

"Visions. What is just and unjust. He wants to help you. This is good. This is just. One day he will see you, again, thus he has spoken."

"You have strong faith in your friend."

"He is more than my friend," spoke Joseph. "He is my brother-in-law, so I honor him. *Heya.*"

Surprised at this disclosure, Katherine said, "My gracious, he has a breed wife! Your older sister . . . in a village somewhere? I didn't realize . . ."

Passing a hand back and forth, Joseph Brings Yellow replied, "No wife. No, my sister, Two Feathers, half white, yes, but she died during childbirth, her daughter, too. Long ago when I was five winters. Our father, a man called Marat, was trading over by the Mother River. He never came back. White Hawk thinks he was killed, so I went to live with him in the land of the *wasichu.* It is good for you to know what I mean when I say my brother hears songs. He understands the loss of your child. He lost both a wife and a child."

"Yes," mumbled Katherine. "Yes, of course."

Martha Jane Canarray, a woman as tall as Katherine Coltrane but with the muscled arms and hardened hands of a sawyer, entered Manny Slaymaker's dining room with Porter Webb. Her appearance drew far more attention than had Katherine's a day earlier, for in less than five years, she had become a frontier phenomenon. A high-spirited woman in her late twenties, her home was anywhere she chose to make it, east and west across the fort roads, the outposts, the way stations, all the way south to Julesburg, Cheyenne, and Denver. Everyone knew her. If they didn't, she made herself known in short order. She was a mule skinner, comparable to any man, and she talked like one and even looked like one, baggy pants, sometimes bibs, boots, a soiled cotton shirt with rolled sleeves, and a big, droopy hat stained with the sweat and grime of a thousand miles of prairie dust. Neither homely nor attractive, she had dark eyes, high cheekbones, and black hair, a tumble of it knotted up high on her head, and when she pulled her hat down, at first appearance, she was a man. The only decoration she wore was a forty-five revolver, to shoot snakes, she said.

There were a dozen people seated to both sides of the long table, including several of the newspaper reporters, and toward the far end, Katherine and Lieutenant Clybourn. Katherine was anticipating this meeting, Clybourn dreading it. Martha Jane Canarray didn't make it to the end of the table where they were sitting. She abruptly stopped near the middle where she recognized a familiar face, a face that simultaneously recognized her. She shouted, "Burly!" and Henry Burlingame, the man from *Harper's Weekly,* stood, stepped over the bench, and shoved out his hand. She firmly shook his hand, gave the correspondent a big embrace and several pats on the back, pushed him back and grinned broadly. "You did me good, Buster," she said, bursting out in a sharp cackle. Jane Canarray didn't laugh—she cackled like a goose.

Henry Burlingame, somewhat flustered, said, "Ah, then, you read my story . . . good, very good. I trust you found it accurate . . . no faults?"

"Got it in my duffle, the whole magazine, I have," she returned. "You made me famous."

"No, Miss Jane, I think you had achieved that status before I came alone. You are a colorful woman of some repute—"

"Most likely, ill repute," she interrupted, and laughed harshly once more. They talked briefly while Porter Webb, with only the trace of a small smile, moved on by and joined Katherine and Thomas Clybourn at the end of the table.

Directly Jane came, only partway, and as though she had forgotten something, she turned, lifted her hand, and dangled a shiny gold watch by its chain. "By gawd, Burly, ain't no measure of time where we've headed, only the sun and the moon, but you'd probably feel as naked as a jaybird without this, now, wouldn't you?" With another laugh, accompanied by a few chuckles from those along the table, she returned the watch she had filched from Burlingame's vest during her brief embrace.

Katherine was in complete awe of this big woman; Thomas Clybourn was in silent disgust, for after the short introductions, Jane Canarray had seated herself next to him on the bench, and with a sly wink, Porter Longstreet Webb eased in next to Katherine. As expected, it was a conversation dominated by the woman called Calamity Jane, and by the time the supper of greens, ham and beans, and cornbread was half-finished, she was calling Katherine "partner" and Clybourn, much to his chagrin, "bluebird" and "shaved tail." Anyone, including Porter Webb, was "buster." To Clybourn's utter dismay, her conversation was spiced with other words much more descriptive and commonly used by fatigued troopers after an arduous patrol. Her lack of propriety didn't particularly disturb Katherine. She had been among mule skinners and frontiersmen before and had listened to the angry tongues of the old Lakota women and their smutty stories. She found herself actually smiling (and felt the nudge of Porter's knee) when Jane emphasized one of her rambling phrases with a particularly harsh expletive.

Afterward, toward sunset, Jane left. She had a few chores to do before the early departure the next morning—arrange her pallet in her freighter, wash some clothes down at the river—and she thought she just might cross over and pay a visit to some friends at Jack Sander's hog ranch on Currant Creek. With a wave, she left; and offered "Kate" a helping hand in the morning if she needed one.

"Horrors!" sighed Thomas Clybourn, watching Jane Canarray stride away.

"She has friends over at that place?" questioned Katherine. "Did she work there, too?"

Lieutenant Clybourn shrugged. "Who knows?"

"I don't think so," answered Porter. "These doves . . . they flit about, sometimes, from one place to another. I reckon Jane knows most of them from along the line somewhere." He grinned dourly. "She might not find much time for talking over there tonight. Not with all of these soldiers moving out tomorrow. Big heads and empty pockets."

"Doves, indeed?" wheezed Clybourn.

Webb rested back and began packing his pipe. He sang lowly in a mellow voice, his own rendition, "Rye whiskey, rye whiskey, rye whiskey she cries . . . gonna drink rye whiskey 'til the day that she dies."

Chapter Three

The Game of Tricks

"Oh, I see your sentiments," Jane Canarray said. She stirred the pot over a small fire. "A woman always lets sentiment get in the way, and this ain't the best way out here ... too damn unpredictable, Kate. You have to be more practical. What I'm only saying, is that maybe you made a mistake not taking up on Porter's invite to go on down to his place and wait around 'til this mess is over, you know, making your move then. No telling what those redskins are going to do when all these soldier boys show up." She grinned at Katherine. "Now, taking some comfort for a while down with that buster, Porter, to my notion, is a lot better than trailing along with a train of shitty bluecoats. Always did like that cuss, right handsome feller. A sight different, he is, not your regular cut."

Undaunted, Katherine said, "It's not all sentiment, and it does have a practical side to it. Who knows? Maybe there'll be no fighting." She stared around at the conglomeration of wagons. This was at the headwaters of Spring Creek, the site of General Crook's camp the first night of his army's move up the Bozeman Trail. "Mercy, I've never seen so many men and wagons in all my born life."

"A practical side is it?" questioned Jane. "Just what you planning that's so damn practical, I'd like to know? How you going to be finding that little girl? Fetching her out, away from her people?"

"I said it was a chance, didn't I?"

"Hah! Like grabbing at straws in a dust devil! You counting on a peace parley? Walking in there with the troopers and snatching her up? Not likely, from what that breed Joseph told me. Some of those redskins are his people, too, Miniconjou, onerous as the Oglala, he says, mad as hornets. Like Porter said, 'parley time is done past ... time for fighting and killing again.' Old man Crook will attack any vil-

lage in his way." Jane gave the bean pot another vigorous
stir and cast a skeptical look at Katherine Coltrane. "Now,
say there is some big fighting ... you ain't planning on
sneaking in the back door, are you? ... trying to fetch that
girl out of there, something crazy like that?"

"I'll try anything. I certainly don't like the idea of her getting trampled by some idiot's horse ... or shot."

"Shot? More likely, they'll round 'em up like a passel of
horses, herd 'em back to Standing Rock or Pine Ridge ...
separate the women and children. That's what they do. Get
'em all split up, and you can go right in and snatch the girl.
Pisses off the bucks when the blue bellies do this."

"Separate them? Bull!" Katherine said bitterly. "They
shoot and run over anything in the way, destroy everything
they can, and you know it."

It was dusk, scattered fires flickering up and down the
long line of freighters, and far to the front, soldiers were
milling about, forming lines in front of the awnings along
the mess tents. More than a thousand soldiers and officers
had to be fed. Pulling a covered pan from alongside the hot
rocks, Katherine lifted the lid and peeked in. The biscuits
were big and brown. She placed the pan aside and moved a
small tin of syrup next to the hot rocks as Jane Canarray began ladling out the beans and several large chunks of pork
into two bowls. This was food out of Jane's private larder,
a collection of assorted staples and tinned goods she had fi-
nagled from army stock, either by outright theft or trading
for favors with a supply sergeant at some future date. Jane
Canarray seldom spent money for food. Whiskey, yes, and
she often gambled, but very rarely did she squander money
on supplies. She bartered, cajoled, and sometimes she
begged. Calamity Jane was a very persuasive person. Even
the men's clothing she had procured, for Katherine, had
come by way of donations from army "pals," she claimed.

Katherine didn't question this; she was grateful for the
boots, the work pants, hat, and loose-fitting jacket, and as
Jane had advised, Katherine had wound her long hair into a
bun and wore the broad-brim cavalry hat low, almost covering her ears. Jane Canarray had a theory—when a woman
looked like a man, worked like a man, and was all businesslike, except for some casual jawing, most men kept their
proper distance. They usually didn't come sniffing around
looking to bed down with you in the bushes, under the

wagon, or wherever you happen to throw down your bedroll. Looking and acting like a man tended to put most of them off. There were exceptions, she explained, always a few rambunctious ones around, particularly young trooper recruits—the privates. Except for at payday, most of them didn't have a cent to their name. They came into the army as white trash, and some of them still were white trash, expecting to get a piece of tail for next to nothing, cheap bastards.

As the women ate, Jane began discussing the business aspects of the journey, how profitable it could be, that is, if Katherine wanted to triple her teamster pay of a dollar a day.

Wide-eyed, Katherine said, "What! What do you mean triple my wages? If it's what I'm thinking you mean, well, I'm not interested. I only came on this trip to try and get my baby back. Consorting! Mercy, Jane!"

Jane explained with a grin, "Ain't no difference you being with that Injun buck, 'cept you get paid for it, and in your case, since you're a good-looker, probably right handsome pay, too. Just a couple minutes for most of these busters, 'cause they ain't going to be liquored up ... not on the trail, and it's all over before you know it, just like rabbits, that's all. It's all business, gal, all business."

"Sneaky business," Katherine said with a frown. "Sordid. Unscrupulous."

"Yes," agreed Jane Canarray. "Yes, I allow you're right. All depends on how finicky you are, how much you need the extra dough. You can be choosy, too. Ain't like the cabins down below. You don't have to split the money. You only have to take the best of the lot, the sergeants, the ones with their pockets jingling, and you have to keep it quiet-like. Some of the officers get all uppity." Setting her bowl aside, Jane grinned again. "Just thought you might be interested in the possibilities, that's all. Now, if you ain't, that's all right, too. If some buster goes giving you trouble and you need some help, well, I reckon we can get that notion out of his head in a hurry. Ain't no profit in doing a trick if you don't want to, and I surely do understand this."

With a grimace, Katherine said, "Good Lord, Jane, you're a caution, you certainly are."

Calamity Jane shrugged indifferently. "That's what they say, so I reckon you're right. I do what I damn well please, I do, and that's the nut of it, taking the best of it with the worst, and I've seen both, I have. It's a helluva life, for sure, but there ain't no flies on me. I have to keep moving, Kate, all the time moving, 'cause I ain't never met a man my equal who's asked me to settle down." She stopped and sighed. "Can't even imagine what that'd be like, settling down, maybe raising a family." Staring across the small fire at Katherine, she said, "A woman wants security, first. Maybe a good man, but security, first. Ain't no security out here, not a lick of it, and I've been from hell to breakfast. Not many good men either. You ever think about it? Ain't this what a woman wants, security?"

"Security? Yes, I suppose," returned Katherine. It was almost dark now, and a few gnats were flitting about. She brushed at her forehead, thoughtfully stared across the shadowy tumble of stage, buck brush, and the winding line of willow along the creek bottom. "I think of peace," she finally said. "Peace of mind, that kind of peace . . ."

"Yes, that little girl. I can understand that." Jane took up the small coffeepot, reached out, and refilled Katherine's tin cup. She said, "One of these days, you're gonna have to get her away from that buck you had, her pappy. And, knowing how these Injuns are about family—"

"Find her . . . first, finding her."

"He'll kick up a fuss."

"He'll be disappointed, of course."

"Mad as a wet hen?"

"No, disappointed. He came to respect me. My needs."

"You liked this buck? What's his name?"

"Standing Bear."

"You liked him?"

"No, not at first," replied Katherine. "I hated him. I hated everyone. He raped me."

"The dirty bastard!"

"My sentiments at the time," sighed Katherine with a dark look. "He raped me four times. Raped me until I got used to it, like breaking a two-year-old, a wild filly." She sipped at her coffee, then went on reflectively. "He never tamed me either, not until after I had Julia, and that was certainly strange, how it changed everything, my baby, how it changed him. So strange, almost unbelievable."

"Hah, you tamed *him*, the son of a bitch!"

With a small blush, Katherine Coltrane confessed, "We started to enjoy each other, became affectionate. When I wanted him, he came crawling. In time, I suppose you can get used to anything, learn to enjoy it."

"It ain't so strange, Kate," said Jane. "Ain't so strange at all. Hell's bells, gal, it's all in the way a buster treats you. Why, when I'm turning a trick, I can tell right off if he's aiming to please me as well as himself. Most men are fools. Ain't many who know a lick about a woman, you know, and when I find one who stirs me up, I sure as hell give him his money's worth." She cackled. "Likely the buster's gonna come back for more, too."

"Good heavens, Jane, that sounds like . . . like lust, not security."

Jane's laugh reverberated down through the creek bottom, and somewhere, the laugh of a man came back. "It sure as hell ain't love, just good loving, and that's about as close as I ever come to the real thing. It's all over too soon. Get yourself up and all washed, come back, and the buster is gone. If he does come back for seconds, you get a little excited, that's all. Never get your expectations up. Ain't likely a piece of good tail's gonna make for a marriage. Take yourself, gal. All your years with that buck, and you'd bolted away with your little girl first chance. I know it just the way you talk about it. I'd say it's damn lucky you had that child . . . made you survive. Just likely you'd never lived to tell about it otherwise."

"I'll get her back. Sooner or later."

"I know you will," said Jane. "I like your grit. You sure as hell ain't no prissy woman. By gawd, we'd make a real pair to draw to, wouldn't we."

"I don't know," Katherine replied doubtfully with a silent smile. "I've never met anyone quite like you. That writer, Henry Burlingame, says you're one of a kind. This doesn't leave much room for another, does it?"

"Well, now, this all depends, Kate . . . depends on you, how you take to learning my rules of the road if you're interested. Why, I reckon you're looking at one of the best teachers around these parts. You're a good talker, gal, got some brains to go along with your grit. Since you're on your own, that buster, Porter, told me to watch out after you, give you a hand, and I intend to do that." Jane stopped abruptly. "Say," she said. "whatever happened to your kinfolk, anyways? Porter says since you went and lost your brother, you ain't got a lick of kin."

"That's true. My father and an aunt got killed in the raid on Lawrence ... the war. My mother died the second year we were in Cheyenne. Yes, I'm on my own."

"Don't cotton much to drinking and gambling, do you?"

"A glass of wine?"

"Just makes the heart warm, that's all. No gambling?"

"Never."

"See? You already got a hand up on me."

"You break your own rules?"

Jane cackled again. "For a fact, I do, but it's different with me. I been doing it for five years, now ... habit, can't break it, and 'sides, I got nothing else to spend my money on 'cepting the good times. I figure you might have some plans down the road. You got some schooling, that girl you're gonna get back, that house you got down in Cheyenne. Hell, you're young yet. Maybe you can even fetch yourself a good man down the line a piece. Now, you see, I never figure on these kinds of things."

"Why not?"

"I don't rightly know. Hell's bells, it's just the way I am. Hell-bent, I reckon."

"You have other rules, I suppose."

"First one is survival, and you already know about that. Getting yourself killed out here is easy. Staying alive is work. Second rule is looking out after yourself. The hell with the rest of the busters."

"That's a bit selfish, isn't it?"

"What I'm meaning is, you don't let them take advantage of you. You have to turn it around, see? You take advantage of *them*. If you don't, they're like to grind you under a boot like a piss ant. Don't mean you can't like someone. Just means don't trust 'em no farther than to our wagons over there; wait until they play out their whole hand before you give 'em a second look."

Staring at the dark forms of the wagons, Katherine smiled. "Sort of like the golden rule. Do unto others ..."

"Exactly," returned Jane. "You do it to them, 'fore they do it to you. When you're alone out here, that's the way it is. Just ain't much room for trust. This is goddamned lonely country, Kate."

Eyes on the wagons once more, Katherine said, "I hadn't thought much about it, but do you realize we're at the end of this outfit? ... the very last two."

"This is where Quinlan wanted us."

"Less trouble, I suppose ... that it?"

Jane grinned against the flickering flames. "Pete knows how I deal the cards, what I'm up to, consorting. 'Sides, it's safe. Sentries around the perimeter. Get up in the Powder country, and we'll probably be in a goddamned circle. No privacy at all. Even have to watch when you take a pee, take a bath when it's dark, less you like showing your stuff to a few troopers, and I ain't one for giving nothing for free, not even a look." She chuckled. "More of my rules of the road."

"I had that problem once in a while when we had our own wagons, always worrying about the other drivers watching me."

"Men like to ogle, and I'd say you have a lot to ogle, Kate."

"Porter didn't tell me you were such a good teacher, just said if I needed any help I could count on you. That's trust, isn't it?"

"Well, that buster Webb is a different breed. Wants to help you get that little girl back. Oh, he's one you can trust, all right, a straight dealer." She snickered and said, "Didn't say nothing about me teaching you how to make a lot of extra money with that gold mine between your legs, did he?"

"No. I think someone said you had considerable experience in this line, though. The way you spend the cold months. 'Soiled dove' was the expression. I told them I was tarnished merchandise, myself."

Jane huffed back, "Tarnished? Soiled? Who in the hell knows the difference? Listen here, now, your goodie never wears out, gal, and you know it. 'Sides, beats freezing your butt off all winter on a wagon, and on a trip like this, turning a few tricks pays damn good wages. I like to strike while the iron's hot, you know. Once we get up north, things might get a little busy ... downright nasty."

General Crook's big parade north lumbered along for another day and another night. Katherine once again saw familiar landscapes, rocky sandstone buttes, sage-covered hills, and a few brushy creek bottoms where the jays, flickertails, and magpies darted about and joined each other in raucous chorus. She also continued to hear Jane's familiar enticements, the matter of prostitution, getting a good grubstake.

This night Jane again cajoled her. "Damnit, Kate, you're gonna need a nest egg, ain't you? You need a big wad to get yourself on the trail again. It's like you got no use for money. You don't hear a word I'm saying."

"Heavens, of course I need money!" Katherine whispered harshly. "I'm dead broke." Why in heaven's name was she whispering? Why was she so agitated? All of this, the very idea, was absurd, sordid, disgusting. "I just don't think I could handle something like whoring. The very thought of bedding some stranger is appalling, Jane, and that's all there is to it."

"Well," countered Jane, "it doesn't have to be a stranger, you know. And it ain't much work, either, for what you get out of it." She grinned. "That is, if you want to call it work. There's some big money on this train, and I aim to get some of it 'fore we reach the end of the line."

"Big money? What do you mean by big money?"

Jane idly poked at her big hair bun. She clucked her tongue once, and looked away, calculating. "Oh, I reckon maybe a couple of hundred apiece if we got real picky, took the best of the lot. Wouldn't want the cheap busters, those fifty-cent bastards."

"Two hundred?" Katherine Coltrane swallowed once. Mercy! Tempting thoughts finally began to flirt with her scruples, skittering around in her mind like tiny water spiders.

"Interested?" she heard Jane asking.

"No. No, you make it sound too easy. It's not easy, not at all, at least not for me. I can't even imagine—"

"Told me you got used to that Sioux buck, didn't you?"

"That was different. The man became my husband."

"Turning a trick or two is just as easy," grinned Jane. "Get paid for it, too. That's the difference."

Katherine's mind spun, whirled around like a gillywhiffet. Mercy, what was happening here? Had Jane's nagging persistence finally overwhelmed her? Or was this just simply her own curiosity. Illicit riches? After a moment, an agonizing moment, Katherine huddled close to Jane. She spoke lowly, almost furtively as though she were preparing to hatch some kind of foul plot. She asked, "All right, say I might try it, just once to find out what it's like. How much would I get paid? What kind of wage are you talking about?"

"Ah," smiled Jane, "you're warming up to the notion, then?"

"I'm just asking, damnit! I'm curious, that's all."

"Oh, is that it? Just curious about all that money sitting out there."

"*You* said it was out there," whispered Katherine. "I didn't."

"Well, now, let me see." Jane pushed up under her hair again, momentarily worked at her tight strands with her fingers. Her long black locks suddenly tumbled down over her broad shoulders. And removing Katherine's big hat, she began loosening her hair, too, talking at the same time. "I'd say up here, a beauty like you can negotiate . . . high as four dollars, maybe down to two. Yep, at one or two tricks a night . . . well, I reckon you can make yourself up to two hundred on the trip up, allowing thirty or so days on the campaign. Maybe you can make another two hundred on the way back."

"Mercy! That's four hundred, not two!"

"Well, I plumb forgot to calculate it round-trip." Grinning, Jane said, "I got the feeling you're beginning to like the idea. All that money can take you down the road a long way when we get back . . . up the trail to Pine Ridge agency, too, if we don't get your girl out of one of the villages on this trip. Now, what do you say? We'd make a damn good team, you know."

Katherine nervously wiped at her brow. "Mercy, that's a lot! I never realized—"

"Down at the hogs, lucky if you get a dollar a throw. Makes Quinlan's thirty a month working with these shit-assed mules look right miserly, don't it?"

"Yes," Katherine whispered huskily. "Yes, indeed, it surely does."

"Feel up to trying it, then?"

Katherine sighed fatefully. "I can try. Yes, I can try, see what's it like. It's a start, isn't it?"

"A damn good start," opined Jane Canarray. "Better'n down below at the hogs, for sure . . . 'less you decide you're interested in doing it for regular wages. That case, you can get yourself on down to Cheyenne City . . . Denver, get in one of those fancy houses where the big money is. Some of the busters down there get right careless with their wallets . . . big tips, too."

"Lordy, this is outrageous! I've heard about those places . . . never thought about working in one of them. I'd go crazy. I'd die. I'd simply die."

Jane gave Katherine a hug and said, "Well, that'd be up to you, honey, see if you like it and all. Who knows? With your looks and long legs, I reckon there ain't a house down there that'd turn you down."

Katherine stirred uneasily. Jane was stroking her hair, combing it with her long fingers. Katherine finally asked hesitantly, "When do you plan on dealing your cards? Doing something?"

"We've already frittered three nights away," Jane replied. "I reckon I could mosey around tonight, see what business looks like."

Katherine stiffened. "Tonight!"

"You ain't up to it?"

"Why, I've barely had time to think about it."

Jane chuckled. "You been thinking about it for two or three days, ever since I asked you."

"Nonsense!" Katherine felt a blush. She turned away, saying, "I'm scared silly. I don't know the first thing about this . . . what to do, what to say. I don't even have . . . you know, the things I need."

Jane gave her a reassuring pat. "I'm your teacher, ain't I? Got me a whole little box full of stuff, everything you'll need. You just be sure your buster washes himself. And you check him, too. Ain't no use catching someone else's misery."

"Oh, my God!"

"Don't you worry, Kate. Like I told you, ain't no different than what you been doing already, 'cepting get paid for it." Jane smiled. "And if you want to get started tonight, I think I got someone for you, too, regular gentleman, he is."

Katherine suddenly went limp. "Good lord! You didn't even know if I was interested in doing this kind of thing. How terrible! How embarrassing! How in the hell did you make such an arrangement? Who, for God's sake? Who did you talk to about me?"

"I didn't talk to him," Jane said defensively. "I didn't say one word about you turning a trick, so help me, but it was Pete Quinlan. He asked me about you the other day . . . if you were in the business. I told him I had no idea. Well, the buster upped and flipped a ten-dollar gold piece in front of my nose. He said he'd give most anything to get inside you. Reckon you sure caught his eye."

"Ten dollars! So much?"

"He's a good-looking man, ain't he? Keeps himself right presentable and clean, too ... not one of them youngsters, and he's a real good start for openers. Leastways, no stranger."

"Mercy!"

"Look honey, for the ten, let him bed down with you for a couple of tricks. Ain't gonna be like all night, you know. Pete's got too many chores ... up before dawn getting this train all ready." She gave Katherine's head a little tousle and smiled. "Long time since you had that Sioux buck, ain't it? Two or three weeks?"

"Longer," sighed Katherine. "Maybe a month ... I don't remember."

"Well, look at it this way, it's damn good beginners. Ten dollars for doing something you wouldn't mind doing anyways. A month is a mighty long time for a woman who likes it right regular."

Feeling a deep blush, Katherine Coltrane retorted, "Good heavens, what makes you say such horrid things! How do you know what I want? How I feel? I'm so confused, I can't even think straight. I told you, I'm frightened."

"Weak in the knees, is it?" Jane smiled. "Well, that's a surefire sign, so I reckon we better get some things together. Get ourselves ready for a little gold mining the easy way."

Wilting inside, yet feeling a tiny spark of anticipation, Katherine Coltrane mumbled, "Yes, the easy way ... get ready."

On her pallet in the narrow confines of the big wagon, it was still quite dark, but Katherine had heard a bugle somewhere in the distance—faintly heard it, for she had been in a deep sleep. A big tarpaulin covered the back of the wagon, good shelter from the cold dawn air of the prairie. She carefully eased out from under her quilt, and began searching about on the crates above her for her bundle of clothing. She was still naked, and after some maneuvering in her corridor of illicit love, she managed to dress, then edged past her empty basins and the coal oil lantern, and found her boots under the tailgate of the wagon. Jane Canarray was already up and fully clothed. A blanket thrown over her shoulders, she was sitting in front of a small fire putting up her hair, while nearby the little coffeepot was steaming and the two tin cups were warming on a flat rock.

Half turning, Jane smiled at Katherine and said, "Good morning, Miss Kate. Allow you slept well, eh?" And she let out one of her cackles, but it was subdued, not one of her usual raucous outcries.

Observing the rising sun, Katherine returned, "Good morning." Now, a mocking smile of her own. Yes, of course, she had slept well, exceedingly well. After Pete Quinlan had given her a parting kiss and crept away like a whipped dog, she had collapsed, oblivious to all of the night sounds, and had heard absolutely nothing until the bugle. She quickly found her soap and towels, and headed for the upper reaches of the willow-lined creek. Security there. She saw a few mule skinners crouched in the early morning light down below her, and as she departed heard Jane call: "No trouble, was it?"

"Not a bit."

"Told you it was easy, didn't I?"

Waving a handful of towels, Katherine disappeared in the brush. Later, when she returned, she saw a man standing beside a big brown horse talking to Jane. Oh, mercy, could it be! Yes, it was—it was Quinlan. Quinlan making his rounds of the train, or Quinlan on a social call, not looking for seconds, of course, because she had given him seconds and that must have been around eleven o'clock. He was a wagon master, her first gentleman, and he had been that, too, certainly not crass and uncaring. She had been lucky, very lucky, and she knew it.

Pete Quinlan also said good morning. He tipped his hat and smiled, too. "Just passing by, that's all," he said. "If you two need a hand with the teams, give me a shout." He remounted, turned, and grinned down at Katherine. He admitted sheepishly, "Had some trouble getting in the saddle this morning. Worth it, though." And, with a little chuck, he urged the brown back up the line.

Jane grinned, too, and looking over at Katherine Coltrane, she said, "But I'll bet the buster didn't have trouble getting in your saddle last night, did he?"

"No, not that I recall."

"You don't remember!"

"It was . . . confusing. I didn't know if I could . . . well, then it got all mixed-up. I guess I forgot it was one of those tricks. I think I made a fool out of myself."

Jane held up a warning finger. "Well, don't be forgetting it's a job, honey. 'Course, like I told you, Pete's a cut above most of the busters 'round here."

Katherine Coltrane fished a big coin out of her pocket, held it up in the morning sun. It glittered, gold. "Look at this, will you!"

She sat next to Jane by the fire. Jane did look, and she whistled lowly, then said, "For crisesakes, gal . . . a double eagle!"

"Yes," sighed Katherine, "twenty beautiful dollars."

Jane Canarray shook her head and moaned. "The son of a bitch ain't that rich, honey. What in the hell did you do, put a spell on him?"

"I destroyed him." Katherine giggled once, and added, "He's coming back, too . . ."

"Next time it won't be at that price, I'll tell you that."

"Anything from two dollars up will do nicely. Just a little more than regular rates is all right. I don't intend to be greedy, you know."

"No," returned Jane, "but you sure as hell catch on fast."

"Good teacher, good learner."

Katherine pulled a big tortoise comb out of her back pocket, turned her back, and let her new teacher work at finishing up her hair, and Jane did so willingly, began slowly combing it into a long brown curtain. There was a small, tin box now sitting on one of the rocks alongside the fire. Head gently swaying to the steady pull of the comb, Katherine said, "What's that . . . that box?"

"Breakfast."

"Breakfast?"

"Pete dropped it off," said Jane Canarray with a little chuckle. "Said he picked up some biscuits, syrup, and bacon up at one of the soldiers' mess tents. Thought we might like some free army grub. Been on a train twice with that buster, and he never did nothing like this before. Reckon it has something to do with you . . . you know, destroying him that way. Ain't hot enough for him to go getting himself crazy with the heat. I can't figure it. Maybe the damn fool is taking a regular fancy to you . . . sort of setting his hat . . ."

"Ridiculous! After the first night?"

"It happens," said Jane. "Seen it before. Some buster

swoons, and a woman goes grabbing at that security." Giving Katherine's head a final pat, she said, "There, now let's eat."

"There's no great measure of security in running freighters," Katherine said. "Not by my way of thinking, anyhow. I lost my brother, six wagons, and five years of my life to the Oglala freighting. No thanks. Even if Pete has some notion, which I don't think he has, I'd say no. And, besides, thinking about last night, I just have some notions of my own. And, you're right, too, this work can be very lucrative. I'm in no position to be choosy. Another thing, too . . . it was nothing like I thought it was going to be. And you realize, I made almost a month's wages in . . . in, well maybe an hour." Katherine laughed. "I certainly wasn't keeping time."

"Oh ho, you did like it!"

"Well, it wasn't bad."

"Figure you're in the game, now?"

"I'm in," Katherine said. "I have another notion, too. I know this is going to sound crazy. I've been thinking about this. Maybe this is only a beginning, but those houses in Cheyenne and Denver . . . the ones you were talking about—"

Jane cut in. "Hold it, hold it! Now look it here, gal, I thought this was a temporary job of sorts, a little tricking on the side 'til you got the little one back. Why, you ain't even got your feet wet, and you're thinking about the big time! For crisesakes, you planning on taking your little breed daughter down there with you?" Jane heaved her big bosom, then spat to the side. "You ain't got a lick of sense, woman!"

Katherine parted a biscuit, carefully layered it with several strips of bacon, and took a bite, then said in between chewing, "If I have to get by that way for a while, I will. I can find a way. Grit? Remember? And, I have a house down there, you know . . . two bedrooms in it, a parlor and kitchen, too. With the money from this trip, I can fix it up fancy."

"Ah yes," Jane said with a wink. "Yes, now I see what you're meaning."

"You do and you don't." Katherine swallowed and went on, "It would be a start, only a start. You could come down and turn some tricks, too, couldn't you? . . . like you said, in the winter, better than freezing on one of those damn wagons. Yes, to start with, a little house of our own, inviting gentlemen in, not having to split the take ... certainly more appealing than those cheap-paying hog ranches."

"I ain't no beauty like you, Kate. Just a pair of big tits and a firm body, that's all. Tricking together, huh? Tricking and taking care of Julia, is it? This what you're thinking?"

"For openers, as you say. Yes, just a start."

Jane took a long draft of coffee, smacked her lips once, and asked, "And, after this start, then what?"

Holding her cup to the sky, Katherine said, "Shoot the wad. Expand. I want my own place, a big one, a dozen rooms, a saloon, fiddles, dancers, singers, and the hottest women in Cheyenne, Denver, who knows?"

Jane almost choked on her biscuit. She spluttered and coughed to the side, then exclaimed, "My gawd, Kate, you've done and gone daft on me! You taken to swilling red-eye, too? Where in tarnation did you get such a crazy notion? Better'n that, where you gonna get the money for all of this?"

"Just knew you were going to think I'm crazy. I just knew it."

"Well, it ain't such a bad notion. No, the notion is all right. Just seems a little too big for your sweet britches, that's all."

"Where does most of the money around here come from?"

"Cattle, gold mines, the banks, I reckon."

Suddenly radiating confidence, Katherine replied, "That's it, a bank ... don't you see?"

"Oh, shit, now you're gonna rob a goddamned bank!"

"No, no, Jane, will you listen!" Katherine sighed in exasperation. She began dribbling syrup on another biscuit. "Look, I get a loan from a bank, that's what, a damned loan."

"Humph! Need that stuff they call collateral, you do," answered Jane skeptically. "Loan, indeed! Money is what talks."

"Don't worry, I'll be getting myself some of it just like some of the others out here ... by hook or crook." And, smiling slyly, Katherine placed her hand where her legs met. "Rest of the collateral is right up here."

For the next several days, the trail twisted and wound its way slightly to the northwest, most often along the sage and rock-strewn flats and sometimes along the sandy creek bottoms, the headwaters of the Powder River. By day, Katherine Coltrane frequently saw more old trails winding across the prairie, trails she had once traversed with the Oglala searching out the buffalo. By night, in the dim light of her canvas-covered freighter, she saw unfamiliar faces. By prior invitation, the men arrived quietly, and pledged to the secrecy of the game; they only talked in hushed whispers. The occasional little grunts and sighs were only heard in the immediate vicinity of the two wagons, for Katherine and Jane always managed to draw up a good distance away from the rest of the train. Women mule skinners needed their privacy, and Peter Quinlan had issued orders for everyone to keep clear of the area. Jane Canarray opined it was one of the most orderly and properly managed arrangements she had ever known. By Jane's rules of the road, it was all business, strictly women without the wine and the song. And, it was becoming very lucrative, each woman taking two tricks during the evening and early-night hours. By eleven o'clock or shortly thereafter, Katherine and Jane went to the nearest creek, bathed in silence, then returned to share a cup of coffee before retiring. Katherine was happily content with this arrangement, and began marking one of the wagon frames with a piece of charcoal as she stashed her earnings in a leather bag at the bottom of a flour sack.

One morning, not too far from Pumpkin Buttes, General Crook's long train came to a halt. Katherine and Jane learned that one of the scouts, Louis Richards, had returned from the advance party with news of the presence of Indians. Richards was one of the guides in Lieutenant Thomas Clybourn's party. General Crook wanted to determine the hostiles' intentions before proceeding. The Indians soon disappeared; the delay was no more than a half hour, but during this pause, Peter Quinlan came riding down the line accompanied by an officer Katherine remembered from the afternoon tea in Benjamin Bradford's office back at Fort Fetterman. It was Colonel Jason Armitage, General Crook's adjutant, the officer that Porter Webb called Bird Dog. Sometime later, after the tea, Porter had told her the term "Bird Dog" was a carryover from the Civil War, twelve years earlier. Armitage had been a young lieutenant in intelligence, a spy. He was a few years older than Porter, probably around thirty-seven now, a rather dashing fellow with a black mustache and small goatee, and his eyes were almost coal black.

Katherine Coltrane's wagon was the last in the train, and this was where Colonel Armitage and Peter Quinlan stopped and reined about. The colonel smiled and politely nodded to Katherine and said, "I barely recognized you, Miss Coltrane. Quinlan, here, told me you were in our party. Never give up, do you?"

Katherine pushed her hat back and returned, "No, not while there's some hope." She stared curiously at Quinlan, who gave her a wink, and moved away back to Jane Canarray's wagon. Bird Dog. Yes, indeed, Armitage was a bird dog, that sly wink from Quinlan, and now she was alone with the colonel. Instinctively, she knew some intrigue was in the air.

"This isn't any place for a tea, Miss Coltrane," he said, "but Mister Quinlan said he believed you occasionally enjoy a glass of wine in the evening. I was wondering . . . ?"

Katherine Coltrane smiled. "Is this an invitation, Mister Armitage, an invitation to a mule skinner? . . . the way I look, now?"

Armitage replied diplomatically, "This is the trail. I should say any manner of dress is appropriate out here." He paused and added, "Will you consider?"

"Yes, I might, depending . . ."

"Depending on what?"

"Business or conversation?"

"Perhaps a little of both." He grinned. "I think you understand, don't you?"

She nodded. "Tonight? . . . here?"

"No, Miss Coltrane, I was thinking of my quarters . . . at dark. I'll make sure my tent is pitched away from the others."

"That's a bit dangerous, isn't it? General Crook?"

"Not at all," he replied. "This is just between us. Come in quietly from the back." Armitage grinned again. "Dressed in that outfit, no one is going to take you for a charming woman. Will you join me?"

Without hesitation she answered, "I'll be there, Mister Armitage . . . after dark."

"Excellent," he said, once again tipping his hand to his hat. "I shall look forward to our evening."

As he turned away, Katherine called, "I'll need a few things . . . understand? Can you provide them?"

Colonel Jason Armitage waved and nodded.

Jane Canarray was aghast later that afternoon when Katherine told her she had agreed to turn a trick with Colonel Armitage at his quarters. Jane, always wary of officers, fearful of them spoiling her game, thought it was an unwise arrangement, one that might have unpleasant consequences for both of them. She was both surprised and dismayed at Katherine's startling disclosure, for it was well-known that General Crook, as well as some of his aides, despised the presence of women around the troopers, especially prostitutes. Crook himself thought women were bad luck.

Katherine Coltrane viewed her secret engagement with Colonel Armitage much differently. She believed it was a ticket to security for the entire campaign, because before any report got to the field desk of General Crook, it had to pass through Jason Armitage first, and she allowed that once she tricked with him and established a relationship, he would become a trustworthy and valuable ally. No one would dare interfere with their new business. In fact, Katherine explained, she thought such a relationship might even improve business. A very good explanation, agreed Jane, but she still entertained some doubts. Did Kate plan on them tricking the entire army? No. Katherine Coltrane told her; she certainly would exclude old Three Stars Crook.

General Crook's army camped that night alongside a great stand of cottonwoods near the site of old Fort Conner on the upper Powder, wagons and tents arranged in a gigantic half circle. Toward sunset, Katherine Coltrane, head lowered and her hat pulled down close to her ears, took a casual stroll around the perimeter. It didn't take her long to locate the group of headquarter tents, and there off to the side, conveniently set among the shadow of several trees, was the tent of Colonel Armitage. Standing directly in front of it near a small table was the colonel himself talking with two soldiers. Backing away into the shadows, Katherine smiled. Jason Armitage was a man of his word; he couldn't have placed that tent in a better location; it was perfect for secret entry and departure as well. She laughed inside. Oh, what an exciting game this was becoming, the intrigue, the challenge. And the profit, always the profit.

When night finally set in, Katherine packed away a few of her personal necessities, went up the river several hundred yards, bathed, and washed her hair. Fluffing it out, then combing as she walked, she circled around through the brush and gaunt cottonwoods, and ultimately arrived near the back of Jason Armitage's quarters. Momentarily huddling in the shadows, she cast her eyes in both directions, then darted forward, flipped up the bottom of the tent, and scurried under it like a frightened squirrel. There was Colonel Armitage, standing at the other side near the entrance. He turned, cocked his head once, and looked down at her. She, in turn, on her hands and knees, stared back at him. She felt terribly foolish.

"Hello," he said.

She said, "This is a helluva way to come to tea . . . wine, or whatever."

"Yes . . . yes, I'm sorry, but I'm happy you're here." Armitage hurried over, extended his hands, and helped her to her feet. Her big, greenish-blue eyes darted in all directions: the little field table, covered with a cloth, two small, canvas-covered folding stools to each side, wine, glasses, a plate of cookies, a flickering candle next to the wine, and a lantern suspended from a tent pole casting a soft, golden patina over the whole interior. To the side, on a box, lay a bucket of water, towels, and a small, enameled washbasin. It was cozy-looking, even the army cot covered by a white sheet, a pillow at the top, two blankets neatly and appropriately folded at the bottom, but the yellowish illumination in the colonel's well-furnished quarters was much too bright. She whispered, "I think you should turn that down a bit. It casts too much shadow . . ." She went over to a box stand and set aside her little pouch.

Jason Armitage reached up and turned the small lantern knob, lowering the wick, and the interior darkened. "Better?" he whispered.

Katherine smiled and nodded. She said haltingly, "This is all very nice . . . I wish I could have worn a pretty dress, made myself more presentable."

"You're a lovely woman the way you are," replied Jason Armitage. And, reaching out, he touched her hair, stroked it once, then her cheek. "You feel damp," he said. Abruptly turning away, he went to the back of the tent and returned with a long burgundy-colored robe. It was made of the finest wool, very smooth to the touch. After fondling it for a moment, she held it up to her body, measuring it for size. Her eyes met his, almost directly. "It fits," she smiled. "I'm a tall woman ... the Oglala called me Tall Woman."

"Tall women are always most appreciated," he returned. "Go ahead, take off your clothes, if you wish. Wrap yourself up in it ... be comfortable. I'll pour some wine."

Katherine went over to the small cot, seated herself at the bottom end, first took off her boots, her baggy britches, then peeled off her long black stockings, and finally slipped out of her underclothing. Last, she took off her shirt, then stood. The wine had been poured, and as she wrapped the robe around her, Armitage exclaimed lowly, "I've never seen anything lovelier in my life, Miss Katherine. I've thought so from the very first day I saw you in Bradford's office ... when you were sitting there in such a terrible fix."

Katherine replied, "Thank you, Mister Armitage ..."

"Jason ... Jason, please."

"Yes ... Jason. Well, I'm still in a terrible fix." She hesitated, and added, "Maybe more of a fix, now, coming down to this."

"I'd like to help you—" he began.

Smiling at him across the way, she returned, "This *is* a big help, isn't it? Yes, perhaps a big help for both of us. You want something, and so do I. Not exactly the same things, but we're both searching ... wanting."

He then graciously seated her and said, "Yes ... yes, I understand your predicament, of course, I do."

"There's always a means to an end," she said, "and presently, this seems the most practical." Tasting her wine once, she smiled over at him. "This is very good ... not army issue."

"No, not army."

Holding up her glass, Katherine said to him, "Here's to better solutions, Jason ... for both of us."

They sipped wine and talked lowly. Katherine mostly listened, occasionally nibbling on a cookie. He was Jason Armitage, a graduate of West Point, a career officer, once married to a young woman who soon became disenchanted with post life in Omaha and divorced him. He was the only son of James B. Armitage, president of the Penn-Central Railroad. Jason detested the idea of working in an office for the railroad; he enjoyed the rigorous life in the army, and like a few other people Katherine had met, she learned that he respected General Crook as his commander but thoroughly disagreed with his campaign strategies. And, personally, he disliked the general. Katherine thought all of these disclosures boded well for her own present well-being, also her selfish plans for the future. She was a good listener, and as she had told Jane, a very good learner. She was orderly, too, filed away anything and everything in the crevices of her fertile mind. Army or not, Armitage was a wealthy man.

Ultimately, their whispered conversation waned, the silence only broken by the sputtering lantern overhead and a few isolated camp noises outside. She reached over and touched his hand, stroked it several times. Armitage stood, went over to his small footlocker, shortly returned, and placed a few green bills on the table. And, as though he were showing his cards, he slid the crisp bills into the neat shape of a fan, five tens, an impossible hand but an astoundingly good one. Pleasantly stunned, Katherine Coltrane blinked several times, glanced up, and said, "Are you sure?"

"I'm sure," replied Armitage. "I said I wanted to help you. It's worth that much just to look at your beautiful body."

Katherine smiled back. "You're going to be surprised at what it can do. For this much money, I'm staying all night. Get your clothes off, Jason." And by the time she had pulled off the bedding from the cot and rearranged it into a large pallet on the ground, Armitage had shed his clothes. When Katherine slipped out of her robe, she turned and faced him. "Oh, mercy!"

Somewhat embarrassed, he returned. "Yes . . . yes, I think I'm ready."

"My goodness, your wife must have been crazy leaving you." Katherine quickly reached up and snuffed the wick of the lantern. "Shhh," she whispered.

Chapter Four

The Camp at Goose Creek

There was activity somewhere in the coulees to the left, the sound of sporadic rifle fire, followed by faint shouts. Then from above at the head of the column, Katherine heard a bugle, and several riders from the file at the rear charged by, one yelling to pull up and get under the wagon. Katherine did, and moments later, Jane, holding her rifle, joined her. Jane took out her pistol and handed it to Katherine. A few more troopers arrived from the head of the train, quickly dismounted, and took up positions behind the line of army wagons and civilian freighters. By this time, Katherine saw a few clouds of dust along the hills to the west, and then emerging from the billowy haze, at least a half-dozen riders, their blue shirts appearing grayish-black against the afternoon sun behind them. They had their mounts running hellbent for the safety of the wagon train. Directly behind them, mounted Indians began materializing out of the clouds like black ghosts, shouts began to swell into a screaming crescendo, and Katherine heard the first whine of bullets splitting the warm air.

Jane came up on an elbow and positioned her Winchester, looked over at Katherine, and smiled grimly. "Some Sioux friends of yours, I suspect. Helluva way of showing it, ain't it?"

Katherine forced a smile. This was on the Tongue River, only several days' ride from the headwaters of the Rosebud where the Lakota and Cheyenne tribes were supposed to be congregating. Just who *these* Indians were, Katherine couldn't determine, not yet, anyhow; they weren't within range for accurate identification, but she knew without a doubt it wasn't Crazy Horse. "Yes, probably Sioux," she said, "but not Crazy Horse. That patrol probably bumped into this bunch by accident, and the boys are running for their lives. We're getting too close to the villages . . . the big villages."

Directly, the fleeing troopers charged through the train in a blur of blue tunics, and in the distance, about forty or fifty Indians broke off into a long file and whirled around in a gigantic circle. In a ragged, swerving line, they made a parallel pass at the wagon train, discharging their rifles at full gallop. A staccato of shots erupted all the way up to the head of the train as soldiers returned fire, but not an Indian dropped from his pony. Then, as swiftly as it had begun, it was over; the Indians turned and disappeared like phantoms over the hills to the southwest.

"Just a goddamned warning, I reckon," sighed Jane.

Katherine edged back out from under the wagon and sat cross-legged in the shade. "Yes, a bit of a fright, wasn't it?"

"You're damn right, it was! First time for me. Never been in a fracas with them before this." Sitting beside Katherine, she rested the butt of her rifle straight up between her legs and with her other hand, wiped her sleeve across her forehead. "Those buggers always yell and holler? Carry on that way?"

"I suppose," Katherine answered. "I don't really know . . . there were only thirty of us when Lieutenant Clybourn's troops ran into us on the Little Powder. Wasn't much time for shouting, just running. We were laggards . . . half a day behind the rest of our people. Most of the women were in their menses . . . custom, you always move behind when you have the curse."

"How'd you know it wasn't Crazy Horse out there?"

Katherine nodded to the north. "He's up there farther . . . probably camped on the Rosebud by now. That's where everyone was headed a few weeks ago." She turned and peered up the line. Riders were moving about now, up and down the entire length of the train, checking for casualties or damage. "Besides," she went on, "if it had been Crazy Horse, we would have been attacked on three sides . . . middle and the flanks. That's what the army tries to do." She grinned wanly. "He's like me, a good learner." Nodding again, Katherine said, "Well, here comes Pete."

Pete Quinlan rode up holding the reins of his big brown horse tightly; the horse was nervous, chomping at the bit, shying from side to side. "Scared the hell out of him," Pete

Quinlan shouted down. "Everything all right, here? Mules catch any of that lead?"

The women stood, and Jane replied, "Everything's all right, Mister Pete, but I damn near pissed my britches, and that's a fact."

"What are we doing?" asked Katherine.

"Holding fast for the moment," said Quinlan. "The old man and some of his crew are jawing up ahead."

Jane asked, "Ain't no one gonna chase after those busters?"

"No profit in that, Jane. Couldn't catch them if they wanted. 'Sides, the old man is a bit skitterish about splitting the train, maybe running into a trap, or even getting hit from his backside. That's my way of reckoning, anyhow. He might send a couple of those Crow or Shoshoni out to take a look, see where the hostiles went, but that's about all." Reining about, Quinlan headed back.

What Quinlan said was true; a few minutes later, four of the friendlies, Crow and Shoshoni who had joined the train several days earlier, rode off in a slow trot to the west. Katherine and Jane sat down in the shade and shared a canteen of water. Not more than ten minutes had gone by when Quinlan returned with news—General Crook had decided to move back to Goose Creek and set up his war camp; operations for the campaign would be conducted from there; the two converging armies coming south from the Yellowstone weren't expected to be along the Rosebud for another six or seven days, so the general had elected to await scouting reports on their precise movements. Pete told the women to prepare to turn their wagons around.

Jane, with a broad grin glanced over at Katherine. One week at a permanent camp; no trailing, just sitting around waiting and relaxing in the warm winds of early summer and enjoying the long, cool nights. What could be better?

Katherine understood what her dear friend meant, but business notwithstanding, she thought of at least one thing that could be better—the miracle of peace, getting into the village of Crazy Horse and finding Julia. Despite the profitable enterprise in which she was now engaged, thoughts of reclaiming Julia were forever gnawing away inside her like a pack of hungry field mice. However lucrative the new war camp might prove to be, she was also evaluating it realistically—it was only a postponement of the inevitable, the clash between red and white.

Later that evening on the forks of Goose Creek, in the purple shadows of the Big Horns, a great camp was made. It formed a circle, extending along the meandering stream back into groves of evergreens, aspen, and cottonwoods. Katherine and Jane edged their wagons in among a growth of fluttering aspen at the lower end of the camp, a perfect location, and toward dusk, while scrounging for firewood in the nearby woods, they discovered a small, clear pool fringed with watercress and pond lilies. One abandoned beaver lodge, its small dome thatched with branches and twigs as white as sun-bleached bones, stood alone directly in the middle of it. Katherine thought this was a beautiful place. Jane was a bit more practical—it was a damn good place to take a bath, well hidden and far enough away from the turmoil of the camp for privacy, night or day.

The women stretched a large sheet of canvas between their two wagons, removed several crates of tinned and dried food supplies, and two barrels of brined pickles to use as chairs and worktables. At the edge of the canvas awning, Jane gouged out a fire pit, and the women ringed it with rocks from the bank of the nearby creek. It was almost dark by the time they had their coffee, some cornmeal cakes, bacon and fried potatoes; it was also too late to do any soliciting for the night, but not too late for social calls. The first call was a surprise to Katherine. Lieutenant Clybourn appeared out of the dark. It had been his patrol returning from ahead of the train that the Sioux attacked earlier in the day. Two of his men were wounded, fortunately only superficially. He was tired but very happy to be back among friends again, free of forward patrol duty, at least for a day or two. And how was Katherine faring on such an arduous journey so far, driving six mules in the heat, the dust, the constant fear of attack? Was it like old times again, freighting?

Katherine poured a cup of coffee for Thomas Clybourn, the young man most responsible for her predicament, yet her friend. Yes, she told him. In most respects the journey thus far was like old times, with one exception, she thought. Thomas Clybourn thoroughly disliked Jane Canarray. To discover Jane had already introduced her to prostitution, that she had made more money in two weeks than the lieutenant made in a month, would certainly be an abhorrence to him.

Thomas wanted her to take a short stroll with him, away from the camp; the moon was up, beautifully full, the edge of the glade in deep shadows, and she led him through the brush down the winding game path to the little pond. There was nothing here but night beauty and its sounds, silver rays on still water, cries of nighthawks in the air, and the chirps of crickets in the lush grass. They sat near the edge of the pond, and Clybourn said haltingly that he had thought of her more than once during his time on patrol, pleasant thoughts. Sensing his hesitancy, his shyness, Katherine said it wasn't so unusual for men to think about women, particularly when they were lonely. She smiled over at him. "And," she said softly, "the prairie is often a lonely place, even with people around."

After a brief silence, Thomas said, "I was thinking ... when this campaign is over, I'll be back down at Fort Laramie, and if you're waiting around there, or even down at Cheyenne, I'll be having some furlough, and I'd like to call on you, Miss Kate ... see how you're doing, see if you have your daughter yet, or if you need some help ... that sort of thing."

"That's very gallant of you, Thomas, but God only knows where I'm going to be ... when any of this is going to be over."

"I realize this," he replied. "A post? ... perhaps, you could write, keep me advised?"

She had to be candid. She reached over and took his hand, saying, "You're so kind ... understanding, but what do you have in mind? Courting me? A relationship, Thomas? Romance? This is very flattering, if this is what's on your mind. But you barely know me. Courting? My goodness!"

"Yes, courting," he confessed quietly. "I was thinking along those lines. I do fancy you, Miss Kate."

"It's something that's so nice, but all so impossible, Thomas. My God, I'm a mother ... a jaded woman, and you ... you have a good career ahead of you. Good Lord, if we had some kind of relationship, all I could be is a hindrance, that's all. It's five years too late. If this was happening five years ago, why ... why I'd feel like lightning had struck. I surely would. Oh, it still makes me feel a little shaky inside, but ... but no, it's too damn late."

"Listen," he said, "as far as I'm concerned the past is past, Miss Kate. It's not too late, not at all ... it's a new beginning. Anything can be overcome in time ... forgotten. I thought maybe you liked me."

Another moment of silence. Katherine Coltrane was trying to collect her fractured thoughts. She had scars of her own, and now she was about to inflict a small wound on an admirable young man, a caring young man, one with honorable intentions. This was a travesty, a paradox, because her own recently acquired habits were disreputable, regardless of the money. But truthfully, she didn't want to stop. Every time she dwelled on her whoring she shuddered inside, but despite this, she was enjoying most of it and all of the rewards. She couldn't explain this to anyone, except Jane Canarray, who already knew it, and she had no intention of explaining it to Thomas Clybourn.

Finally she said, "I do like you, very much, but you don't understand what's happened to me since I left Fetterman. I should say, you won't understand. Yes, the past is past, but this is the present, Thomas, the practical present, reality ... the shameful present I suppose I should say, but it was my decision, one I had to make if I expect any future at all." Katherine Coltrane shrugged and gave him a helpless look. "So, I've been seeing a few men at night ... taking their money. This is what it's come down to ... at least until I can get myself a stake, a big stake to tide me over." Her smile was thin as she stared across the still water of the pond. She couldn't look at Thomas Clybourn, didn't want to. "One of those soiled doves," she said. "I think that's the kindest expression, anyhow. You know all of the others."

It was some time before the lieutenant could collect his senses, yet in a way he wasn't surprised. Quite simply, she was fundless, and then, of course, she was traveling along with Calamity Jane, which only compounded an already onerous situation. "I'm sorry," he finally said. "I'm disappointed. As you say, it's your decision, and if you believe it's going to help solve matters, so be it, but I don't. I think you've made a big mistake taking this deplorable route. I can't believe you would do this to yourself. There were other ways ..."

"I don't think I had much choice."

Clybourn gave her an imploring look. "You could have gone down to Hawk Springs with Porter ... waited around until things cleared up," he said. "That was an option wasn't it ... one you should have considered."

"A month? . . . two months? . . . maybe all winter, never knowing what's happening. Yes, and without a dollar to my name." She sighed. "I did consider it, and I didn't want it. I want my daughter."

"And you want this, too?"

"Yes, the money," Katherine answered. "It's here, so I decided to take it. Shameful, I suppose. I can't say any more. I'm sorry, I can't."

Back at the wagons, Lieutenant Clybourn tried a parting smile; he casually waved and disappeared into the moonlight, moonlight that was playing shadow games with the solemn trees. Jane was sitting on the ground on a tarp, resting up against one of the big barrels. She had a cup of coffee and was smoking a little pipe, a unique pipe in that it had the carved head of a smiling Indian on its wooden bowl. When Katherine had first seen it, she had commented that it was very inappropriate. Indians these days were not smiling. Jane, watching the form of Thomas Clybourn melt away, said, "That was a quick one, wasn't it? The shaved-tail short on cash?"

"Conversation," Katherine replied. "Just conversation."

"Told you about that, didn't I? No profit in just jawing."

"Yes, I know, but he wasn't interested in getting in me. It was more than that. I like him, too. I think he was looking for my heart. Jane, the young man wanted to court me."

Jane Canarray almost spit out her little pipe. She tried to cackle between her teeth. "Hee-hee, hee-hee, hee-hee." It sounded like the fright call of a startled goose. "Now, by gawd, Kate, that's one I ain't never seen, a buster coming to court one of us ladies of the night. Why, I don't even have a notion what you'd charge for something like that. Courting, is it? And, I reckon you had to tell him you just ain't in the courting business. 'Less it's for money."

"Yes, and I hated to," confessed Katherine. "He surprised me. He was kind to me down at the fort, but I had no idea . . ."

"Never courted in my life," Jane said. She puffed several times and blew smoke with the pipe still between her teeth. "When I was young, always was a tad bigger than the boys. Scared the shit out of 'em, I reckon. You ever have a regular fellow?"

Katherine stared down reflectively at the dying flames.

"Friends, school friends. Once when I was sixteen, before we came out and started the hauling, I had a fellow. Sort of courting behind the bushes. Mama said I was too young. Marshall . . . Marshall Taylor. He was nineteen. It was a big mess. Neither one of us knew what we were doing. He probably has a batch of children by now."

Jane chuckled. "More'n courting, I'd say. Good thing you moved, gal, or you'd be having that batch of young'uns."

"I don't know. I never thought much about it after we got to Cheyenne. We hit it good right off with the freighting. Got so busy, I never had much time to think about anything but where we were headed next. We built a nice house, Mama died, and then it was just Will and myself. Oh, a few young men came around, mostly penniless and without promise. Will didn't cotton to most of them." She stopped and smiled. "I suppose I didn't either."

"You could go back and start freighting again, you know," Jane suggested. "Take your profit and parley those wagons you got into a few more . . . use your goody for some of that collateral, and you'd be back in business again. Hire a few busters. Hell's bells, I'd skin for you, and we could always do a few tricks on the side, just like now."

"What about Julia?"

"Damnation, I upped an' forgot about her."

"Well, I haven't, and don't you either," said Katherine. "Damnit, we're partners, aren't we?"

"Yes, ma'am, we are. Tried and tested, true and blue."

Katherine giggled. "Well, you got the 'tried and tested' part of it right, for sure."

Katherine didn't know how long she had been asleep, perhaps an hour or a bit more, not too long, when she was awakened by several whispers between the canvas flaps at the rear of the wagon. "Psst, psst, Kate . . ." She bent forward, came up on her knees and crawled over her pallet, slightly parted the flap, and stared into the face of Jason Armitage. "For God's sake, what are you doing here?" she whispered. "You want to stir up trouble? . . . someone seeing you?" Reaching out, she seized his shoulder and gave a pull. "Hurry up, get in, damnit!"

"Whew," he sighed. He sat at the foot of her bed. "I used the best night tactics I know getting around the edge down here."

"You're a damn fool," she said, shaking her head. "I saw sentries just below here before I came in . . . watched me go down to the creek, even."

He grinned, leaned forward, and kissed her. He ran his hand down her shoulder, too, and felt her flimsy chemise. "Not dressed the way you are now, I hope."

"No," she said. "I went down naked, let them look at my butt in the moonlight. They enjoy that kind of thing." Katherine pulled up her knees, clasped her arms around them, and tried to make out his face in the darkness. She said, "Kind of late to be visiting, isn't it?"

"No, not at all," he whispered. "We're not moving anywhere in the morning. You can sleep late. I've been thinking about you for the last four days. I think it's four. I've lost all track of time. This campaign has turned me around . . . meetings, strategy sessions, reports . . . you, yes, most of all, you."

"Me, how nice? And what have you been thinking, my sweet? What kind of thoughts have I provoked? Tell me!"

Jason Armitage chuckled lowly. "All kinds, mostly amorous, I confess."

"And, now . . . now, you've come to fulfill some of them?" she asked.

"If you care to, of course, yes."

Katherine skittered on her bottom close to him, stretched her long legs out to either side, then curled and locked them around his middle. "I care to," she replied. A hand caressed her face, and she took his lips in a long kiss. After a moment, she confessed in a hushed voice, "I've been thinking about you, too."

"Passionate? Good thoughts, I trust."

"What else?"

"Aha."

"Yes, I'm glad you came. You should make a habit of it."

"I'd like to," Jason said. "I'd probably go broke, though."

"Oh, but it would be my pleasure to break you." She laughed. "And when you're broke, maybe if you're extra nice, I'll loan you more . . . and more."

"By gadfrey, I can't lose!"

"No, of course not. We'll both be winners."

Later, her head was resting on his bare chest; she listened to the steady, deep thumping of his heart, heard his voice, the low incantation of what had transpired at a meeting with General Crook that night after the return of two scouting parties. One of the scouts, Frank Grouard, and two Crow had returned from the north, another scout from the west. Morning Star, the Cheyenne chief whom the Sioux called Dull Knife, was camped on the Rosebud. Two Moons's people were with him, and their numbers totaled in the thousands. Another village was above Morning Star, the village of Crazy Horse, and this is probably where Julia was. Still another village had been sighted to the northwest, not too far from where Crook's long train had been harassed earlier in the day—a moving village. The scout, Baptiste Pourier, said it was the Hunkpapa of the great chief, Sitting Bull. The camp had been about five miles from the attack site. Probably two or three thousand Sioux had joined the Hunkpapa leader, so the report stated, and Armitage said it was most fortunate that General Crook hadn't pressed on. "We'd have run directly into them, and there would have been one messy battle, one with drastic consequences for us. Luckily, we stalled, talked Crook into camping here and waiting for the boys from the north to come down."

"Lucky for me, too," she sighed.

"Everything Porter told us that day, everything . . ."

"The day we first met," she interrupted. "The day you had secret desires about me, Bird Dog."

"Yes . . . but I properly covered my desires with interrogation," he reminded.

"I hated you . . . all of you, a bunch of bastards, all trying to be polite and proper, and I was sitting there in a bunch of hand-me-downs, trying to feel like a white woman again."

"You looked very much like a white woman, a very attractive one, and one most desirous to any man."

"You didn't show it," Katherine said with a little snicker. "Had you, I'd surely have noticed it . . . your . . . your war club."

Jason Armitage sighed in silent amusement. "My thoughts weren't covetous at the time, only appreciative. Not even in my greatest imagination, could I have believed something like this was going to happen . . . in a freight wagon . . . in my tent. Gadfrey!"

"I think I can say the same," she replied. "Certainly, I had no intentions of entertaining the general's best man flat on my back."

"I enjoy being with you."

"The best parts of me?"

"All of you. You're a very interesting woman, Kate. Regretful, isn't it? We've met at the wrong time under the worst of circumstances . . . one of us captive to the army, the other, captive to society. Another time, who knows?"

In her relaxed state of satisfaction, enjoying his closeness, she fell silent. Finally, "Yes, Porter was right, but do you recall what he said about a place called the Greasy Grass? . . . he thought it might be where everyone was going, the gathering place for the big celebrations."

"I remember. You like Porter, don't you?"

"He offered to help me, but that's beside the point," she said, poking his side. "Do you know where the Greasy Grass is?"

"No, not precisely, but the guides do . . . and the Crow."

"Well, I do know where it is. I've been there twice in the past five years. It's over the hills from the Rosebud. It's on the Little Bighorn River, and you better believe it when Porter says there's ten or so thousand Indians meeting there."

Ruffling her hair, Jason said, "That sounds almost like a warning."

Katherine came up and straddled him, knees to each side of his breast. "It's a warning to you to caution old man Crook about trying to get into that place without waiting for help. He'll get cut up and quartered like a hog . . . and I don't want you hurt no more than I do my daughter."

"Grouard says your old friend Crazy Horse is on the Rosebud."

"Now, yes . . . for another ten days or so, that's all."

"Well, we plan on moving directly up the Rosebud . . . that's his decision, not mine."

"Your whole strategy is a month late," Katherine said.

"Oh, ho, and now we hear from another intelligence quarter, do we?"

"Yes. You dumb asses should have moved with your troops a month ago, even two weeks, and scattered the tribes while they were moving in separate bands across the rivers toward the mountains, forced them back to the reservations. You have no intelligence. You should have known all of this was happening, nipped it in the bud."

"Hindsight," he mumbled. "It's a bit too late for that now, my love."

"A damn pity."

He reached up and tweaked one of her breasts. "Is it too late for dessert?"

Katherine lowered herself and kissed him. "No, not if you're still hungry."

"Aren't you?"

"I think I'm always hungry," she replied. "As much as I like you, Bird Dog, this is going to cost you. You realize this, don't you?"

"I do."

Katherine did sleep longer than usual the next morning. She was finally roused by Jane, who set a cup of coffee at the foot of her pallet and whistled loudly. Katherine snaked the coffee inside, crossed her legs, and took a few sips before reaching up for her bundle of clothing. She would have to do a washing this morning; she had only one pair of underpants left, the bloomers given to her by Mary Slaymaker. She quickly slipped into these, squirmed into an army pullover shirt, retrieved her trousers from the box overhead, pulled on her hat, and slid from the tailgate in her bare feet. Before she could hurry away down the trail to the little pond to attend to her personal chores or even exchange a few words with Jane, Peter Quinlan came striding in, coils of rope over each shoulder. He wanted the women to remove the hobbles from their mules. There was a meadow of good bunchgrass down below the camp where some of the men were already busy rigging up a pole corral for his stock.

Tossing the rope near Katherine's wagon, he gave her a smile and a wink, tipped his hat once, and started back toward the big compound; then, as though he had forgotten something, he came back and asked her how she was fixed for time that night. She knew Jason wouldn't be returning so soon, and she cared less about her other customers than she did either the colonel or Pete Quinlan. She told Pete that she was open, the evening was his if he wanted to come, and tipping his hat, but smiling more broadly, he left. Katherine didn't suppose he was in any big hurry to get the mules moved, so she finished her coffee, briefly chatted with Jane, who immediately plied her with a few questions about her late-night visitor. When Jane learned that it had been Colonel Armitage, she was once again appalled. The fact that Katherine had visited his tent earlier was chancy enough, but she was shocked that an officer of Armitage's rank would dare invade the quarters of the mule skinners.

"Get busted down to a shaved-tail if he got caught in your wagon," opined Jane, wagging her head. "Bet he didn't bring his wine bottle, did he?"

"No, but he left me some brand-new scrip." Katherine smiled. "A ten." She lied, it was twenty, but since Jason's pay had been so outrageously high both times, especially compared to the money Jane had been taking in, she felt ashamed to tell her friend the truth. Katherine Coltrane's little charcoal marks on the wagon interior were becoming jumbled; she already had one hundred and sixty-two dollars in her flour sack, and she allowed that Crook's campaign was far from finished.

Her bath in the glade pool was leisurely; she thoroughly cleaned her little assortment of apparatuses, washed her underclothing and stockings, and suspended them on the bushes to dry. By the time she got back, Jane had some bread, ham, and fried potatoes set aside in a pan next to the fire, but Jane was nowhere in sight, not even over where the hobbled mules were grazing. Staring curiously around, Katherine finally shrugged, set her towel-wrapped belongings inside her wagon, and went over beside the fire to eat. Except for the usual camp sounds, some distant shouts, the bray of a mule, and someone pounding a stake, it was a relatively quiet morning. Katherine turned her back to the sun, let its rays warm her back as she ate, and looked into the sunlit forest in front of her. About halfway through her meal, she heard a muffled voice to her right, glanced over, saw nothing, but then heard several familiar little sounds, "ungh, ungh, ungh," coming from the wagon next to her—Jane Canarray's rig.

Katherine gulped once. Heavens, there wasn't a doubt about it! Right in the middle of the morning, Jane was turning a trick! And, she had chastised her for tricking with the colonel in the middle of the night! Not too long afterward, a ruddy face appeared at the canvas opening; the man looked both directions, once, twice, stared at Katherine briefly, then leaped out and walked quickly away into the adjacent bushes. He was hatless, in his undershirt, suspenders dangling from his blue, yellow-striped pants, and he wore high black boots—cavalry. Jane Canarray shortly appeared, too, a towel over her shoulder, and she was carrying her little bundle. She smiled, waved once, and disappeared down the little trail leading to the pond.

Fifteen minutes later Jane reappeared, and after a brief stop at her wagon to stow her personals, she came over to where Katherine was finishing up the last of her coffee.

Jane smiled down at her. "Damn good way to start the day, ain't it? Ready to move those shitters?"

"It's a good thing those wagons butt up against the woods, that's all I can say."

"Yes, my pretty dove, I know my business, I do. Had this all in mind when we pulled in."

Chatting quietly, walking across the compound with their hats pulled down, they went to the nearby pasture and began unhobbling the mules. They rigged neck halters and started leading the stock away to the distant corral, skirting the great circle of squad tents and army wagons on the east side of the camp. They soon found Quinlan's crew busily arranging the slender lodge poles on the last section of a simple jack fence. Several dozen mules grazed inside the compound, and amid a few friendly shouts from the men, Katherine and Jane ran their mules inside, gave the skinners a parting wave, and continued on, circling the camp perimeter at the north end far above General Crook's staff headquarters. On the upper west side, they came upon a cluster of wickiups, small conical, brush shelters erected by the Crow and Shoshoni scouts who had joined Crook. Some distance below this site, there were some new arrivals, civilians, unloading several wagons and pitching wall tents. Thirty or more horses were in their remuda on the far side of the creek. Some of the men were wearing big hats, others were attired in derbies and straws. Surprised, Jane gawked for a moment, then took Katherine by the hand and made a wide circuit away from the group. Once in the brush, the women stopped and silently observed the activity.

Katherine finally said, "The way they're dressed, they don't look much like plainsmen or drovers."

After another few moments of surveillance, Jane said, "They ain't. They're miners ... tradesmen, a passel of everything just wanting to be Indian fighters."

"Humph!" Katherine grunted disgustedly. "From the Black Hills, I suppose."

"I reckon. It's about the only place they could have come without getting scalped ... from the east. Deadwood, Lead, the mining camps, and if they're from the diggings, I might know a few of the busters." Jane squeezed Katherine's shoulder and grinned. "Good prospects, they are. Squatters, some of 'em with fat wallets, money belts, few bottles of whiskey stashed in those packs, I bet."

"You're thinking—?"

"Why not? Yes, I'm thinking we just might do some business, only with the best of the lot, though. Can lighten up their wads a tad. I'll allow some of those busters are rich, already, or they wouldn't be here, would they? They'd be back digging or doing business. Sorta like they're taking a holiday—"

"A holiday! Out to kill just for the sport of it?"

"Well, maybe protecting their interests, too."

"Bullshit!" exclaimed Katherine. "They don't even own the land they're fighting over. It's on the reservation. That's what's behind this whole mess. They're thieves."

"Yes, they are," agreed Jane, "but that ain't the way they look at it, and if we aim to make some money off of those busters, best you be keeping such Injun talk to yourself. No talk, just work."

"Oh, I certainly will," replied Katherine grimly. "I can play thief, too. If they want a piece of me, they'll be paying double. Holiday, indeed!"

Jane cackled lowly. "That's the way I like to hear my gal talk."

They walked along the edge of the trees and buck brush toward their wagons. Wagging a finger at Jane, Katherine warned, "And don't you go drinking whiskey with them either ... dangerous enough what we're already doing. We have a good game going, now don't we? . . . all to ourselves. There's no profit in doing something foolish, taking a chance on getting booted out."

"I ain't going on a toot, if that's what you mean. No, I ain't that crazy, but I reckon a little snort after work wouldn't be so bad, would it?" She chuckled and gave Katherine a wink. "Gets me right off to a good sleep, it does."

"Well, a few tricks will do the same damn thing. You pay attention to what I say, you hear?"

"Oh, I will, partner, I will."

Jane Canarray kept her word; she didn't go on a toot, but she enticed a few of the Black Hills squatters to the wagons.

The men had money and whiskey; she relieved them of both, stowing one bottle of rye behind a freight box to use as a nightly sleeping aid. Katherine Coltrane was true to her word, too; she doubled her fee. On the second night after the arrival of the miners, she entertained a lanky, soft-spoken attorney by the name of Tim Frawley. He was thirty years old. Frawley, who specialized in mining deeds and contracts, and who had several gold claims of his own, was so impressed with Katherine, he arranged for a return visit on the fourth night. He willingly paid, and was so enraptured by this tall, winsome woman and the story she told of her capture by the Sioux and its tragic consequences, that he offered her additional aid and compensation. Deadwood was becoming a booming town; it was the hub, surrounded by the Indian reservations, a most likely place to conduct a search for her missing daughter if her present endeavors proved futile. What's more, Tim Frawley held the mortgage on the Red Bird Saloon in Deadwood and was, in fact, a silent partner with a man named Henry Givens. Frawley was presently in the process of building a hotel over the saloon. He thought that within another month and a half, those bedrooms and a small reception parlor would be richly furnished and ready for use; he had six wagon trains of freight coming in from Bismarck, and they probably would be in Deadwood by the time he returned.

Katherine Coltrane was intrigued, so intrigued, that she invited Tim Frawley down to the secret little pond for an afternoon rendezvous, and before it was over, she had his pledge of security at the Red Bird if and when she needed it, as long as she needed it. Tim Frawley promised that until Katherine located Julia, she could manage the operations on the second floor and reserve the very best of the clientele for herself. In the deep grass and blooming shrubbery, in the shade of the quaking aspen, Katherine turned the first free trick of her short career—a violation of the code, but she looked at it as a down payment on her security in Deadwood, if she ever chanced to get there.

Tim Frawley was mannerly, a gentleman obviously on his way to some financial success on the frontier; he was rather handsome with a long, straight nose, deep brown eyes, and a flowing, black mustache; he was presentable in every way; he was nice, sexually adequate, but she had no particular fondness for him one way or another. While he expressed empathy for her, she knew his interest was mostly carnal. He had a wife and small son in Springfield, Missouri, waiting to join him as soon as some civility came to the Black Hills. She wanted to ask him if helping Three Stars Crook kill Indians was the best way of bringing this about, but she didn't.

Tim Frawley was a lonely man. He hadn't seen his wife and child in over a year, but in his quiet-spoken Ozark twang, he told her she was the best woman that he had ever bedded. This was a compliment of sorts, for she hadn't asked him how many women he had intimately known in his young life; undoubtedly, he had taken a few other doves.

Ultimately, Katherine asked, "About girls . . . women for the rooms. Who are they . . . except me, if I decide on this?"

Tim Frawley pulled his lanky frame into a sitting position and thoughtfully scratched his head. "At the present, I don't know. Givens is advertising for some dancing girls in Omaha." His mouth curled in a little smile. "I think women know what dancing girls do in Deadwood. The girls come and they go . . . different places. I suppose some of the hiring would be up to you . . . as you say, if you decide. There's no big hurry, a couple of months at least."

"What about when your wife arrives?" asked Katherine.

"Susan? What about her?"

"This business, damn it," sighed Katherine. "My heavens, how's such a thing going to strike her? I should think it would be embarrassing to her, you philandering, consorting, running a whorehouse."

"I'm a solicitor," he drawled. "Henry Givens owns the saloon. I hold the papers but I don't intend to participate, only in the profit." He grinned again. "Just as you would profit if you want to manage the upstairs back rooms, and no, I'm not looking for a mistress. Of course, I can't deny there's something special about you."

"You mean how I move on my back or how I think with my head?"

"Both," Frawley replied. "You're a mercenary, a pretty one, too good to be doing this on a wagon train. You're clever, you know what you want and how to go about getting it. I suspected this after our first encounter. After the second, I knew it."

Katherine scoffed. "I'm only a beginner, Mister Tim. Didn't cheat you, did I? You came back, didn't you? Counting the free piece of tail ... dividing by three, it wasn't that expensive. Business is business, you know."

"Yes," he agreed. "It's a pity, Kate. Had you initiated this profession five years ago, you'd probably own the whole damn territory."

Later in the afternoon there was a flurry of activity in the camp, movement of stock, transfer of supplies from some of the wagons, and a general mustering of soldiers adjacent to headquarters. Katherine suspected that General Crook was preparing to pull stakes, to make his move north, however a short time later when Pete Quinlan came down the line, she and Jane learned the general, indeed, was ready to move but he was not vacating the camp completely. Most of the supplies and all of the wagons were being left behind, in addition to two companies of infantrymen who were going to guard the camp. The remainder of the army, including some foot soldiers who had elected to ride mules, was departing the next morning at five o'clock. General Crook, failing to get dispatches regarding the whereabouts of the armies on the Yellowstone, was impatient; he had elected to make his move. It wasn't until after dusk when Jason Armitage appeared out of the brushy darkness behind Katherine's wagon that she learned the rest of the story. Fetching a blanket, she quickly led Jason down the trail to the little pond, where, seated next to each other in the moonlight, he told her it was likely that he might not see her again until the end of summer. The departing troops were taking only four days of rations in their saddlebags and one hundred rounds of ammunition each; they were going to move down the Rosebud, and if they made a successful engagement with Crazy Horse, would continue north and join General Gibbon somewhere in the Yellowstone country.

Katherine's heart sank, and she said, "What do we do? Just sit here the rest of the summer? This is impossible!"

"No, Miss Kate," the colonel answered, "but, for the present, it's as far as you'll be going. We'll send a patrol back ... a few scouts, to determine the relocation of the main camp, might even send everyone back to Fetterman. Quinlan's going to move in a few days, anyhow. He can't sit around here with twelve empty freighters. I don't know yet. It all depends on what we run into up above."

"Crook's a fool," Katherine said bitterly. "He still doesn't believe anything he's been told, the obstinate old son of a bitch." She searched Jason's shadowy face. "Engage Crazy Horse's village? Heavens, there's three or four villages ... probably all joined up by now. What about Julia? ... what am I going to do about her? For crisesakes, Jason."

"I've thought about it, too." He gave her a consoling embrace. "If we get in, we'll do everything we can. I've told Grouard and Pourier her name ... Wicapi Hinto, her age, everything you told me. They both speak adequate Siouan. Be assured, Miss Kate, if there's any roundup, they'll sort her out from the rest. Under the circumstances, this is the best I can do."

"Yes," she said quietly. "I appreciate it. I understand."

"Who knows? Maybe we'll get lucky, find her, send her back with the patrol."

After a long pause, Katherine sadly shook her head and said, "I think it's going to take more than luck, now. It's going to take a miracle ... the Sioux we ran into last week, they know everything that's going on down here, probably have been watching us from the mountains all week." Staring up into his face, she added fatefully, "They're not going to let you get close to a village, Bird Dog, and you won't ... not unless you get a lot of help from the north, some diversion, and for crisesakes, no one seems to know where anyone is, or what's going on. Stupidity! Yes, you underestimate these people, too. They won't run this time ... they'll fight."

Jason Armitage sighed. "Yes, I believe you're right. We always seem to underestimate them, and worse yet, we don't understand them. You probably know as much about them, if not more, than anyone in this camp, but even if you were the oracle personified, the old man wouldn't listen to you, no more than he paid much attention to Porter's intelligence. He's here to fight, has a mind of his own. Besides, he hates women around his command ... probably doesn't understand them either."

"The stubborn old fart! Probably doesn't screw them, either."

There wasn't much room for levity, but this brought a little chuckle from Armitage. They tarried and talked in the moonlight for another fifteen minutes until Jason reluctantly said he had to return to headquarters; he still had work ahead of him before the dawn departure. Katherine knew Armitage was an unhappy man, that he had little faith in General

Crook's plans to seek an engagement with or without support. The great plan of convergence had flown out the door like a scalded cat. And Armitage, the only man she truly enjoyed being with, was in no mood for companionship this night. General Crook, Jason said, had given him a pain in the ass.

Katherine did not feel much better; she was nervous, and had come down with a few stomach cramps. Late that night her monthly cycle of menstruation began. Had she been living in the Oglala village, her former husband, Standing Bear, may have taken this as an omen of bad luck. He seldom undertook any endeavors until all of the signs in his lodge were favorable.

Chapter Five

Retreat

Within four days of General Crook's departure with his army of twelve hundred troops and Shoshoni and Crow allies, Peter Quinlan's freighters had been thoroughly serviced and repaired for the North Platte River Trail the following morning.

Katherine was no longer destitute, but she was disheartened and despondent. There had been no news of Crook's movements and no sign of the patrol that Bird Dog Armitage had told her would return with word on disposition of the Goose Creek war camp. Most depressing of all, two of the guides, Frank Grouard and Baptiste Pourier, who had been assigned by Colonel Armitage to search for Julia had failed to return. With bitter resignation, the last of her faint hopes dissipating in the billowy clouds over the Big Horn, Katherine and Jane finished final preparations to head back to Fort Fetterman the following morning.

Yet, Quinlan's departure was not to be, at least, not for the immediate present. During the night, the thunderheads over the adjacent mountain collapsed, a heavy downpour came, and as it slid away across the valley, two troopers, one of them Sergeant Marvel Hansen and two Crow scouts, came riding into the camp behind the last remnants of the rain. By dawn, the word had been spread to every tent and wagon— General Crook was returning, his advance thwarted, his troops expected back in camp by midday! A big war party of Cheyenne and Sioux had intercepted him on the upper Rosebud, had fought him to a standoff, and the general had made the decision to retreat back to Goose Creek. Peter Quinlan stayed his freighters, but the wagons were not going back to Fort Fetterman empty; they were going to transport fifty-six wounded soldiers. The bodies of twenty-eight troopers would not be among the freight—they had been buried the night before in the rich loam along the banks of the Rosebud.

It wasn't until shortly before noon that Katherine heard more bad news. Marvel Hansen, Thomas Clybourn's trusty platoon sergeant, another of her first friends after her capture on the Little Powder, appeared at her wagon. She greeted him warmly, poured him a cup of coffee, and they sat opposite each other on two empty crates. He had said nothing more than good morning and asked about her welfare before tears welled in his eyes, and Katherine Coltrane knew that he was here with a sad message. In a few halting words, Sergeant Hansen told her that Lieutenant Clybourn had been killed early in the battle, shot twice while he was attempting to rescue a badly wounded Crow scout and another trooper, both of whom had been pinned down in a small ravine by hostile fire. Ultimately, all three had died.

"I'm so sorry," she whispered huskily. Visions suddenly danced in the blur of her lowered eyes, visions of the old holy man, Flat Iron, that evening when she and young Thomas listened to his singing in the captives' tent at Fetterman. *To die in battle when one is young is honorable. The old, the wretched, die with toothaches, and the bluecoat was not going to die with a toothache in his head.* Brushing at her eyes, Katherine mumbled, "He had so many good thoughts about others . . . so many songs to sing . . ."

Marvel Hansen looked over curiously. "Songs?"

Smiling sadly, Katherine said, "It's nothing . . . just an expression."

"Well," sighed the sergeant, "Mister Clybourn was a good one, all right, always was that way, looking out for someone else, first, doing what he thought was best for his men. Best friend I ever had. Talked about you a lot, too, you know. Told me just after we got jumped the other day, he'd like nothing better to find your little girl . . . be the one who brought her back to you."

Seized by a big sob, Katherine doubled over. "Oh, mercy!" she choked into her lap. "Thomas, Thomas, dear Thomas!" She felt the touch of Marvel Hansen's hand patting her gently on the back. "It's all right, Miss Kate. It's over . . . I wish you wouldn't be carrying on. Look, I'll give you a hand." He gripped her shoulder firmly and said, "I have to be going now . . . you need anything, let me know."

Disconsolate, Katherine wandered around the perimeter of

the camp up toward the corral where Jane had gone to check on the condition of the women's mules. Now, there was more activity at the north end. Katherine, finding shade under one of the cottonwoods, saw a long file of troopers winding down the train alongside the creek; she squinted, saw a few officers at the head of the column, and as they drew closer, she recognized several; among them the bushy-faced General Crook and directly beside him, Jason Armitage. He had come from the fray unscathed, at least bodily. His mind? She knew him all too well. His mind would be one tormented by frustration and bitterness. No victory here. No capture of villages, no rendezvous on the Yellowstone. As the troops filed by, Katherine Coltrane had mixed emotions; Crook's troops hadn't been annihilated; many lives had been spared, and this was good; the village of Crazy Horse hadn't been sacked, no threat to Julia's safety there, and this was good, too. She had to rationalize, had to face the reality of all of this—the quest for her daughter was regretfully stalled, only stalled, not over, and if this were only the beginning, she would persevere, somehow continue the quest. She wasn't about to give up, ever.

The file of tired troopers grew longer; a few civilians rode by, but she didn't see the Black Hills attorney, Tim Frawley. In fact, she saw only several of the so-called Indian fighters from Deadwood, could only assume that most of them had already left for home from the overnight camp on a fork of the Tongue. Then Katherine saw the wounded, more than fifty of them, a few bandaged, riding loose in their saddles, others stretched out and covered with blankets on mule-drawn travois. The procession was painfully slow, disheartening to watch. These men were soon taken into two large, adjoining tents, a hastily rigged infirmary, where two army doctors and several aides who had administered emergency treatment in the field were now preparing to save a few lives.

Katherine met Jane at the corral; they walked slowly around the perimeter to the north, crossed the creek, and headed back toward their wagons; the small clearing where the men from Deadwood had camped was deserted, indeed, the miners had cleared camp. However, a short distance below, the women encountered several of the newspaper correspondents, including Henry Burlingame. Burlingame, fatigued from the journey and resting under the shade of a big fir tree, gave them a polite greeting and called them over. The rotund writer had a dark-colored bottle in one hand, a cigar in the other, and his faded brown hat was on the ground beside him. Katherine could see that he was a tired, bedraggled fellow. Obviously, the short campaign hadn't gone well for him either. Because the women seldom wandered too far from the extreme lower end of the various campsites along the way, this was their first meeting with Henry Burlingame since Fort Fetterman. He simply nodded when they approached; he was too weary to get up and make a gracious bow, and brushing at a bit of foam on his mustache, he said, "I heard a rumor a week ago that you two were riding herd on some wagons at the back. One thing and another, I never managed to get back and arrange a chat with you." He looked at Katherine Coltrane, and went on, "You sure you haven't got some kind of a story to tell me now . . . after this fiasco?"

Katherine gave him a negative wag. "I should think you'd have plenty to write about, Mister Burlingame."

"Oh, I do, I do," he nodded, "but not too much of it good, I fear. A companion feature story would be nice."

Jane Canarray, pointing to the dark bottle in his hand, said, "Is that malt liquor? Where in hell did you get it?"

"Cold stout," he smiled. "Yes, the finest of brew," and he pointed his nose toward the creek. "I managed to bring along a case. Hid it in the freight."

A hand went jauntily to her hip, and she cocked her head at him, saying, "Goddamn it, Burley, least you could do is offer us ladies a drink."

Henry Burlingame chuckled. "The way you're dressed, I'd never have known you were ladies, but you get on over there and help yourself . . . several bottles stashed below that little riffle."

"By gawd, I'll do just that," and Calamity Jane headed for the stream.

Henry Burlingame, puffing several times on his cigar, smiled up at Katherine. "I knew she would. Damndest woman I've ever met in my life."

Katherine Coltrane agreed, saying, "Yes, I know." She seated herself in the shade opposite the writer and asked, "What happened up there? How much of it did you see?"

"Not all of it, but enough," replied Burlingame. "Enough to know Mister Crook was prudent in withdrawing to his present position here. I should say the red chaps surprised the hell out of the general with their skill and tenacity."

Burlingame went on, relating all of what he had seen and later heard from some of the officers in the field. To Crook's surprise, the Indians had attacked his troops in the canyon area on the upper Rosebud, and had pinned the soldiers down for the better part of one day before retreating themselves. One of the scouts, Louis Richards, who later followed the Indians north for more than ten miles, said they were Lakota and Cheyenne, at least one thousand warriors, probably led by Crazy Horse and Two Moons, one of Chief Morning Star's most capable tribal leaders. At one point, Anson Mills, a battalion commander, had ridden clear of the fray with eight companies of cavalry in an attempt to locate the village downriver and attack it, but he had been recalled by General Crook, who feared an ambush and who also realized that because of the ferocity of the battle, he could not support Mills. Captain Mills, according to Louis Richards, never got near a village. The Sioux and Cheyenne hadn't waited for their great camp to be attacked; instead, they had ridden almost twenty miles up the Rosebud to attack Crook's troops—a strategy unprecedented and totally unexpected.

After taking a long draft of his beer, Henry Burlingame said, "I can't fault the soldiers, not at all. They fought bravely, and had they shown any signs of weakening, it would have been a complete disaster ... they would have been overwhelmed." He sighed once. "And, most likely, I along with them. Oh, I've heard all of the reports about the fight, saw some of it, and I tell you, there's no pride among the officers, and, I hasten to say, they have considerable more respect for their adversaries."

Katherine was silent; Jane, now seated to her side, was quaffing on her bottle of beer, and Burlingame, a weary man, had shuttered his eyes. He mumbled in afterthought. "Richards told me if Mills and his men had reached that village, they probably would never have made it back ... says there's at least two or three thousand warriors up there, Hunkpapa, Oglala, Miniconjou, and Cheyenne ... even some Arapaho."

"Humph!" snorted Jane. "Porter Webb knew that three or four weeks ago ... told that to Colonel Armitage back at Fetterman ... said the hills were full of Injuns. What the hell did Crook expect to find? A bunch of kids swimming in the river?"

"Confirmation," Burlingame smiled thinly, his eyelids fluttering. "Confirmation of the fact."

Finally, Katherine asked, "Do you know what the old man's going to do, now? ... sit around here and mope? I had some hope ... some promises of help in getting my little girl out of there."

"I understand your concern, Miss Coltrane," Burlingame said, "but I don't know what he's going to do. Who does? I heard some talk, that's all, something about reinforcements. Some of his best men are out of commission, now ... all of the Crow and Shoshoni taking off. All I can say, is that General Crook jolly well met his match."

"Reinforcements?" asked Katherine. "My heavens, why, that's likely to take another two or three weeks! Good Lord, Mister Burlingame, that means he won't move for almost a month. What does he expect to find up there by then?"

"Cold campfires, I imagine," he replied wearily. "He certainly won't be capturing any village, and in another month or so, your daughter probably will be on one of the reservations, and I must add, out of harm's way, too. Whatever, it's going to be a long, restless summer for the hostiles. I fear this is only the beginning, Miss Coltrane. I'll tell you one thing, I've had quite enough of this ... this bungling, waiting around to see the culmination of the great design, the great plan of convergence. I'm going back tomorrow with the supply wagons, back to some semblance of sanity. For me, the grand goose chase is over. Truth be known, those chaps up on the Yellowstone Crook's been waiting for are probably lost, bogged down in the river bottom or some damned coulee out on the prairie." He sighed again. "I smell like a hog, ladies. I'm too tired to take a bath right now, so I'm going to take a nap. If you care for another beer, help yourselves." Henry Burlingame settled back against the big tree trunk.

Jane reached down and gave him a pat on his whiskered cheek. "You're a good old boy, Henry. You find some time tonight, you drop by my wagon down by the trees yonder for some entertainment if you want. I'd be obliged."

His drowsy eyes momentarily rolled upward. "Entertainment?"

"Damn right, entertainment ... back of my wagon, just you'n me, Burley." Jane cackled.

"Oh, my," smiled Burlingame, wagging his head. "Land's sake, dear woman, the way I feel now, I fear I'd be the poorest of company. Oh, my, have another beer. Yes, do, and we'll let it stand at that." He chuckled, clasped his hands together over his midriff, and closed his eyes, but there was a little smile playing on his drawn face.

By later that afternoon, all of Quinlan's freighters had been readied for the return trip, a few pressed into duty to haul some of the wounded, hay from the nearby meadows piled high inside them, and canvas stretched tightly over the frame to ward off the prairie heat and the threat of early summer thunderstorms. Katherine's and Jane's outfits were not among the converted ambulance wagons, but the women did cushion their floorboards with some of the fresh blue stem and grama grasses, and were in the process of breaking up a few empty crates to store for firewood, when voices suddenly brought them around. Katherine paled under her floppy hat. Jane was hatless, her long, black hair bundled up in a big knot with a few wisps jutting out like the mane of a horse; she also appeared startled.

"Jesus," moaned Katherine, "it's the old man, himself!"

And, it was—General Crook flanked by several junior officers and Peter Quinlan, obviously on some kind of an inspection tour, a final check of the wagons, those recently renovated to carry his wounded. Just as the little group prepared to move on by, the general came to a halt, turned, and coldly stared at the women. Katherine Coltrane, a broken board dangling in her hand, was speechless, felt like bolting away like a maverick, but it was too late.

General Crook was speechless, too, but only for a moment, and he then snapped at his aides, "Will someone tell me what's going on here? Who is responsible for this? This outrage, these women."

"Teamsters, sir," one of the officers answered crisply. "Along with the civilian train ... mule skinners."

Jane grinned and waved a board. "Making some firewood, General, that's what's going on, getting ourselves all ready to move out."

Quinlan quickly intervened, explaining that he had been short two drivers at Fort Fetterman on the morning of departure. Both of these women were experienced skinners; one, Katherine, was the woman who had only recently been freed from captivity with some of Crazy Horse's people, and hoped to recover her young daughter during the campaign; she also had been in need of a job.

The brief explanation wasn't enough. General Crook recognized Calamity Jane. "I don't like women around my troops, regardless of how experienced they are handling wagons." He glanced back and forth at the captain and lieutenant who were standing to his side, then at Pete Quinlan. Quinlan shrugged, the two officers said nothing, and General Crook exploded, "My God, man, what is this, some kind of a conspiracy? I want some answers."

The captain said, "I didn't know they were along either, sir."

Quinlan offered lamely, "They did a good job getting up here, General . . . right mannerly, too. No trouble."

General Crook continued to glare and finally growled, "Fait accompli." Turning on his heel, "If Colonel Bradford finds need of your freighting services when he sends up my reinforcements, just be damn sure these women aren't along. I don't want them around."

Jane piped up. "I can do any goddamned man's job. What the hell's the matter with you, buster? Superstitious 'bout women?"

"About you, I am," he muttered. "I'll have you taken back to the nearest post under military escort if you dare to show up here again."

Katherine, unable to restrain herself, angrily thrust out her jaw and shouted, "I came up here to get my daughter back, General! You're a miserable, insensitive old fart, that's what you are!"

Peter Quinlan winced; the lieutenant, his brow arched, turned and looked back over his shoulder, and the captain merely wiped his forehead. General Crook, jerking at the brim of his big, dark hat, forged ahead without saying another word.

It had been a hot day. Too hot, Jane Canarray allowed, to prepare supper over a fire, so she took the little coffeepot, snaked out Pete Quinlan's tin food box and a big pan, and headed for one of the battalion mess tents, then directly returned with a mulligan stew, biscuits, hot coffee and two cans of mixed fruits. If somewhere down the line she had to make some price adjustment for the mess sergeant, she thought it was well worth it.

Mentally exhausted by the miseries of the day, stories of battle, the sorrowful news of Thomas Clybourn's death, not to mention the brief altercation with General Crook, Katherine's appetite was almost gone. So was her conversation. She dabbled at her plate of food and had very little to say. Finally, she picked out a few clean clothes, took up her towel and soap, and disappeared down the brushy trail leading to the pond. It was here, sometime later, where Jason Armitage found her sitting beside the bank in the twilight, her towel curled like a giant turban around her damp hair. He stood above her contemplating, staring across the stillness of the water. "Your wishing pond, Miss Kate, and what is your wish this night?"

"Hello, Bird Dog." And then, without hesitation, she said, "To find Julia and get the hell out of this godforsaken land."

Jason Armitage sat beside her, picked up a small pebble, and fudged it like a clay marble into the pond. "We didn't get within miles of the girl," he sighed. "Just as you said back at Fetterman that afternoon, we got our tails whipped. I think it must have been your old friend, Tashunka-Witko. Every time we made a move, he countered it, and I think he let Mills and his men ride on down the river just to thin our lines. Hell, there wasn't a village anywhere in sight down there. The man made fools of us."

"Not you," Katherine said. "Old Three Stars." She gave him an affectionate pat on the arm. "I'm happy you're back."

"The financial aspect of it or romantic?"

She playfully twitched the side of his mustache. "Both, but I'm not quite up to taking anything from you tonight. Circumstances, personal."

Jason nodded. "Oh?"

"It's been a miserable day all the way around."

"Sergeant Hansen told me he came down to see you earlier . . . Lieutenant Clybourn, one of your friends . . ."

"A very true, compassionate friend. He was never in the wagon with me . . . kind to me. Before he left for the Rosebud, I told him what was going on. I disappointed him. He thought I was worthy of better things. What do you think?"

"Oh, I agree, but I learned long ago never to question the decisions of a woman. A general, yes, but never a woman.

Besides, you never disappoint me." He paused, then flipped another small stone across the surface of the pond. "I'll be disappointed to see you pull out in the morning, though. I'll miss your company."

"Likewise." Katherine smiled.

"I'll keep a lookout for your daughter when we move north. We'll do everything possible."

"The general won't appreciate that," she said.

"Yes, I heard about your little confrontation." Jason Armitage chuckled, put an arm around her, and pulled her close. "It provided a few laughs among the men. We haven't had much to laugh about, and you're right. He is a miserable old fart, sometimes."

"How long will you stay here?" she asked.

"Until we get resupplied, more men . . . perhaps three weeks. In the meantime, the General wants to do a bit of fishing, some hunting . . ."

"Jesus! Oh, for God's sake, fishing . . . hunting!"

"That's what he says . . ."

"I hope a grizzly bear eats out his asshole!"

"Well, he's come to the conclusion there's a formidable enemy out there . . . not a grizzly, either, some fearless Sioux and Cheyenne, willing to fight. The element of surprise is gone. From here on out, it's going to be slow and tedious, a long, hot summer."

"Yes," she lamented with a long sigh. "Such a tragedy, such stupidity. Why can't these people be left alone in their own land? That's all they want . . . not a damn thing more, just to be left alone."

"The politics of society . . ."

"White society."

"Yes." Jason Armitage stared up at the starlit heavens. The moon was almost full. He said, "I hope through all of this, you don't wander too far. I may not see you again until fall."

Katherine Coltrane put her head against his shoulder. "I'll be around somewhere along the North Platte. Quinlan says he has other irons in the fire . . . hauling freight up from Cheyenne, Chadron, all kinds of skinning jobs. Who knows, I might even go to Deadwood. The reservations are no more than a day's ride in any direction."

"What about Cheyenne, your house?"

"Yes, I've thought about that, too. I plan on fixing it up

... a good place to winter, if need be. If I find Julia, maybe an extra room or two, until things get better, until I can see some daylight again. You can't imagine the ideas I have."

Jason Armitage smiled into her damp turban and mumbled, "Oh, yes I can."

"Well," concluded Katherine, "if you get stuck in the cold at Fetterman or Laramie this winter, you're welcome to come down and stay with me if I'm in Cheyenne. I'll keep more than your feet warm, Bird Dog." She kissed his cheek. "You bring a couple of bottles of your fine wine. Take some furlough time. I won't charge you for board and room."

"But you'll charge for other amenities?"

"You bet your boots, I will."

"Yes," sighed Jason Armitage. "Yes, I figured as much."

Chapter Six

Alva and Buford

The first day down the Bozeman Trail was miserably hot and muggy; thunderheads building in the west, and by late afternoon, lightning, thunder, followed by a huge downpour beset the wagon train and trooper escort. Shortly, everyone was soaked, everyone except the wounded in the ambulances and canvas-covered freighters. They weren't wet, but several were gangrenous and filled with fever, and despite the valiant efforts of the surgeon, Major William Bosely, they were dying. The long train came to a halt. Unlike General Crook, Major Bosely welcomed the presence of Katherine Coltrane and Calamity Jane; he welcomed their assistance, their willingness to try to help ease some of the misery of his men. As the late afternoon drizzle continued, the women and Bosely's two medical aides went through all of the wagons tending the bedridden, changing bandages, removing soiled long johns, aiding those able to relieve themselves outside, supporting them under the protection of an awning. Some were in pain, others in shock, some too sick and miserable to show any embarrassment at the presence of the two women. Some moaned, other cursed, and some said, "Thank you, sister."

From her wagon near the end of the line, Katherine Coltrane continued to hear a few groans and an occasional nightmarish outcry throughout the night. By morning, the rain had moved out across the prairie to the east; by morning, a burial detail was on the fringe of camp; blanket-wrapped soldiers, two of them, were lowered into shallow graves; no fanfare, no rifle shots, only a prairie burial with a short prayer, "may the Lord take your soul, rest in peace," and the wagon train began moving on again, south toward Fort Fetterman.

They made two stops this day, one for a noon mess, another to attend to the needs of the wounded, and once again,

Katherine and Jane lent their helping hands. Major Bosely was grateful. With a weary smile, he told them they had already lifted the spirits of a few of the men. Jane, with a wry smile of her own, replied that in several cases while sponging a soldier or two, more than their spirits had been lifted. Toward sunset, the wagons pulled into a half circle on Crazy Woman Creek where camp for the night was quickly established, and since no hostiles had been sighted, only a small guard was posted. Because of the earlier exodus of Lakota and Cheyenne to the north, neither Captain Martin Stanford, in charge of the escort company, nor wagon master, Peter Quinlan, believed there was any danger of a hostile encounter. However, Katherine, while taking her bath a hundred yards above the camp, did have an encounter, not with Sioux or Cheyenne, but instead with two bushy-faced men dressed in buckskins, one of whom wore a large hat trimmed with rattlesnake hide. The other man had his long, speckled hair partially covered by a faded, red bandanna; a gold earring dangled from the lobe of his left ear; around his neck, hanging down over his chest, were several strands of Lakota beads. Bathing in the rippling water, Katherine hadn't heard their approach, but there they were, sitting on their horses, trailing a heavily packed mule, grinning down at her through their whiskers.

Annoyed, slowly hunkering in the deepest pool, trying to cover her breasts, Katherine spoke first. "You should have called out . . . at last, given me some warning, you rascals!"

"Well, I reckon so," the one with the gold earring said, "but we was just as surprised as you. Didn't allow we'd be seeing a white woman way out here. Wasn't our notion to be intruding."

The other man snickered. "Ain't much use you trying to hide either, 'cause we already saw everything there is to see, and I'll swear the good Lord set me down in heaven, 'cause I ain't never seen anything so damned pretty in my whole life, and that's the gospel straight from ol' Alva, it is."

"Will one of you get your butt off your horse and toss me my towel, please? Go on, step to it, damn it."

"We can ride on, let you finish," the first man offered.

"The towel . . . throw it out here. I am finished."

The appreciative one, the one called Alva, leaped nimbly from his horse, snatched up the towel, waded part way into the stream, and gave it a toss. Katherine snatched it. "Turn around," she commanded, and when both men had averted their eyes, she quickly wrapped the towel around her body, and splashed away over toward her clothes.

"Name's Alva," she heard the one call. "Alva Tompkins. This is my partner, Buford Reasons, and we sure didn't mean to rile you none, miss."

"I'm not riled," retorted Katherine. Turning away, she sat on the grass, threw her slipover shirt on, then tried to pull up her underpants over her wet legs. They stuck, and she tugged, and since the men, as the one had said, had seen everything there was to see, she finally stood, presented her bare bottom to them, and proceeded to hike up her pants. "Lord, Lord," she heard one of them gasp.

Then, rubbing her hair briskly with the towel, Katherine said, "You've been in the hills too long, carrying on this way, like seeing a woman for the first time."

Alva went over to the bank, knelt down, and splashed water over his face. Smoothing at his mustache, he replied, "Well, I reckon you're right there. Been back up the cricks aways nigh on a month waiting for the Injuns to clean country, but that has nothing to do with how pretty you are. I'd say that same about you if I'd only been up there a day or two."

Katherine smiled. "You've never seen a naked woman, then?"

"Never saw one made out of a piece of heaven."

Katherine burst out laughing. "Nonsense!" Turning, she stared down at Alva Tompkins. He was sitting cross-legged, still staring at her. She looked up at Buford. He was staring, too, but at the same time, attempting to bite off a chunk of twisted tobacco. After a moment of appraisal, she asked curiously, "What were you boys doing up here in the first place? . . . don't you know there's a war going on? There were hostiles all around here a couple of weeks ago."

Alva looked up at Buford furtively. Buford hunched his shoulders innocently; Alva replied in a whisper, "Looking for the old Lost Cabin mine diggins, that's what. Telling you, but no one else. It's secret-like."

"Lost Cabin?"

"Making like you never heard of it, eh?" Alva grinned.

"I haven't. Truly."

"A pilgrim, are you?" asked Buford from atop his horse.

"Pilgrims in those wagons? . . . coming back from the Montana Territory, are you?"

"No," Katherine said. "Wounded soldiers in a lot of those wagons. Coming back from the Tongue River. They had a battle on the Rosebud . . . Lakota, Cheyenne. We're taking them back to Fetterman. My name is Katherine . . . Katherine Coltrane. I'm a mule skinner."

There was a gasp from Alva Tompkins. "Jesus Christ!" he exclaimed, tossing a startled look at Buford Reasons. "Coltrane! Why, you must be Will Coltrane's sister. We knew young Will. Injuns got him . . . thought they got you, too. Well, I'll be damned!"

"They did get me," she replied.

"Land 'o Goshen," whispered Alva. "Well, you sure ain't much for the wear and tear of it, living with those heathens all that time, a regular nosegay, you are, and that's a fact. Lord a'mighty!"

Buford, his cheek bulging, spat once to the side, said, "Bless your lucky hide, we're mighty glad to meet you, Miss Coltrane. Reckon this is our lucky day, too, seeing we had a mutual friend, that brother of yours. He was a good one, he was, young Will. You wouldn't happen to have some spare rations, would you? All we have left is some sowbelly and a little flour. Not a lick of coffee."

Katherine smiled and shook her head. "It always gets back to a man's belly, doesn't it?" She retrieved her soap, draped her towel over her shoulder, and said, "Well, come on, gentlemen. You've already had a free look. I think I can spare you some supper, too."

Back at the wagons, the two men confronted Jane Canarray, an old acquaintance but not a dear old friend. To Jane, they were two bastards, and she greeted them thusly, telling Katherine that the sun had hatched them from two turds a crow had expelled somewhere on a prairie rock. And, once the two men were eating their supper, Jane took Katherine aside and enlightened her further—Alva and Buford were thieves; they stole anything not nailed to the floor or tied to the nearest post, everything from hardware to horses. Not only this, they were niggardly busters, too, always begging a drink or a meal. Buford was a drunkard; he didn't cotton to women. Alva was a different breed, like a fox on the scent, a peter as big as a cucumber, but he was as cheap as they came, claiming he was down-and-out, and offering no more than a half-dollar for a piece of tail. They were a couple of blowflies, and when Jane learned they were heading across the valleys for Deadwood, she hoped a dust devil would rise up to help them along their way. Jane Canarray detested Alva Tompkins and Buford Reasons. Of course, Katherine was to find out later, neither of the men held Jane in very high esteem either.

The next morning, Jane thought Alva and Buford had cleaned country. They had made the fire, prepared coffee, but they were nowhere in sight. She gloated. Good riddance. Her gloating was short-lived for there was their mule, fully packed, tied on behind Katherine's wagon, and Katherine, clad only in her nightgown, was sitting on the wagon gate, drinking coffee and feeding dried apples to the shit-grinning mule. Damn! Where had the old bastards gone? Hunting for some fresh meat, explained Katherine. The men said they wanted to earn their keep. They promised there would be meat in the pot tonight, meat enough to make a good, hot broth for the wounded soldiers, too. Alva Tompkins had assured Katherine that he and Buford were patriotic men, that in this time of distress, they wanted to do all they could to help the troopers. Jane cackled at that. Peas in the pod, she said derisively, just like most soldiers, poor white trash who still chewed food with their mouths open and who looked around for a corncob every time they went to the brush to squat. As long as they were around, Jane warned, it would be wise to keep a sharp eye on everything.

Wily codgers, notwithstanding, the men kept their word. Toward mid-afternoon, they intercepted the wagon train about ten miles above Crazy Woman Creek. Slung over the backs of their horses were three antelope that they later quartered and distributed to the three mess sergeants, all but the livers and one hind quarter, which they kept for the women's pot. Additionally, Alva pulled out a big mess of greens from a canvas sack hung from his pommel—mustard, poke, dandelion, and onion.

Here, on a fork of the Powder River, not too far from where Thomas Clybourn had found Katherine, where she had become separated from Julia, Katherine washed the greens in the stream, with tears on her cheeks and tragic memories overwhelming her heart. Making the rounds that evening with Major Bosely, she moved among the wounded as though she were in a trance. She smiled, though; she patted the men and tousled their hair; they were appreciative; they didn't know she had been wounded too—by remembrances.

Beautiful white clouds were scudding across the pale blue sky the next morning, a warm day, but not hot, a day to enjoy, and when Alva Tompkins offered to handle Katherine's team, she didn't protest. She padded the back of her seat with a blanket, made a headrest with another, and with the brim of her hat blocking the eastern sun, relaxed for the first time in what seemed like an eternity. She dozed several times, but she became alert when Alva called some distant sight or landmark to her attention. She listened, too. In his soft-spoken but blunt way, he was informative, often humorous. He was a big liar, but unlike many other men on the frontier, he freely admitted it. He had almost lost his hair to Indians a dozen times (actually only twice); had fought several hand-to-hand battles with braves (actually only once); had fornicated with Indian women many times (actually twice), and over in Deadwood, he and Buford had staked out a dozen claims. In truth, they had two, both practically worthless, but he had plans to increase their value considerably. What he and Buford did have were two homesteads and a spacious cabin on Bluegrass Creek up in the hills above Chugwater. It was their home during the cold winter months. Most other times, he and Buford were out scavening, preparing for winter. Was he a thief? asked Katherine Coltrane. Yes, he admitted, but everyone on the frontier was a thief. In twenty years, he hadn't met one man who was honest through and through. Without exception, everyone had a trace of avarice.

Katherine had heard this story before, Jane's version: trust no one, get everything you can, and run like hell before someone gets it back. She looked over at Alva, his out-thrust jaw accented by his whiskers, crow feet at the corners of his greenish-blue eyes, and a small scar parting the hair over one of his brows, sustained in a skirmish with a Pawnee years ago—so he had told her. Probably was a handsome man in his youth. He said he didn't rightly know how old he was but he was still agile, his rugged body as tough and sinewy as buffalo hide.

"Do you ever work?" Katherine asked.

Alva Tompkins gave the reins a little flip. "Depends on

what you're meaning by work. Ain't much work skinning mules or scratching for gold. I never cared much for making wood, though. Never cared much for being beholden to no one but myself ... or looking out for ol' Buford. We sorta look after each other, I reckon. Never did like the sound of that word, work."

"What about those diggings?" she asked with a twinkle in her turquoise eyes. "That Lost Cabin place you were talking about ... did you boys find it?"

Alva cocked a wary eye at her. "Told you it was a secret, didn't I? Have to keep things like this mum, Katie."

She poked his leg. "Well, come on, did you?"

Alva chuckled lowly. "Ain't nothing left of that cabin ... a few burnt logs, that's all, fireweed all in bloom. Ain't nothing left of those ol' Swedes who built it, either. Injuns got all but one or two of 'em ... scalped 'em, ate their livers."

"One of your tall tales, Alva?"

"No, Katie, no tall tale, 'afore your time out here, though. Maybe ten, twelve years back. One of those ol' boys shows up down on the Platte with a pocket full of nuggets ... all he managed to get out. Injuns just plain hacked up his partners and the outfit, dust'n all, ten thousand dollars worth, so he claimed, back there in those foothills below the big mountains, eh? Buford'n me been scouting around that place off and on ever since. Ain't safe, you know, damn Sioux always after our hair. Fella has to be mighty careful up there. Have to pussyfoot it, you do. Go using a sluice box too much, and it riles the water ... Injuns see that right off, know damn well it ain't no beaver making muddy water."

"You found something, then?"

"Said no such thing."

"Well, you found what was left of the cabin, didn't you?"

"Ain't no mine up there," Alva said flatly. "Nothing but a crick running up through this gully and some skinny ledges of white quartz. Now, a man goes picking around right careful below the rocks, and he's apt to find a few specks of yellow iron, all right, nuggets, too. That's my notion on it."

"How much yellow iron?"

Alva Tompkins clucked his tongue and gave Katherine a sly wink. "Oh, I reckon maybe about a dozen pokes ... enough to fill a couple of pickling jars."

"Oh, mercy!" she whispered.

"Good for salt."

"Salt?"

"Yep, salt, leastways, some of it."

"I don't understand."

And, Katherine listened in quiet amazement as Alva Tompkins explained one very interesting and deceiving aspect of prospecting for gold. Alva and Buford, indeed, were heading back for Deadwood to finish up a little work on their two claims several miles above the town, claims that had produced only a trace of color. Actually, they now weren't going to dig for gold on their properties; they had already done that, and had discovered it was almost nonexistent. What they were going to do was carefully "salt" a few crevices and some of the gravel, cash in a few pokes at the bank, thus revealing a rich strike, since they both had reputations for disliking too much work, they were going to sell their lodes for a handsome price. Then, they were going to head for the hills above Chugwater.

Katherine Coltrane stared incredulously across the seat at Alva Tompkins. "That's terribly dishonest!"

He chuckled. "Sure as hell is, ain't it?"

"Good grief!" Katherine sighed. "Jane was right. You are two unscrupulous farts."

"Hah, ain't she the one!" huffed Alva defensively. "That's the pot calling the kettle black. Why, I could tell you some tales 'bout that woman, I could."

"I've already heard most of them. She's been kind to me . . . a good partner on the trail. Two sides to every story, you know."

"Drinking, brawling, whoring—"

"There's been very little drinking on this trip, I'll tell you. She's been sober all the way. All business."

"Business? Little whoring business on the side? You, too?"

Katherine Coltrane felt a small blush under her floppy hat. She said what she had said before, the first thing that came to her mind. "Sometimes, you have to strike while the iron is hot, Alva . . . under the circumstances, take what you can, and make the most of it."

"Yep, I sorta figured that," he said. "Well, I've seen a few doves in my time, Katie. Ain't never seen one the likes of you, though. You just don't palaver like one . . . just don't seem to wear that kind of collar, either."

"Sometimes looks are deceiving."

"I reckon you know what you're doing, most of 'em do. 'Course, ain't nothing that's forever, 'specially out in this land. Survival is the work, eh?"

"Oh, until I get my daughter back, I'll survive. This won't be forever, but in the meantime, one way or another, I'll live. It takes life to love life. That's what they say, anyhow."

"For a fact," Alva said with a grin. "Damn lonely life at times, but sure as hell, there ain't nothing to love when you're a goner." He gave the reins a ripple, just to let the mules know they weren't alone. "Gaddap there, you darlings, move along. Heigh—ahhh!"

After a while, Katherine Coltrane smiled over at him and said, "Jane says you're a regular philanderer, always chasing after women. Is this just another tall tale?"

"Look here, now," Alva protested, "don't you go believing everything you hear from that woman. She's the biggest damned liar above the North Platte, barring none. Why, you oughta know that by now after skinning with her for a month. Land alive!"

"Yes, but is it true?"

"Well, I can't deny it," Alva finally confessed. "I reckon I've seen the best and worst of 'em from here to Independence in my day, Calamity being one of the worst, but I've turned my head to every pretty one along the trail. Fell in love with most 'em, too. Funny thing about me, you know, still got a lot of rattle in my tail. I never had a hankering for settling down, the marrying itch. Women got what men ain't got, that feeling within . . . seem to have a knack at that mind reading stuff, like one of them Madam Zsa Zsas reading those glass balls."

"Fortune-tellers . . ."

"Yep, you got it, Katie. I'll allow all women are fortune-tellers, damned if they ain't . . . fortune-tellers and fortune seekers. Always see right through me, for sure." Alva Tompkins chuckled and gave Katherine a wink. "I love women, though, I surely do. I don't trust 'em no more than a man, but I love 'em."

"Is that why you're sitting up here with me today?"

"Beats the hell outta sitting back there riding longside Buford, it does. Hell, I've been with that ol' boy for nigh on ten years, now. I know every goddamned word he's gonna say, even before he says it."

"That's sort of like mind reading, isn't it?"

"No, it's plain ol' habit . . . like a chaw of tobacco. Everytime you bite into a plug, you know damn well what it's gonna taste like. Chew and spit, chew and spit. Hell, that's all me'n Buford been doing all these years. Just ain't much to talk about when you getting to know someone this good, so sometimes I end up talking to myself."

"They say a lot of people out here talk to themselves. Some of those wounded troopers in the wagons up ahead have been doing it, too. Sometimes, it only means you're lonely."

"Damn good reason for talking to yourself, I'd say," Alva Tompkins said, pointing his chin whiskers to the side. "Prairie is one helluva lonely place."

Katherine Coltrane was both intrigued and delighted; Jane Canarray was chagrined; Alva and Buford stayed with the wagon train, enjoying Katherine's hospitality and conversation, and the daily free fare from the army mess during the final three days back to Fort Fetterman. There was a practical side to this; Katherine (pledged to secrecy) hadn't disclosed to her partner, Jane, the pokes of gold from the Lost Cabin diggings that the two men had stashed away in their saddlebags and the pack on their mule. Alva and Buford had elected to ride along under the protection of the troopers down to the river trail instead of chancing some dangerous meeting with hostiles by taking the shortcut across the prairie. Though Katherine hadn't seen the pouches of gold, there was no doubt they existed. On the second day out of the Crazy Woman Creek camp, Alva had plucked five shiny nuggets out of one of his pockets and had shown them to her. One was as big as her thumbnail; her eyes had sparkled. She thought that a handful of those nuggets would be a nice addition to the gold coins, silver, and new scrip that she had hidden in the bottom of her flour sack. She didn't suggest this to the men, but it was on her mind. Yes, it was true—without exception, everyone had a trace of avarice.

The return to Fetterman wasn't any occasion for a celebration. The news of General Crook's retreat on the Rosebud, the damage inflicted upon his troops, preceded the wagon train's arrival by several days. This was the "Indian telegraph" at work, that seemingly mysterious interchange of information across the great prairie between the scouts and camp runners of the wandering tribes. But, despite the woes of the command and the miseries of the wounded, it was a homecoming of sorts. Captain Stanford, in charge of the returning troops, and the surgeon, Major Bosely, made their reports to the post commander, Colonel Ben Bradford. The incapacitated were housed in more comfortable surroundings, and after taking care of their teams, Katherine and Jane found lodging at Manny Slaymaker's boardinghouse.

Though Katherine dwelled on her own failed mission, she received condolences from the Slaymakers and Colonel Bradford, as well. The colonel, saddened at the loss of his aide, Thomas Clybourn, talked briefly on the porch with Katherine, and inquired about her immediate plans. Her plans were tentative, in somewhat of a muddle, but she thought she might return to her house in Cheyenne first, then work on one of Quinlan's freight lines up to Deadwood where she could be near the reservations where she anticipated the Oglala would return in early fall. Hope and faith were her companions, she said with a wan smile.

In parting, Colonel Bradford thanked her for her assistance to Major Bosely with the wounded. "The doctor said your services were invaluable ... the woman's touch, as it were, even brought a measure of civility to some of those roughneck soldiers."

"Some of them were in no condition to be otherwise, Colonel," Katherine said.

Benjamin Bradford studied her for a moment. Her long brown hair was clean again, swept back and pinned at the back, and she had on a skirt and blouse, and her button-up, pointed shoes. She was a lady, yet not quite. Bradford grinned, and said, "Bosely said you had a few words with General Crook just before you left ... some parting words, something about disliking his attitude."

"Humph!" Katherine smirked. "Not exactly in those words. As I recall, I called him a miserable old fart."

Bradford laughed. He held her hand. "Very appropriate, Miss Coltrane. You're not alone in your appraisal, but from any of the rest of us around here, that would be intolerable, an act of insubordination."

"Bird Dog thought it was funny, too."

"Ah, good old Jason," mused Ben Bradford. "Down in his cups because of all of this, I suppose?"

"Who isn't?"

"Bird Dog, is it?" He scratched up behind his hat and grinned at her. "I trust you got to know Jason somewhat better, then? Didn't impress you too much at our first meeting, his questions . . ."

"Oh, I know him," she said. "Yes, I surely do."

"Well, he'll feel a little better when he returns," Bradford assured her. "Some new orders have been cut . . . came in several days after you people left. He's going to have a command of his own. Bird Dog has a promotion, Miss Coltrane, so you stay on the good side of him. He's a brigadier general now . . . being recalled to take over at Fort Robinson."

"Oh, mercy, mercy!"

"Yes, precisely my sentiments." He paused on the steps and looked back. Benjamin Bradford told Katherine he was going to pen a note of introduction for her, something she could present to the commandants at the forts and the agents at the reservations, something to give her assistance and make her task of finding Julia much easier. "I'm going to try and put a few troopers at your disposal, when and if you need them," he said with a grin. "Jason would like this."

Katherine Coltrane was breathless. "Why . . . why, I appreciate this very much."

With a little wink and a tip of his hat, Colonel Bradford replied, "Yes, I thought you would."

Warm feelings suddenly rippled through Katherine. Oh, how she would enjoy sitting across from Jason this night, sharing a bottle of his fine, red wine, lifting her glass to his, congratulating him. Yes, the very best to you, General Armitage! To life and the love of it, to the lonely hearts sharing it. Will there be a slight fee? Oh, you bet your boots, there will! Katherine laughed inside. She took some of her money and went to the post mercantile; she bought all of the women's apparel she could find, a dress, a suit, underclothes, stockings, and a small brass-trimmed trunk with leather straps. Perhaps she was no lady, but if and when the occasion arose, she certainly was going to look like one.

Outside the store, she met Alva Tompkins, and he offered to carry her trunk and purchases back to the boardinghouse. Through the generosity of the mess sergeants, he and Buford had found temporary quarters in a barrack in back of the mess hall, but Alva said they had a small problem—as usual, they were practically fundless. At least, he explained, they had no coins or scrip to spend, and they needed a few items for their trip back to Deadwood. With all the mule skinners and post loafers hanging round, it was foolhardy and downright dangerous to be flashing any gold. Alva wondered if Katherine might loan him twenty dollars. Somewhere down the trail, he surely would pay her back.

"You told me never to trust anyone," Katherine reminded him. "Why, it's likely I'll never see you two again. You said it yourself . . . this country's so big a man can get lost and never be seen again."

Alva grinned. "Did I say that?"

"You surely did."

"Told you a secret, didn't I? 'Bout that Lost Cabin mine."

Katherine Coltrane opened the door of her room, took the trunk and her clothing, and set them on the bed. Alva stood aside expectantly, and after delving into her bundle, Katherine came back and handed him three new ten-dollar bills, some of the scrip Jason had given her. Alva grinned and said, "I'm obliged, Katie, and you can trust me, too." Then, he broke out in a chuckle. "More'n I expected . . . might just buy me some new duds, too." Suddenly, he leaped in the air and clicked his boot heels together, and dancing down the small hallway, he glanced back over his shoulder at her. "Didn't think I could do that, did you?" He disappeared.

"Mercy," Katherine moaned to herself, "I must be crazy! Damn it, I am crazy, loaning money, talking to myself . . . crazy, lonely, I don't know . . ."

Later, after supper, she sat on the porch by herself, staring at the distant river and observing the last of the activity around the fort. Jane had disappeared, probably had gone across the river to have a few drinks at the hogs. At dusk, Pete Quinlan arrived to pay his respects and deliver wages for the recent trip—forty dollars. Colonel Bradford had hired him to return to Goose Creek with six wagons of freight for General Crook, but he was going to be delayed for another week until the troop reinforcements came up from Fort Laramie. In the meantime, Quinlan had six empties that needed to be skinned back to Laramie. Was Katherine interested in handling one of the teams? She was, and she promptly agreed; she had decided to return to fix up her house in Cheyenne before moving north to Deadwood.

Later, Mary Slaymaker joined Katherine on the porch where they chatted quietly until darkness set in. Once back in her room, Katherine lit the lamp on the small table and began preparing for a good-night's sleep. After slipping out of her clothing, she sat on the side of the bed and began attending her hair, head to the side, ear attuned to the tiny crackles as her tortoiseshell comb made its long, deliberate sweeps. Thus, she was busily engaged when she heard the faintest knock on her door. Katherine quietly slipped the latchstring, wedged the door, and peeked into the faint lamplight of the little hall. A small leather pouch was resting against her nose, and behind it, a whisper came: "Decided I couldn't wait till I met you somewhere down the road . . . here, I'm paying you back, now."

"Shhh!" Katherine whispered back, and she opened the door and quickly pulled Alva Tompkins into the room. "Don't make a sound," she whispered again. Throwing her gown over her shoulders, she took the pouch of gold and went over to the lamp. Oh, it was heavy! Oh, it was gold, too, and how it glittered and gleamed as she doffed the little pebbles and flakes into the palm of her hand. Mercy, how she had wished to get her hands on those little bags of gold, and now, deliverance, dear Alva, bless his soul, the bearer! Alva now came up behind her; he was staring down, too, chuckling. He smelled as though he had bathed in a tub of mint. "Ain't mica. Real stuff, it is. Your troubles 'n' all, thought you'd be needing a grubstake. One bag full."

"Baa, baa, black sheep?" she said in a hushed voice. "Am I the little girl in the lane?"

"I reckon that's right," he whispered back. "There's more where that came from, and we're going back next spring to get it."

Katherine Coltrane reached up and stroked the side of his face, ran her fingers through his hair. It was still damp from his bath. She picked up the lamp and held it to him, yes, a new shirt, new trousers. Why, he was dressed and pruned like a guinea hen. "Just what are you up to, Alva?" she whispered teasingly. "Coming here in the dead of night?"

"Only wanted you to know I'm mighty obliged for the way you went and treated me 'n' old' Buford, that's all. No one's ever done that before, you know. No one gives us the time of day, for a fact."

"This could have waited until the morning," Katherine said. "Anything else on your mind?"

He grinned and replied, "Like I said, a woman's the best damned mind reader going, 'course anything else is up to you, Katie. Ol' Alva here, and someone like you ... so pretty 'n' all, I don't know how you feel. Why, I reckon I'm old enough to be your daddy."

She touched a finger to his lips. "Now, you keep quiet, hear? And, don't belittle yourself. You're a proud man, and fifty isn't what I call old, Alva." A compassionate warmness swept through Katherine. Oh, indeed, she knew the mind of Alva Tompkins and her own devious mind, as well. Was this part of avarice? Perhaps, but strangely it was a sensuous and affectionate feeling too. Very strange. Tall tales. Older men. She couldn't help but wonder. What Jane had said about the prowess of this man had been on her mind, too, shamefully. Bags of gold be damned, she wanted to find out, and she would. "Now, I'll tell you a secret, Alva," Katherine whispered. She carefully set the lamp back on the stand. "I've been wondering about you. Does this surprise you?"

"Nope," Alva whispered. "I think you had the evil eye on me once or twice. Sometimes those damn buckskins don't hide much." He chuckled. "Want me to take my clothes off then?"

"Yes, I want you to stay for a while ... but mercy, we have to be very quiet about this. Do you understand?"

"I sure do."

Alva shed his clothing, and in the faint glow of the lamp, Katherine saw all of him, a surprisingly sturdy, physical specimen of a man, sinewy and well proportioned from head to feet. Her preliminary examination went by the wayside, for Alva Tompkins suddenly knelt before her like a veteran knight. Katherine felt his rough hands gently caressing her knees, parting them. Then he slowly began melting kisses up her thighs.

Oh, this man, this gentle, caring, lustful, unpredictable man! Mercy, mercy! Her troubled mind suddenly collapsed; every memory was erased; she was now living only moment by moment in the wonderful realm of ecstasy.

Chapter Seven

Cheyenne

On July 8, Katherine Coltrane stepped off of the stage in Cheyenne and received the first of several surprises; the town had mushroomed dramatically; no longer was her house on the outskirts; several business had sprung up along the street, and the station, a large new one, was only a stone's throw from her front yard. The front yard, that was something else, too; the pole fence had been recently white-washed, the grass shortened with a sickle, and flowers were in bloom around the porch. Momentarily, she stared in silent awe, wondering if some squatter had taken over the place. But, no, there in the back she could see the Coltrane freight-ers, behind them, the big barn, its doors closed just as she and Will had left them.

Hoisting her small trunk to her shoulder, she forged ahead toward the front door, realizing that she had long since lost her house key to Standing Bear, her Oglala husband. She had explained its use, a key to open the lodge of a *wasichu*. He had interpreted it spiritually. It was the key to her inner self; thus he would wear it around his neck to retain her charm.

A small voice cried out from the street. "Miss Katherine! Katherine Coltrane, is that you, child?"

Katherine whirled about. Ye gods, old lady Pryor! Emma Pryor, God bless her soul! The woman was now rushing for-ward, a man directly behind her—Samuel Pryor, her hus-band, and moments later, they were through the gate, Emma trying to fasten her sunbonnet, and Sam nervously adjusting his big, yellow straw hat.

"Yes," Katherine finally managed to shout, "I'm home." Tears flooded her eyes. "Yes, Misses Pryor, I'm home."

"Oh, dear me," Emma said breathlessly, "let me look at you. Why, you're all grown-up into a regular lady. Oh, my, my, Miss Katherine, the Lord has blessed you." And the two women traded fond embraces.

Samuel Pryor spoke up. "Been expecting you, we have ... read all about you in the paper ... being found. Everybody gave thanks to the Lord. Why, I told them all the time, you'd be back. Never found your body at those wagons up above, and I told them. I says that little woman has gumption, and if she's alive, she'll be back one of these days. That's what I told them."

Emma Pryor was weeping. "Oh, God bless you, girl," she sobbed.

After wiping away a few tears of her own, Katherine thanked them for their concern, and directly, Samuel had a key in the lock of the door, explaining that Will had given it to him five or six years back in case of an emergency. Before they entered, he bowed his head and offered a prayer of thanksgiving. The parlor was hot but conspicuously clean, and as Katherine opened several windows, Samuel Pryor explained that he and Emma had taken the liberty of entering the house every week or so to keep things proper-like. Samuel had even drawn water from the well to keep scum from settling on the surface. Yes, everything was as clean as a church, and Katherine Coltrane slumped in a rocker and wiped her wet eyes.

Her second surprise came when Samuel Pryor told her that the people at the stage station wanted to buy the Pryor property and Katherine's as well. Freight yards, he went on to explain; the railroad was planning to extend tracks up through Chugwater and on north to Laramie; a livestock yard already had been staked out for the east end, and a spur track and siding would run right through the middle of the Pryor and Coltrane properties.

"But this is ridiculous," Katherine said. "I've been away five years. I finally get home and find out I'm going to be without a house. My heavens, I can't even think about it ... not right now. My mind's already in a quandary."

"You come over to supper this evening," Emma said. "Come over when you get yourself settled. Samuel can explain it. I'm going to fix a special meal for you, Miss Katherine, a celebration meal."

"Are you selling? How soon is this ... this expansion taking place?"

"Year or two," Samuel answered. He went to the door

with Emma, looked back at Katherine and said, "All in the planning stage, but we're selling, all right. Big money, plenty to build a better place, and that's something a young lady like you will be wanting to consider."

"Big money?" she asked. "Like what? . . . have they said?"

"Eight thousand for our place," Samuel returned. "Since you got all that property to the east, that big barn and all, I'd say maybe ten thousand for you, only a guess, though. They might go twelve if you got your dander up."

Katherine quietly mumbled, "Jesus!" Neither Emma or Samuel heard it. They were out the door, waving, reminding her that supper was at six o'clock.

Yet another surprise awaited her this first day of her return—at the Wells Fargo bank where she appeared at two o'clock in the afternoon to deposit her earnings from the recent trip north with General Crook's army. She had three hundred and eighty dollars in cash and she had a pouch of gold, which brought a look of surprise from the teller when she slid it through the cage. He took out a scale, and she watched him weigh the small leather sack. And, after a moment of calculation, he told her that she had exactly four hundred and sixty dollars worth, making her net deposit eight hundred and forty dollars. Katherine Coltrane was quietly astounded; she only smiled and nodded, signed her deposit slip, and stuffed the receipt into her small purse.

She did some swift calculations of her own—Alva and Buford, those wily rascals, had at least four or five thousand dollars tucked away in the packs on their flop-eared mule! Mercy! Katherine wanted to laugh aloud, but she was walking along the boardwalk with others now. She could only dwell on those last few tumultuous weeks on the prairie above Fort Fetterman. Oh, how she had longed to share her secret about Alva Tompkins with Jane, her dear friend Jane, now somewhere on a freighter headed for Deadwood. Why, Jane would fall off that wagon in a dead faint if she really knew the truth about Alva and Buford, those poor, miserable codgers. Tall tales, indeed!

And, Alva, bless him, rough as an old corncob, but within, as warm and mellow as a sweet persimmon. Oh, how he had surprised her. No one had ever roused her passions as he had that night in the boardinghouse. Yes, she certainly would see him again, either in the gulches of Deadwood or high in the mountain meadows of Bluegrass Creek; she had promised. She would take his gold again, too. Unscrupulous? Conniving? She didn't want to dwell on principles, only the sensuous satisfaction he had given her. Alva Tompkins idolized her, and because of her own selfish desires, never, never, would she deny him any of his.

Katherine's walk in the afternoon sunshine was brisk, the stride of her long legs stretching her suit skirt to its limit. Indeed, she was a good looker; she knew it, and she had plans to look even better: some tailored suits, pretty shoes, fancy boots, beautiful silk underclothes only fitting for one in her new profession, and yes, several dashing bonnets, brimmed and feathered, and last, but not least, riding apparel, perhaps a parasol, too. Colors? Oh, the colors, the shades of blue and green to match her turquoise eyes, the richness of burgundy and purple, too; she adored all of these hues. Then there was the potions place for the small assortment of intimate personals she needed. Oh, she would have it all, everything befitting a soiled dove. Not a whore.

Katherine slowed her gait at the stage station, hesitated, then found a seat on a long bench under the shade of the great, overhanging roof. A new sign dangled over the eave—"CHEYENNE." People were moving about, and at the end of the boardwalk, an olive-colored coach with a team of six black horses was awaiting passengers. This was the Cheyenne–Deadwood stage, bound for the North Platte River Trail with connections east and west. The stage she would board within the next few weeks to continue her quest for Julia in the middle of the Indian nation. Small trunks and bundles were being arranged on top of the coach by two men. Another man with a dark blue apron wrapped around his middle was standing below, observing, and at the clatter of an approaching wagon, he moved to the side. The wagon slowed beside him, and Katherine saw that one of the two men in it had a shotgun propped between his knees. Then, the aproned attendant removed a small, metal-bound box, carried it over to the stage, and hoisted it to the awaiting hands of one of the drivers. One of the men called, "Where in the hell is the dummy?"

Dummy? Katherine curiously leaned forward, then saw another man emerge from the station carrying a similar box that was transferred and placed behind the driver's seat. Moments later, the last passenger boarded, the door was shut, and with a holler, the reins were snapped, and the stage trundled off down the dusty street directly in front of Katherine Coltrane's white pole fence. Finally, it made a wide turn north and disappeared behind a line of huge cottonwoods.

She looked up. The man in the apron was standing in front of her, and he asked, "May I help you, ma'am?"

She said, "I'm a neighbor. My name is Katherine Coltrane. I own the house down the street . . . the land down to the creek, and that trail you're using around the corner. All of that's my property."

"Good God!" the man exclaimed. "Why, you're the woman the Injuns . . ."

"Yes," she cut in. "Yes, I'm the one."

"Name is Anderson," he said. "Rolly Anderson." Bowing slightly, he went on, "I'm pleased to meet you, Miss Coltrane. I'm the assistant stationmaster. Saw you when you came in earlier today, but I didn't realize . . . you don't look like someone who's . . ."

"I know, I know," Katherine said.

"Well, is there anything I can do for you?"

Katherine dabbed a handkerchief at her forehead, and said, "I understand they plan to run tracks . . . put in rails, a landing or some such thing. Are any of these railroad people around?"

No, Rolly Anderson told her. The man in charge of the development had an office in town; he came around occasionally, but was in the field most of the time working with a surveying crew. It was true, though, a rail line was going to run north through Chugwater to the North Platte, and right-of-way agreements were already underway. He thought actual construction of the new route was still several years away.

Katherine thanked Rolly Anderson. "I plan on leaving for a while in several weeks," she said. "I don't know exactly when I'll return. Indefinite plans. Yes, there is something you can do, Mister Anderson . . . tell someone to drop by my place. I want to discuss the sale of it, and the sooner the better."

"I certainly will do that," he returned. "It's a shame you're leaving so soon, after just getting back from all that time up there, and our boys are sure having a bad time of it, aren't they? It's damn good you're out of there. Place isn't safe, not at all."

"Yes, and I have to return," she said with a tired smile. "Some unfinished business."

"North of the river?" Anderson asked cautiously.

"I'm afraid so."

And then Katherine received another surprise, a shocking surprise. Rolly Anderson exclaimed, "Good Lord, Miss Coltrane, the place is on fire! Everything is in a terrible mess. Haven't you heard? . . . seen the dispatch in the morning press? It's horrible!"

No, she hadn't. Rolly Anderson disappeared in the station, directly returned with a copy of the Cheyenne *Democratic Leader,* and shook out the front page in front of her. Headlines. Bold headlines. "Massacre. Annihilation." And, as Katherine perused a few lines, she heard Anderson speaking to her side.

". . . News came around the horn from Bismarck, one whole command wiped out by the hostiles, half of another. Place called Little Big Horn. See here, that General Custer . . . twelve days ago."

Katherine was swiftly reading ahead, leaping from one paragraph to another, looking for some mention of General Crook's command. Oh, dear Bird Dog. Not a word. It appeared that the great convergence trap had a rusty spring. She sighed, then said almost vehemently, "Custer wasn't a general. He was a lieutenant colonel, a pompous ass."

Rolly Anderson, his eyes wide, asked, "Did you know him? . . . meet him somewhere up above?"

"I have dear friends who knew him, and the Lakota I lived with certainly knew him." Handing him the paper, she said, "Ironic, isn't it? They called him Long Hair, the Butcher of Washita, and he ended up on the meat block himself." She walked away without another word, and left a confused Rolly Anderson staring at her swaying backside.

For the next several days, Katherine had visitors. Emma Pryor came in the afternoons, bringing vegetables from her garden, and a Methodist minister and his wife came another day. They brought an invitation to come to church, and they also left a prayer book. A young newspaperman appeared on the porch the third morning, and since Katherine had been sleeping late in the luxury of her very own bed again, she was still in her robe. He wasn't the stalwart, veteran type like Henry Burlingame. He was young, had a batch of angry red pimples on his forehead, and Katherine thought he was also very nervous because of her flimsy robe and bare feet. She told him she was sorry, but the life she had lived with the Lakota was very personal, and she declined to be interviewed. He understood, he said, and he left in a hurry; his ears were red, too. On this afternoon, Katherine withdrew three hundred dollars from her account and went shopping. She purchased everything she had wanted, and was fitted for two suits and two pairs of fancy handmade boots—one black and one brown.

She had four new pairs of stockings, quite sheer, she thought. She could easily see her hand through them, two new fancy girdles, too, and three pairs of garters: pink, white, and black. One of the lace-trimmed silk robes she had bought was also black, so in the privacy of her bedroom, she soon attired herself entirely in black—underpants, stockings, brassier, and girdle, and after fastening the second stocking, she stood in front of the half mirror of her dresser. Turning first one way, then another, she smiled. This was all very delightful, at least, from her midriff up. The half girdle exposed her belly button nicely yet discretely hid the top of her curly brown mound. Then, tilting the mirror, she examined her legs, which Bird Dog Armitage declared were the most beautiful legs he had ever seen.

She was admiring herself when she heard a sharp knock, then a rattle of the front screen door. Not Samuel Pryor, for he always shouted out her name; not his wife, Emma, for she always appeared at the kitchen door, either with a bowl, pail, or covered dish. Katherine hastily donned her new black silk robe, and in her stocking feet, glided across the parlor.

Through the screen she peered at the fuzzy image of a man. He was wearing a tan flat-brimmed hat, white shirt with the sleeves rolled, brown pants, and tall boots that laced all the way up the front. Under one arm was a fat folder. From his attire Katherine knew instantly it was the railroad man, and as she edged behind the wall with only her head and shoulders showing, he spoke, saying, "Miss Coltrane? Stanley Howard, here. Colorado and Southern Railroad." He grinned. "Everyone calls me Howie."

"Not Stan?" she replied, smiling.

"Howie. Inconvenient time for you?"

"Yes and no. It all depends on your taste. I'm trying on some new clothes."

"I have good taste, Miss Coltrane, but I don't have much time. I'm on the road tomorrow again. One of the men down at the station told me you wanted to see me. The sooner the better, he said. I made it sooner. . . ."

Pulling her silk robe close, she edged back and said, "You better come in, then. I don't want you flying the coop on me, because I don't plan on being around here too long myself."

"Fine and dandy, Miss Coltrane," and Stanley Howard removed his hat, entered, gawked at her once, and said, "Egads!"

Sitting on the davenport, Katherine told Howard to take a seat, and he did, in the nearby rocker, placing his hat and the folder on the floor in front of him. "Those are quite some clothes, all right. Black is quite a fetching color in the boudoir. I don't care much for it on the street . . . always reminds me of misfortune, someone is distress. My Uncle Henry died when he was forty-eight. Aunt Flora outlived him by thirty years. Wore black the rest of her life, a black hat with an ugly white lily on it. Rather an eccentric old biddy, anyhow. I think they buried her in that damn outfit, too."

"I hadn't planned on walking the streets this way."

"No, that would be a tad too provocative."

"Your wife, does she wear black? The boudoir, you said."

"I'm not married," Stanley Howard said. He smiled under his black mustache, which was broad and edged sharply at the sides, not twisted into a fancy loop.

Katherine curled her legs back and carefully covered them with the robe. "To business, Mister Howard . . . Howie," she finally said. "What's this place worth to your railroad? My neighbors tell me your people already have been looking around, so what's the price?"

"Ah, the valuation," Howard replied, and he began delving into his folder, pulled out a sheet, reached over, and handed it to her. "It's broken down . . . house, well, barn, acreage, etcetera, even the water rights on the creek."

Tracing her finger down each item, Katherine came to the bottom of the page, the figure there, underlined—$10,500. "Is this your estimate? Did you figure it?"

"No, one of my appraisers did."

"It's not enough," Katherine said flatly.

He sighed. "Yes, I know, everyone says the same thing about their property."

"I'm not everyone."

"No, you're not, Miss Coltrane. It's quite obvious. You're not the typical property owner around these parts."

"The barn," she said, casting her eyes on the paper. "Five hundred. Ridiculous! It would cost me a good thousand to build a barn like that one. The water rights—"

"But, why would you want to build a barn? Your business is down. You don't have a mules. Egad, you're not planning on going into freighting again, are you?"

Katherine shrugged. "I don't know exactly what I'm going to do, but that's not the point. The point is—"

"No, wait," he protested gently. "Wait, wait, wait. Maybe we should discuss this over a meal . . . this evening. I can come back."

"Oh, no, Howie, no meal for the Colorado and Southern, not on your life. The railroad should be buying *me* a meal, not the other way around."

"But, Miss Coltrane, it is," he said imploringly. "You and I . . . we can have dinner, discuss this."

"We? You want me to go to supper with you?"

"Why not? It would be my pleasure. You're a very fetching woman, probably a good businesswoman, too."

"You said black was a very fetching color. You weren't speaking about me, were you?"

"Well"—Stanley Howard grinned—"it does depend upon who happens to be wearing the black."

"So, you want to bribe me with compliments and a meal."

"I'd like to try. Show you some reasoning behind these figures."

Unfolding herself from the sofa, Katherine said, "All right, Howie, I would enjoy your company. You're a fetching gentleman, too." She eyed him mischievously. "I don't suppose I should wear black, do you think? You know, your dear old Aunt Flora."

Stanley Howard grinned. "Looking at you this way, I don't think anyone would be much interested in eating, Miss Katherine."

"Is that so." She followed him to the door, and he pushed through the screen and replaced his hat. Slipping the sash from her black gown, she whispered, "Howie, what time are you calling on me?"

He half turned. "Six o'clock . . . egad!"

Dinner. Stanley Howard called it dinner, not supper, and it was dining, not supping, not eating, but dining. Whatever, it was exquisite, and she felt absolutely grand about herself, her beautiful blue dress, her matching blue leather shoes, her white shawl. How the people in the hotel dining room stared, nodded, and smiled at her. And how Stanley Howard beamed and nodded graciously to everyone when he later escorted her out under the flickering glow of the glass chandeliers. Who was this beautiful woman, this newcomer to the elegance of the Palace Hotel dining room where the most fashionable gentlemen and women met to quietly gossip, discuss business, and enjoy the finest cuisine in Cheyenne? Katherine Coltrane smiled to herself. Oh, if they only knew! And she hadn't discussed business; she artfully talked around it, said barely anything about her adventures, or recent misadventures; she purposely led Stanley Howard into discussions about himself, his work on the frontier. He was an ambitious young engineer, twenty-seven, one year older than she. He loved the West, the challenge it presented, the opportunities it offered. He was in charge of land acquisition for the Colorado and Southern in the Wyoming Territory, and he directed the survey crew working north toward Chugwater. And everytime he broached the subject of her property next to the stage station, she gave his hand a pat. Later, she would tell him, not now, this was too nice to muddle up with business.

It was nice, and it wasn't finished. Katherine crooked her arm through his, and he escorted her down the block to the Grand Theater. How delightful, a play, and in a small box to the side, they watched the performance of *A Southern Rose*. She enjoyed every minute of the long evening, undoubtedly the most sociable time that she had ever had. That it was her first such experience, she neglected to tell him.

Samuel Pryor had fixed the porch swing and repainted it the day before. Here, Katherine and Stanley Howard sat, the matter of the property sale still unresolved. She went inside to light several lamps. She told him that there was a pitcher of sassafras tea that she had made earlier in the day; it was in the cellar in the back. Perhaps, over a glass of tea, they could reach some kind of mutual agreement, a compromise, but she knew she wasn't going to settle for less than twelve thousand dollars. He didn't.

Holding one of the lamps, Stanley Howard went to the cellar, located the pitcher of tea, and directly returned to the kitchen. The glasses were there on a round table, two chairs pulled up, too, but there was no sign of Katherine. Stanley sat. He stared around the kitchen; it was spacious, plenty of cupboards, and from what he could see in the faint light, they were well constructed. Perhaps, he could arrange another five hundred on the kitchen, and the barn, well, she probably was right about that—it was big, had ten stalls down each side and a blacksmith shop in the front. He looked at his glass, picked it up, and idly twirled it around several times, and then Katherine returned, a different Katherine. She was wearing a white robe; she was stunning, absolutely gorgeous, and he was speechless as she filled the two glasses. Sugar. Yes, sugar, and she went to a cupboard, and along with two spoons, set it on the table.

Katherine sat down opposite him. "I'm forgetful," she said. "I'm not used to entertaining."

"That's a very pretty robe."

They talked, Stanley producing the valuation sheet and making notations with a slender piece of graphite. He thought eleven-five was a more appropriate sum for the property, but Katherine said she couldn't figure out what difference five hundred dollars more would make to a big railroad company; she wanted twelve thousand.

"Probably wouldn't make a darn bit of difference," he said. "It's what the property is actually worth, Miss Katherine. It's also something called principle, deciding what's right and what's wrong, working on my own honest convictions."

"Sort of like scruples?"

"Well, yes, in a way. We bend over backward to please everyone, but it's reciprocal. Do you understand?"

"I surely do." But, this wasn't what she considered the rules of the road that she had been recently taught. Well, she would think about it, let him know when he returned from his trip. She had told him nothing about Julia, and very little about her life with the Sioux, but with the northern plains in such turmoil, there was little use in her leaving Cheyenne and heading for Deadwood for another ten days or so. She could wait, give him an answer when he returned. How long would he be gone?

"Five days or thereabouts," he replied. "I'd like your company for dinner again when I get back."

"Yes, I'd like that very much, Howie." Katherine reached up and impetuously put her arms around him. "I surely enjoyed tonight. Here, I'll give you something so you won't be forgetting." She closed in on him with a firm kiss, then slightly opened her lips and pressed harder.

Finally parting he gasped, "Egad!"

Katherine reached up and stroked his cheek. "Now, you hurry back, you hear?"

"Oh, I will, I will," he promised, and disdaining the few steps, he leaped out to the stone walkway. Stanley Howard disappeared in the darkness, but Katherine could hear him whistling. With a sly smile, she locked the screen and closed the door.

Bright and early the next morning, Katherine, attired in her trail clothes, was out in back working on the three Kern freighters she and her brother had left behind on their last trip, Will's fatal trip. They were rugged wagons, and even though neglected, had fared much better than she had expected. One had a split tongue; she had forgotten about that; the other two had a few weathered sideboards, but otherwise were in fair condition. She began greasing the axles and making a few other minor repairs. If Jed Bollinger, the owner of Bollinger's Cartage, came over, she wanted them as presentable as possible. Bollinger was interested in buying, but as everyone else on the frontier, from prostitutes to railroad men, he wanted to dicker. He thought two hundred apiece for three old, well-used wagons was a fair price. Katherine didn't doubt that, either, but she allowed that three hundred each was a more appropriate figure. She knew Jed was stingy, seldom gave anyone more than they could put in their eye, so she pitifully pleaded her case, one of destitution; she was downright broke, and would have no money coming in until the sale of her property, and that, she told him, was going to be a long way off. Remember the good old days, Jed, when we all helped each other? He did, but as always, he was closely guarding his wad. Katherine went to the cellar, poured herself a glass of tea, then sat in the shade of the little porch in back, contemplating the sale of the wagons, the nine hundred dollars, and how nice it would be to make another deposit in the bank. It had been two weeks since she had turned a trick, that tremendously porfitable one with Alva Tompkins, God bless him, and she still couldn't get that night out of her fertile mind. Katherine never believed she would be sharing thoughts of fornication with her deep longing to have Julia with her again. How contrary, how shameful, how fickle the mind, and how lonely the heart!

Riders. Riders coming, two of them, circling, looking her way, searching for someone, and she heard a distant call, saw the wave of a hand, then, "Hey, Kate, is that you?"

Katherine stood, squinted out through the hazy sunshine toward the trees. That slouch, that drover's hat turned up on the side. Oh, lordy, lordy, yes, it was Porter Webb, and alongside, it had to be Joseph. Katherine's heart swelled, and she shrieked, "Yes, yes, it's me, Kate!" She ran out across the back past the wagons to a distant back gate. "This way . . . this way, come on."

Slowly nudging their horses ahead, the men circled back. They came, and at the gate, they all met. Porter and Joseph Brings Yellow dismounted, each gave Katherine an affectionate embrace. After they moved the horses into the tall grass next to the barn to graze, she took them into the kitchen.

"My goodness," she said, "such a delightful and unexpected surprise!" As Katherine brought food for them, Porter told her he and Joseph had met one of Quinlan's skinners at Chugwater the day before. He told them that she had left Fort Laramie on the stage bound for Cheyenne, and since their immediate business was in Cheyenne, they thought it only appropriate to pay their respects and see if she needed any help. Porter Longstreet Webb was expecting four Appaloosa brood mares coming in from the west on a Union Pacific cattle car the following day. It was an opportune time for a visit. Over the impromptu meal they discussed the news of the fighting on the northern plains, and Joseph said the last he had heard, General Crook was still camped on Goose Creek. Except for the humiliation on the Rosebud, his troops had seen no action. The fact that Jason Armitage was now a brigadier general and was going to take command at Ford Robinson didn't surprise Porter Webb, but he was somewhat amused when Katherine kept referring to him as

Bird Dog. With a wry smile, he finally said, "You got to know him pretty well, I take it."

"Yes," she replied with a smile of her own. "In a manner of speaking, yes I did."

"More than speaking? . . ."

"Yes, but business, and none of your business."

"Ho, ho," Porter cried out. "Well, now, don't tell me that damned Calamity got to you? Showed you how to turn a profit on a trip. By God, Kate, for all your troubles, you went and cut yourself out for some more. You're a regular caution, you are."

"It wasn't all of Jane's doing, my good friend," she returned. "I had to make the decision, you know. Bird Dog is a very generous and understanding gentleman . . . in more than one way." She grinned.

"Yep, I should have warned you about him. That's another reason we call him Bird Dog. He's a lady's man, all right."

"I know."

Joseph Brings Yellow said sagely in Siouan, "A man who pays to mount a woman is a foolish man. He pays and pays but he never owns her. She never works for him, and she never makes a meal for him. This is foolish."

"Heya, heya, kola miye, waste wakage," returned Katherine, pretending to drop coins into the palm of her hand.

Porter Webb chuckled, and Joseph nodded, saying *"Hau,* pretty woman. There is more to life than making good."

"Well, brave one, I do not want any man to own me. Owning a woman is the Lakota way. I worked and I cooked and I fetched dung and wood for Mato-Nazin. I will do this again only for my daughter, no one else."

"Yo, you will have no man then."

Katherine Coltrane pressed a finger against the end of his nose. "I will have plenty of men. *Otapi wichasha.* I will be master. This is the way of Tall Woman. *Heya, hechetu welo.* This is my lodge. I am master here, and no coyote dares come to piss on it. If you argue with me, I will throw you out. You will have no food."

Joseph Brings Yellow playfully snapped at her finger. "Tall Woman speaks with the tongue of an old woman, but she does not look like an old woman. I hear your words. I love you as a sister. I will say no more."

Katherine Coltrane laughed. She kissed the tip of her finger and pressed it to the smiling lips of Joseph. The young breed didn't snap back.

Stretching her slender body out in the chair, clasping her hands behind her head, she said, "Oh, you can't imagine how happy I am to see you two scamps. I've been so damned lonely. I only wish you could stay around a week or two. Heavens, I could even buy me a horse and a mule, pack up, and ride up to Hawk Springs with you. Catch a stage there up to the diggings."

Porter Webb said, "Then, you've made up your mind? Deadwood? Hang around there for a month or so?"

"It's as close as I can get to her, isn't it?"

He stared thoughtfully at her for a moment, then replied, "Safest, I reckon. No guarantee your little plan is going to work, though, 'less the tide turns. Soldier boys got the shit kicked out of them. Might be this thing will go on for another year or two, and your old Oglala friends may take to roaming again. Not likely, of course, but it's possible. Anything's possible."

Katherine's face fell. "You're not very encouraging, Porter."

Joseph Brings Yellow said in English, "He never is. Until the sun shows its face, he never sees it. This is his way."

Katherine told them that Colonel Bradford had written out some orders for the commandants of the northern forts to assist her in the search for Julia, even to supply an escort of troopers. Well and good, commented Porter, if the Indians all returned to the reservations. If not, of course, she still had several options. Since her house was in such good repair, and she still had three freight wagons, she could ride it out in Cheyenne until conditions normalized above the North Platte River. And, of course, the latchstring was always out on his ranch at Hawk Springs, too.

This pleased Joseph Brings Yellow, and he said in English, "A good idea, Miss Kate. You can come and cook and make wood for us. Maybe later, I can go back with you and pick up Julia."

Katherine Coltrane forced a smile. She was selling her house, she explained, selling it to the Colorado and Southern Railroad. Additionally, she met a businessman from Deadwood up at Goose Creek; he had offered her a job managing a new hotel, a hotel of sorts, sometime in August, and because of the proximity of the town to all of the reservations, she was seriously considering the offer.

Porter Webb almost choked on his sassafras tea. "Oh, shit," he moaned, "a manager, is it? Goddamn it, Kate, they call 'em madams, not managers, and it's not a hotel, it's a brothel . . . a cathouse . . . a whorehouse . . ."

"A house of ill repute," smiled Joseph Brings Yellow. He shrugged offhandedly, and looked at Porter. "But, my friend, can you blame her? It's a better offer than we have. No making meals and wood either. She will be the master . . ."

"Mistress, I'd say," drawled Porter.

"You don't approve?" asked Katherine innocently.

"Well, who in the hell am I to approve or disapprove? You'll probably make more money than I'm making with my herd of shitters."

"You should start raising more cattle . . . cows," suggested Katherine. "That's where the money's going to be, you know. Buy more stock . . . or rustle it." After a moment, Katherine Coltrane hunched forward in her chair. Honey and money were on her tongue. "Porter, I love you—"

"Aw, Kate, please—"

"—As a brother," she smiled. "You need money, I need more money, and I have a notion . . . thought about it all last night."

"You're full of notions, all right."

"Shhhh! Now, listen." Katherine went on seriously. "I met two older men, sort of drifters, when we were coming back with all of the wounded. They were telling me about their homesteads up on Bluegrass Creek—"

"Oh, hell!" exclaimed Porter Webb. "Buford . . . Buford and Alva!"

"You know them?"

"Who doesn't know them? . . . anyone that's been around these parts for a month or two. Damndest pair of panhandlers and no-accounts as you'll ever meet, that's what."

"Hmm," Katherine intoned almost musically. "Why, sure, they don't look like much, I'll agree, but they treated me most ladylike. Yes, truly they did."

Joseph grinned, saying, "Why not? You are a beautiful woman. They wanted to mount you."

A small blush came to Katherine's face. Mercy, had they noticed? She quickly went on, "Look, this doesn't concern them, only what they told me. They only had those claims legalized a year ago, and there's a lot of land below them, all the way down to the river, even along it—"

"Open range," interceded Porter. "Public grazing land, and some of it nothing but thin straw, cheat grass." He looked across the table at her. "Just what you getting at?"

"I think we should stake out some homesteads down the creek bottom north of Chugwater," she said proudly. "All we can get."

"Cattle running through there now and then," Porter Webb replied. "Old man Slaughter has a spread about ten or so miles above Chugwater. No one likes sodbusters. I don't either."

Katherine Coltrane tilting her head back and forth, said mockingly, "Sodbusters . . . sodbusters, I don't like sodbusters! Well, listen, damn it, I don't give a shit one way or another about them, but the goddamn railroad's going to be moving up through there in another year or so, and if we don't get off our butts and get moving to get our hands on a thousand acres or so of that bottom, we're going to lose a bundle of money."

Porter's brow suddenly hiked. "Land acquisition? Rights-of-way? Is this your notion? Wouldn't be worth all that much, Kate, not unless . . . whoa, hold on here, hold on—"

"Not unless we had a cabin, few sheds . . . maybe some chutes, a bit of development going on," she finished.

"She makes good sense now." Joseph smiled. "A good mistress."

In a muse, Porter Webb drummed the table with his fingers for a while, occasionally emitting little "hmmms." He finally said that he had another idea, one almost foolproof. He knew about railroads, had been working on bringing a line up through Hawk Springs to enhance his own operation; he knew how railroads sometimes took a circuitous route to avoid right-of-way problems. He also was very familiar with the Chugwater Creek Valley, the high and low spots, and where a few canyons bordered the creek. Porter Webb concluded it was worth investigating. Katherine said it wasn't wise to wait too long—the survey crews were already working south of Chugwater. She also said that if Porter could stake out seven or eight claims and get legal names, she had an attorney friend who would draw up the necessary papers free of charge, who would even come down to Cheyenne to handle the deeds prudently and properly.

"And," asked Porter Longstreet Webb, "just who is this solicitor?"

"A friend in Deadwood," Katherine said. "He specializes in deeds and claims, and I just happen to own a little piece of him."

Chapter Eight

Deadwood

"Is one more night of this worth five hundred dollars, my dear Howie? You haven't had such loving in all your life."

Indeed, Stanley Howard had returned, and after another night of dining with him at the Palace Hotel, Katherine was turning her first trick in a month, one she knew was going to be a very profitable one.

Stanley Howard mumbled, "Tomorrow night? You want me back?"

"Of course . . . if you want to."

"Egads, but yes, Katherine. Yes, anything you want."

"You know what I want, damn it."

"Yes, yes, and I suppose I'll have to agree to terms. Ahgh . . . holy smokes!"

"Oh, mercy, me!"

"Katherine, sweet Katherine."

Nibbling at his neck, she whispered breathlessly, "Twelve thousand?"

"Tomorrow night?"

"I'll be waiting. You want to stay the rest of the night, sleep with me?"

Howard emitted a long sigh of desperation. "I can't. You'd own the whole railroad by dawn. You're very mercenary."

She laughed. "I've been called that before."

"I want to stay but I can't . . . have to be out by six o'clock, and I want to go out walking, not crawling. I'll be back tomorrow night, the whole night."

"It'll give you something to think about, then . . . pleasant thoughts."

"I've had those ever since I met you . . . and, you're right. I've never experienced anything like this in my life. Could I fall in love with you?"

"No."

* * *

Another day. Jed Bollinger came; he thoroughly inspected the three Kern freighters; he hemmed and hawed. Katherine said it was up to him, that she had another interested buyer over the mountains in Hawk Springs. Jed Bollinger wanted those wagons; he relented and wrote Katherine a bank draft for nine hundred dollars, and she gave him a big hug, then a kiss on his hairy cheek.

Another night in the seduction of Stanley Howard: this time, he stayed the entire night, and he and Katherine slept late into the morning. Over breakfast, the agreement over the sale of her property was concluded. Since she had decided to leave for Deadwood within the week, Howard agreed to deposit her settlement check in the Wells Fargo Bank when negotiations were completed at the main office in Denver. How soon would she return? She didn't know exactly what her plans were, but when she did return, a letter would precede her arrival. Someday, Katherine told him, she might build a grand house in Cheyenne, a place with chandeliers and mirrors just like the ones in the Palace Hotel, but, she added laughingly, it was only a dream.

Four days later, Stanley Howard of the Colorado and Southern Railroad, saw Katherine Coltrane off on the Cheyenne–Deadwood stage. Would she think about marrying him? She was stunned. No, she was terribly sorry. He was such a dear, but she couldn't possibly do that. When the stage trundled off and swung around her house, Katherine was crying. She stuck her head out of the window, though, and called out to Emma and Samuel Pryor, who were standing in the yard. Dear old Sam held up the key to her house and waved it, a key that would never adorn the necklace of a Lakota brave. Katherine had given all of her household belongings to Emma and Sam, and they were mighty appreciative because Miss Katherine was one of the finest, sweetest young ladies they had ever known.

Four days, three layovers, two Concord coaches, and how many changes of teams she didn't remember, but here she was, her head poked out the window, getting her first glimpse of Deadwood. And it took her only several moments to realize this was no Cheyenne City. Such a conglomeration of buildings, such confusion, and such an assortment of wagons, Katherine had never seen in her life, not even in her earliest days in Cheyenne. The long street leading up to the stage depot was clogged with rigs of every type, from freighters to lumber wagons. Men of every description, from miners to businessmen, were along the boardwalk, and they were dressed in every conceivable way. Some wore fringed buckskin, others brocaded vests. They wore blue cotton shirts, canvas pants, and outsized boots. Katherine saw one miner wearing dress pumps, probably, she thought, because his boots had worn out. The men were walking, talking, and a few were lounging on benches in front of the saloons, many saloons. New construction was everywhere, workers still hammering and sawing in the late-afternoon sunshine. And Katherine noticed with a tired smile, among all of these people she saw exactly four women, two of them Orientals, probably the wives of shop owners. Despite its ugly, primitive appearance, Katherine allowed that Deadwood was going to be a promising place for business, particularly her type of business.

A young man wearing a white straw hat helped her from the coach, and when her trunk and two suitcases were set aside, two boys immediately rushed up and offered her help with the luggage. The Red Bird Hotel, she told them. They eagerly forged ahead up the street; Katherine, in her long suit skirt, almost at full gait trying to keep up. They shouted in glee when she gave them a dollar to share.

The Red Bird. Finally, here it was, and the sight mildly surprised her. It was a large clapboard building with two floors, recently whitewashed, four windows across the front, and two doors. One door to the side, one she assumed led to the upper floor to the rooms of the legitimate hotel. Tim Frawley had told her he planned to construct divided housing facilities, eight rooms and a parlor in the rear for women and their gentlemen guests. The second floor in the front of the hotel wasn't going to be her entryway, she knew this, so she pushed through the other one into the saloon. She was surprised once more, for the interior was spacious and well lighted, many lamps suspended down from the ceiling, each fixture with four transparent shades, and there were three big oval-shaped mirrors behind the bar. Next to the bar, she saw a raised platform, a stage for musicians. Fortunately, the saloon had only a few customers at this hour of the day, a table of cardplayers, and four or five men standing at the bar, businessmen. They were all dressed in dark suits, white

shirts, and were wearing string and bow ties. There were two
men behind the bar, and Katherine had walked no more than
halfway across the room, when one hurried around and met
her. His name was Henry Givens, the manager, the partner of
Tim Frawley, and when she identified herself, he beamed
broadly and promptly and courteously escorted her to a table
near the door, and seated her. She ordered wine. He brought
her luggage in, then went to the bar and came back directly
with two glasses of Burgundy.

Henry Givens was ecstatic. He toasted her with his glass,
and, after a sip, he said, "You couldn't have arrived at a better time, Miss Coltrane—"

"Kate," she said. "Most everyone calls me Kate . . . Mister Tim, too."

"Said you had a good business head on you." Givens
smiled. "Didn't say what a beauty you were, didn't know for
certain you were coming."

"Thank you, but I don't feel worth a damn," Katherine replied. "I'm dirty. I'm tired. I could have done better coming
up here on a horse."

"Well, we'll take care of this soon as you finish your
drink." He grinned, and went on. "Not quite done upstairs . . . Oh, hell, drink up, Kate, and we'll go up, show
you the place, and get you settled in. Frawley's going to be
surprised to hear you're here."

Katherine drank, set her glass aside, and stood. She was
ready, could hardly wait to take a bath and get some rest.
She carried one suitcase, and Henry Givens, a stout, partially
bald man with a ruddy face, hoisted the little trunk to a
shoulder and picked up the other suitcase, then moved
briskly ahead, past the bar, through the kitchen, and out the
back door to the rear stairway. And, it was as Givens had
told her—three of eight rooms were doorless and only partly
furnished. The rest of the doors and furnishings were to be
installed the next day. The small reception parlor and the
bath were ready for use, the bath facing the back of the hotel. Katherine looked in. It contained several commodes and
two big tin tubs, a fireplace for heating water, and a drain
that went through the back wall to a long pipe leading down
to the alley. But no wood, no water, no hot bath, Katherine
complained. Water was not a problem, Givens told her. He
would have two or three barrels brought up within an hour,

but wood? Well, that would have to wait another day. Katherine said she could manage.

Katherine's room was at the opposite end of the hall, well furnished with a small table and two chairs, a small cupboard, throw rugs, velvet curtains hiding the one window, and a large bed with a beautifully scrolled headboard. The bed was covered with a dark blue velvet spread that matched the curtains. Givens opened the door to the closet; here many boxes were stacked, filled with sheets, pillowcases, and an assortment of towels and washcloths for the girls.

Katherine gave him an inquisitive look. "What girls?"

"Our girls," Givens said, smiling. "That's what I was saying, you couldn't have shown up here at a better time. I'm expecting three young ladies day after tomorrow ... first three. Including you, that'll be four, enough to get you started. You can pick a couple more later on." He grinned again and winked. "I'll start doing a little word-of-mouth advertising next week ... give you plenty of time to get organized, anything you need. Frawley says he wants this place to be the best in town, very high-class, so this is what we're going to do, money be damned."

Katherine Coltrane smiled back. "Good, Henry, I'll look things over, start making a list tomorrow. The first thing I want is that water." She went over to her door and looked down the hallway. "The second thing I want is this floor covered with a thick carpet. We want a quiet place, don't we?"

"Yes, quiet but busy. I'll see to the water, Kate." Turning away, he said. "You want something, come downstairs to the kitchen, let me know. You can eat in the saloon anytime you want, or go next door to Brown's Café ... charge you over there, though."

Henry Givens was halfway down the hall when Katherine called after him. "Where does Frawley hang out?"

"Has an office down Main Street ... name on a board over his door," Givens called back. "Probably won't be there now, but he has a room at the Cosmopolitan, new boardinghouse up a block on the other side of the street."

Katherine was very tired, tired and lonely. She went over to the bed, removed her button-up shoes, and stretched out. Visions of Julia were dancing behind her shuttered eyes.

It was late, almost six o'clock, by the time Katherine had bathed and dressed. She wore a summer dress, her hair was covered with a white shawl that draped down over her shoulders; she was very pretty, this she knew, and therefore wasn't surprised when she drew admiring stares as she walked up the street to the Cosmopolitan boardinghouse. Admiring stares? She smiled to herself. More like covetous stares. Despite all the frenzy, the gold, the gambling, the drinking, there were many lonely men in this bawdy, boisterous town; lustful men, too, and it was in her mind to sort out the best of the lot, help relieve them of their loneliness, yes, and their gold.

A bespectacled man sitting by the window reading a periodical looked up in surprise when she appeared in the small lobby. Katherine gave him a kind smile. Setting aside his newspaper and folding his spectacles, he quickly got to his feet. But before he could speak, Katherine told him she had come regarding a business matter with her attorney, Timothy Frawley. The man promptly stepped aside and peered around a drapery into an adjoining room, then nodded back at Katherine. Mister Frawley was having supper; was he expecting her? Propriety? Katherine thought. Here? In Deadwood? Ridiculous, or did he suspect she was a whore? Silently amused, she said, "Please tell Mister Frawley that his client, Katherine Coltrane, is here," and she went over and took the chair the man had recently vacated. Moments later, the drapes parted; Tim Frawley came striding happily toward her, smiling, graciously bowed, took her extended hand, kissed it, and in a low, but excited voice, he said, "Oh, my dear lady, by God, what a pleasant surprise ... you came, you came!" He gave her hand a gentle squeeze. "Come. Please come, join me. Have something to eat, and we can talk."

Katherine did join him; she had supper with him, and they talked at great length about the new saloon and hotel, about each other, and he related news of the recent wave of Indian depredations, the attacks by hostiles on the isolated settlements and ranches springing up around the Black Hills. A few people had been killed, cabins, sheds, and haystacks had been burned. The marauders were Sioux and a few Cheyenne who had disbanded after their early summer victories on the Rosebud and Little Bighorn. Warriors who had escaped the army dragnet were still roaming free. Frawley told her that some of the agency Indians had returned to the reservations where they were now being treated as prisoners of war. Conditions east and west of Deadwood were discouraging. Settlers shot without question at any Indian in sight, and the army still refused to protect the residents in Deadwood and Lead. Frawley told Katherine that he had no news of the whereabouts of Crazy Horse and his people. Perhaps, in another month, when fall set in, conditions would normalize and some of the Oglala would return.

"Squatters all around," Katherine said almost bitterly. "I'm one of them now."

Tim Frawley nodded understandingly. "Still have some sympathy for those people, even after what they did?"

"Yes, I do. This place, everything around us here, belongs to them. At least they gave me some insight about the *wasichu,* those without any understanding or compassion for others. Oh, but I didn't come here to preach a sermon or kick people in the ass. I came to steal, too, rob the *wasichu* of gold." Katherine smiled across the table. "Digging *my* way, Mister Tim, and shoveling all of it I can under my bed."

Frawley grinned. "Mercenary."

"Yes, so you once told me. Isn't that why I'm here, to help us get rich?"

"And find your daughter Julia, or have you forgotten?"

"Oh, I haven't forgotten that," Katherine replied. "Not a day or night goes by that I don't think about her. I'm letting you know in case Henry objects in another month or so, long before Winter Man comes, I'll be taking a few days off now and then, visiting the agencies, the forts, and for this very purpose, I've made a few friends along the way."

Chuckling, the young attorney said, "Oh I believe it, Kate, yes I do. Everything with you is a means to an end, a profitable end, but that's what I like about you. Do you realize that in four months, you've come from a destitute young squaw to a madam in a fancy house of pleasure. That's quite an achievement in itself, since your apprenticeship was so brief."

"I met the right people. I met you."

He said with a wry grin, "Those beds I bought, they're the very best, build for the long haul."

"I'm only interested in the short, profitable hauls . . . except on very special occasions, Mister Tim."

"Would your arrival be one of those special occasions?

Say, like maybe later tonight? Renewing our deep friendship for one another."

Katherine leaned close and whispered, "We've only been sitting here a little less than an hour, damn it, you mean to tell me you already have an itch for me? My gracious, Tim!"

"I do," he confessed.

Whispering again she said, "Well, you're just going to have to tie a pretty ribbon around where you itch and save it for tomorrow night. I've been riding stages for four days, and I'm so tired I could drop. Besides, we're not officially open for business yet."

"Business? A little business tomorrow night, then?"

"Strictly business."

"What! You mean . . . you mean I pay?"

In another whisper, Katherine said, "You bet your boots, you pay. Look here, you had your free trick up on Goose Creek at my private little pond. That was against my rules of the road, Timothy Frawley. No, sir, not again."

"You used me, you did."

"Yes, and you liked it, too!"

Katherine slept well in her new bed this first night and was awakened the next morning by an assortment of sounds: the carpenters had arrived and were setting in the three remaining doors, and movers were on the stairway at the back, bringing in the last of the furniture. When Katherine, clad in a robe and wearing slippers, looked out from the bath window, she saw another man unloading firewood and stacking it in a covered bin next to the shed housing the toilets—six toilets, three appropriately labeled, "LADIES." No sooner than Katherine had attended to her personal chores, Henry Givens appeared in the hall with a long measuring string. What color of carpet did she want for the hallway? A nice, rich red, she told him, and he laughed at this. They went to the kitchen where she ate breakfast, and he sat opposite her drinking coffee detailing the operation plans for the hotel and saloon, some of which she had already heard from Tim Frawley. Profit from the back rooms was to be split equally between Katherine, Frawley, Givens, and the women employees, excluding tips, and the women were to receive two meals a day from the kitchen. Profit from the saloon and six guest rooms partitioned off from the working rooms was to be divided by Frawley and Givens, and the cost of daily cleaning and laundry service would be paid for out of the saloon-hotel profit. Katherine was optimistic, envisioning salaries of at least sixty to one hundred dollars a month for the women, and with good fortune, double that for herself. She was satisfied, and told Henry that it was much better than skinning mules. He agreed; a woman with a head for business and a body for pleasure like Katherine had no business parking her butt on the top of a freighter in the first place. She agreed.

Katherine spent most of the day inspecting, making adjustments in five of the rooms for the private comfort and convenience of her doves, and she set aside three other rooms solely for the use of their business with the gentlemen. It was the best she could do; on a night of brisk trade, the girls would just have to use their own rooms, and from what Jane Canarray had told her, this was quite common anyway.

The smell of fresh varnish was still in the hallway when Tim Frawley made his appearance, her first customer; he brought wine and a tin of bonbons; they had a pleasurable evening, and he left about midnight without grumbling about the exorbitant price of her entertainment, thirty dollars. After all, Katherine told him with a sweet smile, it was an equitable arrangement; everyone profited. The split was ten dollars each for Frawley, Givens, and her, not bad for the impromptu hotel inaugural. "Mercenary," his often repeated term, and he gave her a kiss on the tip of her nose and left.

The next day at ten o'clock, Katherine and Henry Givens sat together at one of the front windows awaiting the appearance of the stage from Bismarck. It was nearly a half hour late, but when it stopped a block down the street, the first three passengers off were women, a most pleasant sight to a few gawking men who were seated on a bench in front of the stage depot. The women were tired but joyous, happy to be off the rollicking coach, and they were provocative, readily trading smiles and bawdy remarks with the men gathered around. Packing up an assortment of luggage, boxes, suitcases, and several parcels, Katherine and Henry, walking abreast up the boardwalk guided the girls to their new home and place of work. About an hour later, toward noon, refreshed to some degree, they were seated in the little reception parlor partaking of a small pail of beer and eating sandwiches that Henry had brought up from the saloon.

Ida Hamilton, Margaret Meacham, who called herself Meg, and Carrie Colyer were their names. All were in their mid-twenties, and all experienced prostitutes. Two, Meg and Carrie, were actually entertainers, both having sung and danced. This was good news to Katherine; they would also be useful to Henry in the saloon when he had fiddlers working. Ida, a winsome woman with auburn hair and almost as tall as Katherine, was the talkative one, bringing a laugh from everyone when she said that the only entertaining she did was on her back, and she was good at it, too.

Since they were familiar with their trade, Katherine wasted no time on procedure, only the routine. They could use daytime hours at their own discretion, could turn a trick in the afternoons if they desired, but no gentleman would be allowed in rooms during the morning. Some decorum and privacy had to be observed, she said. With exception of tips, everyone would share equally in the profit, and once established, once known for its quality, she expected a thriving business in the new house with only the best of customers, mostly rich miners and successful businessmen. There were twelve other establishments of similar nature in the town, Katherine said, none of which compared with the Red Bird, and the girls were going to have some fun making thirteen a lucky number. If there were any problems, Katherine said she would handle them discreetly and properly. She considered excessive drinking a detriment to business; she thought several drinks during the evening was an acceptable standard. Preliminary entertaining could be done in the parlor. Personal cleanliness was mandatory. Only the finest ladies attract the best men, she explained. Katherine told them that no girl had to trick a gentleman she disliked or mistrusted for any reason. Men who were boisterous, crude, and unmannerly were not to be tolerated.

Katherine said, "I won't entertain any man who isn't clean and decent, and I don't expect you to, either." She smiled at all of them. "Are there any questions?"

No. They all smiled back at her. Their Miss Kate was going to be a working madam.

For the next several days, the women of the Red Bird relaxed and became accustomed to their new home. On a Sunday afternoon, Henry Givens rented a wagon, and they went for a picnic in the mountains above the town; they picked gooseberries and wild raspberries, enough to make two pies in the hotel kitchen. By Monday night, their house of pleasure had been readied for opening, and Henry made it a gala affair, setting up platters of baked ham, oysters, cheeses, a variety of pickled dishes, and a big basket of apple tarts, the latter of which Ida Hamilton declared the most appropriate offering of all. Henry Givens invited some of his best customers to the festivities on the upper back floor—the mayor, E. B. Farnum, came; so did five members of the city council. Sheriff Con Stapleton, a gambler who had come over from the Montana Territory to mine and play cards, also was among those in attendance, and a half dozen of Deadwood's leading businessmen were present, too, including Farley Graham and Art Merrick of the *Pioneer Press*. Katherine Coltrane and her three girls served wine to the guests, and a few of the celebrants became very jovial, for indeed, these young women were seductively charming. The social lasted for three hours, and when the guests departed, some of them vowed they would return. Six of them did, later that very same night.

The next morning, Katherine Coltrane took out a small ledger and carefully penned in the names of those who had attended the opening and those who had returned to be entertained privately. This was the beginning of her diligent record keeping, which she thought might have some political advantages at a later date.

Several weeks sped by and business was brisk. Then one morning in late September, Katherine's fourth dove came in from Bismarck. Little Ruby Danforth, a young breed darky girl Tim Frawley had met in the territorial capital where she had been working as a chambermaid—a mulatto, Tim had called her. While Frawley hadn't admitted it, Katherine suspected he had seduced her in his room; Ruby had previously worked as a prostitute and was looking to catch on somewhere. Katherine knew this kind of intimate information didn't come by way of casual conversation while someone was changing sheets or taking out a chamber pot.

Whatever, Ruby Danforth was a welcome addition to the house: she had good manners, her grammar was adequate, and she was quite pretty, having a rounded face, large brown eyes, and pouty lips. She was proportioned superbly: her legs shapely, her buttocks firm, and her breasts plump and full without any sag. Ruby was from Memphis; she was twenty-two years old and was golden-brown in color. She also was apprehensive of her new surroundings, wondering how she would be accepted by her white sisters of the Red Bird. Some whites, she told Katherine, didn't like Negroes any more than they did Indians. Katherine knew all about prejudice, and she told Ruby not to worry, everything was going to be just fine. "I'm your friend," Katherine told her. "If you ever feel lonely, you come and talk with me. I'll understand." Katherine held Ruby's hand. Ruby gently squeezed. Katherine gave Ruby the room next to hers.

A week after Ruby's arrival, Henry Givens appeared at Katherine's door shortly before noon; two men, drover types, had registered at the guest hotel in front, and one of them who signed his name Porter Webb had inquired about her. The other man, who looked part Indian, had simply printed his name in big, bold letters—"JOSEPH." Katherine's heart leaped. They were dear friends, she told Givens, and she gave Henry a quick kiss.

Would he be so kind as to set up a table near the front windows? For a change, she was going to entertain two gentlemen in a most ladylike fashion. Givens smiled. Of course, anything Katherine wished, but they didn't look much like gentlemen: they looked pretty rough and trail-worn, and they both wore revolvers. She gave Henry a reassuring pat on the shoulder, telling him that she had been fooled by appearances several times in her young life. Sometimes men had gold in their hearts instead of in their pockets, and then momentarily thinking of Alva Tompkins, she winked at Henry, and added, sometimes they had both.

But Katherine Coltrane soon discovered Porter Webb did have gold in his pockets, a little more than two thousand dollars worth from the sale of a herd of horses he and Joseph Brings Yellow made early this morning to a group of squatters trying to ranch along the Belle Fourche River. Joseph, spooning his soup, momentarily stopped and grinned at her. He nodded at Porter and said in Siouan, "Man called White Hawk will see some of those ponies again before the Hungry Moon. Our brothers will steal them. White Hawk will buy them back for half the price, and we will sell them again."

Katherine stared over at Porter for confirmation of such an outlandish scheme. Shaking his head, he explained sheepishly, "His idea of humor. We did that a couple of times, but it doesn't work too well anymore. Too risky. Bucks show up below the river these days moving stock and everybody gets nosey."

"That's a crooked game." Katherine said, "It's dangerous, too."

Porter only smiled, but he slid a hand behind his vest and pulled out several sheets of folded paper. "So is this," he said, placing the papers beside Katherine's soup bowl. "Those land claims along the Chugwater me and some of my hands staked out ... eight of them, and you better get your solicitor friend moving ... get some names on them, get them filed all legal-like ... or illegal."

"Lordy!" Katherine exclaimed. "You did it, already!"

"Your little plan, isn't it?" Porter said. "It's what you wanted."

"Our little plan," she corrected.

Joseph Brings Yellow lifted his bowl and drank the remaining bit of his soup. After a little grunt, he said, "A joke. This would make our people laugh. You are right, Tall Woman. It is crooked. The *wasichu* comes and steals our land with crooked promises. Then, they steal the land from one another. When the human beings were here alone, the land belonged to everyone. No one had to steal from his neighbor, only a few ponies, a game. Now everyone is a thief. Everyone steals but it is no longer a game. A joke, but a very bad joke, one without honor."

"*Heya,*" agreed Katherine.

Porter and Joseph had brought some hopeful news with them—they had encountered several bands of Lakota on their trip, small villages moving back toward the reservations. Some were Brule and Miniconjou, but a few were Oglala, and most of them had been up in the Big Horns during the summer. During smokes with them, a few admitted to Porter and Joseph they had participated in the battles along the Rosebud and Little Bighorn. But, now the valleys below the River of Yellow Stones was not a good place to be. Many longknives had come from all directions; they were angry, and they were seeking to kill and destroy, so the tribes had disbanded, some fleeing across the valleys to hide, others choosing to return. It was going to be a bad winter for everyone. Whether Crazy Horse, Dull Knife, and Two Moons's people were moving east, they didn't know. However, Sitting Bull and his Hunkpapa were still fighting somewhere north; the longknives had not been able to defeat or capture any of the Hunkpapa or Oglala. Katherine asked Porter how long the fighting was likely to continue before the tribes were subjugated. He didn't know, but he agreed with what the returning Lakota had told him—it was going to be a long winter for both the Indians and the soldiers. "Indians will run all winter, and the soldier boys will freeze their asses off chasing them."

Joseph Brings Yellow said solemnly, "Hungry bellies make fast moccasins."

"Yep," Porter Webb said, "that's what it's all about—whoever runs out of rations first. Hunger never had a friend, not that I know of, anyway."

"Oh, Julia," lamented Katherine softly. "Dear God."

Porter reached over and took her hand, saying, "Maybe not so bad. They always look out for the little ones first . . . you know that."

"Yes, the people do," Katherine finally sighed. "The soldiers seem to make a habit of forgetting, though."

After a sip of his coffee, Porter Webb casually said, "We were thinking about cutting through the mountains, down to the Cheyenne River on our way back, crossing over and checking the agency at Pine Ridge. Might find someone who knows something." Katherine's heart leaped, and she looked at him sharply. "A little out of our way," continued Porter, "but, what the hell . . ."

"I want to go," she said. She stared anxiously at the two men.

"Aw, hell, Kate, you'd be better off . . ."

"No, damn it, I want to go, too."

"Well, well . . . what about this place? . . . your job. And how in the hell you going to get back by yourself? Still hostiles out there, and the weather's going to start turning cold one of these days."

Katherine Coltrane knew the country, too, and she had a ready answer. She had been preparing for a chance like this. "I can take a week off. I can take the stage back out of Chadron or Luck. They're close to the fort. All I need is a good horse to ride out with you two, that's all, a bedroll and some extra grub."

Joseph said, "The song is still within her, my friend. You have two bad ears. Listen to what she says."

Porter Webb looked at Joseph and shrugged, and the

young breed grinned over at Katherine. "You can make wood . . . make meals for us like the old days with the Oglala," he suggested. "Make a plenty good feast for us on the trail."

Shoving back in her chair, Katherine got up, went around, and kissed Joseph on the cheek. "You have bad ears, too, *misunkala*. Didn't I once tell you no man commands me? Ho, I will find you a prairie bone to chew upon. *Sunka wayatanin*! Yes, feast well, oh dog."

Katherine went to the kitchen where she talked briefly with Henry, who wasn't surprised about her decision to visit the Sioux reservation, for after all, this was one of the reasons she had come to Deadwood. Frawley had told him this, and Ida Hamilton was capable of managing the rooms while she was gone. It was an amicable agreement. Katherine was all smiles. She took a pot of coffee back to the table and filled the cups of Porter and Joseph. Not too long after this, Carrie Colyer and Ruby Danforth came in from the back and prepared to take a table to eat breakfast. Katherine Coltrane was proud of her girls. Would Porter and Joseph like to meet two of her prettiest? Before the men could reply, she was beckoning them over, introducing them, then directly Katherine brought extra cups and more coffee. Ruby Danforth sat next to Joseph Brings Yellow; for a half hour she barely took her big brown eyes off of him. When Porter and Joseph finally left to go find Katerine a horse and saddle for the planned departure the following morning, Ruby watched young Joseph all the way to the door, then looked over at Katherine and sighed. A smile came to her golden face. Yes, Ruby admitted, she surely did like Joseph: he was handsome, he was very polite, he was brown like she was, and she thought it would be very nice for him to visit with her in the parlor that night. She wanted to know him better.

Katherine asked, "Much better?"

Ruby Danforth nodded, and her tongue delicately traced her lips. "Yes, Ma'am, Miss Kate, much better."

With a little smile, Katherine explained that Joseph was a young man not inclined to spend his hard-earned money on enjoying the companionship of a woman. Joseph believed a man should own a woman, not simply pay for her use. The young men in Joseph Brings Yellow's old tribe often gave ten or twelve ponies to claim a maiden.

Smiling back at Katherine, Ruby replied in her low,

throaty voice, "I didn't say nothing, Miss Kate, about taking his money, did I? I'm no maiden, either. 'Sides, what am I gonna do with a dozen of those ponies?"

"He's an honorable young man. He may be a virgin."

"Oh, my, my, Miss Kate, oh, my!"

BOOK TWO

Chapter Nine

Pine Ridge

Excerpts from an interview with Henry Burlingame.

As I think I mentioned, the first time I met Katherine was at Fort Fetterman, the very day she came back from all of those years with the Oglala Sioux. She was a distraught woman and in no mood to sit down for an interview with me. I saw her several times on the Crook campaign, and from the stories I heard, this is when she began to sow some of her seeds of fortune, or misfortune if one wants to look at it this way. Of course, after the Crook debacle on the Rosebud, it was obvious that reclaiming her daughter was out of the question, if it ever were a sane endeavor. One can't imagine the immensity of that country until one begins to travel it. It was a very dangerous place for the un-initiated, the so-called pilgrim or greenhorn. Oh, Kate had plenty of spirit, grit if you will. She did, however, captivate a few men on this capricious journey of Crook's, one of whom I distinctly remember, Colonel Jason Armitage. Armitage was a rarity because, unlike most officers in the Army of the West, this one had some intelligence and understanding of the Indians. The Frawley fellow I had never met at this point in time, but for Kate, this was the beginning of another long and very influential friendship. He was a Deadwood attorney at the time. He was the one who later employed Kate in Deadwood. He had money, and the rumor was that she took a good portion of it.

Joseph Brings Yellow, the French-Indian who was a very close friend of Katherine, told me that her main purpose of setting up business in Deadwood was so she could be near the Sioux. I never doubted this. She always had that little girl on her mind, and every time

I met the woman, she was still planning some escapade to reclaim Julia.

The shadowy game trail, once carpeted with pine needles and golden leaves, was now pocked and littered from the hooves and dung of a thousand horses and mules. Blue smoke from the canyon camps of miners mingled with the ghost mists of early autumn in the sacred Black Hills. Katherine Coltrane looked across from her pony at Joseph Brings Yellow. He was silent and somber. Did he remember riding these mysterious mountains when only a child, when the face of Mother Earth wore a smile, when the air was clean and the evergreens shed no tears? Or, was he too much *wasichu* now to feel the distressed spirits of the ancient ones hovering and wailing about him along these once-majestic mountain trails? Katherine often wondered about Joseph. What would his future have held had Porter Webb not taken him from the Miniconjou? What had happened to his white father, the trader called Marat, who had one day left for Fort Pierre to buy supplies and had never returned. Like Porter, Joseph Brings Yellow never discussed the past—*nunwe,* forget it—but could any Lakota forget the once-pristine beauty and sanctity of these mountains?

Katherine Coltrane thought about her own past, these hills, a village near the hot springs. To the west, on the Powder River, was where Julia had been born. Wicapi Hinto, Blue Star. It seemed like only yesterday that her world had been turned upside down, and all she had to show for it was Julia, and Julia was lost.

Katherine's departure earlier in the morning had been fraught with some consternation on the part of everyone except Henry Givens, who thought it would be good for her to get away for a week and perhaps lessen the anxieties about her daughter. While Ida was a bit apprehensive about taking over the management upstairs, she had no compunction about working in a few extra tricks during Katherine's absence. With hostiles reported in the vicinity, the other three girls deplored the very thought of Katherine riding into the mountains. Porter and Joseph were resigned to her company. Katherine herself was anxious to get on the trail. The horse the men had saddled for her was what Porter referred to as "borrowed." He saw little sense in buying a horse for her when he already had more than a hundred on his ranch at

Hawk Springs, so he and Joseph had gone back to one of the new ranches at Spearfish before dawn where they retrieved a mount they had sold the previous day. Joseph Brings Yellow thought it was funny, his idea of Lakota humor, selling a horse to a white man, then stealing it back. The horse even had Webb's Circle-W brand on it, as did the horses he and Joseph were riding.

The saddle Katherine was sitting on was something unusual, a well-used one Porter had bought for twenty-five dollars, and she swore she had seen it before, or one exactly like it. Alva Tompkins had such a saddle, an old McClellan with a tilted horn that made it look like the whole saddle was askew. The black cantle came halfway up to the small of her back. "Plenty good to keep her from toppling off if the pony suddenly reared" were the words of a grinning Joseph. Katherine could only believe that her dear friend, Alva, had bought himself a new saddle when he and Buford returned to Deadwood to sell their salted claims and cash in their gold from the Lost Cabin diggings. She assumed the two scamps were now living high on the hog up on Bluegrass Creek, where she had a standing invitation to stay.

Since she was now a horse thief, at least one by association, Katherine found herself occasionally glancing over her shoulder at the back trail. It was Porter, in the lead, who first observed two riders winding their way down through the brushy trail ahead. Joseph and Katherine came abreast and stopped to either side of him. After a moment, Joseph mumbled, "Miners." Indeed, they were miners. They were trailing a fully packed mule decorated with picks and shovels; two horses were tied on behind the mule, and as the men approached, Porter finally held up his hand in greeting. The man in the lead, heavily bearded and wearing a tattered gray hat, one that once had been black, called out a hello in return and directly reined up about five yards away. His partner, sporting a flaming red beard, came up alongside. He nodded once and spat to the side. Porter began exchanging a few words with them. They were prospecting along the western rim, the first man said with a short laugh, searching for the mother lode.

Katherine was wearing her new hat with the broad brim, had her long hair neatly tucked up under it, but both of the miners took note that she was a woman, and directly the first man tipped his fingers to his hat and said, "Good day, ma'am. Mighty rare to see a woman riding in the hills around here."

Porter Webb explained that he and Joseph were taking her to the railroad at Chadron to catch a train east, and at the same time, his sharp eyes noticed the canvas bundle suspended from a pick tine on the mule. The bottom of the canvas was caked with dried blood, and Porter said, "Hunting was better than prospecting, I see. Got yourselves some fresh meat, anyhow."

The miner, grinning behind his whiskers, replied, "More 'n seven hundred dollars worth of meat. Ain't much for eating, though. Injun heads . . . three of 'em. Aim to sell 'em in Deadwood. Two-fifty each. That's what they're paying."

Katherine suddenly shuddered. A chill of horror coursed her entire body, and she gasped, "Heads!"

At this moment, the only thing she heard was Porter's command. "Hold your horse!" His forty-five revolver came out of nowhere, and a resounding explosion brought her pony up on its back legs. From the side of her widened eyes, she saw the horses of Porter and Joseph dancing sideways. Simultaneously, the miner directly in front of her was bucked and thrown. He was dead by the time he hit the ground. Then, a second shot shattered the quiet bottom and the red-bearded man's arms flew backward; his head jerked violently several times. He, too, fell but his right foot caught in the stirrup; his frightened horse bolted, and began dragging the man's body, the mule, and the trailing ponies down toward the little canyon creek. Joseph Brings Yellow kicked off after them. Dismounting, Katherine Coltrane went over and sat under a big fir where she held her head between her trembling knees. For a moment, she thought she was going to vomit, but then Porter was beside her, holding out his canteen.

"Jesus," she choked.

"Better take a long swig, Kate," said Webb. "Riles my belly, too, the bastards."

Shortly, Joseph brought back the spooked stock, but not the body of the redheaded miner. Joseph's face was dark and grim; his lips were tightly compressed; his jaw set in iron. Katherine knew he wasn't going to make a joke of this. She took a long draft of the water, and wearily set aside her hat and looked over at Porter. He was already removing tools from the mule pack, a pick and a shovel, and he tossed the pick to Joseph. Katherine stared in disbelief. "What are you going to do? . . . bury them, for God's sake!"

"Nope," Porter replied, "not them . . . their game—the Indians."

"Oh, mercy," moaned Katherine.

"Their land, isn't it? Least we can do. Who in the hell are these poor people? We don't know. Go getting caught by your brothers hauling around bloody freight like this and likely we'd meet the same fate before we could go explaining ourselves."

Joseph Brings Yellow was untying the stained canvas. "What about the two *wasichu*?" he asked lowly.

"Piss on them."

"*Heya,*" returned Joseph. "I will."

Katherine wiped at her eyes and buried her face again; she couldn't watch; she heard the men working nearby with the pick and shovel; she heard the sound of the pick hitting rock, the sound of the shovel biting, the sound of the earth sliding from its blade. Crawling away to the other side of the tree, she stared up through its drooping boughs. The sky was almost hidden; it was a dull blue, but to Katherine, it looked black. Then, there was a low moan from behind, and the moan grew into a mourning wail. It was Joseph.

His saddening cry suddenly died, and she heard Porter cursing. "The sons o' bitches . . . the dirty sons o' bitches!"

Katherine was afraid to ask, but she gulped once, and did. "Who are they?"

For a moment, barely a sound, only the chatter of a squirrel in the pines. Porter finally said, "An old man . . . and an old woman, and . . . and a child, a little boy it looks like."

Katherine Coltrane let out one great sob, leaned back against the tree trunk, and bawled uncontrollably.

It was nearly a half an hour before they left. Porter and Joseph removed all of the equipment from the stock, stacked it to the side, and turned the animals free. There was good grass in the canyon bottom, plenty of water; the animals would roam, eventually find their way to the foothills below, hopefully to be reclaimed by Lakota. Porter and Joseph took nothing from the dead miners, not even their rifles, nor did they attempt to identify the men. Joseph Brings Yellow told Katherine that he didn't urinate on them, either; the smell of urine would discourage scavengers, the bears, the wolves, and the coyotes.

They rode steadily the rest of the day, only stopping several times to relieve themselves and water the horses. By sundown, they were rounding the southern slopes of the great mountain the white men had named Mount Harney. In a small, secluded draw far from the goldfields, they made camp. It was very peaceful here. Katherine, huddled in her blanket, sat on a gray lichen-covered boulder, and watched the sun set beyond the troubled valley below.

The following afternoon, Katherine saw the first Sioux lodgepoles thrusting skyward against a backdrop of yellowing cottonwoods along the Cheyenne River. Joseph told her that this was the northernmost tip of the Pine Ridge reservation, a day's ride from the agency headquarters to the south. They soon discovered that the small village wasn't Oglala; these people were Sans Arc and a few Blackfeet Sioux, friendlies who hadn't participated in the summer battles across the valley to the west.

Porter and Joseph spoke with several of the men, who said they were postponing moving back closer to the agency as long as they could for fear of losing their horses and what few weapons they possessed. They reported that the army had confiscated many rifles and ponies from both returning Lakota and Cheyenne tribes as punishment for leaving the reservation during the Moon of the Green-up Grass, regardless of the reason. The men said that perhaps, by the season of the Hungry Moon, all of the furor would be at an end, they could strike their lodges, and once again set up their winter village closer to the agency where they now received their rations, their chuckaway. The white man's government was very angry because of the humiliating defeats inflicted upon its soldiers by the warriors of Crazy Horse, Sitting Bull, Low Dog, and Cheyenne braves under the leadership of Dull Knife and Two Moons. Because of the oncoming winter and the threat to the women and children, many people were returning to the reservations; some were remaining defiant, Crazy Horse and Sitting Bull among them. One of the Sans Arc men said that at last report, no one knew the whereabouts of Crazy Horse. Three Stars Crook and General Bearcoat Miles were chasing Sitting Bull's Hunkpapa far to the north, and Dull Knife had taken his Cheyenne into the Big Horn Mountains.

Katherine Coltrane sitting to the side of the small circle

where the men were smoking and talking, listened sadly. This would be a long winter of suffering.

Though the visit in the little village was cordial and warm, to Katherine it was depressing, and once they had made their farewells, she was relieved to be on the trail south again. By dusk, the trio had reached the White River where camp was made in a nearby flat ringed by a few scraggly alders and grease wood thickets. Porter Webb made coffee, black and strong, and Katherine prepared the last of the ham, beans, and hard rolls she had packed at the Red Bird Saloon.

Their conversation was subdued as they ate around the small fire; it was not a happy land, and there was nothing joyous to talk about, but ultimately, Joseph Brings Yellow told Katherine to go make wood for the night fire; the night was going to be a chilly one. Smiling, she took him by the hand and led him away to the riverbank where they scavenged together for driftwood. They found several pieces of logs, banked them high in the fire pit, and arranged their bedrolls and tarp covers to the side of the big flaming skunk. To the sound of popping wood and the occasional yelps of distant coyotes, Katherine finally removed her boots and wedged herself in between the security of her two companions, her beloved brothers. She thought it strange how she could be so troubled and yet paradoxically, so content. She couldn't remember when she had felt so comforted and at peace with herself. Oh, how she loved these two men. If only Julia were here, too, why, it would almost be like a family.

The following day before noon, Katherine and the men saw the first indications that they were nearing some of the villages—a few women and children foraging for fuel in the brushy bottoms and foothills. Obviously, the Sioux still had ponies at their disposal. A few of the gatherers had travois rigged behind their horses, and some of these were already piled high with dead limbs and logs that they had scavenged from downfall in the valley. A short time later, a scattering of lodges began to appear, some along the flats, others tucked away in groves of trees, some colorfully decorated, others drab, and a few covered with faded, white government-supplied canvas, a poor substitute for the thick, weatherproof hides of the buffalo. The day was sunny, the October air brisk, women, children, and their ubiquitous mongrels everywhere, little indication of the strife and turmoil in the valleys to the west and north of them. By now, Katherine's anxious eyes were probing every small gathering of children, searching for familiar faces, playmates of Julia, or miracle of miracles, the face of Julia herself. As she, Porter, and Joseph wound their way through clusters of camps, there were a few shouts of welcome by the little boys, friendly waves from the girls, and silent, curious stares from the men and women, but not one cry of recognition. Porter and Joseph pointed and made comment, and occasionally spoke aside to someone nearby; most all of the lodges were Lakota, but there seemed to be only a few Oglala about, and no Hunkpapa at all. Porter, with a glum look, told Katherine it didn't look too promising. Pine Ridge was the reservation where Red Cloud's Oglala congregated, but many of the old chief's followers had deserted him; many of them were still in the unceded territory following their new war leader, the victorious Crazy Horse.

Soon the lodges thinned, and in the proximity of the agency stockade, there were only a few cabins, sheds, and corrals, and a conspicuous absence of people, only several agency Indian police loitering in front of the gate. Near the gate was a long, slender lodgepole and a freshly dug hole. Katherine saw Porter shake his head and trade a tired smile with Joseph Brings Yellow. "Still trying to run up the colors over your brothers, Joseph, on their own land. Bastard never learns, does he?"

As they approached the agent's small house, Porter said, "This fellow is an asshole of the first water, Kate, but he should know something about the traffic coming in here. Name's Saville, some politician's man, and like most of them, doesn't know a goddamned thing about these people or how to treat them."

"Not exactly a friend of yours?"

"Only met him once," grinned Porter. "Once was enough."

Joseph Brings Yellow said solemnly, "The Lakota do not smoke with him."

Before they could dismount, J. J. Saville, agent of the Pine Ridge reservation, attired in a long black coat, and wearing a black hat with a wide brim, was already on the porch, and he immediately recognized Porter Webb. If there were any animosity between the two men, it didn't surface immediately. Saville politely tipped his fingers to the black hat and said, "Good day, Mister Webb ... madam," he added, curiously staring over at Katherine. "What brings you up this way? Long way from home, aren't you?"

"Heading home, right now," Porter replied. "Just passing through." He nodded at Katherine. "This lady is Kate Coltrane. She's looking for some news of her little girl, running with some of Crazy Horse's people. Thought we'd stop here before riding on up to the fort."

With another tip to his hat, Saville said, "Miss Coltrane ... yes, I heard about your misfortune, some talk here on the place about it, but those hostiles ... the ones you were living with, well, we just don't see 'em 'round here much." He held up one of his hands. "Oh, not that we won't be seeing them one of these days. No, from what I hear, we'll be getting a new batch in here before the year is out. Some newcomers, renegades already here, but I sure don't recall hearing about any breeds among 'em, no little ones. Course, there's always a lot going on 'round here I don't hear about either." He shrugged apologetically. "Damn big place, you know, and there's the Rosebud other side of us. Understand there's a couple thousand of the beggars over there."

"Beggars?" questioned Katherine.

"Just a manner of speaking, ma'am. On the dole ... wards, that sort of thing. Damn notional, they are ... some not very respectful, 'specially the new ones, a troublesome lot."

"Notional?" huffed Porter Webb. "Seems like you got it ass-backwards, Mister Saville. It's the goddamned politicians and government that're contrary and notional. Indians above the Platte sure as hell never settled for all of this shit you're heaping on them."

"Some of the chiefs did," Saville retorted. "As I recall, you did some talking for them, didn't you? Seems like you wanted to bring the soldiers into this. Well, Mister Webb, you got your wish."

Katherine glanced over at Porter, who was staring coldly at the agent. "You know damn well what Baptiste Pourier and I told the commissioners," Porter finally said. "None of this would have happened if the army had done its job ... patrolled the perimeter and shut off that north and south trail through the Black Hills."

Katherine Coltrane, small green sparks in her eyes, thrust her chin forward and said, "Stop it, will you! Both of you!

I didn't ride all the way into this godforsaken reservation to hear two men quarrel over spilled milk, what could have been or not have been. I'm looking for my daughter, damn it. Don't you understand? Now, let's get on with my business, please."

"I beg your pardon, Miss Coltrane," Saville said. "I don't think your daughter is here . . . leastways, not right yet, but I can send a couple of the police out . . . take a look and ask some questions. Might take a day or two."

Porter Webb said, "That's not good enough."

"Do you have a better idea?"

"Yep," replied Porter, turning his horse. "We can't hang around here a day or two. We'll take a look ourselves."

"I'd rather you not," said Saville. "I'm having enough trouble now without you poking around my reservation, maybe getting some of these people all stirred up again."

Porter laughed sardonically. "Don't worry about it. First place, it isn't your reservation. You only work here, Saville. You're supposed to be taking care of these beggars. Second place, like I told old Three Stars' boys last spring, time for talking is done and past. They didn't listen, and now they're damn well paying for it. I'm sure as hell not looking to stir up any more trouble."

"If you go in without my permission, I'll have to inform the post commandant," Saville threatened. "I'll have General Armitage call out a patrol to remove you."

Porter Webb abruptly turned his horse about and almost collided with a stunned Katherine Coltrane. Staring at Porter, she said, "Jason? . . . Bird Dog?"

Porter called to Saville, "Armitage, you say? Where in the hell did he come from?"

"General Crook's command," replied the agent. "Arrived here three days ago, and I'll send a message up to him if I have to."

Sidling his horse close to Katherine's, Porter asked if she had the paper of introduction and request for assistance that Colonel Ben Bradford had written for her. She did, inside her coat pocket, and she pulled it out. Porter took it and rode close to the porch steps and handed the paper to Saville. "Here," he said with a grin, "have your messenger boy deliver this to General Armitage, too. Have him tell the general to set aside some quarters tonight for three guests, one room with a tub of hot water in it for the lady here. She's a very special friend of his."

Agent Saville was reading the paper when Porter reached the gate and called back, "And you better get rid of this god-damned flagpole, or I'll tell some of the renegades down below to come up and make kindling out of it again. You sure have a thick skull, Saville. This is an Indian reservation, not a goddamned military post. They don't want your flag flying over their property."

Within another half hour, both Porter Longstreet Webb and Joseph Brings Yellow encountered acquaintances from the Miniconjou, who in turn directed them to a village on Wounded Knee Creek where a few Oglala had recently arrived from the Powder River country. Whether these Oglala had been part of the huge village on the Little Bighorn and had participated or witnessed the early summer's battle there, the Miniconjou professed not to know, or were disinclined to talk about it. It was dangerous to talk too much with the agency police always snooping around, and no one went about displaying a scalp stick.

Porter, Joseph, and Katherine soon discovered the trail leading down the creek to the village, but three women washing clothes along the water's edge saw them first. One, throwing her arms into the air, went shrieking back to the village; the other two dropped their wash, and began waving and shouting, and Katherine, in turn, leaped from her horse and rushed forward to embrace them. Tall Woman had returned to the Oglala.

By the time Katherine and the men arrived at the ring of lodges, small clusters of mostly women and children were already forming a ragged line and setting up tremolos. Katherine, elated, yet embarrassed by the warm reception, waved, and finally threw back her head and screeched out a tremolo of her own. This was a truly Lakota gesture that immediately set off another resounding shriek from her responsive sisters along the line. Beyond the line, Katherine saw a group of blanket-covered men, several of whom she immediately recognized, and in the middle of them, partially supported by his staff, was the holy one, Flat Iron. The smile on his wrinkled face was barely discernible, but he was nodding at her in approval. Flat Iron also nodded at Porter Webb, the *wasichu* who had given him tobacco and a pipe on the Little Powder, who had sat and talked fluently with him in Siouan.

After the formalities of greetings, the new arrivals sat on robes in front of the medicine lodge; the sun was at its highest point; the sky was cloudless, and as the pipe was passed, the aroma of red willow, kinnikinnick, and tobacco was fragrantly sweet. Some of the women who knew Tall Woman sat in a circle to the back of her and the men. They knew why Tall Woman had come. They knew what was going to be said in this smoke, and they wanted to be a part of it. They would share Tall Woman's grief, for they all knew her daughter, Blue Star, was not here. They all knew that Tall Woman's man, Standing Bear, had been killed on a hill overlooking the Little Bighorn River.

Porter Longstreet Webb, the *wasichu* everyone called White Hawk, spoke. He honored all of those present; he honored all of those who had been slain on the Rosebud and Little Bighorn, and he drew grunts of approval when he said there would be no peace for the soul of Pahuska, the Long Hair chief of all thieves. He said Tall Woman had been proud to be adopted by the Oglala, but now she was lonely for the love of her child; a daughter's place was beside her mother, away from all the trouble and fighting. Tall Woman's time with the Oglala had come to an end; her family had called her home.

Chief Red Dog spoke. Beside him was Red Horse, who had been on the Little Bighorn, who because of the threat of Cold Maker to the women and children had brought back many of them to the safety of the reservation. Red Dog said, "Others will soon follow. Our people cannot hunt and make war at the same time during the time of the Hungry Moon. Like hungry wolves, the soldiers are everywhere in the valleys." Raising his hand in a benevolent gesture to Katherine, he said, "Standing Bear will not come. Standing Bear's spirit is alive. His body is buried in the valley of the Big Horn." Katherine grasped Porter's hand and slumped in silent shock as her sisters behind began moaning in unison. She barely had time to suppress a sob when she heard Red Dog say, "Some of our people are with our Hunkpapa brothers above the Mother River. Some are with Tashunka-Witko. We are told that your daughter, Wicapi Hinto, and her grandmother, Huhuseca-Ska, left the Oglala and went with her cousin, a Hunkpapa woman. By now, they are safe from the soldiers. The Blue Elk watches over them. They are in the Queen Mother's Land where there is no war."

BOOK THREE

BOOK THREE

Author's note:

By the end of 1877, the United States Government's military adventure against the Indians of the northern plains had been concluded. Sitting Bull and many of his followers were in Canada; the Oglala, never defeated in battle, were on the Pine Ridge reservation. Crazy Horse surrendered on the false promise of General Crook that he and his people would be granted land on the Powder River. Later, during a guardhouse brawl on the reservation, Crazy Horse was bayoneted by a soldier and died of the wound.

His father and mother buried his remains at an undisclosed site along the Chankpe Opi Wakpala, the creek called Wounded Knee. In November of 1877, Chief Joseph of the Nez Perce, after valiantly leading his people across the Idaho and Montana territories, surrendered in the Bear Paw Mountains. Some Nez Perce, along with the Sioux, made successful escapes into Canada where for a number of years they lived unmolested. The Indians were relatively peaceful, but the white men now began to fight among themselves.

Chapter Ten

Valley of the Chugwater

Deadwood, Dakota Territory, July, 1878.

Fred Evans had more than nine hundred men working for his freight company, hauling every conceivable kind of supplies into Deadwood from Bismarck to the east, and Cheyenne to the south. Nine hundred men and one woman, Martha Jane Canarray. When Jane wasn't on the trail, she was at home in her small cabin at the end of Lee Street; when she was home and not in her cabin, she usually was at either Kelley's Saloon or Saloon Number 10. On several occasions when she was jailed for disorderly conduct, an old friend, Katherine Coltrane, the madam at the Red Bird Hotel, went down to Sheriff Seth Bullock's place of business and bailed her out. In the person of Katherine Coltrane, Jane always had a good, steady shoulder upon which to weep. Since the killing of her dearest friend and sometimes lover, Wild Bill Hickok, by Jack McCall, she frequently ended up in the Red Bird's second floor reception parlor expending the last of a crying jag on one of Katherine's receptive shoulders. Not too good for such a place of high-class business as the Red Bird, opined Henry Givens, so Katherine often doused Jane in one of the tin tubs, gave her some black coffee, bedded her down in one of the spare bedrooms, and kept her old teacher out of sight.

On this particular early-July afternoon, Jane Canarray had wasted herself in Kelley's; she came into the parlor inebriated and weeping, and Katherine and Ida quickly spirited her into one of the vacant rooms. Within ten minutes, Jane was blubbering and snoring. Katherine, exhausted mentally and perspiring profusely, promptly took a cold bath in one of the big tin tubs. Wrapped in a towel, she returned to her room and began dressing when a knock came on the door. In came Tim Frawley, all smiles. He had been gone for almost three weeks on a business trip to Cheyenne, and Katherine knew some of that business was closing out the Chugwater deeds. Time was precious, for she had heard that her old property in Cheyenne had been cleared. Stacks upon stacks of rails were being stored there, according to her friends Alva Tompkins and Buford Reasons, who had recently stopped by the Red Bird after cashing in a few pokes from their secret Lost Cabin diggings. Alva had happily left for the return trip to Chugwater wearing new boots and a derby hat, and minus one poke of gold, but with a promise from Katherine that she would be down in the valley before the summer ended to check on the homesteads Porter Webb had marked out.

Tim Frawley had a packet in his hand, and he slid it on the small table next to Katherine's bed. "You owe me for this," he said. "These papers are right out of Cheyenne. Everything has been filed and recorded."

Katherine glanced at the package once, smiled back at Frawley, and joyously exclaimed, "The deeds! Finally! Oh, mercy, everything went through!" She kissed him.

"Eight of them. Porter has four, you have four."

"Eight! How did you do that? Eight pieces of property?"

"There are other papers in there," Frawley replied. "Had some of the girls' names on three of the homesteads, Todd Chatham, Henry's, and my name on three, you and Porter on two, but the rest of us, well, that's what the other papers are all about. We all sold our land to you and Porter . . . three hundred dollars per parcel. That's over fourteen hundred acres. The girls aren't interested in this kind of business, and Henry and I can't go getting mixed-up in your railroad negotiations later on. It wouldn't look right, and besides, it would take up too much of my time."

Collapsing on the edge of the bed, Katherine sighed, "Oh, my gracious, that's . . . that's eighteen hundred dollars, Tim!"

"On paper"—he smiled—"only on paper."

"Porter and I . . . we don't owe you?"

"Well, I didn't say that."

Katherine grinned and nodded knowingly. "That's one helluva lot of tricks, eighteen hundred dollars worth. I hope you get that house finished, and Susan gets out here in a hurry. Ruby and I'll be working for nothing for a year or two at this rate."

"I didn't say anything about Ruby."

"You didn't have to, Timothy," Katherine replied with a foxy smile. "I don't see everything that goes on up here, but I'm a good listener. She says you fancy her . . . like her little brown body."

Tim Frawley brushed Katherine off with a nervous laugh. "Women talk too much," he said.

"It's not the truth?"

"No one compares to you, Kate," he offered lamely. "Honestly."

"Shall I believe you? Shall I believe any man?"

"I would call you Katherine the Great."

"There's honey on your tongue."

Tim Frawley shrugged and said, "Besides, the end is right around the corner, anyhow. That's some more of my news. Susan and little Tim are due in here on the sixteenth. Letter was waiting for me when I got back to the office. Should have the house ready by then, too."

"Wonderful!" exclaimed Katherine. "That's simply wonderful."

"Yes, wonderful," Frawley agreed. But he added somewhat regretfully, "We'll have to do business through Henry from now on. I won't be using the back stairway anymore."

Standing, placing a hand affectionately against his cheek, she said, "I appreciate everything." She held the packet out. "You've been very good to me, Tim. I won't ever forget it."

"I shall say likewise, Kate, between all of my work . . . my work, and you, you've made it less lonely. We've been good for each other." He smiled fondly at her. "I suppose I'll have to settle for a drink right now."

"Men!"

"You love men, and you know it."

Katherine leaned forward and kissed him. "I love their money. Most of them don't know what they're doing when they get in bed." She brought a bottle of wine and two tumblers, and after slowly pouring, she handed him his drink. "This may stimulate your desires for something else, you know."

"I know." He grinned. Raising his glass, Frawley said, "Here's to the new landowners. Both of us, Kate. More news . . . I bought a lot in Cheyenne, not too far from that corner where your house was."

"A lot? Whatever for?" She sipped and watched him curiously.

"Office building," he casually replied. "Looking down the line, the future, I plan on expanding my practice down there . . . more stability. Cattle business is forever. Gold isn't, not placers, not Deadwood."

"I'm happy for you," Katherine said. A small smile touched the corners of her mouth. "Do you know, I sort of had that notion in my head, too . . . about Cheyenne. A business for myself. Yes, a very exquisite hotel, mirrors, chandeliers, twenty or so rooms, very spacious ones on the upper floor, a two- or three-room suite for me . . . one of my dreams." She laughed lightly and said, "Whoring is that kind of business, you know. It's forever, too."

"Well, here's to dreams and good business, then," quipped Timothy Frawley. He touched his glass to Katherine's. "May we have the best of them."

They drank. She finally took the glasses and set them aside, then led him over to the edge of her bed where she began removing his coat, then his tie. "I don't think there's any reason you should be sneaking out of here and knocking on Ruby's door, is there?"

"No. No, I see no reason, but . . . but for God's sake, is this going to be worth eighteen hundred dollars?"

"We'll just have to see, won't we?"

It was toward midnight when Jane Canarray awoke. Her eyes were filled with sand, her lips parched, and it felt as though a nest of mice had taken up quarters in her mouth. Kate had put a robe on her, a silk one, and there was some sense of luxury in this. Stumbling about in the darkness, Jane found the pitcher of water on the little commode; she tipped it up and quaffed, gargled once, and spat in the basin. Finally, the lamp. She scratched about and found the matches, and with a trembling hand, brought up a small flicker, enough light to find her clothes neatly hung over the back of a chair. Slipping into her pullover shirt, next her baggy underpants, was a chore in itself, and she stopped to rest back in the chair, heard the faintest of a giggle from the room next door, someone turning a trick, she supposed, something that presently was the farthest thing from her mind. She needed some sustenance, a good belt, perhaps, something to get her going, but most of all, and she had to admit it, she badly needed to put her miserable life in order again. Pants, boots, and fumbling her fingers through her hair, she went over to the window, stuck her head out, and took a deep breath of fresh air. For a moment, she surveyed the bright sky, the fuzzy dark hillside in back, spires of the pines perched up there on the dim skyline, then the building next door, black windows, and near the back of it at the alley, the small orange glow, a few sparks, and an ominous pall of smoke. Jane focused her bleary eyes for a second look. Fire! The goddamned building next door was on fire!

Moments later, she was in the hallway, shouting and pounding on doors. Confusion reigned. Several of the girls, grasping robes, popped out, directly followed by two men, one clothed, the other attired in nothing more than his shirt, and carrying a pair of shoes. Katherine, wide-eyed, appeared from her room at the end of the hall. By now, it was worse—the flames were licking up the back of the Red Bird, too, and three or four men were already dashing about in the alley toting buckets.

Ruby Danforth came up behind Katherine, took one frightened look, and said, "Miss Kate, we better get our little asses out of here 'fore they get scorched!"

Back in the hall, Katherine quickly accounted for all of her girls. "We don't have much time," she said. "Gather up what you can ... bundle up everything in your bedspreads, and get down the stairs ... hurry, hurry, now!"

Jane came out of the bathroom carrying one of the tin tubs in her big arms. She promptly set it to the side of the stairway, took one quick look at the flames below, and tipped it over, cascading water down the steps. There was a resounding hiss and a spew of stream at the bottom. Directly, Meg Meacham and Carrie Colyer, burdened with two large bundles, hurried down the stairs. Jane came back with the second tub partially filled with water, and she quickly gave the stairs a second dousing. By now, the hallway was filling with the acrid smell of smoke, and flames from the adjacent building were eating into the wood of the Red Bird.

Henry Givens appeared at the top of the stairs as Ruby and Ida hurried by toting all of their belongings. Jane now was rolling a water barrel toward the landing, and Givens shouted, "Where in hell is Kate? For crisesakes, is she still back there?"

"Got her stuff there," Jane said, pointing, "but she had to go back ... forgot some kind of shitty papers ... deeds, something like that." Wheeling the barrel into position, Jane gave a mighty heave, and once again flooded the smoldering stairs. Henry Givens, holding a bandanna to his face, disappeared down the smoky hallway.

Shouting, "Look out below!" Jane gave the empty barrel a shove, and it crashed in a pile of staves in the bright glow of the alley. She turned, and snatching a damp towel from the bath, rushed back to the hall, only to be met by a coughing Givens, who was pulling Katherine by her outstretched arms. Givens cried, "Give me a hand . . . catch her by her feet."

"Where's the papers she wanted?" Jane shouted through the towel.

"Scattered all over hell . . . floor. No time for that, now."

On her hands and knees, Jane stumbled along through the smoke. The papers were there, and amid chokes and burning eyes, she gathered them up, hurriedly slipped them inside her pullover, then clambered back to grab onto Katherine's dragging feet. Henry Givens stopped momentarily to give Katherine's bundle of clothing a kick; someone down below quickly retrieved it; then, together he and Jane carried Katherine down the smoldering steps. Minutes later, the entire back of the Red Bird was engulfed by crackling flames, and the stairway collapsed.

Katherine was shortly revived with a wet rag on her forehead. There were sounds around her, shouts of the fire laddies who were valiantly trying to save adjacent buildings, the sobs of her girls who were huddled close by, and Jane Canarray's raspy voice telling her to breathe deeply. When she finally sat up, she stared at disaster—the Red Bird and Brown Café were flaming skeletons, and she knew that her days in Deadwood waiting for news of Julia were over. What a terrible loss for Timothy and Henry, she thought, as tears coursed down through the grime on her cheeks.

Both Frawley and Givens appeared the next morning at King's Hotel where Katherine and her girls had taken refuge; the men were going to rebuild, but the women had already decided to move on—Carrie Colyer and Meg Meacham were returning home to visit relatives, and Ida and Ruby were going to Cheyenne to find a new place of work, for neither had any relatives who would claim them. Katherine was to accompany them as far as Chugwater. Katherine had no relatives at all, but she had a few old friends, also, some pending business with the Colorado and Southern

Railroad. Jane appeared at the hotel, too, all spruced up in a new dress, high-button shoes, and a large summer bonnet, adamantly declaring that she was off booze. Fate had intervened on her behalf; had she not awakened from her late-afternoon stupor, her charred bones could well have been a part of the blackened rubble of the Red Bird. She was leaving the next day on a freight run to Bismarck with twenty other skinners to pick up forty thousand pounds of flour. Since Carrie and Meg were heading east, they were most welcome to ride along. The two girls politely declined; they abhorred the thought of camping out along the way; they envisioned more lucrative opportunities riding the stage with gentlemen packing greenbacks in their pockets.

Katherine rationalized. Even though everyone was temporarily out of a job, and this was now by choice since they all had refused offers to work in the less prestigious houses in Deadwood, the Red Bird disaster might be a welcome respite. Everyone had worked hard; a brief rest was needed, and perhaps better days were ahead for all of them. Katherine expressed her thanks to Jane Canarray for all of her help during the fire, and saving the Chugwater deeds, for it would have taken months to replace them in Cheyenne, and she knew she no longer had that kind of time. Progress on the railroad was gaining momentum. She briefly wondered whether her old friend, Stanley Howard, was still directing the surveys and land acquisitions. If so, oh, what a surprise he was going to get.

By afternoon, all of the young women had withdrawn their savings from the bank, had purchased new leather-bound trunks, and were fully prepared to leave on their respective stages the following morning. Attired in their finest dresses, they accompanied Henry Givens to a dinner in their honor at the Cosmopolitan this last evening. The silent partner, Tim Frawley, didn't attend, but he left boxes of bonbons for the girls at King's Hotel, and a note encouraging them to return the following spring to a more plush and spacious Red Bird Hotel.

Katherine was packing her last suitcase when Givens reappeared. He had forgotten something, and he pulled out a small revolver from his coat pocket and a little leather pouch with a few extra shells in it. "It's a Plants forty-two," he explained. " 'Oughtta fit right nice in your purse. 'Course, you can get a holster if you want."

"Oh, mercy!" said Katherine. She turned it over several times admiring its gleaming steel and brass and the rosewood handle. "But ... but whatever am I going to do with it? Hold up a stage?"

Givens chuckled. "Who knows? Woman shouldn't be moving around alone these days without some kind of protection ... all that money you're toting. Some ruffian starts bothering you, shoot his balls off." He laughed at that, gave Katherine a kiss on the cheek, and left, calling back, "I'll see you off on the stage in the morning."

Katherine Coltrane held the pistol out, aimed, and took an imaginary shot at the window. "Pow!" She grinned, and tucked the revolver into her purse with the Chugwater deeds and the deposit draft for four thousand dollars in greenbacks in her new money belt. Her stay in Deadwood had been very profitable. Nevertheless, she was glad to be leaving because, despite its booming, boisterous heart and despite all of its riches, Deadwood was a lonely place.

Several nights later, Katherine Coltrane, Ida Hamilton, and Ruby Danforth stepped off the Cheyenne–Deadwood stage at the Chugwater way station. Katherine's two companions had only a three-hour ride left to Cheyenne, but it was almost nine o'clock, they were all train-weary, dusty, and exhausted, and the thought of arriving in an unfamiliar city, at midnight or thereafter, was discouraging to Ida and Ruby. When the stage driver told them a day coach came through the next day around noon out of Fort Laramie, they eagerly accepted Katherine's invitation to stay the night in the Star Hotel adjacent to the station. The women were cordially welcomed, and soon discovered that Luther and Maybelle Hatch operated the little saloon-hotel. A small café was partitioned off from the bar on the main floor, and a stairway inside next to the dining area led to six rooms on the upper floor. As in the former Red Bird Hotel, a back stairway also led to the rooms, but unlike the Red Bird, there was no parlor and the small bath had only one tin tub. Whatever, the little hotel by frontier standards was clean; curtains were fluttering in the open windows from a small breeze coming down the hall from another window at the front; the bedspreads were colorful, homemade quilts, and pinewood-framed mirrors were tacked into the log wall over the small commodes.

Luther and Maybelle were in their fifties. Luther, who had a gimp leg, tended the bar and hotel registry, and Maybelle tended the kitchen and washed the hotel linen. Together, they owned the Chugwater livery next door and a two-room cabin in back of it. All of this, Katherine, Ida, and Ruby learned by the time they had deposited the last of their baggage in their rooms. They were the only guests, but Luther Hatch predicted better business ahead. Within another year, the railroad was coming through, and everyone knew that business always accompanied the railroads—merchants and purveyors of all kinds. Best of all, the cattle business was beginning to mushroom, several spreads down the river, and a big one over the hills thirty miles to the east at Hawk Springs. Luther Hatch was going to build loading chutes and a small stockyard, already had the skinned poles coming down from Bluegrass Creek.

All of this information came in an incessant rush, but the last bit of news left Katherine Coltrane staring in silent surprise as Luther Hatch hippity-hopped down the hall to fetch a few kettles of hot water, as he said, so the ladies could freshen up before bedtime. Over the hills; only thirty miles to Porter Webb's spread; poles coming down from Bluegrass Creek, the homesteads of Alva and Buford, all very interesting and intriguing to Katherine. Of course, it already had been in her mind to have Alva and Buford help her get a firsthand look at the property she and Porter now owned, just where it was, and how far along the Chugwater River it extended. Then later, with some time on her hands, and in no great rush to get to the bank in Cheyenne, perhaps she could entice Alva to guide her over to Porter Webb's spread to make some plans and see how he was developing his cattle herd.

It was almost dark now, and Katherine lit the lamp, undressed, slipped into a robe, and then shook the dust from her traveling suit out the open window. She went down the hall to the window facing the front, braced herself on the sill, and looked out into the shadowy darkness of the street. Not much to see: to the right, the front of Hatch's livery, beyond it, several small houses with yellow light filtering out from the windows; to the left, the stage station, now deserted, and adjacent to it, a saloon with two horses at the hitching pole. Across the street, a mercantile of some kind, and a small frame building that looked new. A rustle and quiet laugh brought her around. It was Ruby, holding a pot in one hand, in the other, dangling three cups from her fingers.

"You already looking for some business, Miss Kate?" Ruby asked. "No gentlemen 'round here, far as I can see, 'cept that Mistuh Hatch."

Ruby Danforth was wearing a robe, a very low-cut robe, and she obviously had very little on under it. Katherine said, "Oh, mercy, don't tell me you went downstairs looking like that? Oh . . ."

"Didn't even see a boogerman." Ruby giggled. "Got us some coffee, though, from the kitchen. Lady says we want something to eat, just let her know. I said we were going to take a bath and go to bed . . . not much interested in nothing else." Turning, she padded down the dim hall in her bare feet, provocatively swaying her bottom.

Katherine shrugged hopelessly, and followed. "Missus Hatch? Lordy, what she must think."

"Big-eyed chick, Miss Kate. Thought I was hired help for you and Ida." Ruby turned into Katherine's room. "First nigguh gal she ever saw out here, that's what I think. Told her no different, but she took a good look." Pouring coffee for Katherine, she giggled again and said, "Everybody takes a good look at little ol' Ruby 'cause I got something good to look at."

Sighing forlornly, Katherine said, "Will you ever stop using that term, 'nigguh'! You're a woman of color, damn it. A breed, a mulatto, part Negro, if you will, but, mercy, not nigguh. I hate that word. I hate Injun, redskin, all of those words. God, I can't believe the shit people pile on one another out here."

"Do it in Memphis, too," Ruby returned. "That's civilized." She handed Katherine the cup of coffee, then turned away, stuck her head out the hall and called, in an affected, stilted voice, "Oh, Missy Ida chile, your little woman of color is serving coffee in the parlor. You come and get it, you hear?" Grinning back at Katherine, she shook her head violently and whispered softly, "Nigguh, nigguh, little sweet-loving nigguh!" She pursed her lips and blew Katherine a kiss.

They waited for Luther to bring their hot water. They sipped coffee, Ida seated on the bed, Ruby, her bare legs crossed on the throw rug by the bed, and Katherine, in a chair by the open window. They were so intoxicated by exhaustion, they were silly, and every utterance from any one of them brought a comment, frequently smutty, and they all bent over in laughter. They were the girls from the Red Bird, and despite their companionship over the past two years, laughing together, crying together, often consoling one another, they were never closer than on this last night. Luther finally came and cautiously peeked through the slightly opened door. No, they weren't drunk, no, not at all. They were just three lovely, vivacious women, and never had he seen such a rare mixture of beauty in one room. There was harmony here, and Luther Hatch spoke hesitantly, reluctantly, fearful of breaking the charm.

"Ladies ... ladies, I put two kettles in the bath. Bringing another right away." He forced a stubby laugh. "Have to draw straws to see who gets first bath."

"Thank you, Mister Hatch," Katherine said politely.

"No straws," said Ida. "That's a very big tub."

"We're together," smiled Ruby. "Been riding that stage for almost three nights all pooched together like butter beans and okra. No straws, Mistuh Hatch. You bring on that other kettle, and don't you pay us no mind. These two white ladies want some color, so we're all gonna get in that tub together, see if some of mine washes off."

"Oh, my ... oh, my goodness!" Luther's head disappeared, and the women heard his hurried hippity-hop gait fading away down the hall.

Katherine Coltrane snickered in her lap, Ida fell back on the bed laughing, and Ruby Danforth giggled and said, "I was just joshing. I'm not getting in that tub with either one of you. Might be the other way 'round, that white washing off on me, and you be turning me into a damn spook."

The rattle of a wagon, the clomp-clomp of a horse, woke Katherine. She stretched once and sighed. Oh, mercy, it was one of the best sleeps she had had in ages, a sleep without dreams, prairie dreams, Indian dreams, dreams of the men in her life, or dreams of Julia lost in the far north. She had been in oblivion for hours. She bathed her face in cold water, disdained the chamber pot, and throwing her robe around her, darted down the back stairway to the privy. Beyond it, over a small picket fence were several large elm trees, lilac bushes, and what appeared to be a small rock garden. Sitting in the shade were Ruby and Ida, both fully dressed, chatting gaily, eating breakfast at a long plank table as though they were on a picnic. They waved, shouted good morning, and kept right on eating.

It was almost twenty minutes later before Katherine joined them. They were drinking coffee and discussing the possibility of staying in Chugwater for another day. They had been overcome by the hospitality of Luther and Maybelle Hatch. Certainly, the Hatches must have suspected they were soiled doves, but did it matter? They were being treated like part of the family, an unusual happening for Ruby and Ida, neither of whom had experienced such kindness in their misguided lives, at least, not since childhood. And directly Luther came out from the back of the kitchen carrying a big tray, on it a plate of hotcakes, bacon, and scrambled eggs. He set it in front of Katherine, said good morning, wheeled about, went back to the kitchen, and shortly returned with a pot of coffee. He refilled the cups of Ida and Ruby, poured for Katherine, and finally sat down at the end of the table. Smiling, he said, "Nice place out here in the early morning . . . no jays or blackbirds in these trees to go crapping on you. Fresh air, and right peaceful." He pointed to the flowers in the rock garden. "Ol' lady Bigelow fixed that up a couple of years back. Maybelle keeps it up. Womenfolk seem to glory in the presence of posies."

"It's all very nice," said Katherine. She stared at her plate. She couldn't remember when she had seen such a sumptuous breakfast. She was hungry; she was going to eat every bit of it. Had she been out on the prairie with the Oglala, she might have saved some for her pouch, something to feed Julia later in the day; she had always done that, always had shared the extras with Julia. Katherine munched; she nodded over at the pretty flowers, and between swallows asked, "This Missus Bigelow . . . the lady who did that, what happened to her?"

"She owned this place, she and Charlie. Sold out a couple of months ago," replied Luther. "Got a cash deal, and moved on down to Cheyenne City. Charlie was a tinsmith by trade. Not much tinning here, and this place wasn't making much of a profit." Luther chuckled. "Got impatient, I reckon. Couldn't wait for the iron horse no longer, so Charlie upped and sold the whole lash-up."

Katherine smiled across the table at him. "And you, Mister Hatch, you have patience? You think you and Maybelle can turn a profit?"

Luther Hatch puckered and doubtfully shook his head. "I'm no hotelman, Miss Coltrane, but I know what the railroad and cattle are gonna do to this country." He motioned to the distant corrals, the livery barn, and the small house. "I'm all staked out over there, waiting. Maybelle and me, we don't own the Star, just running it, that's all. For a friend of yours."

Katherine glanced up, her fork dangling. "A friend of mine?"

"I reckon so. Have your name on a piece of paper. Kate Coltrane." Luther clucked. "Damn fool, I am, but Maybelle remembered, and last night 'fore we shut down, she went and fetched the paper, looked at the register, compared the names, and said it was you in the flesh upstairs in your room. I was supposed to be looking out for you later in the summer, and well, when three of you ladies showed up, it sorta bucked me. Alva said he was expecting you ... wanted me to show you how to get up to his place in Bluegrass."

Katherine gulped once, and stared over at Ruby and Ida. Ruby's mouth was agape, but Ida found her voice and said, "Alva ... Alva Tompkins, that old coot?"

"One and the same," replied Luther. "Alva owns the Star Hotel, lock, stock, and barrel. Paid Charlie eight thousand for it."

Ruby Danforth puckered her lips and whistled. Ida stared at Luther in disbelief. "Eight thousand dollars! Wherever did he get that kind of money?"

With an offhand shrug, Luther answered, "Never asked. Diggings, I reckon. He and Buford been running back and forth above the Platte for nigh on three or four years, all over that infernal country. Never know what those boys are up to. Most times stay up above in the winter, but when the bluebirds start making nests, you never know where they'll be ... or what they'll be doing, either. No good drifters, some say." He grinned at Katherine. "Surprised the hell out of me, too, and I was telling Maybelle last night, I just couldn't figure out where he met a fine lady like you."

Katherine smiled back at him and replied, "We crossed trails several times."

* * *

Ruby Danforth and Ida Hamilton decided to move on to Cheyenne, and since Katherine planned to say in Chugwater for a week or two, the girls promised to send a letter via the stage as soon as they were relocated. There were tears behind their smiles at departure, and Katherine Coltrane suddenly found herself alone again.

Later, Maybelle Hatch fixed her a sandwich and brought her a cool glass of buttermilk. Luther went to his livery and hitched up a buckboard, and sketched out a map in the dust. Pointing with a stick, he showed Katherine where to turn to catch the trail up to Bluegrass Creek. She packed one suitcase and a small bundle of personals, and Luther took the rest of her belongings and stored them in the bedroom in his house. It was almost one o'clock when Katherine snapped the reins across the back of the big gray horse. The little wagon lurched ahead, and she was off for the distant green meadows and fir-covered slopes to the west. She crossed Richeau Creek, followed the winding ruts up through rolling hills decorated with blooming sage, patches of daisies, larkspur, and lupine. The high country came on in all of its splendor; the mountain air was warm but invigorating.

Following a little wagon road down through a patch of willows, she forded Sybille Creek, and then ahead, tumbling down through a long green meadow bordered by more willow and groves of aspen, was Bluegrass Creek. At the tip of this meadow, surrounded by tall pines, was a sprawling cabin with a big front porch, the top of it adorned with a set of sun-bleached elk antlers. But before she had driven halfway up the meadow, she saw two figures materialize on the porch; she saw the frantic waving of arms, then heard a lusty, piercing outcry, almost like an Oglala war whoop. Katherine screamed back, and when she looked a second time, Alva Tompkins and Buford Reasons had locked arms; they were spinning around together in a wild jig. Tears of happiness flooded Katherine Coltrane's eyes. She had never been to this place, hadn't even pictured it in her most imaginative mind, but in one fleeting moment of exhilaration, she thought she was returning home.

They hugged her, they kissed her hand; they seated her in a rocking chair on the porch, and they brought her a drink of cold water. However, the men weren't quite prepared for her early arrival. They had built a place for her whenever she visited, a room of her very own, but it wasn't quite finished. Shortly, they gathered up her belongings and led her through the cabin; it was spacious, a large front room with a huge rock fireplace, two bunks up against one wall, a long table, and four chairs. The room was clean but cluttered with items of every conceivable nature, trinkets, hardware, pelts, pictures and weapons suspended from the log walls, pots and earthenware stacked in one corner, and an assortment of Indian regalia—even a feathered ceremonial lance. Katherine didn't ask the origin of this conglomeration; she knew, she was in a den of thieves. Alva led her through the kitchen, resplendent with another fireplace, but also an iron range. A big black pot was resting on top of it, its lid gently rattling; Katherine hesitantly lifted it and peeked in—a bubbling stew of some kind, a meaty smell, spiced with sage and pepper.

"Over here," Alva said, grinning. He was standing in front of a newly installed door, one made of planked, unfinished pine. Cocking his head, he rapped smartly on the door, stood back, and in a melodious, feminine voice, answered himself. "Please, come in." Alva pushed the door, and without so much as a squeak, it swung open into a bedroom, a bedroom filled with the fragrance of fresh pine. There was a new bed with a brass headboard; it was unmade, but cotton sheets and a colorful quilt were neatly arranged at the bottom of it. Buford Reasons looked at Katherine and smiled. "Alva and me built this," he said proudly. "We're calling it the guest room, and you being our first guest, I reckon it's all yours . . . so long as you want to visit, and anytime you're wanting a place to bed down." He pointed to the bed. "That's a real mattress. Ain't no damn hay in it either."

Katherine Coltrane stood between the two men; she put an arm around each of them, alternately looking into their smiling, bearded faces. "Everything is so nice," she said. "I don't know exactly what to say, only that you've made me very happy."

"Nothin' more than you'd be doing for us," Alva Tompkins said. "Ain't a woman in the land as good as you, and we ain't ones to be forgetting friends."

"Well," declared Buford with a cackle, "we just plain and simple ain't got many friends, Miss Kate. Been bucking the wind most of our goddamned lives till you came along, people shucking us off like blowflies, always staying upwind feared we're gonna blow some stink their way."

"Two rascals," she smiled. "I love you both."

Buford held up his hands and protested gently, "Now, don't you go getting all sentimental-like. You just get yourself all rested up for a couple of days, and we'll give you a hand with those homesteads, get 'em all sorted out for you. Shoot fire, woman, we're gonna be neighbors, least anyways as long as you hang 'round the Chugwater."

"I'll need some help."

"Well, we figured that, all right," Alva said. "But what we ain't figured, is what you're gonna do with all that land. You got some notion about it?"

"No, not precisely," Katherine replied. She said Frawley had given her a small map with the deeds showing the claim locations in relation to the Chugwater River. She didn't know much about it, but it appeared that Porter Webb had staked them out strategically on both sides of the river, several extending to the east toward Sybille Creek, and one of the parcels had a cold-water spring marked on it.

"I'll have to check with Porter," she finally said. "Lay out some plans . . . maybe a building or two, something. Speculation. Frawley said there's no way the railroad can get through the valley without crossing our property somewhere, and if those people try to swing around it, it's going to cost them a fortune. If they're homesteads, we have to do something with them. Make a farm, till some land. Something."

"You ain't no sodbuster, Kate," Alva said.

"You're not any hotel operator either," she returned.

"I'm a hotel owner, by gawd!"

"Yes, so I discovered. Why in heaven's name did you buy that place?"

Alva grinned down at her. "Like you said, speculation. Some of those big-shot railroaders are gonna need a place to stay one of these days, people coming and going like piss ants. Might be more money there than meets the eye."

Buford threw back his head and guffawed. "He's a damn liar, Kate. He bought that hotel for you. Yep, that's what he had in mind. Said when all the ruckus starts down there, a smart woman like you can make a fortune off'n those dumb nutcrackers."

Katherine smiled up at Alva. "Is that what you said? You want me to turn that place into a fancy house for you?"

With a weak grin, Alva replied, "Aw, that was just a notion, that's all. Crazy talk. Naw, it's a place where you can stay right close when you're down this way. Fact is, you can do what you want with it."

"And stay right close to you two, at the same time, I suppose?"

"Hell, ain't no harm in that either." Alva grinned. "I was thinking, one of these days that ol' Sitting Bull's gonna come down out of Canada, and you can fetch that little girl back, maybe make yourself a right good living here in Chugwater. Fix up that hotel and saloon to a fair-thee-well. Hells bells, you can't stay in that Red Bird place forever."

Katherine sighed sadly, "The Red Bird burned to the ground five days ago. Your old friend, Calamity Jane was sleeping off a drunk in one of the rooms. She helped us get out of the place, maybe even saved a life or two, including mine."

Buford Reasons, scratching up under his bandanna, emitted a low whistle. "Good gawd'a mighty!" Alva just shook his head and muttered to himself.

"So," concluded Katherine, "I'm out of a job for a while. I'm not going back to Deadwood ... not until some news comes down from Canada about the Hunkpapa. I'll stay here for a while, get my business done in Cheyenne, maybe even help out Luther and Maybelle down at the Star if things get busy." She looked up at Alva curiously. "Say, what kind of wages you paying, Alva? Not counting what I could make on the side."

Alva Tompkins was silently stunned. The good Lord had delivered the fairest woman in the land to his doorstep; she was no longer poor, no longer destitute, but here she was, the tallest, most beautiful lady in the Wyoming territory asking him for wages. And that Buford had called him crazy for buying the Star! Why, in the presence of Kate Coltrane, the damn place already had paid for itself. He said boldly, "You take fifty percent, and as long as Luther and Maybelle want to hang on, I reckon they can have the other fifty."

"My gracious!" exclaimed Katherine. "What about you? You own the place."

"Kate, you know me. I don't give a hang about money, just the fun of getting it, that's all." Katherine said she would think about his proposition.

Buford Reasons took her by the hand; he wanted to show off the rest of their two homesteads. They went out the back door of the new bedroom and here was a shed, inside a stand with a basin and pitcher, a big tub, and a pipe with a spigot on the end of it. The pipe disappeared through a hole in the wall. Alva pointed to the distant creek where it terminated. This was his idea of running water. To the side of the meadow she saw a big log barn, corrals, and a few horses and mules. On the other side of the kitchen facing north was a cellar. Buford pulled up the door and a cool rush of air enveloped Katherine; she stepped down and peered into the dimness, and could hardly believe her eyes. Mercy, this was amazing! Tinned foods, cans of every size, jars and bottles, were stacked high on three sides, enough to feed an army, and upon closer inspection, Katherine discovered this was exactly where most of it had been purloined—the U. S. Army.

At another small shed hidden in the pines, Buford Reasons showed her his pride and joy. First, asking Katherine to close her eyes, he stepped nimbly by her and swung open the door. She heard a swish of something being removed, like a tarp or a piece of canvas, and when Buford finally told her to look, she did; she was staring directly into the muzzle of a small cannon. It was an eight-pound howitzer mounted on wheels, and to the side of it, a ramrod, four black balls, and a small, wooden box of black powder.

"Oh, mercy . . . oh, my gracious!"

"Pretty little devil, ain't she?" Buford said admiringly.

In utter disbelief, Katherine sighed, "Oh, yes."

"There she was, sitting all alone outside Laramie one night," Buford explained. Katherine gasped and stared at the men. They were grinning like two possums in a sorghum pail. "How . . . how did you get it out?"

"Well, now," replied Alva, "that was a chore in itself. Had to go down to the compound and steal a wagon, and getting that damn gun in the box, well, Buford threw out his back. Went limping around for a week like ol' Luther Hatch." Pointing to the ammunition, he said, "Took us a couple of months before we latched onto that stuff. Spent half of one night tinkering with a lock on one of the ordnance sheds."

"Why?" Katherine asked. "Whatever for? Whatever possessed you to steal a howitzer? And what the hell are you going to do with it?"

Buford puckered and shrugged and looked over at Alva. "Don't rightly know, Kate. We ain't figured that out yet.

Like Alva says, it's just the fun of getting it and, we take pride in our work, we do."

"Maybe we'll blow a hole in a bank somewhere," Alva joked. "Hells bells, maybe we'll hold up a stage with it. Scare the shit outta someone. Who knows? We're calling her LuLu. Little LuLu."

It was a warm night, so Katherine raised the window fully, and easily, too; it moved as though it had been oiled. After emptying her bathwater over the back doorsill, Katherine sat on the edge of the bed, a bed every bit as good as the ones Tim Frawley had bought for the Red Bird, but it took up almost half of the room. In expectation of Alva's arrival, for surely he would soon come calling to offer his sensuous worship, she unfastened her robe and began combing out her hair. Once finished, she took care of other little details—water in the basin on the commode, and extra towels draped over the chair next to the bed. She had just finished turning the lamp wick down to a faint glimmer when his soft knock came at the inside door.

Katherine smiled and, mimicking his afternoon call, she said, "Please, come in."

He did, laughing.

Katherine thought Alva had never looked more stalwart and handsome, his beard neatly trimmed, his arms sinewy and muscled, and his bare chest sparse of hair. He was a young man at heart, and in body, too.

He wore trousers, but no shoes.

After one long, adoring look at her, Alva said, "Expecting me, were you?"

Katherine placed her hands on his shoulders. Her damp forehead met his, and she replied in a low voice, "You devil."

"When I'm next to you like this, Kate, I feel like I must have curled up and died and woke up in heaven, 'cause for certain, ain't no one like you walking on God's green earth."

"Well," sighed Katherine, "I can't say that I've ever met anyone quite like you either . . . least, not one so blessed and knowing how to please a woman the way you do." And after this, Katherine Coltrane said nothing more.

Chapter Eleven

Confrontation

What a wonderful new day along the Bluegrass! The morning sun was brilliant, the surrounding hills breathing with the verdant life of midsummer. Katherine Coltrane, dressed in a white robe, her legs pulled up under her, was sitting on the porch bench, her hands around a cup of coffee. Buford Reasons was down below the creek turning out the stock into a lower meadow. Alva, dressed in faded blue denims, his eyes half-closed, was resting back in a chair, his boots propped up against the pole railing of the porch. Occasionally, his right eye would pop open to make a casual check on Katherine's well-being. For Katherine, the morning had been a leisurely one. She had slept late, bathed in a tub of warm water that Alva had kindly heated for her, eaten a breakfast of sourdough pancakes with Buford, and had taken a short walk in her bare feet through the damp meadow grass. She was so relaxed and happily content she decided to wait another day or two before riding back down to the valley to check on the new homesteads, and her future plans were no longer indefinite. After the night with Alva, she had made up her mind to help Luther and Maybelle at the Star; Alva and Buford agreed to assist in any work she decided to do on the homesteads, and if this entailed too much labor, she would find several hands and board them at the hotel. Also, there was no great rush to deposit her bank draft in Cheyenne. And she could ride over the hills to see Porter Webb and Joseph at any time. Katherine thought this was a practical, businesslike arrangement. So did Buford and Alva, particularly Alva, who knew, as well as Katherine did, that her decision had a pleasurable side to it, too. Admittedly, she now had no inclination to ride away so soon from something she had warmly anticipated so long. She remembered a saying, "what's good only deserves repeating." It was astonishing how he had overwhelmed her, this older man she had taken because of empathy and curiosity, and of course his gold. His adoration seemed as endless as her passion, and now it was more than his gold—it was because of the incredible satisfaction that he gave her. Katherine had to laugh about this. She and Alva were a perfect match in bed. If she were insatiable, so was he. Fate had brought them together on the prairie, she searching for Indians, Alva hiding from them.

Across the porch, Alva's eyes shifted toward her again. It was as if he were reading her mind, and with a little smirk, she said, "You devil, you, why do you keep looking at me that way? Are you getting some notions?"

Alva grinned sheepishly and looked away, gazed down the meadow where Buford was moving the stock. "I always get notions when I look at you, Kate, and I just have to keep checking . . . making certain those pretty long legs and white toes ain't skipping away to some fancy place down the trail. I'm counting my blessings. Ain't too much on the gospel you know, but I reckon the good Lord had something to do with setting you down on this porch."

"Oh, I think you had a great deal to do with it, too," she smiled. "Besides, my toes wouldn't run away. They like your kisses."

"Like it up here in the high country, do you?"

"You know I do."

"You make it a helluva lot prettier," Alva said. "I never knew how pretty this place was till I came out here and saw you sitting on that bench. You sorta blend right in with the whole shebang like all of this was meant for you."

"I'm very happy. You and Buford make me feel this way."

"Like me a little, then?"

Setting her cup aside, Katherine got up and went over beside him. She gently tousled his hair, kissed his forehead. She whispered, "I like you inside and out, Alva, your *wochangi,* your soul, your spirit. My Oglala sisters once told me that to see a man truly, one must look within." She gave his head a pat. "You have good *wochangi. Heya, siće, waon welo.*"

Looking up, he said, "If you was up to it, I thought you might like to take a little ride up the canyon a piece, cut up to the ridge, look over the country . . . nigh on to nine thousand feet up there. Fair day, you can see all the way to the big river. Got an extra saddle or two in the barn, and I can fit you out right proper."

Katherine pushed a finger against his nose. "Bought a saddle in Deadwood last time you were there, didn't you?" She laughed. "I thought it was kind of funny, you buying one instead of stealing one."

"Now, how in the hell did you know that?"

"Because, I rode that old McClellan you used to own. I rode it all the way from Deadwood down to Fort Robinson. The trip I made with Porter and Joseph. What's more, those two fools put that crooked thing on a stolen horse, a horse they had just sold the day before."

Alva chuckled. "Looks to me like those Deadwooders were the fools, letting those two anywhere near a herd of horses. Porter and that breed used to be the best two rustlers in the territory."

"Used to be?" Katherine asked. "Meaning, maybe, you and Buford are better?"

"Oh, no," Alva quietly protested. "No, siree bob. We do a little thieving now and then just for the hell of it, but not horses. No, we ain't into horses. That's hanging stuff." He nuzzled his nose in between her robe. "I always figured I'd rather die in bed than at the end of a rope."

"Well, you better stop this kissing right now, Mister Alva. If you don't watch out, you'll be riding me in bed instead of a horse up the canyon. Yes, and if it's nigh to nine thousand feet up there, as you say, you have to save your wind . . . at least until we get back."

Alva Tompkins stood up beside her, gave her a hug, and then shook himself like a big bear. "Damned if you ain't some kind of a special woman!"

Katherine was surprised by the immensity and diversity of the land, timbered draws of pine and fir, hillsides splashed with juniper, outcroppings of weathered rock, and always the grassy slopes and ubiquitous clumps of sage. From this high lookout on the ridge, the small creeks and streams coursing down through green bottoms far below appeared to be no more than shimmering strands of silver thread. There was water there, good grass in the bottom and in the sheltered draws, and tiny seeds of opportunity began to germinate in Katherine's fertile mind. She controlled some of that land down below, fourteen hundred acres of it; Alva and Buford's homesteads were near the top, and all of the range in between, from Sybille down to Richeau Creek, to whom did that belong? Open range, Alva told her, the government, the Territory of Wyoming. What did she have in mind? Well, just offhand, she didn't know, but Porter Webb knew all about these things; he owned a big spread over those distant hills to the east, and she had a notion that she should talk to him about the possibilities of cattle ranching, just how profitable such a venture might be. He had grazing rights on a lot of land.

Alva Tompkins was resting back against the trunk of a big fir chewing on a stem of grass, but this brought him upright and spitting. "What in tarnation you thinking, woman? You don't know a damn thing about raising critters. Hells bells, you don't even own one. Profitable, maybe, for those that knows, but most likely you'd lose your pretty silk panties trying a fool notion like that."

"Look here, Alva Tompkins, you don't give me much credit, do you? Besides, it's just a notion, that's all, and lately, I've been having lots of notions about spreading my blanket somewhere. One of these days, Julia . . ." and her voice trailed off.

"Notion was that you were going to spread it with Buford and me, down at the Star."

"Well, I am," she replied. "But, we have to do something with those homesteads, don't we? You said it yourself, I'm no sodbuster. And, whose idea was it to stake out those homesteads in the first place?"

"Looking to profit on rights-of-way, wasn't you?" retorted Alva. "You sure didn't have no other notions, guarantee you that."

"I do, now."

"Land o' living, Kate, ain't a fit notion for a lady like you . . . ain't a woman's work either."

Katherine whirled about, straddled him, and pinned his arms back. "Damn you, Alva, you know good and well I can do anything any man can do, and most of the time, a helluva lot better, too."

"Can't pee up a straight rope, can you?"

She bounced on him, and he winced. "Whoeee!"

"I'm going to look into it, Alva. Talk to Porter, see what he thinks. He could help. So could you. It'd keep you busy and out of trouble. If you don't watch out, someone's going to catch you and Buford pilfering. You'll end up in jail, and I'll end up having to take care of everything."

"I don't like critters," Alva said. "Contrary and onerous, worse than mules, they are. 'Sides, the way me and Buford been looking at it, you're gonna be looking after all our things one of these days, anyhow. We ain't got a lick of kin, y' know, and we sure as hell don't want no goddamned sodbuster moving in and taking over our land. They do that, y' know."

"Shhh!" Katherine said. She rested back on his lap and pressed a finger to his lips. "Don't you be talking such nonsense. We just might have a lot of work ahead of us. I'm depending on you two. Do you understand?"

"Oh, I reckon we ain't going no place right soon, but a feller has to look down the trail a piece. Life is short, Kate, and full of blisters, and me and Buford got our share of 'em. Just wanted you to know we figure you as a partner, now. You're one of us, and that's the way it's gonna be."

Katherine Coltrane pressed her forehead into his chest. She felt ashamed. So much generosity and love for the meager kindness she had given them on the trail more than two years ago. And her thoughts at that time had been tinged with avarice, how she could get her hands on more of that Lost Cabin mine gold. "You're too good to me," she muttered. "This isn't the way it was supposed to be. I came as I promised, to visit. Nothing else is necessary."

"You don't want to go in cahoots?"

"That's not it."

"Think we'd mess up your life?"

"It's already messed up." Katherine tucked him under his whiskered chin once and smiled. "You two have made it better, though."

"Well, there you are!" Alva exclaimed. "Until something better comes along . . . until you get your little Julia back, you just hang around the Chugwater and Bluegrass. Partners, damn it, Kate, and we'll all take care of each other right fair and square." He winked. "Got a notion it's going to be worth your while."

A deep roll of thunder suddenly sounded behind the rocky ridge, and Katherine stared down at Alva. "You think that's an omen?"

"No, ain't no omen. It's a fact. If we don't get moving down the trail, we're gonna get our asses wet."

Rain came that night, and after Alva left her bed, Katherine fell asleep listening to the steady downpour on the shakes overhead, but by morning when she peeked out the window, only a residue remained, puddles below the eaves, limp grass, and a buttermilk sky. Alva and Buford had decided they would make a day of it, staking out boundaries of the homesteads, so after breakfast, they tied on three saddle horses behind Katherine's buckboard, threw in her belongings, and headed down the ruts for Chugwater and the Star Hotel. It was mid-morning when they arrived. After a few pleasantries with Luther and Maybelle, they took three rooms upstairs, and a short time later were headed north up the river road, Katherine wearing her boots and denims, a drover's hat and her Plants forty-two tucked in a holster that Alva just happened to have stashed away in one of the corners among an assortment of other stolen goods.

Porter Webb had done his job well. The sack of new stakes Buford had brought along were only needed in several places along the Cottonwood and Alder bottom where a few markers were either missing or had been kicked away by stray cattle. With the aid of Tim Frawley's map, by mid-afternoon Katherine, Alva, and Buford had covered six of the eight homesteads; the plots were all connected, several joining both sides of the Chugwater. The final two extended from the bottom up to some tree-lined bench land where a nearby depression was ringed by a tall stand of aspen. Katherine reined up and quietly surveyed this bench and the huge shade trees scattered about its perimeter.

Buford Reasons, mounted to her right, pointed and said, "Call that spot Indian Wells . . . marked on your little map, 'spring,' but that's what they call it, Indian Wells. Years ago, Cheyenne used to camp around it making powwows, least that's the story. Good water, it is."

"A sacred place?"

"Wouldn't know about that. Not much sacred about water, is there?"

Katherine smiled across at him. "To the people I lived with everything was sacred, Buford, the land, the water, the sky, everything . . . sacred and respected."

"Amen," he said quietly.

And, after a long, second look at the bench, Katherine surprised the men. "That's where I'm going to build a home, right up there in those trees below the spring. A big house

... room for all of us, a long porch overlooking all of this down here."

"Why ... why," sputtered Alva, "why, you're joshing! You ain't needing a big place. Shoot fire, Katie, you already got yourself a hotel in town and our place up on the Bluegrass. Now, what kind of a crazy notion is this? I thought you were gonna talk to Porter about this, this infernal cattle thing."

Kicking ahead, Katherine shouted excitedly, "Let's go look."

"You're plumb daft," Buford shouted. "You go spending your money for a big ol' house, and you're not gonna have a cent left for critters."

"We'll borrow some," she laughed. "We'll get some seed from Porter."

"Bullshit!" exclaimed Alva, riding up beside her. "Last time we was that way, Porter didn't have more'n a hundred head or so on his range ... more horses than cows."

"I want my home up here," she replied. "Don't you understand? Everyone needs a home sometime. Rich men, poor men, beggar men, thieves. Even an orphan prostitute." Her face flushed, she pulled up in the green grass where a rivulet coursed down and disappeared in a little marsh. With Alva and Buford obediently following, she rode around it and on up to the tumble of gray rocks and crevices, the source, Indian Wells. Katherine happily cried, "Mercy, mercy, look at that lovely water!"

"Never cared much for water," Buford mumbled, " 'cept for washing."

"Look here," she said, pointing. "Why we wouldn't even have to dig a well, just bury a pipe and run it right down to the house, almost like up at your place."

"Gravity flow, they call it," Alva said dryly. He cocked his head, measuring the distance, scratched his whiskers once, and declared, "Figuring the slope, and about forty yards to the trees, I'd say we could put in a tank down there, cover it with a shed or a lid to keep out the bugs and bird shit, fix up one of those spigots inside, take it right into the kitchen."

Buford Reasons threw back his head and chortled. "By gawd, Alva, if you ain't the one! One minute you're calling Kate crazy as a bedbug, next thing you know, you've got her goddamned kitchen all built and watered. Man, you're a caution, you are!" He reined around and trotted toward the trees. "You call me when supper's ready," he shouted back.

"Man ain't got a lick of imagination," Alva grumbled.

After a drink at the spring, Katherine and Alva joined Buford in the shade of the cottonwoods by the river where they rested briefly and watched the northbound Cheyenne–Deadwood stage rattle by, this shortly followed by two riders coming up along the edge of the trail directly toward them. Buford swung his horse around for a better look, and promptly recognized one of the men—Matt Slaughter, the son of Jeb Slaughter owner of a ranch about eight miles down the river. Young Slaughter and his drover-partner, an older man with a black beard and wearing a broad-brim Texas-style hat, reined up a few yards away. Matt called Buford and Alva by their names. The men were searching for strays. The beginning of the brief conversation was cordial until young Slaughter noticed the sack of stakes hanging from Buford's pommel.

Nodding at the bundle, he said, "Damn it, Buford, we been seeing those markers off and on for a year. Thought it was the railroad people making survey. Now, I see it's you boys doing the marking. Just what the hell is going on, anyways?"

"Marking, I reckon," Buford replied.

"Marking what?"

"Property rights ... claims."

"Down here? Aw, for crisesakes, who you bulling?"

"All along here," Alva Tompkins cut in. "All the way to the bench yonder ... other side of the river, too. Fourteen hundred acres, in fact."

Matt Slaughter stared incredulously at his dark-haired companion, then back at Alva. "This is open range," he declared. "Ain't supposed to be sodbusters along here. We're running some of our stock up this way, you know that." He cocked his head and eyed the men curiously. "You for certain about this? My pa just might have something to say about it. Ain't another one of your jokes, is it? Now, come on, boys!"

"No joke."

"Well, who's claiming all this land? You sure as hell ain't. Farmers? Something sure smells fishy here."

Katherine Coltrane spoke up. "I'm claiming it."

Matt Slaughter, leaning forward in his saddle, took a long studied and curious look. "And, who might you be, Slim?" he finally asked.

"My name isn't Slim."

"You . . . why, you're a woman! What the hell?"

"That's right, mister. These aren't apples I'm wearing under my shirt."

Alva chuckled and said, "This is Kate Coltrane, your new neighbor, Matt. She's aiming to settle here, make herself a spread. You're sitting on her property right now, you know."

"I didn't know."

Katherine said crisply, "Well, you know now. I'll have some poles along here later to remind you, and maybe you can teach your critters to stay down below where they belong. I'm going to irrigate part of this bottom, grow some hay." This brought both Alva and Buford swinging around with blank looks. This was outrageous.

"But, ma'am, you can't do this," Slaughter declared. "You just can't close off the bottom and take all this water. We drive this way, taking stock to Cheyenne. We winter stock here, too."

"I've already done it," Katherine answered. "Your father can come up to Chugwater and talk things over anytime he chooses . . . run your cattle through here for another year, but come next summer, I'll be fencing my property down along here and up to the bench." She pointed to the bluff. "I'm building a house up there. And that land across Sybille and on up to Bluegrass. I have twelve thousand acres filed for grazing rights, too, all recorded on the books in Cheyenne, and I have an option to buy it." Katherine smiled at young Slaughter. "I think we'll be good neighbors, but I thought I'd better tell you this so there's no misunderstanding or trouble down the line."

The older man with Slaughter grunted once and spat to the side. "Trouble?" he snorted. "Woman, this most likely'll stick in Jeb's gullet like a chicken bone."

"Hells bells," Alva said, "Jeb has all of the Laramie forks country! How much does the ol' man need?"

Matt Slaughter said, "That's not the point. It's getting moved off what we been using for the last three or four years. Squatter's rights."

"I'll settle this with your father. I'm not looking for trouble."

"Can't promise that, miss," Matt Slaughter replied. "He's hard of hearing."

"Oh, I think he'll listen. I have my men around, too, you know."

Looking over at Alva and Buford, Slaughter scoffed, "Those two rusty buzzards! Come on, lady, now you *are* joshing."

Pointing her chin to the east, she answered, "No, over the hills there . . . Hawk Springs. I have a few men over there who don't take to talking too much."

"Hawk Springs? That's Webb's spread . . . Porter Webb."

"Yes." She smiled. "Porter Webb is my partner."

This ended the conversation. Slaughter wheeled about but paused long enough to shout back, "We'll just have to see about his, Miss Kay-Cee."

Watching them ride down the trail, Buford Reasons scratched under his faded bandanna and questioned curiously, "Kay-Cee? Called you Miss Kay-Cee?"

"Kay-Cee," Alva repeated. "Kate Coltrane . . . a *K* and a *C*, you ignoramus, her two marks." And then he said with a scowl, "Those scamps are gonna bear watching, Katie. Jeb is a cranky ol' fart."

Staring at the parting men, Katherine said pensively, "K-Bar-C. That's a pretty good brand, isn't it? We'll have to thank that young man one of these days. We'll register it in Cheyenne, too. The K-Bar-C Ranch, and every unmarked critter that wanders in here will get that scorched on its rear."

Alva Tompkins mopped at his forehead and grinned. "By gawd, Katie, you ain't only the best looking fillie-loo in the territory. You're the biggest damn liar, too. Porter . . . your partner! And twelve thousand acres! Grazing rights! Whooee, woman, what a stretcher! Why, that beats the hell outta anything me and ol' Buford ever did come up with. Yassir, you're some woman!"

Katherine winked at him. "Lay yourself down with a dog that has fleas, Alva, and you get up with fleas."

Chapter Twelve

A Box of Greenbacks

Excerpts from an interview with Henry Burlingame.

There were always rumors as to where Katherine got the money to start that operation in the Chugwater country. Well, it was a known fact that she received a rather handsome sum from the sale of her property in Cheyenne. It wasn't worth more than four thousand dollars, but some say she got three or four times that much for it. No question about it, she took the Colorado and Southern for another ride on those homesteads along the Chugwater River bottom, but Porter Webb was in on this, too. The last time I saw Jane Canarray she told me Katherine had been the recipient of a considerable sum of money from the sale of two placer claims in Deadwood. Well, Katherine never owned any claims. I know this. It was a matter of record. A few people pointed fingers at Alva Tompkins and Buford Reasons. These two drifters were only part-time miners. By reputation, they were two of the worst pirates in the West. They had several claims and some of Katherine's wealth could have come from the sale of these. She was friendly with the men, had befriended them on the trail during that horrid trip back from the Rosebud. She once told me that Buford and Alva felt indebted to her. What those claims were worth, she didn't say, but it must have been considerable. Joseph Brings Yellow told me that Katherine saw these two fellows frequently. They owned homesteads above her land on the Chugwater River.

Porter Longstreet Webb's first reaction was one of shock, and shock gave way to dismay. Shaking his head, he said deploringly, "I can't even see how you could get such a cockeyed idea. If I'd known you were setting to get your ass so deep in trouble, I'd never have staked out those damn parcels in the first place."

Katherine Coltrane, resting back in a chair on the porch of Porter's rambling log home, was staring down the length of her long legs at her dusty boots. She was twiddling her thumbs in her lap and not getting one bit of encouragement from her dear friend, Porter Webb. Joseph Brings Yellow was there, too, sitting below her on the steps. He was amused, but he understood the tenacity of Katherine Coltrane better than Porter did. Katherine finally said, "It was only a notion . . . a notion until we went up to that acreage along the bluffs, and that little draw where the springs come out."

Porter said, "That acreage was accidental, just to connect with the end ones along the river and tie up the bottom. The rails would have to make two switchbacks to get around on the left side where those springs are. They wouldn't even consider that land."

"I considered it," she smiled. "I took one look at it. I aim to build my house there. And then I got to thinking, I should do something with all that land down below, develop it, run some water through the fields, make hay, make it more valuable. I certainly don't want to sell it off to sodbusters and be looking down on a bunch of farmers the rest of my life."

"Now, what the hell can you do with a thousand acres or so all parceled out that way?" Porter asked.

"Control the bottom."

Exasperated, Porter sighed, "Damn it, I know that. I mean ranching. So, you get yourself a few hundred acres of hay, plus a helluva lot of work, and where do you range your stock?"

"Well, I thought all of the land in back of me. Those hills running across Sybille Creek and up to the Bluegrass would give me more than enough range." She wagged a finger at him. "You told me once that country was full of rocks and cheat grass. Well, I've ridden up through there twice now, and there's forage all over the place and plenty of water, too."

Porter Webb held up his hands defensively. "All right, all right, Kate, so there's plenty of range. So, you build a house, maybe a barn, a few sheds, some corrals, a bunkhouse. You build everything it's taken me almost ten years to build here.

Course, all of this takes money, and I haven't the slightest notion how you're going to come by it. But then, there's the matter of cattle, cattle which you don't have, and the matter of hired hands, which you don't have. For crisesakes, Kate, you don't even own a horse. Now, come on, woman, let's be realistic about this."

"I have two hired hands," Katherine retorted. "Alva and Buford. They're cutting poles right now to fence off the springs and the bluff, all the way down to the river."

"Those two geezers," huffed Porter Webb. "Lord, Lord, woman."

"They already have some ideas on the house, too."

Joseph Brings Yellow finally spoke. "They will help you make the lodge one day. The next day, they will steal it."

"They said you two were the best horse rustlers in the territory," Katherine returned with a little smile.

"Now, that's a bald-faced lie," countered Porter. "We haven't stolen a horse in years. Fact is, we've been selling horses to buy the goddamned cows we've been bringing in."

"You stole that horse I rode down to Fort Robinson."

"That was an exception."

Joseph Brings Yellow said, "It was a coup against the *wasichu*, who are the biggest thieves of all."

"Well," Katherine sighed with resignation, "you do have some good points about my ranch. I really thought you'd have some good ideas, too, to help me get this started instead of belittling me."

"Money," Porter answered with a long sigh. "Advice I have. Money, I don't have, and my advice is go back to Deadwood when that Frawley fellow rebuilds his hotel. Save the money you have for something more sane when you get your girl back."

"Money? Well, I figure you'll have three thousand dollars when the rights-of-way are finished. That should buy a few more cows for you, shouldn't it?"

"Three thousand? How do you figure that?"

Katherine Coltrane began explaining. Ivan Poindexter, a landowner near Horse Creek received four thousand from the Colorado and Southern for the rights to pass through his property. She thought that since Poindexter's holdings weren't as extensive as the ones she and Porter controlled, perhaps she could get six thousand from the railroad people. She knew how to bargain much better than men did. Oh, she was a sly one, Porter agreed, but he asked her where she got all of her information on the right-of-way transaction.

"At the hotel from Luther Hatch," she replied.

"The liveryman? . . . that Hatch?"

"Hotelman, too," she said. "He and Maybelle. And myself. We run the hotel now."

"You? You're setting up business? Oh, aw, not in Chugwater! And what the hell happened to Charlie Bigelow?"

Katherine Coltrane grinned. "You're not going to believe this, either one of you, but he sold the whole works for eight thousand and moved on to Cheyenne. He couldn't wait any longer for the railroad to come in. Alva Tompkins bought it. Alva can't stand the place, though, so he sort of turned it over to me."

Joseph seldom laughed, but he did, now. Tall Woman was a very clever woman. *"Hau, hau!"* he exclaimed.

Perplexed, Porter Webb frowned and asked, "Where in hell did Alva get the money to buy a hotel? Why, he and Buford never made an honest dollar in their lives. Those two pack rats never even had a job in their lives, not that I know about, anyway."

"They have a job," Joseph said. "They make wood for Miss Kate. Soon, they will make a house for her."

To Porter, Katherine replied, "I don't know where Alva got his money. I have a good idea, though. They had a couple of claims up above Gold Run Creek in Deadwood. They sold them a couple of years ago, so I just suppose—"

"Claims were probably worthless," mumbled Porter.

"Yes, that could very well be, but they did sell them." Katherine paused, then said, "Anyhow, I thought we could split the six thousand for the rights-of-way and use it to buy a few cows from one of the big spreads south of Cheyenne, maybe Colorado . . . herd them up here next spring or summer."

"Ah," smiled Porter Webb with a little glint in his eyes. "Yes, my lady, now I'm seeing your mind . . . me and a few of the boys driving up some seed cattle for you. Well, for your share, three thousand might get you forty or fifty cows at best, hardly worth the effort. Now, if we was to move a thousand head, that might be more profitable in the long haul of it."

"I have a couple of thousand dollars from Deadwood,"

she said. "I could pitch that in, and we could borrow some, couldn't we?"

Porter grinned and wagged a finger at her. "You're always saying 'we' and I'm trying awful hard not to hear you."

"Well, we are partners, aren't we? Sort of."

"Those four pieces of land don't mean a bean to me, Kate, only for what the railroad can pay. Sure, I can use that money, but once we split, you can have them ... like you say, make some hay fields out of them."

Katherine said hesitantly, "That Slaughter boy ... said he didn't think his father was going to like me fooling around with that bottom range land. I think he was wondering how I got so many homesteads ... legality, that sort of thing."

"I don't wonder," replied Porter. "Old Jeb is running up around a thousand or more head now. He used that bottom right regular."

"But, we own it."

"Like I said, as far as I'm concerned, it's your land. *You* own it."

"I just had the notion Slaughter might make some trouble."

"Well, work something out with him," suggested Porter. "Talk it over. Damn, you can talk an egg out of a rooster, anyhow."

"The boy ... Matt, said he didn't think his father would be interested in talking with a woman." She grinned mischievously and said, "I told him he could try talking with you, only, you weren't one for talking too much. I told him you were my partner."

"Oh, law, law, woman," moaned Porter Webb.

Joseph Brings Yellow chuckled.

Katherine stayed the night at the Circle-W spread, ate supper with the men and Porter's two hired hands, Jesse Talley and Hank Morrison, both young and both with peach-fuzz mustaches adorning their upper lips. They were fascinated by her beauty, her tall, willowy presence, and there wasn't a hint from either Porter or Joseph Brings Yellow how she had made her living for the past couple of years. She doubted if such a disclosure would make any difference one way or another, at least, to most of the men she had met, it didn't. There were exceptions—out of necessity she had destroyed young Lieutenant Clybourn's romantic interests at Goose Creek, and he had died with her name on his lips.

They all talked over the supper table in Porter's dining room, the young drovers, Jesse and Hank, ogling her, plying her with questions about her life with the Oglala, for in their short tenure on the range, they knew little about Indians, hostiles or friendlies. At dusk, there were a few last chores for the men. Charlie Lemm, the Chinese housekeeper and cook for Porter, heated two kettles of water for Katherine, and she bathed in a big tub on the back porch. There were two bedrooms in the ranch house: Joseph Brings Yellow graciously insisted that she use his for the night. He arranged a clean pallet for her, took his bedding, and went down to sleep in the bunkhouse with Jessie and Hank. All in all, it had been a very pleasant day and evening. Katherine dozed off listening to a new sound in the night, the occasional bawl of a cow searching about somewhere on the range for her calf. She thought she could become accustomed to that sound. She also felt the breath of little Julia against her cheek, and Julia was a thousand miles away.

Charlie Lemm, always smiling, always clad in a funny little black hat, made her a good breakfast the next morning. Porter ate with her, and though he hadn't acquiesced entirely to her ranching idea, he had mellowed somewhat, admitting that if any woman on the frontier were capable of such a venture, it was she. Indeed, she was a shrewd manipulator; she had determination, and a very good nose for money, but he didn't think she was going to make enough of it turning tricks in a watering hole like Chugwater. Katherine surprised him. She declared that her days of turning tricks were over.

Ready to make the long ride back over the trail to Chugwater, Katherine, her bundle across her shoulder, followed Porter out to the barn. Joseph Brings Yellow already had saddled a horse, only it wasn't the one she had borrowed from Alva. It was the same caramel-colored gelding that she had ridden down from Deadwood in the fall two years passed. Alva's black mare, fitted with a halter and lead rope, was standing alongside the gelding. Katherine stared at Porter. He smiled, and said with an offhand shrug. "Buck wanted to meet you again. I reckon he sorta took a shine to you."

Katherine replied, "You're a liar, but I love you. Thanks."

She reached up and kissed him. "Does this make us partners now?"

"Hell, no, 'cepting on the money from the rights-of-way."

"I owe you for Buck, then?"

"Didn't say that. The horse is a gift. I already got paid for this horse once, didn't I? Wouldn't be square to sell the damn thing twice now, would it? 'Sides, like I told you, it's pretty stupid starting up an outfit without even owning your own horse." Giving her backside a pat, he said, "Now, get moving before the heat catches up with you. Keep me posted on that railroad money, damn it."

Katherine mounted. Webb fastened her canvas bundle behind the saddle while she cinched a knot in the mare's lead rope to the pommel. It was then that she noticed a small wisp of grass braided around one of the bridle straps, and leaning across Buck's neck, she examined it more closely. Sweet grass. Only one person could have done this. As she turned away, Katherine Coltrane said, "Tell my Lakota brother, Joseph, that Tall Woman loves him, too."

Shortly after one o'clock in the afternoon, Katherine dismounted in front of the Star Hotel where she was promptly greeted by Luther Hatch, and after she slipped off her pack and exchanged a few words, Luther led her two horses to the nearby livery. Katherine, tired and thirsty, went through the hotel to the backyard. She drew a bucket of cold water from the well, first took a long drink, and then proceeded to douse the rest of the pail over her head. When she approached the kitchen, Maybelle, towel in hand, met her at the back door. By the time Luther returned, Katherine was half finished with a sandwich of sourdough bread and cheese, and was sipping cider. Luther's news was scant. Several railroad men had stopped briefly the previous afternoon at the little office building across the street where they unloaded a few items from a wagon. After supper in the hotel, they rode back to Cheyenne. Luther learned that they were planning to finish surveying south of town in another week or two, then would begin work to the north. At least three men would be taking rooms in the hotel for several weeks. When Katherine asked about names and offered a description of Stanley Howard, Luther simply gave her a negative nod. No, he hadn't heard that name, nor did either of the two men fit the description of Howard.

In other news, Alva Tompkins and Buford Reasons, tired of working on the jack fence at the Indian Wells property site, had ridden into Cheyenne earlier in the day to pick up a wagon load of supplies. What kind of supplies? Luther shrugged. By the time Katherine retired later in the evening, Alva and Buford had not made an appearance at the hotel, but by mid-morning the next day, the men did arrive—on their horses, and from the north, the opposite direction of Cheyenne. This was about fifteen minutes after the south-bound Cheyenne–Fort Laramie stage went through, and one of the station hands had brought Katherine a letter from Jason Armitage at Fort Robinson. In the letter, the general informed her that he was being transferred to Fort Abraham Lincoln within the month, and though it would put him far from the Lakota reservations to the south, he would be in a much better position to monitor news coming down the Missouri River on the activities of Sitting Bull and his followers in Canada. Armitage also disclosed that he had arranged for the dismissal of the contentious agent, J. J. Saville, at Red Cloud's Oglala agency. On this last bit of news, Katherine Coltrane offered a silent prayer of thanks, folded the letter, and slipped it in her back pocket. Saville hadn't been a servant or a friend of the proud Oglala.

Buford and Alva were happy to see Katherine again. It had been six days since they had last been together, and no, they hadn't been gallivanting around Cheyenne all night; they had ridden through Chugwater shortly after midnight, unloaded a few things at her home site, and had taken the freight wagon back to their cabin on the Bluegrass. Also, during the last few days the spring had been closed off and a pole fence erected the length of the flat below the bluff where she wanted to build her house. They reminded Katherine that all of this work was contrary to their usual routine. They also informed Katherine that they were now tired of working and were going to take a few days rest at the cabin, but not before they took her down the river to see what they had accomplished.

While Alva went to the livery corral to get Katherine's horse, Buford untied a gunnysack hanging from his saddle horn, and stepping lively back to the bench on the porch where Katherine was sitting, he carefully opened it and gave her a quick look. Had she been blindfolded, she would have known; the fragrance of fresh peaches wafted up and caressed her nose. The sack was half-full, and reaching in, she brought one out, sniffed it, and smiled. Why, the only peaches she had seen in years were the halves out of army cans. She exclaimed, "Where on earth did you get these! Mercy, just look at them!

Buford grinned. "Stole 'em, we did. Had a whole box when we left Cheyenne City, but damn, we got to feasting, and well, Alva says if we want Maybelle to make us some cobbler, we just better put some aside 'fore it's too late. Put 'em in a sack this morning, and brought 'em down."

"Stolen sweets?"

"Getting dark, it was," Buford explained. "We was in a hurry to get some things done. Couldn't wait till morning for the market to open, y'see. So, here's all these boxes on the rail siding, and while Alva's talking to this feller, I sorta sneaked around the back and snitched one."

"You rascals, well, did you buy anything?"

"We sure did. Two kegs of nails, strap iron. Sorta borrowed a tool or two we found lying around, yassir, and we borrowed those sweet peaches, too. You reckon Maybelle can make us some cobbler for supper?"

"Give me that sack," Katherine said with a smile. "If she can't make you some cobbler, I certainly will."

The jack fence extended along the bottom line from the cottonwoods up the bench and it enclosed the springs. An antelope could jump it, a horse could not; a deer could snake through it, a cow could not. Alva and Buford had done a good job. From the distance, she saw two large, erect, and freshly peeled lodgepoles, another spanning them at the top. It was a gateway! Surprised, she shouted gleefully and kicked Buck into a trot, and soon reined up in front of it, silently stared for several moments before breaking out in a wide grin. Alva and Buford were to either side of her, and they were grinning, too. A beautiful sign made out of two planks and held together by strap iron hung down from the ridgepole. It was slick and shiny from fresh varnish, and burned deeply into the wood at the top was "K-Bar-C Ranch." Below this, in huge, bold letters was the word "coltrane." Katherine was momentarily speechless, but Alva Tompkins wasn't.

"Makes it official, Katie. This is the beginning."

"Right damn pretty, ain't it?" Buford said.

"Oh, mercy, yes. It's a wonderful sign," and Katherine looked back and forth at each of them, then said, "So, this is what you were doing in Cheyenne!"

"And stealing us some peaches," grinned Buford.

Alva said, "We can do a lot of things, Katie, but we decided there was no way we could make one of these signs all professional-like. Luther couldn't do it, either, so we just skedaddled into town. Yassir, that's the size of it, I reckon."

Spitting to the side, then pointing his chin, Buford added, "All we need now is a house right up there aside the trees. Make your trail to the left, take a curve to the right, and you're right at the front porch."

"Put the sheds . . . a big ol' barn and some corrals over there on the right a'piece back from the house, downwind," Alva said.

"Yes . . . yes," sighed Katherine Coltrane. "It all fits so well. In time, I suppose, in due time. It all seems so far away . . . so much work to be done."

"Well," concluded Alva, "if being a tad touched helps any, I'd say you'll get it done, one way or another. Takes someone with the ol' Ned in him to try some fool thing like this." He gave her a sidelong glance. "Course, takes some savvy, too . . . brains, and you ain't short on that, either."

"Porter thinks it's nonsense, too, Alva."

"Doesn't doubt you can do it, I'll wager."

"No," she replied. "He knows I have enough money to start the building, getting some men up here to help us . . . carpenters, that sort of thing. But stocking the place . . . cattle, horses, turning a profit. Well, that's another thing, and he doesn't want to be a partner in it either."

"Can't blame him for that," opined Buford. "Man already has enough shit on his boots without coming over here and asking for more."

Katherine sighed again. "For openers, at least five hundred critters, Porter says. Down the line three or four years, two or three thousand. Mercy!"

"Well, hell's bells," exclaimed Alva, "it ain't something you're gonna be doing overnight, for crisesakes! I ain't ever seen this Rome place, but I'm always hearing it wasn't built in no day."

Buford Reasons chuckled. "Build yourself a herd that size, for certain, you're gonna need a passel of bulls, Kate."

Katherine stared up at the big sign again. "You two are so

nice to me, you know, always thoughtful. I appreciate this
very much."

"Well, go on and ride through," declared Buford. "You be
the first."

"And be sure you make like you're following the road to
the house," Alva said.

With Alva and Buford behind, Katherine rode through the
big gateway, took an angle to the left up the incline, circled
back to the right, and finally came to a halt in the shade of
the trees. Down below, a small cloud of dust fanning up behind it, the northbound Cheyenne–Deadwood stage suddenly
appeared on the road, the two men perched on the driver's
seat swaying back and forth in unison like stringed puppets.
It passed quickly and disappeared behind a line of cottonwoods, and Katherine said thoughtfully, "Deadwood. I'm
glad I'm not going back."

"Amen," Alva said. "I think me'n Buford better start getting some logs down here for the house. Don't hanker for
the work, y' know, but what the hell else we got to do?"

Buford Reasons, staring down at the murky trail, ran a
hand under his red bandanna, emitted a disdainful grunt,
then a sigh, and finally a long, conclusive, "Hmmm," as
though a revelation had been born out of the little dust cloud
hanging over the river bottom.

Alva gave him an inquisitive look. "Something ailing you,
Buford? You ain't coming down with the mokus, now, are
you?"

"Naw, I'm as fit as a fiddler's bitch, I am," he drawled.
"Just had a notion about that stage." He adjusted his bandanna and shrugged. "Just a crazy notion, I reckon. I was
just wondering to myself—"

"Well, spit it out, boy. Ain't no secrets among us, here, is
there?"

Katherine eyed him curiously. "What kind of notion,
Buford? What're you thinking?"

Buford grinned at them sheepishly. "Jest wondering how
much money they's packing in that box. Wondering if some
of that money would buy Kate some cows to put on this
place . . . sorta get her started."

"Judas priest!" exclaimed Alva Tompkins, recoiling in
horror. "You mean robbin' the goddamned stage! Man, man,
you have got the mokus, for sure. Why . . . why, we'd likely

get our asses shot off trying something like that! What a fool notion!"

Appalled, Katherine shook her head, saying, "Mercy, mercy, Buford!"

Buford puckered. "Well, like I said, it was just a crazy notion. That's one thing we ain't never done, you know ... heisting a stage, and I always sorta had a hankering to see what it was like. Oh, not so much for the ol' do-re-me, just the hell of it, that's all. But, now, seeing Kate could use some of that loot ... well, it just went and struck me, and I says to myself, there goes a big herd of cows in that goddamn stage, and all we have to do is help ourselves."

"Whoeee! Why, you're a regular caution! 'Sides, might be no more'n a few hundred bucks in the box. Who know? And I ain't one to be fixing to get myself shot for that, I'll tell you." Alva gave Buford a look of disgust, puckered his tongue several times, and said, "Come on, let's get the hell back to town ... see if Maybelle's making that cobbler."

"You're thinking about your consarned belly, and I'm thinking about money."

Alva kicked away. "I can't think about things like this on an empty belly, Buford, and that's a fact. Fact is, I don't even want to think about it, riles my belly, it does."

Katherine Coltrane fell into a muse and rode in between the two men. When they neared the bottom, she finally said, "There are two boxes, Buford, and I recollect that every Monday, a supply of scrip goes up to Deadwood for those squatters and the mining companies, trading in their illegal gold. This is what I remember.

With a cocked eye, Alva stared across at her. "Illegal? Well, damn it, it ain't legal robbing a stage, is it?"

"Tit for tat," said Katherine.

Alva asked, "How in hell do you know about the boxes?"

Katherine explained that when she was in Cheyenne negotiating the sale of her house, she frequently stopped by the stage station and chatted with the assistant manager, a man by the name of Rolly Anderson. Rolly Anderson liked her and felt sorry for her because the Indians had killed her brother and destroyed the Coltrane freighting business. She learned a lot about the stage operation from Mister Anderson, and she was very observant.

"Whoa!" Alva suddenly called out. Holding up a hand, he eyed Katherine warily. "Now, wait a minute, here. You ain't catching the mokus from Buford, are you? You ain't letting that sucker put those crazy notions in your head, too, are you?"

"No," Katherine replied. "No, robbing a stage is very serious business. As you say, it would be pretty stupid to get shot over a few measly pieces of gold . . . a box that was practically empty . . . or if those drivers threw down a dummy box and then rode away with the good one. No, that would be very foolish and stupid, a bad risk."

Buford Reasons leaned forward in his saddle and asked, "What day is this? Lately, all this damn work, I done lost track of the days. Saturday, mebee? . . . Sunday?"

"Saturday, I figure," Alva said.

"Saturday," confirmed Katherine.

"Two days till payday," said Buford.

"Hell's bells, will you stop it!" growled Alva.

"You ain't even considered my notion!"

"No, sir, and I ain't likely, too, either. If I didn't know better, I'd swear you been on the goddamn rye again."

"Boys, boys," implored Katherine.

"Oh, great day, great day!" Buford suddenly shouted. He whirled about, dancing his horse sideways. "I got it, Kate, I got it! All the time I knew the good Lord was just waiting for the proper time to give me The Word, and glory be, this must be it! Oh yes, let there be light, let there be light!"

"He's gone daft, Katie. I told you about him, how he's taken to fits, sometimes, like a dog with the tempers, chasing himself in circles."

"Our cannon!" cried Buford gleefully. "Little Lulu!"

Alva's brow hiked. "Little Lulu?"

"Boom!" shouted Buford Reasons. "Boom! Right down the trail a ways, right in the middle of the trail. Scare the shit right outta them! Boom!"

"Incredible!" Katherine exclaimed. "Do you really think it would work?"

"Crazy, that's what," put in Alva. "Never heard of such a crazy notion in all my born life."

"But, will it work?" asked Katherine, staring at Alva.

Alva Tompkins poked his hat back with his forefinger, looked first at Katherine, then over at Buford. Finally, a small grin began to curl up under his mustache. "Well, like Buford says, it'll scare the shit outta them, for certain, it will."

* * *

Katherine Coltrane didn't have to make peach cobbler. Maybelle Hatch had baked three big pans of it, and she served it in heaping bowls at the evening meal along with a pitcher of fresh milk, milk that came up every other day on Darrell Blankenship's produce run from Cheyenne. Three mule skinners enroute to Fort Laramie with a load of staples, and several Chugwater locals, dined in the hotel that evening and shared in the fresh peach delicacy. By dusk, Katherine had a few belongings lashed behind her saddle and was headed for the Bluegrass with Buford and Alva.

They had important plans to discuss for a very dangerous game, a bold, daylight robbery of the Cheyenne–Deadwood stage. Every time Katherine thought about it, she felt the cobbler in her stomach curdling. She was frightened. Alva, fearful of Katherine's welfare and participation, was cautiously optimistic, but Buford, beset with anxiety and a nagging urge to fire the cannon, radiated confidence. He envisioned the planned holdup as one of historic proportions. He had been kicked about on the frontier all of his life, and now he was going to retaliate in grand fashion, with a stolen, eight-pound army howitzer. Buford Reasons felt like crowing; he was the highest stepping rooster in the henhouse, an old rooster, albeit a proud one, for after all, this was his idea.

It was dark by the time they reached the big cabin, and while Buford set about taking care of the stock, Katherine lit the lanterns and Alva kindled a fire in the kitchen range to make coffee and heat a few kettles of hot water. Several hours later, Buford's resonant snore was floating across the parlor into the kitchen.

The next morning, seated together on the front porch drinking black coffee, Katherine and her two partners completed their plans for the activities of the night and next day, with an alternative strategy in case of mishap.

It was a long day on the Bluegrass for Katherine, who relived her life and all of its bizarre twists and turns a dozen times before nightfall. She watched in awe at the ingenuity of Alva and Buford as they lashed the howitzer's tongue to a single tree, securely extending ropes from the rings to their saddle horns. Another rope was double hitched around the muzzle, this trailed back to Katherine's horse as a security measure to assure control of the gun on the steeper part of the descent.

In the dark of night, they made the trip down to the Chugwater Trail without any problems, and in a brushy draw on the west side of the river, they hid the cannon and its ordnance equipment. This site, selected by Buford, was within ten yards of a rock-strewn gully in the trail, an area usually ankle-deep in water during the spring runoff. Here the howitzer, he, and Alva would be stationed. The cottonwood grove about thirty yards away from the gully had been selected as Katherine's position, and at the proper time when she emerged, she would be fully masked wearing a tattered hat, a duster, and riding an unbranded mule. Satisfied that nothing had been left undone, the trio backtracked and spent several hours obliterating any trace of wheel marks made by the howitzer, finally getting into bed after midnight.

The early morning hours on Monday dragged tediously. Anxiety reined again. Toward afternoon, Buford finally brought down two saddle horses and a mule from the barn; Alva carefully checked all of the rifles, and then, clad in an assortment of tattered clothing, the three roadsters hit the trail for the Chugwater River. Step-by-step, all the way to the river trail, Katherine repeatedly rehearsed her part in the bizarre plot.

After a few wishes of good luck, a kiss from both of the men, Katherine took up her position in the cottonwoods where she could watch the little road coming down from Chugwater. Her visibility was unobstructed for almost a quarter of a mile, and after about a half hour wait, she saw the stage approaching. After a shrill scream to alert Alva and Buford, she pulled down her floppy hat, adjusted the big blue bandanna until it covered all of her face but her eyes, mounted the mule, and last, she checked her Plants pistol and cocked her rifle. She was ready. Down below, Alva and Buford, both masked, had wheeled the cannon around in the middle of the road, Buford standing to one side with a fire brand, Alva on the other, holding a white flag in one hand and a rifle in the other. The menacing howitzer, leveled at the rear by a piece of log, was pointing directly up the trail.

Suddenly, almost before Katherine realized it, the stage was trundling alongside her, the driver rearing back on the reins and shouting, his armed companion swinging a shotgun into play, then lowering it and leaping clear of his seat.

Katherine heard one of the men cry out, "Everybody out! Some fool's getting ready to blow this rig to kingdom come!" She saw a passenger clambering out of the stage onto the rocks on the other side of the road.

As Katherine trotted her mule out from the cottonwoods she shouted, "Everybody just sit . . . hold it still! They're not going to touch off that howitzer unless you put up a fuss about this. Throw the box down." Pointing her Winchester at the other man she ordered him to get rid of the shotgun. He set the gun aside, put his hands up and stepped away.

From high atop the coach, a box came flying down, landing only a few feet from the mule. "You got it, young feller," the man said.

Katherine laughed nervously and called back, "One more, mister, come on. Toss the other one down, now . . . the real one. Hurry up, before my partners down there get impatient."

The second box landed near the first one, and at this point, Katherine aimed her rifle directly at the driver, saying, "Well-done, men, well-done. All right, now, everyone aboard. Move out, and hold on to your seats. He's going to set that cannon off as soon as you get clear."

After a snap of the reins, the coach lurched ahead, and Katherine, moving out to the middle of the road, watched as it approached Alva and Buford while the driver cautiously edged around their position. Then, with the four horses in a gallop, the stage began to pick up speed. She saw her two companions turn the cannon; Alva covered his ears; Buford set off the charge; the explosion was a resounding one. Katherine's mule bucked once, almost throwing her, but she recovered in time to see a small black blur sailing across the horizon, and startled birds were cascading out of the trees around her, flying in all directions. Down below, Buford was screaming joyously, and leaping up and down beside the smoking cannon.

Minutes later, up in a forested draw above Sybille Creek, the men broke open the two boxes, one almost empty, the other one filled with greenbacks. They didn't take time to count the money, but emptied it into the gunnysack Buford had used earlier to carry the stolen peaches. Later Katherine carefully sorted them out, one by one, on the table in the parlor of the cabin. Alva stretched out on his bunk, chuckling to himself, Buford was on the front porch drinking whiskey. They were two happy coots, just happy to be alive back in the sanctuary of their cabin, happy to be in the company of Katherine Coltrane, who, in their minds, just happened to be the greatest woman who had ever set a foot on the frontier.

Ultimately, Katherine shouted to the sky, "Fifty-two thousand!"

From the porch: "Hallelujah!"

From Alva's bunk: "Buy yourself a lotta cow shit with that, Katie."

"Oh, mercy!" Staring nervously at the open doorway, Katherine began stuffing the money back into the sack. "We have to find a place to stash this," she said. "Can't just go throwing this in a corner somewhere."

"No, can't do that." Alva laughed. "Not when the woods are full of thieves."

"Where?" she asked.

Turning on the bunk, Alva grinned over at her. "Secret place, I reckon. Mebee like in the wash shed? Where you sit your pretty ass in that tin tub . . ."

"Alva!"

Alva rested back again, clasped his hands behind his head, and said, "Well, you just go look under that tub. Pull up two of those boards. Couple of tin boxes in a hole. Just shove that sack in there. Safe enough, I reckon."

As Alva had said, under two loose boards, down in a deep recess, lay several metal boxes, and a canvas bag. First, she hoisted out the bag, a very heavy bag cinched at the top with rawhide. She was curious, but she refrained from looking inside it; she knew by its weight, by feeling the bulges what it contained—gold. Mercy! Katherine's heart began to pound. She carefully pulled up the first tin box, also quite heavy, and lifted the lid. Oh, lordy! It was partially filled with coins and scrip of every description. She couldn't calculate how much money was in the box, several thousand dollars, at least! The remaining box was much lighter, and inside she found several papers neatly folded. These were the property deeds, but at the bottom were several stacks of greenbacks. They were hundred-dollar bills! Katherine Coltrane felt her knees trembling. She hastily emptied out the stage money into the last tin box, shoved the second one back in place, and pushed the canvas bag on top of them. Next, the boards went back, then the tub.

Confronting Alva Tompkins back in the parlor, she whispered harshly, "Are you sleeping, you rascal?"

"Sorta dozing, I reckon," he mumbled.

"Why didn't you tell me about all that damn money in the shed? You could have loaned me some . . . enough to get started."

Alva cocked one eye open and stared over at her. He replied drowsily, "We thought about that, all right, Katie, we sure did. But, then you see, well, what the hell, it would have spoilt all of Buford's fun. The ol' boy had his heart plumb set on shooting off Little Lulu." Alva sighed. "By tonight, he's gonna be on one of them crying jags having to give the goddamned thing up. Can't have it 'round here anymore, y'know."

"Well, that's a relief."

"A pity, it is."

"Someone will find it and tell the army."

Alva came up on an elbow. "I was thinking mebee about you 'n me riding down there tonight . . . just to take a look. By tomorrow, most likely some deputy from Cheyenne will be snooping 'round. Ol' Buford won't be in no shape to go, but we could lash onto that thing and drag it down the trail a'piece."

"Good heavens, whatever for!"

"Jeb Slaughter. The ol' man has a hay shed 'bout four miles down. I just had a notion we could park that cannon there . . . let him explain to the law how it got all tangled up in his hay."

Katherine came over and glared down at him. "We'll do no such thing, Alva Tompkins, not tonight."

"You got a better idea?"

"I surely do."

Alva grinned. "I figured you did."

It was late Tuesday afternoon by the time Katherine returned to the little community of Chugwater. She rode directly to Luther Hatch's livery, turned Buck to pasture, and headed for the back door of the Star Hotel only to be met by a flustered Maybelle Hatch, who began spilling out a bizarre story about a robbery of the Cheyenne-Deadwood stage. All day she had been serving extra meals to men arriving from Cheyenne to investigate the daring holdup—several territorial deputies, two newspaper writers, a bank official, and a few curious citizens who had wandered in off the street to partake in the excitement. One of the lawmen, a newly appointed U. S. marshal in Cheyenne, had rented a room in the hotel. Katherine, feeling a quickening of her pulse, put her canvas bundle aside, donned an apron, and busied herself washing the dishes that had stacked up on the long table. A short time later, Luther Hatch, poking his head into the kitchen to call out another meal order, saw Katherine for the first time. He immediately came in and added more to what Maybelle had already told her. He said that it was the damnedest thing anyone had ever heard of. A gang of men held up the stage with a cannon, and they had even tried to shoot the coach after robbing it! Katherine knew this was absolutely untrue; Buford and Alva had purposely elevated that round; the ball had sped far above the stage, well out of harm's way.

Apparently, from what Luther reported, news of the robbery had gone by telegraph from Fort Laramie to Cheyenne late the previous day, and it was already quite obvious that the reports had been embellished—the coach had been surrounded on both sides; one bandit, armed to the teeth, had chased several passengers out of the stage and had threatened to shoot them, and the perpetrators undoubtedly were experienced road agents with full knowledge that the stage was carrying two money boxes. All in all, it was a very professional job; the only clue left behind was the army cannon, and it was rather a useless one because at this point in the preliminary investigation, no one knew anything about a missing cannon. One of the deputies had just left with a team of horses to retrieve the howitzer. Luther, shaking his head, went back to the front of the hotel, and Katherine, with a fretful sigh, continued washing dishes. Experienced road agents, indeed! Mercy, two old men and a woman! She touched the back of her hand to her damp forehead, but thinking of Alva and Buford, she had to smile. They would howl when they heard this story.

For the rest of the day, Katherine kept her ears attuned to the gossip in the restaurant and bar. One of the deputies had found a multitude of tracks along the Chugwater bottom, including marks from the howitzer's wheels, but all of the signs ended in a rocky draw, obviously the place where the bandits had hidden the gun prior to the holdup. One lawman and the two writers returned to Cheyenne that night; the

U. S. marshal planned to form a small posse and continue the investigation the next day.

But in the morning, the sky was a dirty gray and rain was coming down. The marshal sat at a table under a lantern, glumly watching the water drip from the porch eaves, and not another man was in sight. After a while, Katherine took a pot of coffee and another cup with her, and went to the table. She refilled his, poured one for herself, and sat down opposite him. Katherine thought he must be in his early thirties. His name was Jake Cardwell. He had the usual flowing mustache, but at the moment, there wasn't a trace of a smile hiding under it. He had his jacket collar turned up hiding his long hair, and his big hat was on the table beside his cup. He had already seen Katherine working in the hotel when he had returned from the river road last night. She was part of the staff, the prettiest part, and Jake Cardwell welcomed her company to help brighten this very miserable morning. His investigation, he told her, was at a dead end, and the incessant rain, more than just a thunderstorm, had made matters worse. With such inclement weather, he couldn't recruit any men to help him, and even if he did, finding tracks, much less following them, was problematic. He had done all that he could in Chugwater, and as soon as the rain subsided, he was riding back to Cheyenne. Trying to make the best out of a poor situation, Jake Cardwell finally grinned and said, "They'll be talking about this one for a long, long time. A cannon. Damn hard to believe, I'll tell you. I couldn't believe it until I saw that thing sitting there in the middle of the trail."

Katherine grinned back at him. "Soldiers, maybe," she suggested. "Deserters looking to make a stake and get back home."

"Well, they got a damn good stake," Cardwell replied. "Over fifty thousand, the bank man says, if they were soldiers. No, the operation was too clever. These boys picked just the right spot to do the job, and they knew what that stage was carrying, but now in the hell they stole that cannon puzzles me. Has to be from one of the forts. And someone had to freight it up the Chugwater. All of this is a lot of trouble, and I just get the notion, it was planned to be one helluva joke as well as a holdup."

"The bankers in Cheyenne and Deadwood won't think it's very funny," opined Katherine. "Somewhere, there's some celebrating going on, though ... five or six men, jolly fellows, splitting up all that swag. Mercy, fifty thousand!"

Jake Cardwell smiled. "Yep, and that's about all I have left to go on, the celebrating, a fifty-fifty chance. These boys always run the same pattern ... either they den up like prairie dogs for a couple of weeks, or they go off on a toot of drinking, gambling, and whoring. Tip their hands damn quick that way sometimes, and we've got the word out already. Deputies will have their eyes and ears working every saloon and hog ranch in the area for the next couple of weeks, watching and smelling for new greenbacks."

Katherine said, "I thought you said these robbers were clever?"

Jake Cardwell sipped, and set his coffee mug back beside his hat, and with a very faint smile replied, "Beggin' your pardon, Miss Coltrane, but when a man gets himself liquored up and some dove goes sitting on his lap, she gets prettier and prettier, and the first thing you know, the man isn't so clever anymore. He sorta just has one thing on his mind, and he tends to get careless ... forgets, if you know what I mean."

"Oh, mercy!" Katherine exclaimed quietly. "You mean—?"

"Yep, he either lays his money on the card table or the bed, and that's where some smart sheriff or a deputy, even a bounty hunter, comes to the party. Every gambler and whore knows the smell of fresh money."

"Reward?"

"The bank man says probably five thousand for this job. Shoot, most people around in this country would sell their souls to the devil for that kind of money."

"Heavens, this is a very nasty business, Mister Cardwell!"

"Yep," the marshal agreed. "Lot of nasty people in the territory all looking for the same thing—money, the easy way."

Toward noon, the rain dissipated and the heavy clouds drifted across the foothills toward Hawk Springs. A fuzzy sun began to appear through the ragged mists. Katherine had planned to ride into Cheyenne with the produce man, Darrell Blankenship, on his return trip to the city, but since she thought she would have some use of a horse during her day or two of business, she elected to accompany the marshal, Jake Cardwell. While she saw some ironic humor in this, there also was some practicality in it. After all, she valued his protection; she was carrying her Wells Fargo deposit draft of four thousand dollars, and another three hundred in cash, the latter which she intended to use to cover her expenses and buy a few new clothes.

Luther Hatch brought Buck around to the front of the hotel and lashed on her belongings behind the saddle. It was something of a surprise to Jake Cardwell, who was waiting on the porch, when Katherine appeared wearing her riding boots, long pants, a denim jacket, and a drover's hat, the brim nattily curled up on both sides, more so when he saw the Plants forty-two neatly tucked into a holster on her hip. He made only one casual inquiry, though—did she know how to use a revolver? She assured him that she did, and what with road agents and scoundrels about, she thought it wise and entirely proper for a woman to be packing a gun. Jake Cardwell only smiled; Katherine Coltrane was quite a lady. They kicked off in a brisk trot, and soon passed the wagon of Darrell Blankenship, and later down the road, paused briefly to watch the northbound Cheyenne–Deadwood stage go by. Katherine noted with a small smile that an extra rider with a rifle resting in his lap was atop the coach with the baggage. Chatting most of the way, Katherine and Jake Cardwell made it into Cheyenne shortly before three o'clock, and after getting a stall for Buck at Jed Bollinger's livery and freight depot, and renewing old friendships with Jed for five minutes, she toted her bundle and trudged away to find lodging. The Palace was still the best hotel in town, and despite her trail-riding attire, she knew that she was an attractive, imposing woman. She told the desk attendant that she was in Cheyenne on business, at least for two days, and signed the register with a flourish. When she paid for her room with a crisp hundred-dollar bill, the clerk, Delbert Finney, didn't bat an eyelash. He did, however, stash the bill at the back of his cash box. This greenback was fresh, obviously uncirculated, and Delbert Finney always had an eye out for the unusual.

Katherine visited her room only long enough to stow her bundle, wash her face, and run a comb through her long hair. Within the next hour she visited the bank, Dooling's Millinery and Fashion Shop, and Cowhick's Mercantile. She purchased several blouses, some silk underwear, and a smart ankle-length maroon skirt and matching jacket. She also bought a pair of high-button shoes, not the color she wanted, but the only slippers that fit her slender, long feet. Satisfied she had done her best in such a short time, Katherine returned to the hotel. It was almost six o'clock. She had only an hour to prepare herself for dinner in the fancy Palace dining room.

A few minutes before seven o'clock, Jake Cardwell, attired in a white shirt, black string tie, and suit coat, appeared at Delbert Finney's registration counter in the hotel. This wasn't his customary way of dressing, and it took a moment for Finney to recognize the marshal. "Well now, Jake," Finney said with a smile, "never saw you so all spiffed up, but let me tell you, this is a coincidence because it's going to save me a walk over to your office. I've been thinking about you. Have something I want to show you."

Jake Cardwell groaned. "Business?"

"I'd say so."

"Damn, Delbert, can't it wait until the morning? Can't you see I'm taking the night off?"

"Ah, yes. All slickered up, you are." Finney grinned, pulled out the cash drawer behind the counter and held a hundred-dollar banknote under his nose. He wafted it back and forth several times. "Nothing like the smell of new scrip, Jake. Look at this. Some woman named Coltrane checked in here several hours ago. Gave me this. Coltrane. Said she's on business here for a couple of days. Interesting, isn't it?"

"The money or her business?" Jake Cardwell asked dryly. He took the new bill, momentarily studied both sides of it, then handed it back.

Finney's brows hiked. "Now, where do you think something this fresh came from?"

"Government mint, I reckon."

"Aw, come on, Jake! Newspaper says those stage robbers got a whole box full of these." Delbert Finney shut the cash drawer and said, "Since you been chasing around the Chugwater for the past three days, thought you'd at least be interested. For God's sake, this is a brand-new bill!"

Jake Cardwell casually removed his hat and hung it on a nearby brass coatrack. "Probably would be, Delbert, if some drifter floated it by your nose or fanned it out on a poker table."

"Woman has a side arm, too. Plain as all get-out, hanging

there on her hip." He turned the registration ledger around. "Right here. K. Coltrane."

"Katherine. The K stands for Katherine. Kate Coltrane." Delbert Finney stared. "You know the woman?"

"I do," Cardwell answered. "What room is she in?"

"Eighteen." Finney's face brightened. "You plan on checking this out, then?"

"No," replied the marshal. "No, I'll allow Miss Coltrane is carrying more money on her than we make in a year. Now look, if you'd been around this country any time at all, you'd know all about Kate Coltrane, damn it. She owns all that property east of town where the rails are setting up. She owns the Star Hotel up in Chugwater, and she's claiming over fourteen thousand acres of land up that way. A lady rancher, that's what. Judas Priest, Delbert! Hell no, I'm not investigating her. Fact is, I rode half the day with her. I'm taking her to supper."

Chapter Thirteen

A Transaction

Excerpts from an interview with Henry Burlingame.

By chance, I met Katherine again in, let's see, maybe it was in the summer of seventy-nine in Cheyenne. I had this thorn in my side, how to finish a series of stories I had written about a young gunfighter by the name of Hardy Gibbs. I left New York and settled in at Julesburg, the last place Gibbs had been seen before he disappeared on the frontier. I went up to Cheyenne for a few days and this is where I met Katherine again, of all places, at the courthouse. She was as comely and cordial as always. She never was one to discuss her personal business to any great degree, but in this instance she was quite elated. She told me she had come to visit two of her friends from Deadwood who had gone to work in one of the so-called "houses of entertainment." Well, we were at the courthouse, and I thought this rather strange, far from a house of entertainment, you understand. She said that she had just concluded business concerning some acreage up on the Chugwater River. She was going into the stock business. I was taken aback. Oh, not that she wasn't capable of raising cattle. Within reason, I think this woman could do about anything she set her mind to do, but this was a venture requiring considerable capital, or financial backing. I knew she had friends, some wealthy ones, too. I wished her well. I didn't find out until several years later that she had also bought a lot at the edge of the business district. It was right next to one purchased earlier by Tim Frawley, the attorney from Deadwood. Frawley was the one she met during the Crook campaign and who backed her in Deadwood. He was not only a business associate. Rumors were

that at one time, he was also her lover. As I look back
on all of this, it was as though the woman had laid out
a detailed set of plans to keep all of her old friends
within finger touch. I didn't know it, maybe she didn't
either, but Frawley had his sights set on politics, big
politics.

Alva Tompkins was astounded when Katherine said that
she had bought a lot in Cheyenne for five hundred dollars,
more so when she disclosed that she wanted to build a saloon and twenty-room hotel, a spacious house of entertainment. Buford Reasons wasn't surprised at all. He thought
Katherine's idea was a very good one; Cheyenne needed a
first-class whorehouse, and only an innovative lady like
Kate could manage such a lucrative enterprise. Katherine delivered this news to the men the day after her return from the
city, a warm sunny morning up on the Bluegrass homestead.
They were seated on the cabin porch drinking coffee, observing the peaceful Chugwater Valley below. Katherine had
related the details of her journey, the legal work at the courthouse regarding her ranch land, her visit with Ida Hamilton
and Ruby Danforth, the pleasant dinner with Marshal
Cardwell (chuckles from Alva and Buford, here) her contact
with the Tarkalson brothers, the carpenters whom she engaged to build the ranch house, and a surprise meeting with
the *Harper's Weekly* writer, Henry Burlingame. Her plans to
see Stanley Howard, the railroad man, went awry; he was
out of the office. The disclosure that she had bought the city
lot came last.

And after a groan and a despairing shake of his head,
Alva Tompkins said, "You done went and bit off a big
mouthful with this ranch-to-do. Now, this! Where in tarnation did you ever get such a crazy notion, anyhow? Ain't no
need either, not anymore."

Buford added, "Well, money or not, Alva's right. You
ain't tricked for a long spell, Katie."

"It's a business deal, and it can be very profitable, too."

"Hawg wash!" mumbled Alva. "If you're building a
ranch, y' can't go diddling around in a cathouse, and that's
the nut of it. Ain't that many hours in the day ..."

"Or night," grinned Buford.

"I had this idea of building a nice house of pleasure long
before I met either of you two rascals," Katherine said.

"When Jane once told me how much money I could make—"

"Jane!" Alva snorted scornfully. "Damnation, what does that ol' baggy drawers know about such things? Why Calamity ain't seen the likes of fancy houses of mirrors in her whole miserable life. Best she ever did was the Six-Mile Hog Ranch, and by gawd, they tossed her lard-ass outta there, too!"

"She's my friend, Alva," reminded Katherine. "Probably saved my life, too." She smiled at Alva Tompkins and patted him on the knee. She said sweetly, "And I wouldn't be sitting here with you, would I?"

"Humph!"

"Besides, I don't plan on running the place ... if I can come up with some money to build it. The bank didn't know how much they could loan against what I have, collateral, that sort of thing. Yes, and at better than twenty percent interest. Well?" She gave Buford an innocent look.

"You know where the money is," he said. "Y' take what y' need, gal."

"Alva?" she said, leaning toward him.

"He said it," Alva returned glumly. "Better spent on getting your critters, I'd say. That's my notion."

"I think I could do both, buy and build."

"And if you don't run the place, who does?"

"I thought I could help the girls, Ida and Ruby. Put Ida in charge. Give them a chance to make some big money. Ida will run the entertainment downstairs, Ruby the rooms upstairs. I can look over the operation every month or so, check the books, and take our cut."

Alva said, "You mean you wouldn't be turning no tricks?"

"Ain't no need, anymore," drawled Katherine with a smile. "Aren't those your words?"

He grinned back. "I always talk up the best I can, Kate."

"I know you do." And, after a pensive pause, she said, "I like that name, Alva. 'House of Mirrors.'"

The next morning, Alva and Buford were up shortly after dawn. Since the carpenters, Ralph and Alfred Tarkalson, were due at Indian Wells within a week, the men had a half-dozen piles of barked lodgepoles to skid down to the building site. Not only this, they had another forty logs to skin. Worst of all, they disliked sawyer's work, or for that matter, as they readily admitted, they detested work of any kind. However, when Katherine Coltrane appeared on the Bluegrass earlier in the summer, work had become more tolerable, and after all, they were now partners.

Meanwhile, Katherine, after a cup of black coffee, rode down the little road to Chugwater in Luther Hatch's buckboard. Except for her continual longing for Julia, always that inner haunt, she was in good spirits. When the time did come, Julia would have a splendid home; Julia would have what every young woman should have—security, and a life free from want, and someone always to look after her welfare.

After unhitching at Luther's livery, she entered the Star from the rear and greeted Maybelle, who promptly brought her a cup of coffee, hot bannock, and some honey. Katherine ate and passed some small talk with Maybelle until Luther came into the kitchen in his usual hippity-hop gait. Greeting Katherine, he hiked his thumb back toward the door into the small dining room. Two Colorado and Southern Railroad men were in there eating breakfast, and one of them had been asking about her.

Luther Hatch said, "They took two rooms. Said they're fixing to stay a few days. All business. Maybe business with you, I reckon ... the right-of-way down the river, eh?"

Katherine quickly set aside her plate and went to the doorway, where she peeked into the room. It was Stanley Howard! His associate she had never seen before, and stepping briskly out, she walked up to the small table and extended her hand to Stanley. "Mercy, mercy, Howie, how nice to see you again!"

Obviously, the feeling was mutual. Stanley Howard flashed a broad smile under his black mustache. He stood and grasped her hand. He was very cavalier; he kissed it, and then introduced his companion, a tall, well-tanned man by the name of Timothy Aubrey, a surveyor recently discharged from the Army Engineers. And after Howard seated Katherine he spoke in a rush. How long had it been since the transaction in Cheyenne? Katherine felt a small blush. Transaction? Certainly it had been more than a transaction. Howie had professed his love for her, and indeed, she had enjoyed his company in all ways. But at that time, it had been an impossible situation. As he recalled, she had a business venture in Deadwood. Had it been successful? Had she recovered her little girl? One by one, the answers came.

Finally, Katherine asked, "How did you find me?"

"I didn't," he confessed. Nodding at Tim Aubrey, he said, "He found you ... after a fashion. His crew ran into a line of pole fences and stakes down the river about seven or eight miles. Markers all over the place. Some cowhand said a woman named Coltrane was responsible. You see, we found no record of any deeded property along there last year."

Katherine smiled. "You will now. Everything is legal, filed in Cheyenne. All of that land and half of the western foothills is part of the K-Bar-C Ranch, probably fourteen thousand acres worth."

Katherine Coltrane knew that Alva and Buford would be working with the logs for the next few days. She also knew that it would take several days for Stanley Howard and Tim Aubrey to settle with her or get a fix on a new route down the Chugwater Valley. Katherine Coltrane wasn't in any particular hurry. Her builders weren't coming for another week, and her plan to ride over and talk cattle business with Porter Longstreet Webb could wait for another week or two. The business at hand was with Stanley Howard, profitable business, she hoped, and after seeing Howie again and remembering what a wonderful time she had had with him in Cheyenne, she had other thoughts, too. Stanley Howard was a gentleman; he was also an innocent, loving joy, no master lover, not as attentive and lustful as Alva, but honestly affectionate. She remembered. She had fallen asleep in his arms. He had held her closely all night long, and sometimes a woman enjoys such comfort and tenderness.

It was shortly after eleven o'clock this night when Katherine heard his tread near the door. She had the door partially open, the lamp on her little table turned low, and she was seated in one of the two chairs. He had come at her invitation, an invitation she knew he wouldn't refuse. First, he kissed her hand, her arm, and then her lips. Then, he surprised her. Sitting down across from her, he reached out and extended his hand. She took it, and he said, "After this work is finished, I'm going to Denver. Why don't you come with me? Come down and stay awhile, enjoy the city."

Katherine Coltrane faltered. This mildly shocked her, for she was never at a loss for words.

"I would like it very much," he continued.

"Why, it sounds so wonderful," she finally managed. "But, mercy, I just can't ride out of here now. I'm starting to build. I have this place to consider, too. And the stock. I have to buy cattle, make the arrangements, find a broker." She squeezed his hand. "Oh, Howie, Howie, you are such a dear one, so kind. Mercy, I just can't believe this. It's so sudden."

"I do enjoy your companionship. You are a stunning woman, Katherine, one anyone enjoys being around. I told you this before. My beliefs haven't changed."

"You're very sweet."

Stanley Howard sighed. "You know, this is a helluva way to do business . . . in your boudoir. It's not conventional in the least, Katherine. And what's more, it's hard to believe you're getting into this cattle business."

"I'm committed. Besides, it's something I want to do. Some of my friends believe the future in this country is cattle. That's where the money is." She touched her lips to his hand. "I'm mercenary. Remember?"

"Yes," Stanley Howard agreed. "Yes, and you're a smart woman, too. You knew we wanted a river-grade rail down this valley. You knew all about the railroad taking this route."

"So did others."

"But you bottled up the whole bottom in that canyon area!"

"It's a good thing I did, too," Katherine said. "Yes, I'll admit it. I wasn't thinking about a ranch at the time, not until after I saw the land: those hillsides and meadows up above, those cold-water springs. Originally, I was thinking of only the money, but now I need that bottom. I can hay down there. I can put in a stock siding. After they pay me, I can give the Colorado and Southern people some business in return."

Stanley Howard grinned. "Pay you a good price."

"Of course." Katherine Coltrane stood. She was barefoot. She wore a long black gown. It was very quiet in the room, but outside the crickets were in concert. "It's time for bed, Howie," she said. She slipped out of her gown.

He protested gently. "I just can't bring myself to discuss cost when I'm in bed with you. It's unnatural."

"Then don't."

It took Stanley Howard two more days to conclude his right-of-way settlement with Katherine Coltrane. He had to inspect the property and evaluate it; he had to estimate the cost of an optional route through the eastern foothills, and his work necessitated a ride around the entire Coltrane property. Yes, and there was the problem of the siding, pens, and loading chutes that Katherine had proposed. To Stanley Howard's way of thinking, it was more practical to build a siding by Jeb Slaughter's spread. A better location, toward the middle of the valley. Katherine objected. Her ranch would be more suitable for several reasons. First, it was closer to Porter Webb's ranch to the east, and second, when the train passed going south to Cheyenne, the engine could take on gravity-flow water from Indian Wells. No one would have to pump or haul it from the river into the tower tank. And besides, she wanted some leverage to keep Jeb Slaughter in a peaceful mood. He would have to come across her land to load his stock. If he ever got too cantankerous, she could shut him off, and then he would have to foot the bill for his own private siding.

Finally, after more nightly discussions in Katherine's bedroom, she and Stanley Howard came to terms: the Colorado and Southern would pay her seven thousand dollars for the right-of-way and construct a siding adjacent to her property to be used by the three area ranches.

Two of Timothy Aubrey's survey crew arrived on the day Stanley Howard left. Aubrey moved north with his assistants and survey wagon; Howard stepped into his wagon and headed south for Cheyenne. At departure, Luther Hatch opined that all of the wrangling had exhausted young Stanley; he looked tired. Katherine Coltrane agreed. It had been quite an ordeal.

Chapter Fourteen

The Bushwhacker

Office of the Commandant
Fort Abraham Lincoln
Territory of the Dakotas

August 14, 1879

My dear friend Kate,
I trust this post will reach you at Chugwater. This very
day one of my scouts, Louis Richards, and three army
volunteers returned from the village of our old neme-
sis, Sitting Bull. I commissioned them for this detail
several weeks ago believing they might find Julia, and
with the aid of the Canadian authorities secure her release. I am sorry to report the mission was unsuccess-
ful, at least on the latter score. My men were treated
like interlopers. Mr. Richards did make contact with
the grandmother's family. Your daughter is faring well.
The Sioux were unwilling to make any concessions
whatsoever, and since we have no jurisdiction up
there, our quest was futile. Mr. Richards was escorted
from the village as though he were a spy. Additionally,
our party was attacked by a few renegade Cree on the
return. I know you will be disappointed to read this
news. I fear we can do nothing about this deplorable
situation until the Sioux decide to move south. Dearest
Kate, when this will be, only God knows. I think of
you often. I deeply value your friendship and love.

My fondest regards, Jason

A saddened Katherine Coltrane sat on the porch at Porter
Webb's place, three days after she had made the settlement
with Stanley Howard.

Porter, a grim look on his face, had just finished reading

the letter she received in Chugwater from General Armitage. He handed it to Joseph Brings Yellow, then said to Katherine, "Well, you can look at it this way—it could be a helluva lot worse. At least, you know she's alive and well. That's something you didn't know. And another thing—this might put a damper on the notion we can somehow sneak in there and spirit her away. Jason stuck his neck out trying this stunt, but knowing him, I'll allow he'll get way with it. That scamp always covers his tracks."

"Had she been a white girl, a captive, it would have worked, I'll bet."

"A breed's a breed, damn it," Porter said. "A breed's Indian, not white, and that's the way everyone looks at it."

Silence on the porch, crows squawking in the nearby cottonwoods. Katherine stared across the drab, olive-colored landscape. The land was getting ready for the golden touch of autumn and the Moon of the Drying Grass, September. Her eyes flooded, and she finally blurted, "She'll be seven years old next month. Oh, mercy, mercy!"

Joseph Brings Yellow finished the letter, carefully folded it, leaned over, and placed it in Katherine's lap. He said solemnly in Siouan, "Among our people, it is said that some things when lost, if they are very good and powerful, always come home. Remember this, Tall Woman, for this is how we look at the world in this camp."

"She is only a child, my brother. What power does a child possess?"

"She is a child, and in children there is always goodness. With goodness comes power."

"And how long must I wait?"

"Until the Great Spirit speaks."

Porter Longstreet Webb winced. He tossed his young brother-in-law a pathetic look and said, "Look here, Joseph, just because Bird Dog goes saying 'only God knows' doesn't mean this is a spiritual thing. Damn it, let's face reality. We won't get our hands on Julia until Sitting Bull wears out his blanket up there ... until he gets his butt kicked out and Bird Dog catches him on the way back. That's it, damn it, pure and simple. And listen, Julia isn't lost. For crisesakes, her home has always been where her people are. The poor girl probably doesn't even remember her father, Kate either, by now."

"Oh, mercy."

Silence on the porch again, until a misty-eyed Katherine heard Joseph say, "Among our people, the bond of unity in a family can be tested but never broken. They say sometimes it takes many winters to travel the Great Circle to discover the purity of the North and return to the South, the source of life. In time, Julia, Blue Star, will return to the source of her life, Tall Woman. *Heya,* this is the way we look at the world in our camp."

"That's virtuous, Joseph," Porter said.

"The virtue of faith," Joseph Brings Yellow replied in English. "Kate has faith. Patience is what she needs." He stood up and grinned. "That's what both of you need."

Porter Webb smiled and said, "Is that the way you look at it in this camp?"

"*Heya.* You people don't have any patience for life."

Katherine had impressed Porter with her news about the deeded land along the Chugwater bottom, and particularly the deal she had struck with Stanley Howard to put in a cattle siding. All of the land was in her name now, but as she had promised, she intended to split the seven thousand dollars with him. She was ready to put a burr in his britches, and she told him that he needed the money worse than she did. Indeed, this amused Porter Webb. Here was a novice rancher, a woman at that, without one critter to her name, without a house or barn or hired hands, telling him he needed the money worse than she did. And Katherine knew exactly that this was what he was thinking. It pleased her when Porter agreed to accompany her back to Chugwater the next day to look over the property and her building plans and make an assessment of what she would need in the way of equipment. Later, at supper, Katherine dropped her ton of hay on Porter Webb.

With a smile over at Jesse Talley and Hank Morrison, Porter's two cowhands, she said, "How would you boys like to trail a herd up here from Colorado, maybe Nebraska next spring?"

Young Talley stared at Katherine. "Why . . . why, it'd suit me all right, Miss Kate." He looked over at Porter. "Have to ask the boss about something like that, though."

"Well, Mister Webb would be along. Yes, he'd be the trail boss of the outfit."

"Now, wait a minute," interjected Porter. "I told you if

you wanted some seed, you could pick up a few heads down in Cheyenne at the yards, enough to get you started."

"Yes," she said, "and you said you weren't interested in bringing up four or five hundred head and splitting them . . . wasn't worth it. Oh, I remember what you said. I'm not only long in body, Porter. I'm long in memory, too. I don't forget, and you said if we had a thousand or so, it might be more appealing. Didn't you say that?"

Joseph Brings Yellow stared at Porter. "I think you did say something like that. She's right."

"Well," huffed Katherine, "how about if I said I'm prepared to buy not a thousand head but more like, say two thousand head if we can broker them at a fair price? How does that sound?"

The fork in Porter Webb's hand dangled. He slowly placed it on his plate and touched a finger and thumb to each side of his mouth. Finally: "Sounds crazy as hell, that's what. Where'd you get such a notion? Better yet, where you planning to come up with that kind of money? I sure as hell can't play in a high-stakes game like that."

"Oh, yes, you can. All it will cost you is the time away from here, some of your men and equipment. We'll split the herd. I'll take a note on your share without any interest. Or you can pay me back out of your first good crop of yearlings." She cocked her head and looked up at him. "Won't get a deal like this from any bank, you know."

The rattle of a pan came from Charlie Lemm's kitchen. Everyone stared at Katherine. Finally, Porter said, "You're serious about this, aren't you? You really have the wad to do something like this? You said you were putting all of that railroad money into your house. You didn't have a wooden nickel for stock. Should I be asking where all of this money is coming from?"

"Should I be telling you?"

"I reckon it's none of my business."

"You reckon right, Mister Webb. What I'm asking is if you're interested in trailing the critters. Are you? Is it a deal?"

After a moment, Porter Webb said yes. There were grins all around the table. Everyone continued eating.

Early the next afternoon, Katherine, Porter, and Joseph Brings Yellow rode down off the trail from Hawk Springs at the north end of Chugwater. There was a small rise to the east ringed by a few big cottonwoods. The little cemetery was here, not more than a half-dozen markers popping up from the tall dry grass. The three riders abruptly stopped. Squinting against the afternoon sun, Katherine first saw Andy Everhard, the owner of the general store. Andy was walking toward the road adjusting his hat. There was a small group of people not far behind him, not more than five or six, and Katherine recognized Luther Hatch, and next to him, Alva Tompkins. Her heart throbbed. She heard Porter Webb said, "Looks like they just planted someone."

Andy Everhard came closer, and Katherine asked, "What's going on? Funeral?"

Staring up at the three riders, Everhard said, "Buford Reasons. We just put ol' Buford to rest."

"Oh, Jesus!" cried Katherine.

"Buford?" asked Porter. "What the hell happened to him?"

"Shot. Bushwhacked, they say. Down the river where Miss Kate's building her place. That's about all I know. Shot out of his saddle. Alva found him plumb dead last evenin'. Told the drivers on the southbound stage to tell the marshal." He removed his hat to wipe at the perspiration on his brow. "Yep, that's about it. Afternoon, mam, gentlemen." Replacing his hat, he strode away.

Katherine sobbed quietly several times. She and the men dismounted, and soon everyone was milling about, some talking quietly, others just shaking their heads. Katherine put her arms around a sorrowful Alva, gently patted him on the back in quiet consolation. He muttered, "One of Slaughter's men is a bushwhacker, Kate."

Once at the hotel, Katherine, Porter, and Joseph sat around one of the tables, drank coffee and listened to Alva's story. He had discovered Buford's body near some corrals in the creek bottom at dusk. It was too late in the day to investigate, so he had hoisted Buford's body back onto his horse and came into town. He stayed at the hotel and helped Luther Hatch make a coffin after breakfast. It was true what Andy Everhard had said—the stage drivers were going to send one of the marshals up to investigate, but Alva didn't think there was anything to investigate. There wasn't a doubt in his mind about the shooter, only his identity. It had to be one of Jeb Slaughter's men.

Porter Webb pulled out his watch, briefly checked it, and then slipped it back into his leather vest pocket. Katherine tried to read his face, but most often that was impossible. No one could ever read any emotion in the face of Porter Webb. And Joseph Brings Yellow could just as well been Porter's twin brother instead of his brother-in-law. He was also emotionless. She said, "What are you thinking?"

Without hesitation, Porter replied, "That it's none of my damned business. It's for the law."

Joseph put in, "The sign is already old, Kate."

Katherine suddenly bristled. "You're a Lakota, goddamn it! What the hell are you telling me? Sign is never too old for a Lakota!"

Joseph returned impassively. "You want to go look? All right, you are my sister, I will take you."

Katherine Coltrane looked over at Porter. "Porter?"

"Oh, shit!" He pulled himself up and glared at her. "Hell yes, I'll go, but you keep your butt in that chair. You stay here with Alva. We'll get back in time for supper, maybe just in time to meet the goddamned marshal."

"I'll do no such thing! No one tells me what to do or not to do. I'm going." She looked at Alva. "So is he. We're all going." And they left—together.

It took nearly a half hour to get to the gateway that Alva and Buford had erected several weeks earlier. A shaft of brilliant sunshine struck the face of the Coltrane sigh. It was ablaze like a golden banner. Porter took one brief look at it and gave Kate a thin smile. "I reckon you weren't joshing about your ranch. That's quite a marker."

"That was Buford's idea," she said. "It's a monument, now, isn't it?"

Turning toward the bottom, Porter asked Alva if he knew anything about the confrontation Buford had; how he determined his friend had been bushwhacked, shot from ambush. That had been simple, Alva told him. The size of the hole where the bullet had exited. It had entered from the side of the chest in front and exited behind the left shoulder blade. "Could'a shoved a banty hen's egg in that hole," Alva said. "That's a rifle, boy. Ain't no revolver makin' a hole that big."

"Tracks?"

"Didn't look. Didn't have time. Just wanted to take care of poor ol' Buford . . . get him the hell outta of this bottom."

He pointed ahead. "Right over there's the place ... poles all knocked down, too."

Shortly, they dismounted. The fence was broken in two places, poles scattered randomly about, and cow tracks were everywhere but most of them were small ones. After one look, Porter said, "Dogies. The little bastards probably went under the poles or poked between them, and Buford was trying to get them out. All the cow tracks are over here, and they're heading down the river ... running tracks."

Pointing toward the east across the river, Porter said to Joseph, "Shot had to come from over there somewhere. If he's moving the critters out, he's hit in the right side of the chest, right? The slug comes out his left side. Go up along that brush line and take a look for horse sign. One rider or a couple, eh? They'll double somewhere, going and coming, but where they end on the right is where the shot came from. Sure as hell Alva's right, too. The tracks are going to go right back down the valley to Slaughter's place."

"Already knows that." Alva grumbled. "That ain't provin' who did it, though, not by a damn."

"No, we'll just let the marshal decide how he's going to handle that end of it."

Alva Tompkins replied sarcastically, "Y' mean someone fessin' up to it! Oh, I can see that, I can." He held both hands high, and in soprano squalled, "I did it, I did it." He gave Porter a look of disgust. "Damnation, Webb, if you ain't a rag-assed mule!"

"Alva!" Katherine said. "Please! Let's get on with this."

Shortly, a hail came from the rim on the other side of the stream, and directly Joseph Brings Yellow came sloshing back across the river. He reined up in front of Porter and tossed him an empty cartridge. "The marshal might be interested in that, eh? A center fire."

Porter Webb sniffed at the hole. He grinned at Alva. "Bushwhacked. Bushwhacked by someone using a Winchester, a model seventy-three, the only rifle that shoots a center fire." He nodded to Joseph Brings Yellow. "You have good eyes, my brother."

"I carry the medicine of Spotted Hawk."

Alva's brow hiked. "Is that a fact? Spotted Hawk, eh? Well, tell us, what does that hawk say about the tracks up there."

Joseph Brings Yellow pointed to the north. "One man, that way."

"I figgered. Didn't leave a name, did he?"

"No, but he won't be hard to find. He used a Winchester. His pony gaits to the left. A rear shoe is loose. It may be off by now."

"Holy shit!"

Katherine Coltrane said, "Well, Alva, you asked, didn't you?"

"Damn Injun!"

Porter Webb was against it, but he was outvoted, three to one. Even Joseph Brings Yellow wanted to follow the tracks, as he lamely explained, "just to be certain." It was near four o'clock when the four riders came to the hay shed several miles south of the Slaughter ranch, the very shed where Alva had wanted to hide the howitzer the night after the stage holdup. There were two holding pens made out of lodge-poles adjacent to the shed, and inside of the first one were three men, two trying to hog-tie a calf, the other one standing beside a small fire holding a branding iron. In the larger corral, were a dozen more calves and three horses. The horses were saddled and tied to one of the fence poles. Katherine immediately recognized two of the men from the meeting in the river bottom earlier that summer. One was young Matt Slaughter, the other the black-bearded gruff fellow. The man holding the branding iron was a new face. They were too busy to notice the approach of riders, so it was a few minutes before Matt Slaughter turned and saw Joseph Brings Yellow on the other side of the second corral. Slaughter was annoyed at such an intrusion. Joseph Brings Yellow was examining the horses, their saddles, equipment, and even their rumps, and when Joseph lifted the leg of a sorrel, young Slaughter yelled.

"Hey, what the hell you doing? Get out of there. Get away from those horses!"

Katherine had moved Buck next to the corral where the men were working. Leaning forward in her saddle, she said, "He's just checking them, that's all."

"Well, well," Slaughter said. "It's little miss K. C., the apples lady. Yep, and ol' Alva, too. And what are you doing here? You're on our property, you know." At this point, Slaughter recognized Porter Webb. He said, "Porter, you've got one helluva partner, that's all I can say. She hasn't got a cow on the range around here, and she's closing ours off from the bottom grass up above."

Porter tipped his hat. "Hello Matt. Maybe you should keep your stock closer to home then. Abide by the law."

"We ain't got fences down here. And tell that breed friend of yours to get back where he belongs on the other side of my fence."

Porter said, "A man was shot and killed yesterday . . . just above here a few miles. Tracks of his mount came down this road."

Then the older cowhand with the black beard angrily interceded, shouting at Joseph. "Get away from my horse, you little bastard, or I'll scorch your butt!" He was wearing a side arm but he made no motion to pull it from its holster.

Joseph Brings Yellow quickly climbed back over the poles, and once back to the side of his own horse, he said aside to Porter, "That sorrel has a Winchester on it. It has a loose shoe, too."

"Damn it, Porter, what do tracks mean?" Slaughter said. "A half dozen riders come down through here every day . . . drifters. Someone pots a man up the river apiece, and you come riding here. Bullshit!"

Joseph's quiet, informative aside to Porter wasn't quiet enough to escape Katherine's sharp ears. She was suddenly uncontrollably outraged. She had only felt this way once in her life, long ago when her brother was murdered and left slumped over the seat of his freighter. She hadn't even been able to reach him before being dragged away by the Oglala. But now, in blind fury, she was able to reach her Plants forty-two. She leveled it down over the top pole and shot the man with the black beard in the chest. "You son of a bitch," she cried, "that's your sorrel! You bushwhacked Buford!"

She fired a second shot before Porter swung his horse around and got her away from the corral. She had taken everyone by surprise, even herself, and in a wailing lament, she leaped clear of Buck and slumped down beside the fence.

"Jesus Christ, she shot Billy!" shouted Matt Slaughter. "You crazy bitch, you didn't even give the man a chance to talk. What the hell's the matter with you! You'll hang for this. They'll string you up. Oh shit, look at this, will you!"

It wasn't pleasant to see, not at all. The man called Billy

was flat on his back, blood oozing across his chest, out his mouth and one ear. Matt Slaughter was bent over Billy's body. The third Slaughter man, barely a man, had turned around and was leaning against the fence, his head buried in his folded arms.

Porter climbed the corral and squatted close to Matt Slaughter. He stared briefly at the dead man. Katherine's second shot must have hit him in the side of the head as he was falling. A bit of pinkish, gray matter glistened in his black hair. Porter Webb stared a second time, and said, "Billy? Billy what? What handle was this fellow using?"

"Billy ... Bill Smith. Goddamn it, Porter, he was a good man. Knew everything there was to know about cattle. My dad's gonna have a conniption about this. Oh, Lord!"

"What do you know about Buford's death?"

"Billy told me Buford was hazing our dogies, running the beef off the cows ... said Buford threatened to shoot him. That's it. Sure he was wrong, but so was she."

After a long sigh, Porter said, "Buford wasn't armed. He was shot through the chest from almost seventy-five yards, Matt. Your hired hand lied to you. Yes, and this man isn't Billy Smith. His name is Mordecai Williams. Black Mordecai, a damn good horse thief. I knew him about ten years back. You're right on one score, though. He should know his stock. He's wanted in the Dakota Territory for rustling. Suspected of two killings, too. Never proved, but the rustling is a fact."

Matt Slaughter stared up in disbelief.

"That's right, son. Likely Kate won't hang for this. Fact is, she'll probably get the thousand reward riding on Mordecai's head."

Chapter Fifteen

Sitting Bull

Excerpts from an interview with Henry Burlingame.

I saw Katherine several times during the early eighties, once at her new ranch in the Chugwater Valley and another time at old Fort Laramie. Her cattle spread was extensive. Her home on the bluff by the old Indian Wells was a grand place. There were three fireplaces in the building, a very large parlor and dining area, and as I recall, five bedrooms, three of them on the upper floor. She had one of these fixed up for Julia. It had a canopy bed and a little rocking chair in it. Kate had placed one of those pretty dolls with the painted faces in the rocker. Kate's private quarters were on the first floor, and in back of the kitchen was another bedroom and the cook's quarters. Let me tell you about the cook. This is an interesting story in itself. After that first cattle drive up from Colorado, Kate took a business trip to Deadwood. I never found out the purpose of the trip, but on the way back, she went by Fort Laramie to visit with some sergeant, Hansen, I believe was his name. He was Lieutenant Clybourn's aide on the Crook campaign, the fellow who got killed. It so happened that Manny and Mary Slaymaker were at the fort. Mary had befriended Kate when she came back from all those years with the Sioux. The Slaymakers had sold out their boardinghouse at Fetterman. Too much trouble at Fetterman, they said, shootings, fights all the time at the hog ranch, even a hanging. Well, before all was said and done, Kate invited them to come down to her ranch. That woman never forgot her friends. Kate had running water in that house and a hot-water boiler. She was a very smart woman. When the Colorado and Southern came through with their coal-fired engines, she profited. There was always a huge pile of coal next to her siding. She had rigged that boiler in her house for coal. You asked about the House of Mirrors. I was never in this hotel. I call it a hotel because from what Tim Frawley told me, it was patterned after his Red Bird Saloon and Hotel in Deadwood, the one that burned in seventy-eight. Of course, it was a much larger palace of entertainment. It was built out of brick. And, as Frawley had been in Deadwood, Kate was a silent partner. In fact, I don't believe there were more than three or four people who really knew she owned the place. She had a fancy two-room suite in the hotel. I understand she stayed there once or twice a month. This is more rumor than fact, because Kate was seldom seen in the city. Actually, the listed owner of the property was Ida Hamilton. Ida was one of the original women working in the Red Bird. She and a young mixed-blood named Ruby Danforth came down to the Wyoming Territory with Kate. I can tell you this, the House of Mirrors had a good reputation, if one can consider a house of ill repute as having a good reputation. What I mean is that it was first-class. It catered to exclusive clientele. It was no secret, some of the highest-stake poker games in Wyoming took place in the upper back rooms of the hotel. The entertainment varied: singing, dancing, and what not. I know that it cost Katherine a small fortune to build, but when it came to discussing financial matters, most of the time she gave one no more than her usual pretty smile.

A few of the so-called society women in Cheyenne mounted several campaigns to curb the activities at the House of Mirrors and other such establishments. It didn't amount to much. Tim Frawley's law office building was next door to the House of Mirrors. I don't know if Katherine had this in mind when she built, but that's the way it was. And later, Frawley, who had set up practice in Cheyenne, ran for county attorney and won. Not only that, Kate had another ally. That U.S. marshal, Jake Cardwell, became the chief law officer a year or two later. I really don't know if Cardwell was aware Kate was the owner of the hotel, but I know this—he never gave Ida Hamilton any trouble. He knew Ida and Kate were close friends. And, of course, after Kate killed that scoundrel, Mordecai Williams, she was something of a local heroine. A woman gun-slinger? Peculiar? Well, this is the way it was on the frontier. I didn't write that story at the time, but some of the dime novels certainly embellished it.

Chugwater, Wyoming, May, 1881.

A warm breeze fluttered the leaves of the greening cotton-wood and aspen in the grove bordering the little cemetery. Katherine Coltrane placed the small wildflower bouquet beside the headstone, stood back with bowed head, and said a short prayer. It was a beautiful marker made of gray granite. The inscription simply stated, "Buford Reasons. He was a good man." When Katherine turned away, Alva Tompkins, standing to the back of Katherine, muttered a soft "Amen." He adjusted his black hat with the broad brim. He tucked at his string tie, then buttoned his fancy coat. Holding his head high, Alva Tompkins addressed the spring breeze. "He was a good ol' boy, a real good ol' boy."

Katherine smiled faintly. She knew Buford was "a good ol' boy." She also knew that Alva had never quite gotten over the loss of his dearest friend. "Time heals all," the saying went, but she didn't believe this. The scars were always there, the burdened heart. She, too, carried sorrowful memories.

Placing the flowers on Buford's grave was to be a yearly ritual. Katherine had first suggested it, and whatever she suggested, Alva readily accepted. That first year Alva wasn't too sure flowers were appropriate; Buford would have preferred a bottle of rye. This was Alva's crusty humor to alleviate some of his sorrow. Katherine touched Alva on the shoulder and smiled again, wondering if Buford would approve of Alva now. His unruly beard was gone; his hair and mustache were neatly trimmed. Daily work on the K-Bar-C had put him in fine physical shape. For his fifty-few years (he never admitted his age) he was ruggedly handsome and as agile as a cat. Katherine said, "Alva, you're quite an ol' boy, yourself."

Several short whistles sounded to the south, the sound of wings beating away from the trees, the calls of frightened crows. The whistle came again, and then the faint huff-huff of a laboring engine. "Northbound," Alva said. On the road, Katherine peered down the adjacent tracks and saw the telltale gray burst of smoke. Yes, the northbound Colorado and Southern was coming, headed for the junction at Hartsville. Up the rutted road in the other direction, she saw several men at the depot, among them the stationmaster, Luther Hatch. Katherine felt sorry for Luther. The railroad had not brought the bonanza to Chugwater he had anticipated. There were only a few new stores and some sodbuster shacks, but through the influence of Katherine's good friend, Stanley Howard, Luther had been given the job of stationmaster. He was a proud man. He met two trains each day, took care of a few passengers and the freight. He also operated the new Western Union Telegraph.

Despite the new railroad, a few mule trains and various other freighting rigs continued to ply the old stage route to Deadwood. Luther and Maybelle were still managing the Star Saloon and Hotel, and the small profit it generated went to them. Katherine wanted it this way because she and Alva seldom visited the Star. She was too busy at the ranch, and Alva, now in charge of the K-Bar-C upper lands, stayed at the Bluegrass cabin most of the time.

Prior to this visit to the cemetery, it had been a hectic spring on the range. During late March and early April, over two-hundred calves had been dropped, most of them in the greening grass of the river bottom. Other critters—bulls, steers, barren cows, and yearlings had been foraging in all directions. With only two young hired hands, Jimmy Reynolds and Jack Cuthbert to help her round up her stock, Katherine made peace with Jeb Slaughter. They combined forces, and with Porter Webb as ramrod, conducted a joint cow hunt. All of the calves trailing cows with Slaughter's Slash-S brand went north; the K-Bar-C brands were rounded up and herded south. Everyone pitched in with the branding, even Alva and Manny Slaymaker. Katherine helped cook at Slaughter's spread and also assisted Mary Slaymaker at the K-Bar-C Ranch. It was the most grueling experience in her life, but she told Porter Webb that it was worth it. For the first time since they had brought the big longhorns from Colorado two years ago, she expected her ranch to turn a profit. But she wasn't a poor woman, far from it. So far, her share of the House of Mirror's gambling and entertainment operation had netted her more than $12,000. Only Alva

Tompkins knew this. He wasn't impressed by the money, but he was happy for Katherine.

The shiny black engine rolled by, slowly screeched to a halt at the station, hissed ominously, then panted, "ah-phoo, ah phoo." A small train, it consisted of one mail car, a coach, and three boxcars, these loaded with an assortment of freight destined for customers along the North Platte. A baggage clerk handed Luther several packages, including a small mail pouch, then skidded two cream cans and a box of produce to the doorway. Luther deftly swung everything down to his cart. The stop at Chugwater was over within minutes. The mail-car door slammed; there was a shout from the brakeman, a wave, the engine drive wheels momentarily spun, and the train began moving slowly ahead.

The small crowd dispersed, and Katherine and Alva went into the Star for coffee. They were seated at a table with Maybelle when Luther, his chores finished, entered. Handing Katherine two letters, one in a government envelope, he said, "Since you were here, I sorted these out of the post. That one might be important."

Katherine thanked him. She examined the letters. One was from Jason Armitage, the other in a badly soiled envelope, from Jane Canarray in Deadwood. She quickly opened Jason's letter. It was penned in his usual flourishing style, but the imprint on the letterhead immediately caught her attention. Major General Jason Armitage.

"Major General!" Katherine burst out happily. "Mercy, oh mercy! Look here, Jason's been promoted. He has another star." She read:

My dear Kate,

I believe I have some heartening news for you. Our old friend Sitting Bull has met with a reversal. His appeal to the Canadian government for a reservation and rations has been denied. A U.S. commission has been appointed to meet with him and agree upon conditions for his return. The man has no options left. I anticipate he will be ordered to surrender at Fort Buford in the Montana Territory. At this writing, no definite decision has been made as to where the Hunkpapa will be relocated, however, I assume it will be the Standing Rock Reservation. I will recommend that the few Oglala with Sitting Bull's people be transferred down to Pine Ridge to be with their own tribe. I anticipate no further recriminations against these people. Our military campaign was concluded four years ago.

I find it difficult to believe that you have gone into the cattle business. However, I do look forward to visiting your ranch sometime in the near future. If it's during the fall, I will accept Porter's invitation to hunt elk with him in the Laramie or Medicine Bow Mountains. I will keep you advised of the situation in Canada. I believe some decision will be reached within another month or two.

Respectfully yours with my fondest regards,
Jason

Katherine radiated joy, and with the others at the table listening, she quickly read part of the letter. Everyone was happy. Maybelle kissed and hugged Katherine, then left for the kitchen to get the coffeepot.

After a moment, Alva Tompkins clucked his tongue. "Standing Rock," he said, "why, that's a far piece, all the way up next to the border. Have to ride one of those riverboats up there, Kate. I'll allow it's a three- or four-week trip up and back by the trails."

"No, Julia will be at Pine Ridge," replied Kate confidently. "Jason will see to it. He won't fail me, not after all this time. Don't you see? Pine Ridge. That's only a whoop and a holler now. I can ride a train to Chadron, rent a buckboard." She smiled. "Two days, that's all."

"Already got it figgered, eh?" Luther Hatch said.

"I surely do."

Alva mumbled, "If the ol' chief cooperates, that is."

"Oh, he's a proud man," replied Kate, "but he won't let his people go hungry. Frawley says sodbusters are coming in up there and starting to plant. No cattle, but they're sowing wheat. The game is scarce and the Lakota aren't farmers, not even citizens. Frawley told me last winter it was only a matter of time before this would come to a head." She paused and patted the letter in front of her. "Jason says the time has arrived. This is it, and I'm ready."

Katherine's spirits soared. Too excited about the imminent return of Julia, she tucked the letter from Calamity Jane in her jacket pocket. Time enough to read it when she got back to the ranch.

Katherine and Alva parted company about a half mile

north of Chugwater, Alva riding west to cross the wagon road up to the Bluegrass homestead. They now called it the "line cabin." When the K-Bar-C cattle ranged the upper summer range, Alva, and frequently one of the other hands, supervised work from the cabin. It was almost fifteen miles across the rolling hills and sagebrush flats to ranch headquarters in the bottom. Consequently, Katherine's visits to see Alva were now limited, discreet too, usually no more than twice a month. She occasionally took up supplies and served as the "relief man" for the cowhand working with Alva. Katherine took pride in her efficiency. The occasional intimacies she shared with her lover, Alva, were very private affairs, her own business. Katherine wanted it this way; she detested gossip, excuses, and explanations. Besides, to anyone but her and Alva, who could explain such carnal gratification? Of course, it was an embarrassment. But it was sustenance of a kind, a loving sustenance that despite the frenzied, amorous brevity of it, served to obliterate every other contentious thought or pain from her mind. Who possibly could understand this?

Katherine Coltrane dabbed at moist eyes. She was seated at the table in the big ranch-house kitchen, Mary Slaymaker across from her kneading bread dough. Glancing up, Mary said, "Good news, now bad news. What is it, Kate?"

With a sigh, Katherine said, "Pete Quinlan. Pete's dead. Blood poisoning, Jane says. Up in Deadwood. Probably several weeks ago."

Shocked, Mary Slaymaker exclaimed, "Oh, my gracious! Peter Quinlan! Oh, oh, this is bad news. Why . . . why, I've known that man nigh on ten, maybe twelve years. He never had a sick day in his life, that one. Dead, you say. Oh, dear."

The words in Jane Canarray's letter became blurred. Katherine sniffed once, wiped the corners of her eyes and began all over.

To Kate Coltrane:

    Kate, you know I can't write worth a hang, so your friend, Henry Givens, does this for me. I write to tell you Pete Quinlan died here four days past. His leg was crushed up at Lead last week by a load of logs. Some doctor up there had to take it off above the knee. They brought Pete to the Deadwood Hospital. He got blood poisoning and died after two days. I was at the hospital and was doing what I could which wasn't much. He gave me a paper to claim the stock and wagons he had with him up at Lead. This other paper belongs to you. I made my name on it to bear witness like he asked. Pete said I should take the paper to one of the lawyers and make it proper. I do not trust these busters here. Henry says take it to Tim Frawley in Cheyenne and let him fix it proper. Pete talked about you at the hospital. He said he still had a deep hankering for you. I sure will miss that buster. I heard a story at the Brewery Saloon. Sitting Bull is coming back soon. I hope this bodes well for you getting Julia back. Nobody wants that scamp back here around the town. Will see you next time you come up.

My love, Jane

A postscript from Henry Givens followed:

Dear Kate:

Jane has been on a toot ever since the funeral. She can't hold the pen steady so I have been pressed into service. Pete had no kin that he claimed. What I make of this paper, he leaves what he owns to you. I believe this may be a considerable amount of money from what he marks on the paper. Best you take this to Tim at your earliest opportunity. In case something goes amiss, I have made a record of this, attested by Preacher J. Cooney of the Methodist Church. Pete had a hired hand down at his mule ranch by Spearfish, name of Jack Darby. Young Darby was at the funeral and I told him to stay on and tend the ranch until this is settled. I will pay his wages and we can settle later. I don't know of what use the mule ranch will be to you. It is only 320 acres. Used to belong to some sodbusters but they were killed off in '76 by hostiles. Quinlan picked up those two places two or three years ago. You let me know what Frawley does. Sorry about Pete.

My best regards, Henry.

Katherine set the letter aside. As she unfolded the other paper, she heard Mary ask, "Whatever ailed him to cause a blood poisoning?"

"He lost a leg," Katherine replied. "Some kind of an accident up at Lead. Amputation. He died a few days later in the hospital."

"Such a pity. This is going to set Manny fretting. He's known Peter since he was a young man. Young man? My gracious, I don't think Peter was more 'n forty!"

"Did Manny ever say anything about relatives? . . . Pete's kin?"

"I don't think Peter had any kin, Kate. His folks passed away down in Colorado. He came up and caught on to mule skinning and hauling, oh, maybe in seventy . . . seventy-one. Manny knew his father, Paul. Paul Quinlan was a tinsmith in Denver." Mary Slaymaker picked up her sack of flour and began sifting another batch into the big crock. She tutted once. "My, my, Peter dead! What a worker, he was. Many's the time I fed and bedded him down after one of those miserable hauls up from Fort Laramie."

Katherine reflected with a sad smile. She had bedded Pete Quinlan, too, in her freight wagon, for a handsome sum. Her very first trick. Quinlan, probably more than Jane Canarray, was the one most responsible for her adventure into prostitution. He had been very affectionate, and it was a pleasurable and profitable experience—a twenty-dollar gold piece!

Now, quickly reading the second paper, several lines suddenly leaped out like wildfire at Katherine—"Merchant's Bank, Casper, Union Bank and Trust, Deadwood, National Bank of Cheyenne." Her eyes widened. Perhaps Henry Givens was right—maybe there was a considerable sum of money involved here. "Oh, mercy, mercy," she mumbled.

"What? What's the matter, Miss Kate?"

"This other paper," she said. "Do you know what this man did?" Katherine nodded at the paper. "This is some kind of a will, Mary. He left me everything he owned. Except for a couple of wagons and some mules, he's left me everything, even that place of his outside Spearfish on the river. I can't believe this!"

"My heavens to Betsy! I never heard of such a thing!"

Katherine sucked wind. Neither had she. Peter, dear, Peter, had she meant that much to him in his worrisome, roaming life? Had he secretly nurtured love for her in his heart instead of just having a "hankering" for her? Unrequited love?

Mary Slaymaker went on. "Why, to do a thing like that, I reckon he doesn't have kinfolk. Gracious, Miss Kate, you hardly knew Peter, did you? That freighting for General Crook . . .?"

"Maybe he knew me better than I knew him," suggested Katherine. "Maybe he felt sorry for me, Julia and all. You know, the way it was after I came back from the Oglala. Yes, I think that must be it, don't you? He just felt sorry for me."

Mary Slaymaker's eyes rolled. "Well, I can't say, Miss Kate. Everyone wanted to help. Either he felt sorry for you or he fancied you. Yes, he could have fancied you and just never got around to 'fessing up to it." Her hands plunged into the mass of dough. "That's the way some men are, you know. Oh, let me tell you, I've seen it, I have. When it comes to sweet talking about love, man gets grits in his mouth, but when he's on his deathbed breathing his last, he always manages to raise his head and say, 'Tell the little woman I love her.' But I reckon we'll never know what Peter had on his mind, will we?"

Katherine slowly folded the will. "No, I suppose not."

A busy week sped by. Katherine and the crew moved almost a thousand head of cattle from the valley to the upper range for the summer. A few of the more cantankerous bulls were culled and dehorned, an onerous task no one enjoyed. As soon as all of this was finished, Katherine renewed her irrigation project on a great section of the lower land. No complaint came from Jeb Slaughter. Katherine's earlier peace parley with him included some concessions—water rights. She agreed to irrigate on alternate days; she also agreed to stop irrigating when and if the river became too low. Additionally, a fenced corridor and gate were installed so Slaughter could move his cattle to the holding pens adjacent the new rail siding. Everyone was happy, especially Katherine. She abhorred the thought of any more confrontations with Slaughter. She still had bad dreams about the killing of Black Mordecai.

Katherine had been too busy to take a train into Cheyenne to see Tim Frawley about Pete Quinlan's will. Instead, she had penned him a letter and enclosed the will. In turn, Frawley had sent her an acknowledgment by telegraph; Luther Hatch had delivered the message, and almost two weeks later, one of Frawley's assistants, Frederick Dinsmore, arrived at the ranch. He came up from Chugwater in one of Luther's buggies. Frawley, himself, couldn't come and Dinsmore quickly made an apology for him. Timothy Frawley was, among other pressing business, engaged in an election campaign—he was running for county attorney of Cheyenne.

They had just seated themselves on the porch when young Dinsmore made this disclosure. Surprised, Katherine asked, "Politics! Good heavens, why? I know Tim isn't that destitute."

"No, Miss Coltrane." Dinsmore smiled. "No, he isn't destitute in the least. True, the position is only worth a pittance."

"Well then, why?"

Frederick Dinsmore hesitated, then said, "Since you don't know about the matter, I'd rather not speak for Mister Frawley." He patted the small leather case he was holding. "The Quinlan estate—"

"Tim is not only my attorney, he's my friend." Katherine gave Dinsmore a pretty smile. "What's your notion about it, Frederick? You know, just between the two of us."

He grinned back. "A means to an end."

"Meaning what? What end?"

"Ambition. Something bigger down the line, perhaps a federal judgeship, who knows?"

"Oh, mercy!"

"I thought you may have known." Dinsmore went on. "Some of the cattlemen have joined ranks. They want a voice in the government. Some of them have become good friends with Mister Frawley. Nesters have started coming into the territory. Do you understand?"

"Yes and no," Katherine said. At one time, Jeb Slaughter had believed she was a nester, a sodbuster. And Porter Webb once had expressed his distrust about the nesters, the small farmers who were invading the range to the south along the Union Pacific railway properties. She said, "We don't have any nesters around here."

Frederick Dinsmore grinned again. "The friends of Mister Frawley don't want any, either." He unfastened the ties of his black satchel and casually asked, "Have you seen your friend, Porter Webb, lately?"

"How long is lately?" she replied. "Yes, about three or four weeks ago, I'd say. We were chasing a lot of critters in these hills. Why?"

Sorting out a few legal papers, Dinsmore said, "I suggest you talk to him. He was one of the men who encouraged

Mister Frawley to get into the political ring." Once more, a grin. "I think your name is on the list, too. So, understand, what I've just told you isn't any big secret. As I said, I'm surprised you don't already know."

"I've been up to my neck in molasses, lately. I haven't been able to move out of this place, that's why."

Handing her several papers, Dinsmore said, "Well, when we get through with these, you'll have to extract yourself, Miss Coltrane, get moving if you want to make a quick settlement and claim this inheritance. Everything seems to be in order. We received the deed on your Spearfish property three days ago from Henry Givens. The banks listed in the will were notified and all replied. They may want to take a look at these certified papers, perhaps you as well, before releasing any of the accumulated funds. There's quite a sum of cash involved here."

"You know this?" Katherine asked.

"We are very thorough, Miss Coltrane. The telegraph is a very useful instrument. We even have the account numbers."

Katherine Coltrane took a deep breath and asked, "How much did Pete have stashed away?"

"Give or take a few dollars, almost forty thousand," Dinsmore said. "If you have pen and ink about, we can sign these papers and make everything legal and proper."

"Oh, mercy me!"

The next day, Katherine rode up to the line cabin on Bluegrass Creek to consult with Alva Tompkins. He and young Jack Cuthbert were preparing to ride the upper circuit when she arrived. Cuthbert hiked himself into his saddle and rode off alone. While Katherine seated herself on the porch bench and took out several of the papers left by Dinsmore, Alva scurried into the kitchen and brought back coffee. Katherine, alternately sipping and talking, explained what had transpired during Dinsmore's visit. Alva listened attentively. Finally, Katherine said, "Now we have to make a decision about this. I've taken a lot of money out of the hole under the floor back there, more than my share, to get things in order, the building and all. And you have been very patient with me, and Buford, too, before he cached out on us."

"Amen," muttered Alva.

"Yes, amen, for Buford."

Pushing his hat back, Alva squinted at Katherine suspiciously. "Well, just what you getting at, Kate, this 'we' making a decision. Pete left that money to you. It's yours fair and square."

"True," agreed Katherine. "Yes, that's true, but I got this notion that maybe I should replenish our stash, sock some of this away in the cubbyhole. You know, for a rainy day. Since you're my partner, this seems only fair." Staring across the bench, she looked into his flinty blue eyes, those narrowed slits there, just like Porter Webb's eyes.

After a moment of consideration, Alva grinned. "Y' know, Katie, it just hit me. Don't you realize this is the first wad that's come our way all above board, y' know, like . . . legittymite."

"Legitimate."

"That's right."

"That's not entirely true," Katherine said. "You and Buford had to scrounge for your money. You boys damn near wore yourselves out digging for that gold up at the Lost Cabin mine. You could have been killed up there, too, taking such a fool chance."

"Well, I'll allow you're right on that one. But the rest of that loot came by hook or crook. We stole every damn bit of it, and that could have got us strung up, too." He grinned again. "Yassir, 'specially that cannon stunt of ol' Buford's. Holy shit, Katie, I'd never put you through something like that again, no siree bob!"

"Alva, all of that is the past, damn it! I'm talking about the future." She stopped to press her fingertip to his nose. "The question is, what shall I do with Pete's money? I want your opinion."

Silence again. Then: "Won't do a damn bit of good in the hole, y' know, and I don't have no use for it. Buford 'n me never could muster up one of those bank accounts. No sirree. That's why we used the hole. If we'd cashed in all the gold, sooner or later every damn drifter in the territory would 'a smelled it out and been on our tails like a pack of hound dogs. Same with all that other loot. No bank account, no mam. Hell, the law would 'a come snooping 'round, for sure, wondering where in the hell we were getting all our do-re-me. We sure never busted our asses working till you showed up here and spoilt our game."

Katherine gave his shin a gentle kick with the toe of her boot. "Alva! Damn your hide, I tried to give you boys a little respect. Besides, a man is happier when he has something to do, something worthwhile."

"We loved it, Katie."

"So, what about this?"

"Well, like I said, this is honest money. No use cashing in and shoving it down the hole. If you don't need it, leave it be. At the goddamned interest those banks are charging, likely it'll double in five or six years. Make a good dowry for Julia, won't it?"

"Julia?" Katherine sighed. She almost teared up. "Alva, you're a dear, you are," she said with misty eyes. She shuffled the papers and put them back in the large envelope. "I told Dinsmore I wanted to hold off on this for a few days. I'm glad I did. Transferring these accounts to Julia Coltrane will be a simple matter. It may raise Frawley's brows, but this is it, Alva. I'll post this tomorrow, give him power of attorney, and get it settled. My girl is going to get a better start in life than I did."

Alva Tompkins chuckled. "Well, you ain't done so bad, y' know."

Katherine set the envelope aside, picked up her coffee, and drained the cup. Smiling at Alva, she asked, "How long does it take Jack to make the circuit?"

"Oh, mebee a couple of hours, depending on what he runs into, or don't run into."

Katherine took him by the hand. "I told you a man is happier when he has something to do. So is a woman. Come on, Alva, we have something to do ... right now."

Three days later at Porter Webb's Circle-W spread, Katherine told Porter and Joseph Brings Yellow about Quinlan's death and subsequent developments. Porter was astounded that Quinlan had willed his entire estate to Katherine. Joseph was not. He nodded and smiled at Katherine as though this had been foretold. Katherine quickly revealed her reason for riding across the foothills to visit them—she needed two things. First, some advice. But, she also needed help. First, what should she do with the Spearfish mule ranch?

Porter had a ready answer: sell it. The ranch was too small and too distant to manage. Sell it to some sodbuster for farming land.

Katherine eyed him closely. "I thought you didn't like farmers, nesters. Isn't this what you told me?"

"I don't like them on cattle land. I don't like them squatting around me."

"Yes," Katherine said with a little smirk. "Seems like a few cattlemen south of us are saying the same thing. Least, that's what that fellow, Dinsmore, told me."

"Ah, he talked to you about giving Frawley some support?"

"Only in passing. I found the idea quite intriguing."

"Necessary is more like it," Porter replied. "We're going to need some help down the line, new laws."

"We?"

"Yes, we ... all of us," returned Porter. "And you're a good example of what this is all about. You went and cut off a whole section of land with those homesteads on the river. Now, what if a dozen or so nesters came in and started homesteading below and above you, fencing the whole damn countryside, cutting off the range you need for your cattle? It's legal, you know. It's legal, but it's not right."

Katherine retorted, "This isn't cropland, Porter, and you know it. Bunchgrass, sage, prickly pear, and cockle burrs. Three months from frost to frost." She elevated her nose. "Maybelle has a fit trying to grow a garden behind the Star."

"Well, you tell that to some of those crazy fools coming in down below. Give a man a hundred and sixty acres and a speck of water and he thinks he's King Potato ... or Mother Corn, or I don't know what the hell what. If he keeps poking the ground long enough, he'll find something to grow."

"Wild hay, maybe," Katherine smiled. "He can't sell that, though. Can't eat it, either."

Then Porter chuckled. "Well, what the hell you making it for? Doing all that irrigating?"

"I'm having an over-shot stacker made, too," Katherine returned smartly.

"Oh, shit!" moaned Porter.

"Alva says cows are stupid."

"And what the hell does he know about cattle?"

"He knows about winters, bad ones."

Porter Webb sighed. "Lord, lord, there's over a hundred miles of range between us around here and we don't have that many cattle to eat all the grass, and I doubt if we ever will."

"Please, I didn't come all the way over here to talk about our stock. Dammit all, I have more important things to consider right now," Katherine said.

"I told you a long time ago you didn't need a cattle spread

to give you more headaches, didn't I? You don't listen well, Kate."

Joseph put in, "Neither of you listen. You both talk too much."

"Well," said Porter, "she doesn't listen to me very damned often, I'll tell you that."

"I'm going to sell the mule ranch," Katherine said. "I've just decided. That's listening, isn't it?"

"Now, what is it you said you need help with?" Porter asked.

"I want Joseph to go with me when I go up to get Julia," Katherine answered. "In case I have some trouble with the agency or Standing Bear's relatives. Joseph understands the people, can make better talk. They're not going to be happy to see me, and I don't want any trouble. He wouldn't be gone for more than three or four days."

"Three or four days?" Porter said. "What're you going to do? Sprout wings and fly?"

"Take the train to Chadron—"

"I don't like the iron horse," Joseph said abruptly. "This doesn't please me, Kate. The train has always been bad medicine for our people. Besides, it smokes too much and makes noise." His smile was faint. "But for you, Tall Woman, I'll make an exception. I will be honored to go with you."

"Trouble?" Porter said, looking over at Katherine. "I don't know what kind of trouble you'll have. You're holding all of the cards, damn it. The army's on your side. You have official papers. The girl is your daughter. Ben Bradford is at Fort Robinson now, and he's a general. Hell, no one at the agency is going to buck the brass."

"How do you know what those people are going to do? I don't trust agents."

Porter scoffed. "You remember the last run-in we had up there, don't you? Bird Dog got Saville's ass kicked out. Should be no different now, especially with Ben at Fort Robinson. Joseph and I worked our tails off for him."

"I don't want to cause any trouble, that's all," Katherine replied. "I've had enough of it. This has to be very proper, very diplomatic." She leaned over and put her arm around Joseph. "You'll know how to handle it."

Expressionless, Joseph Brings Yellow stared across the yard out toward the distant corrals. "Maybe I should go alone, eh? When either of you shows up, it's bad medicine. You always shoot someone."

Chapter Sixteen

Julia

Author's note

On July 19, 1881, Tatanka Iyotake, the Hunkpapa leader known as Sitting Bull, surrendered at Fort Buford, Montana Territory. The horses and arms of his followers were relinquished in exchange for a "pardon" for the chief's military engagements against the U.S. Government. Although the Lakota who followed him into Canada were resettled on the reservations—principally Standing Rock—Sitting Bull, contrary to what the U.S. Commission had promised, was made a prisoner of war at Fort Randall.

Fearful of the chief's leadership and influence among the Lakota, the government kept Sitting Bull a prisoner for two years. Only after a series of hearings and bitter negotiations was Sitting Bull freed and allowed to join his people at Standing Rock. To much of the public, he was considered a hero. He was deluged with so much fan mail that a special officer, Lieutenant Colonel G. P. Ahern, was assigned to assist the venerable chief.

The small group of Teton-Oglala who had been with the Hunkpapa arrived at the Pine Ridge reservation July 29, 1881.

It was hot along the Chugwater. Filmy heat waves devil danced above the shiny slick rails coming into the station. Inside the depot, a perspiring Luther Hatch took receipt of a telegraph message from General Jason Armitage at Fort Lincoln, Dakota Territory. After one glance at it, he donned his straw hat, crossed over to the livery, and hitched up a buggy. In a brisk trot, he made straight for Katherine Coltrane's K-Bar-C Ranch downriver. This was momentous news—

Sitting Bull had finally moved from Canada. No more rumors, it was official! The Sioux were returning to the reservations. As far as Luther was concerned, this meant only one thing: Kate's daughter was coming home!

Once at the ranch, Luther became part of an impromptu celebration. Elation abounded. On the porch, Katherine was embraced by Luther, swung once into the air by Manny Slaymaker, and kissed by Manny's wife, Mary. Another celebration followed, this one at the Star Hotel that evening. Jimmy Reynolds, at eighteen the youngest of Katherine's cowhands, had booted up to the line cabin to get Alva and Jack Cuthbert. Everyone was present. After several toasts from Luther and Manny, a big chicken and dumpling supper was served in the hotel dining room. Toward the end of the meal, Maybelle brought out a large cake with a single candle. Everyone cheered and clapped. Coincidentally, it was Katherine's birthday. At thirty-one years of age, she was a very happy mother.

If patience had always been Katherine's enemy, it now became an ogre. Oh, how she hated waiting. It was humid in the river bottom; water spiders skated on the backwater slicks, and silvery-blue dragonflies hovered in the silent, muggy air above them. Work, however, continued. By day, this relieved some of Katherine's anxiety. The new overshot hay stacker came in on a flat car from Cheyenne; her men mowed and raked the rich stand of bunchgrass and grama on the bottom land, and it was piled high in a dozen stacks. They built pole fences around the hay. Supplemental forage for Katherine's small herd of horses (all of them bought from Porter Webb) was stored in the loft of her big log barn. By night, it was another matter. Katherine's mind became a frenzy of fragmented thoughts, all of them frazzled and disconnected. Somewhere in the center of the maze was her dear little girl, Julia, reaching out, waiting for deliverance.

Finally, on the first day of August, the long-awaited letter came. It was from another old acquaintance, Benjamin Bradford, the general at Fort Robinson, the garrison southwest of Pine Ridge. Word had come from the agency—sixteen Oglala had arrived, most of them women and children. General Bradford wrote that he hadn't been to the reservation, but one of his trusted Lakota scouts reported that an old woman named White Bone and her granddaughter, Blue Star, were among the returning Oglala. Since they were relatives and members of the Crazy Horse clan, they already had been honored, provided a fine lodge, and given many gifts. Bradford told Katherine if she wished to stop at Fort Robinson, he would be happy to provide her quarters and an escort if she needed it. Whatever, he hoped they could renew their friendship.

Katherine felt like crying. She didn't. The recurring thought about her mother-in-law, White Bone, rattled her again. Instead of shedding a tear of joyful relief, she grimaced. White Bone loved Julia, too. During Katherine's many moons with Standing Bear, White Bone had cared for both Katherine and Julia. Even in those days, White Bone had been a very protective woman. More than once she berated her son when she thought he was negligent about the welfare of Katherine and Julia. This was some of the family unity that Joseph Brings Yellow often brought into conversations, the kindred bond. Katherine knew that White Bone had love in her heart, had once cherished her as a daughter, and she pained at the thought of turning this love into anguish. Katherine Coltrane had a fitful night of sleep.

The next morning, she sent Jimmy Reynolds over to the Circle-W spread to tell Joseph Brings Yellow she was prepared to leave for Pine Ridge. Later the same day, Joseph, his bundle packed, came riding back with young Reynolds.

Toward sundown a day later, Katherine and Joseph stepped off the train at Crawford, a small community adjacent Fort Robinson. The ride had been an uncomfortable one, hot and sooty. Her summer suit had wilted; so had she. She decided to accept Ben Bradford's invitation. She would stop at the fort first. This pleased Joseph. He had no wish to stay in Chadron. Indians weren't welcome there. He had been there once before with Porter when they were selling horses. Porter had shot out two lanterns in a saloon when he was refused a drink because of the presence of Joseph. Porter then took a bottle of rye at gunpoint, and they walked out unscathed. With the law searching for them, they spent the night in a livery where they slept in the hayloft. With a small smile, Joseph Brings Yellow told Katherine it was good she had left her revolver at the ranch. She and Porter were alike. Maybe she would have shot the hotel lanterns. Katherine smiled back at him. She hadn't left her revolver behind; it was packed in her small trunk with her riding clothes.

Katherine rented a buckboard at the Crawford livery. It was dusk when she and Joseph arrived at General Bradford's headquarters. Bradford had gone off duty but the watch officer directed them to his quarters, a large clapboard house across from the parade ground. The general, some officers, and their wives, were seated on the porch talking under the glow of two lanterns. An assortment of millers already were spinning about and attacking. Someone on the porch shouted jokingly, "Who goes there?"

Katherine called back, "A man and woman seeking lodging for the night. Joseph and . . . and Kate. Is there any room in the inn?"

Laughter ensued. Someone applauded. Then a deep, booming voice came. "Kate Coltrane!" Directly Ben Bradford appeared out of the shadows. He was followed closely by another man, a man Katherine thought she would never see again, Major William Bosely, the army surgeon she and Jane Canarray had assisted on that painful, disheartening journey back from Goose Creek.

Bradford's greeting was hearty and warm. He helped Katherine from the buckboard, and she promptly kissed him on the cheek. Major Bosely bowed graciously and complimented her. She was more comely than ever, he said. Exchanging handshakes, Joseph Brings Yellow smiled broadly. General Bradford fondly patted him on the shoulder. Dear friends, here, one and all. Once on the porch, introductions were made. Katherine quickly discovered the women knew her, at least had read about her, a story in *Harper's Weekly*. Surprised at this disclosure, Katherine nodded and managed a weak, "Oh." This was the first she had heard of any story about her, but she immediately knew the source—Henry Burlingame. Enroute to Casper the previous year, he had stopped briefly in Chugwater; he had visited her at the ranch.

"You are a very courageous lady," one of the women commented.

"A credit to all of us out here," another added. "A lady rancher."

"Yes," the first one said, "if there were more around like you, we women would already have our legitimate rights, wouldn't we?"

Gentle laughter. Katherine winced.

One of the officers said, "I don't think it would be wise to give every woman a gun."

More laughter.

Katherine finally breathed easier. These women looked upon her as some kind of frontier heroine! Obviously, Henry Burlingame hadn't revealed her whole story, only her years in the Chugwater Valley. Bless him, he was a gentleman. He had been snooping on her ever since the Crook campaign. Yes, bless him, he had been discreet.

Fortunately for Katherine, the conversation was brief. Bradford informed the others he had anticipated her arrival; she was passing through on business, and he had invited her to stop at the fort. Perhaps she and Joseph wanted to refresh themselves, then have dinner with him and the good doctor. Bosely, now a full colonel, took his cue and picked up Katherine's small trunk. After Katherine nodded politely to the officers and wives, she followed Bosely into the house. Shortly, Joseph and the general followed.

Bradford said, "My dear Kate, I haven't any idea if they know why you're here, that you have a child on the reservation. However, I must say, I believe you're entitled to *some* privacy in your life." He looked over at Colonel Bosely. "I think Bill will agree."

"Precisely," Bosely replied. "Fame always follows fortune."

A very tired Katherine Coltrane said, "Thank you. I'm indebted to both of you."

"Nonsense," said Bradford. "You and Joseph are colleagues. These are my quarters, and I'm delighted to share them with you."

A faint smile played across Joseph's somber face. Looking at Katherine, he said in Siouan, "This is good. Tall Woman won't have to use her pistol."

Indeed Ben Bradford was a colleague. The next morning when Katherine and Joseph were preparing to leave for the reservation, he gave her a new paper of introduction. Unlike the first one that he had written long ago at Fort Fetterman, the title preceding his name this time was "General," not "Colonel." As Porter Webb had told her, she wielded a powerful hand; she was Julia's mother, and she had the U.S. Army in back of her. However, she politely declined Bradford's offer to supply her with a military escort. She saw no need for this. In fact, she thought it might prove detrimental; the Oglala had long memories; the longknives never had been their friends. No, whatever was to be, the matter had to be resolved by her and Joseph Brings Yellow. The Oglala were brothers and sisters and wouldn't spit or throw stones at them.

So, without further ado, Katherine and Joseph rode away in their buckboard down the rutted road to Pine Ridge. She wore a long buckskin riding skirt and brown boots. Her white blouse had long sleeves, and around her neck was the beautiful beaded necklace Standing Bear had given her when she took him for her husband. Her long hair was swept back and knotted tightly at her nape by a small shell comb trimmed in gold.

Had Joseph Brings Yellow shed his black broad-brim hat, he could have stepped onto the reservation and mingled with the Lakota as one of them. He wore denim pants and a pair of cowhand boots, but from his waist up he was all Indian. He was shirtless, his torso only partially hidden by a beaded, leather vest, and he wore two strands of red, white, and blue beads. Joseph's hair was not as long as Katherine's but it was similarly bound in back by a plain strip of rawhide. However, there was one significant difference in his attire. He had a .45 caliber Colt Peacemaker holstered on his right hip. Unlike Katherine, regardless of the occasion, he never went without it. Porter Webb once told him that a man without a gun might just as well be naked. Joseph had learned this was true.

The ride to the perimeter of the reservation took almost two hours. It was now mid-morning, the heat building. This was early August, and the land was beginning to burn. Joseph Brings Yellow told Katherine the tongue of Mother Earth was parched; Mother Earth was thirsty. Soon, she would take water. Joseph nodded toward the west where a few billowy clouds had begun to mushroom on the horizon. He predicted rain before the day ended. He also saw the white man's practical side of this, too—the train ride home would be less oppressive.

Several whitewashed poles loomed in front of them, markers of the reservation land, and in the distance Katherine saw the conglomeration of shacks and buildings of the agency headquarters. The compound was much larger than the last time she had been here with Porter and Joseph—several new cabins, some additional corrals, and the agent's house had been freshly painted, white as usual. Ben Bradford had told her about the agent. His name was Rudy McKittrick, a political appointee, the Commissioner of Indian Affairs. He had been at Pine Ridge for almost two years. Though General Bradford had no jurisdiction over the agent, he did collect intelligence on the reservation's operations. McKittrick apparently was following the rules; there were no black marks against the man, only the usual Indian complaint that rations were always in short supply. This wasn't McKittrick's fault. It was because of government ineptitude and disinterest. The awesome burden of maintaining dozens of reservations all over the land had been more than the government in Washington had calculated.

Rudy McKittrick's greeting was cordial. McKittrick, like General Bradford's guests, knew Katherine Coltrane, by reputation, to be a wealthy rancher. He was shocked to learn that a young Oglala girl on the reservation was her daughter. He knew nothing about Katherine's capture and later life with the tribe of Crazy Horse. He was also surprised when he read the letter from Bradford requesting him to give Katherine all the assistance she needed. McKittrick quickly checked his register. What Katherine told him was true—he found the name of Wicapi Hinto, Blue Star, on the list of new arrivals from Fort Buford.

Looking up from his desk, McKittrick said, "I'll have to record this."

"Please do," returned Katherine.

"Do you want me to send for the girl?"

Katherine turned to Joseph Brings Yellow. He frowned and glanced to the side. Near the door, standing on the porch, were two Lakota agency assistants. They were tribal policemen. Looking back at McKittrick, Katherine said, "No, thank you. That might frighten her to death."

The agent nodded. "Yes, I understand."

"Do you know where Julia is?"

"Julia? You call her Julia?"

"Her Christian name, yes."

Rudy McKittrick smiled. "Julia. Such a pretty name." He paused and studied Katherine closely. "She has a pretty mother, too. But after all of these years, I wonder if she'll understand . . . appreciate you or her name. Have you thought about this, Miss Coltrane? Her welfare?"

"Night and day for five years."

With a sigh, almost a moan, McKittrick shook his head. "Good God, sometimes I don't know what I'm doing here. This job, these poor people, how they manage to endure. Things like this make me feel downright miserable." McKittrick inked a pen and began scratching a few lines on a piece of paper. He spoke while he wrote. "If this girl once lived with Crazy Horse's people, she's probably up near the forks of the White. Most of the Oglala moved over there when Wounded Knee started drying up. One of my men can show you the way."

"That's not necessary," Katherine replied. "We know the way. We camped a night up there five years ago with some of these *poor* people."

Handing Katherine the paper, he said with a sheepish look, "I'm sorry. I hope you and Julia have many happy days together. Please stop by on your way out so we can conclude this."

Following the White River trail, Katherine and Joseph Brings Yellow first saw the village from a distant bend, a camp of about fifty lodges spread out on a sage-covered flat. Three young boys brandishing bows came rushing out of the brushy bottom yelling, *"Wasichu, wasichu!"* Crooking his arm, Joseph shouted back, *"Kola, kolapila, waon welo!"* The boys laughed and leaped into the back of the buckboard. Joseph asked questions. Yes, one of them answered, this was a village of Oglala, and yes, the people who had been in Canada with Sitting Bull were here. Another pointed. Over there near the big medicine lodge many people were rehearsing for a ceremony. "What ceremony would it be?" asked Joseph. The little boys looked at each other and giggled. One finally said, *"Isha ta awi cha lowan."*

Katherine smiled at Joseph. In Siouan, she said, "The young womanhood ritual, for girls who are becoming women."

Surprised, the boys looked at Joseph Brings Yellow. One asked, "Who is this *wasichu* who talks like one of us?"

Turning, Katherine said, "I am called Tall Woman. Many moons ago I lived with the Oglala far from here in the great valleys of the Mother River."

"Ma-ya!"

"Yes, a land you have never seen, the land of the old ones."

"Hau, hau!" one shouted.

Joseph Brings Yellow said, "She was the woman of a chief in the clan of Crazy Horse."

More exclamations. Then, each in turn, they quickly reached out and touched Katherine. With happy shouts, they leaped from the wagon and disappeared behind the lodges. Katherine laughed. They had stolen some of her medicine.

Joseph pulled up near the perimeter of the village. Three curious women stood silently watching them from the back of a tipi. Suddenly one shrieked, clasped her hands to her head, and came rushing forward. Simultaneously, Katherine reached out with open arms. It was Walks Fast, one of the young women who had been captured with Katherine during the skirmish with Lieutenant Clybourn's small patrol. After an excited exchange, Katherine told Walks Fast that she had come to find Blue Star. This was good, Walks Fast said. After so many moons, Blue Star would be happy to see her mother. Motioning, Walks Fast said she would take Tall Woman to the lodge of White Bone. Katherine was aglow. Yes, this was good.

Looking happily at Joseph Brings Yellow, she said, *"Waśte, waśte, hechetu welo."*

Joseph's face was somber, barely the trace of a smile. "Yes, it is good, Tall Woman." But what Katherine read in his bronzed face, or felt, wasn't good. Her brother was troubled.

A few children came close. Except for small cloths draped below their fat bellies, they were naked. They followed as Walks Fast led Katherine and Joseph behind the row of lodges. Directly, Walks Fast stopped and pointed. Set in the shade of several gaunt cottonwood trees were two tipis. Sitting on a blanket next to the closest was an elderly woman. She was dressed in a sleeveless faded-blue dress. Several pieces of colorful cloth were scattered about, and she was busily wielding a needle, obviously making a dress.

Katherine slowly approached. "Mother," Katherine said softly. "Mother White Bone."

The woman's head jerked upward. She squinted; the needle shimmered in her trembling hand. Her voice quavered. "Tall Woman? Tall Woman, is that you?"

"Eyah."

White Bone wailed once. Shoving her sewing aside, she stood and stared up at the brilliant noonday sun. Eyelids fluttering, she chanted. *"O-ya-te wan was-te ca, ya ha e hi ya . . ."* Tears tumbled down her wrinkled cheeks. Arms open, she cried, "The Great Spirit has brought you home. We are healed. My daughter has come home to her people!"

For a moment, White Bone embraced Katherine. Then, she traced her gnarled fingers up and down each side of Katherine's cheeks. Katherine finally whispered, "I have come home. Yes, I have come home, but only for a while. Before my shadow becomes long, I must go."

White Bone's shoulders sagged. Her voice was a lament. *"Ma-ya,* this cannot be, Tall Woman. You must go? What has happened? Tell me, have the soldiers captured you again? Are they going to take you away to the big soldier's house? No, this cannot be, my daughter."

Katherine pressed a finger to White Bone's trembling lips. "I am free from the soldiers. They no longer claim me." Pointing, she said, "Far beyond the hills, a journey of many sleeps, is my home, the place where the bones of my father and mother are buried. I come from there to see you and Blue Star. Standing Bear is dead. The old days are dead, too, my mother."

"Your husband . . . my son, died with honor."

"I was told this. I also honor him."

White Bone stared at Joseph Brings Yellow. In a hushed voice, she said to Katherine, "Have you taken another husband?"

"No," smiled Katherine. "This is Joseph Brings Yellow. He is Lakota. I look upon him as my brother."

Bowing her head to Joseph, White Bone said, "If you are her brother, then you are my son. You are welcome here, Joseph Brings Yellow." She motioned to her lodge. "Behold, you see, there is room here for all of us."

"You are kind," Joseph returned.

"Are you a good provider? Do you hunt buffalo?"

Joseph Brings Yellow managed a thin smile. He placed a hand on Katherine's shoulder. "Tall Woman has spoken. The old days are dead. The buffalo are dead. Many of our people are dead. Only the land endures, White Bone. As with our people, the land suffers, but it endures."

Katherine looked at White Bone but said to Joseph, "Good Lord, she thought I'd come home to stay!"

"Yes, and her granddaughter will think the same," Joseph Brings Yellow said. "So now you will take them both?"

"Do you have a better idea?"

Joseph returned somberly, "Take the whole tribe. Then nobody will die from loneliness."

"Jesus, you're just like Porter!"

"No, if we had Porter along, he'd have Julia on his saddle. He'd be gone by now."

White Bone stared at them curiously. She finally spoke: "If you make words about me leaving my people to go live among the *wasichu,* your words have no meaning to me. I see goodness in your heart, my daughter, but as the bones of your people are over the mountains, the bones of my people are here. The spirits of my parents and my grandparents live here. I listen to their voices. I listen to my heart. What song would I have to sing if I left this land?"

Katherine had no answer for this. She kissed White Bone on the forehead. "I must see my daughter," she said. "I must talk with her."

White Bone nodded understandingly and replied. "Blue Star does not remember her father, only the legends. It is the same with you, my daughter. She only knows the soldiers took you away. She is made in your image." White Bone pointed her chin toward the big medicine lodges. "Over there you will find her. She is helping her friends prepare for the ritual of young women. Blue Star is also a leader. The girls always come to her for help. It was the same when we were in the Queen Mother's Land. Wherever she steps, other moccasins follow. When you see her, you will know her."

Joseph Brings Yellow asked, "Will you come with us?"

"I am her grandmother. Tall Woman is her mother. This should be a talk between mother and daughter. No, I will wait." She looked down at the pieces of cloth. "See? I make a new dress for her. Ei, the old days are dead. It will be of cloth. I have no fine hides to tan, anymore."

Standing nearby was Walks Fast. She had listened with deep empathy for Tall Woman. There were tears in her eyes, and she said, "I will go with you, show you the way. *Eyah,* but what will you do?"

Katherine shook her head. All of the joyful anticipation in her heart was withering away like the blossoms of summer. "I will talk," she finally replied. "I will see my child, and the Great Spirit willing, I'll take her home with me."

The little boys who had greeted them earlier, were right—Katherine saw a line of girls near the first big lodge. This was a rehearsal. Several men were standing in front of them. To the side were a few women, several old men, and a group of smaller girls. But there in the middle, a head taller than any of her companions, was Wicapi Hinto, Blue Star. Katherine's body went limp, her heart melted, and she heard Joseph say, "There is no doubt who that one is, Kate. Already she looks like a little woman, straight as an arrow, beautiful, just like you."

"Oh, mercy, mercy, how she had grown!"

"In five years, yes," mused Joseph Brings Yellow. "I remember when we took you away. You spit at the longknives. Porter, too. You were very bitter."

"Yes, I've tried to forget that miserable day, but I'm afraid I'll never forget it." Katherine sighed. "Oh, she's a beautiful girl, Joseph."

"A leader, the old woman says. Yes, like you, she has many friends."

Tears suddenly welled in Katherine's eyes, tears of happiness, tears of sadness. She whispered huskily, "You once told me that all good things lost come home. The circle . . ."

"An old, old story. Yes, I remember."

"She looks so happy."

"She is young. She is with her people. The fighting is over."

"Is she lost?"

"No, maybe you were lost."

Walks Fast said, "I will make a motion, tell her to come over. That old holy one, the teacher, doesn't like it when people make noise."

Katherine suddenly put out her hand. "No . . . no, wait. Oh, mercy . . . dear God, how can I do this?"

Taking Katherine firmly by the shoulders, Joseph Brings Yellow said, "Either you talk to your daughter here and now, or we walk out and say nothing. If this child discovers her blood mother is still alive . . . has come and left without seeing her, she may never forgive you the rest of her life. It's true, Julia may not want to leave this village, but as you say, she is only nine years old. This may not be the time to break the circle. Family relationship is *wakan*, Katherine."

"I'm her mother."

"Ei, motherhood is sacred," Joseph softly replied. "But

you see, you've already confessed to selfishness. You have been walking the Blue Road, sister, East to West. You have been distracted and ruled by your senses, living only for yourself. You talk with Julia. She must decide. If this isn't the time, it may come later. One day she may walk the Red Road to the South where the circle both ends and begins, the source of life."

"Damn it, Joseph, East, West, North, South, what difference does it make? I'm a white woman. I'm not Lakota."

"Blue Star is."

Katherine groaned. She stared longingly at her beautiful daughter, her very own flesh and blood, the little one she had once suckled, that she had doted upon day and night, yet now a daughter who knew her not. With a helpless look at Walks Fast, Katherine finally said, "Call her."

Julia had the dark eyes of her father; they were large and deep brown, but her face belonged to her mother, angular, a firm chin, long nose, and a beautiful wide smile. She was tall, too. She was intrigued by this *wasichu* who spoke Siouan, this pretty woman who Walks Fast had said wanted to talk with her. Away from the village, they sat side by side under a cottonwood tree, Katherine nervously trying to regain her composure. She had longed for this day, oh, so many years, this joyful reunion. But this wasn't the way she had envisioned it. She was devastated, heartbroken.

Julia said, "I have never talked with a white woman. Are you from the agency?"

Katherine Coltrane shook her head. She tried to smile. She felt like crying. "No," she replied softly. "No, I come from over the mountains. I have a very big lodge. Many moons ago, I lived with the Oglala. I learned their ways, practiced their rituals, but I was never a true Lakota."

"*Ma-ya,* you talk our language so well!"

Katherine asked, "Do you like being here on the reservation? Does it please you?"

"Yes. Yes, it is good here." Julia's nose wrinkled. "We lived in the Queen Mother's Land. Did you know this?"

Katherine nodded.

Julia went on. "Sometimes it was very cold. Sometimes there wasn't enough to eat. We left that place. My grandmother says this is our old land. I used to live in the river valleys when I was very young. I don't remember this. The old ones remember. They tell stories. I listen."

"Do you remember your father, a man called Standing Bear?"

"No. Only the stories. He was a great warrior." Julia glanced at Katherine. "Did you know him?"

"Yes," smiled Katherine. "Yes, I knew him." Then, she asked hesitantly, "Do you remember your mother?"

"No. I remember when the longknives came. They were bad. They took her away." She looked across the little meadow toward the Sioux lodges. "That woman, Walks Fast, those longknives took her away, too. They brought her to this place. The longknives didn't kill my mother. Long ago she came here looking for me. That's what some of the old men say. They tell stories about her. She was angry with the man who lived in the big lodge at the agency. One day some men came and made that man go away. This is what the old men say. My mother was a *wasichu* like you."

"Did you know what the Oglala called your mother?"

"They called her Tall Woman."

Katherine caught her breath. "May I hold your hand?" she asked.

Julia's small hand darted forward. "Will we pledge a secret?"

Oh, mercy, how innocently sweet! "A secret no longer, Blue Star." The tears filled Katherine's eyes. Her voice was almost a whisper. "I am called Tall Woman," she said. She kissed Julia's hand and sobbed, "My husband was Standing Bear. Yes, I am Tall Woman, your mother."

Julia's big eyes grew wider. For a moment, she said nothing. Her look was one of awe more than disbelief. She finally blurted. "You . . . you are my mother!" She turned and came up on her knees. She was smiling, and her hands went to Katherine's damp cheeks. "Please don't cry, Tall Woman. Look at me, I am happy to see you. See how I smile. My heart is filled with joy."

"I'm so sorry," mumbled Katherine. "My heart is heavy. I have missed you so much. I tried and tried to reach you. Even in the Queen Mother's Land I tried. Nothing ever went right . . ."

"It *was* you!" Julia suddenly exclaimed. "Oh, this I do remember! The *wasichu* came to our village up there one time. They smoked and talked. Tatanka Iyotake made them go home. Those men wanted to take me and grandmother away."

"I missed you. I could never stop trying to reach you."

"Grandmother thought it was you. She said you must have had big medicine to do that."

"White Bone is good. She was always good to me. I'm happy she has taken good care of you." Katherine gently stroked Julia's long hair. "You are very pretty. One day you will become a beautiful woman."

"I will wait," Julia said. Pointing toward the big medicine lodges she said, "Those are my friends preparing for the young women's ritual. I will know the ritual. I help them. Later, they will help me. Yes, and then I will become as beautiful as Tall Woman, my mother."

Now, Katherine's heart began to weep. Her mind raced ahead. Oh, mercy, what kind of future would she have here? What kind of an existence? What kind of a husband? These poor people. My Lord, what little they had left! They had been robbed of everything, even their freedom to roam and hunt. Hunt what? Poor White Bone didn't even own an elk hide to tan and bleach white for Julia's fancy dress. Finally Katherine bravely said, "Do you know that I gave you a *wasichu* name, too?"

"A *wasichu* name?" Julia asked curiously. "But why? I am Lakota. I am Wicapi Hinto. Is this not enough?"

"Yes, a beautiful name," answered Katherine. "You see, I always thought the day would come when I would leave the Oglala. When I was a maiden, they took me away from my people. I wanted to go home."

"They stole you!"

"Yes, it was like stealing. They treated me well, but they wouldn't let me go. The soldiers never came to get me, either."

Alarmed, Julia whispered, "Grandmother never told me this story. No one ever told me this story. This isn't good, Mother."

Katherine held her hand again and smiled. "It no longer matters. It isn't a good story, either."

"What was my *wasichu* name?"

"Julia. In my heart, I always called you Julia."

"Jule-ya. Jule-ya."

"Julia Coltrane," Katherine said. "The man called McKittrick at the agency knows this. It is now written in his big black book. I thought you should know this. Someday in your life this will be important. As you remember the old stories, I want you to remember this."

"Jule-ya. Yes, this is good, Mother. I will remember."

Katherine had now come to the inevitable. Now, she must bare her aching heart. "I came here, my daughter, to ask you to come and live with me in my big lodge far across the mountains. I asked Grandmother to come, too. I honor her. I honor her for treating me like a true daughter when I lived with the Lakota. I . . ."

Julia's hand, entwined in Katherine's, suddenly went limp. "But . . . but you have come here . . . home." She shook her head sadly. "Not to live in our lodge? Not to spread your blanket? Not to live with me and Grandmother? Is this so?"

Oh, mercy, mercy, lamented Katherine, this beautiful child, this wounded little bird, struck by the very same fateful arrow that had pierced her own bleeding heart. Oh, how she shared her daughter's hurt, but she hurried on. "Grandmother White Bone has spoken. She wishes to dwell in her own lodge. Her people are here, and the bones of her forefathers are here. It can't be any other way for Grandmother. It is the same for your mother, Tall Woman. I have no Lakota blood. My home, my people, are over the mountains. With you beside me, I would be happy. Yet, even as I love these people, I would be unhappy in their village."

Katherine looked into Julia's glazed eyes. Little Blue Star, so young, how could she possibly understand? But as Joseph Brings Yellow told her, Julia was Lakota, and Lakota girls often were wise beyond their years.

Julia finally said, "My home has always been with my people. My clan is here. My girlfriends are here, but you are my mother. I honor you, too. If you want me to go across the mountains with you, I will go. *Hechetu welo.*"

Katherine kissed Julia on her damp forehead. "The Great Spirit has blessed you, my daughter. Would you be happy in another land?"

"I will be unhappy to leave this land, my people, my friends, and Grandmother."

Katherine Coltrane had taken risks in her own life, but this was something she couldn't do—gamble with the life of Julia. She should have foreseen that it was coming down to this. Perhaps she had, and was too selfish to admit it. In a spiritual way, Joseph Brings Yellow had warned her of the complexities, the pain this reunion was bound to inflict. No, she couldn't gamble. Her thoughts were now collected; she knew her mind.

Caressing Julia, Katherine said, "It would grieve me, my daughter, to see you unhappy anywhere. You are so young. Such a beautiful blossom. Your happiness is more important to me than anything. I came here believing it was your choice, but you've made it mine, so I shall speak. No, until the Great Spirit decides otherwise, you must stay with your people. My love for you is forever. Can you understand this?"

"Over the mountains isn't so far, is it?"

"No, my child."

Smiling once again, Julia said, "I'm happy to know I have a mother, one not so far away. This is good."

"Yes, it is good." Katherine carefully removed her Lakota beads and placed them over Julia's head. "Your father gave me these when I became his wife. I want you to have them. Wear them proudly, my daughter."

Chapter Seventeen

Good Times, Bad Times

Excerpts from an interview with Henry Burlingame.

I stopped in Cheyenne for a week in June of 1882, election week. It was a rowdy place, oratory of every imaginable kind. Several fancy balls at the hotels, and brawling in the saloons. I wasn't particularly interested in the contest for mayor. I had my eye on Tim Frawley and the country attorney race. The man was a good attorney. He was a better politician. There wasn't any doubt in my mind, the stock growers, Kate and Porter Webb included, were well organized. How much money they put into Frawley's campaign, I never found out. I'll tell you this, though, he won the election going away.

Quite by accident, I ran into Kate on the street the morning after the election. She chastised me for writing a small yarn about her in the *Weekly* without her permission. That was the story about her ranch. She had never read it. Well, I told her it was my job to write stories, and most certainly, I hadn't defamed her in any way. She was quick, that woman. She said it was going to cost me breakfast, so we went to the Palace Hotel. Ida Hamilton was with her. Now, this is the first time I met Ida. Oh, I had heard stories. Kate's friendship with Ida went back to the early days in Deadwood. I think I mentioned that. Well, that was one of the most fascinating morning meals I had ever had in my life. These women were absolute charmers. Oh, the conversation wasn't ribald in the least. Both of them knew everything there was to know about politics in the Wyoming Territory. Certainly, they were better informed than most of the men with whom I came in contact. What's more, they were beautiful specimens of womanhood. They were ambitious women. Successful. I often wondered about this. Any number of men were in love with them. This wasn't rumor, it was a fact. Joseph Brings Yellow told me he thought Kate's ambition and wealth frightened men. They couldn't afford her.

Chugwater, October 1883.

Jeb Slaughter's wife, Gert, joined Mary Slaymaker in the big kitchen at the Coltrane ranch, and Alva Tompkins came down from the line cabin to barbecue the beef. This event culminated the fall shipment of cattle to the stockyards in Omaha. After a three-day roundup of stock from the Webb, Slaughter, and Coltrane spreads, a long train of cattle cars had pulled away from the K-Bar-C siding that morning. Katherine Coltrane was hosting the barbecue. The afternoon guests included most of the cowhands from the three ranches, but there were special guests, too. Cheyenne's county attorney, Timothy Frawley, his wife, Susan, and their two children, Tim and Sally, were present for the festivities. At Katherine's invitation, Frawley and his family had arrived by train a day earlier, and young Tim, now eleven and already an accomplished rider, participated in the final stages of the roundup. He was allowed the privilege of riding beside the ramrod, Porter Longstreet Webb. Another guest, unexpected but welcomed, was the writer, Henry Burlingame, whose appearance had come about purely by chance.

Enroute to Colorado, Burlingame stepped off the passenger coach in Chugwater to stretch his legs and get a quick cup of coffee at the Star Hotel. Standing beside a buckboard adjacent to the hotel was Manny Slaymaker, who had come into town to pick up mail and supplies for the Coltrane ranch. Burlingame and Slaymaker were old friends. Manny knew Burlingame also was an old friend of Katherine Coltrane. So, after a brief conversation, the writer accepted Manny's invitation to partake in the barbecue. Burlingame quickly retrieved his suitcase from the southbound Colorado and Southern and rode away with Slaymaker in the wagon. It had been over a year since he had last visited. This was an opportunity to renew old friendships, not necessarily gather material for another story. As he explained to Manny

Slaymaker, he had just sent a yarn to New York, about one of Slaymaker's old acquaintances, Alfred Packer, a drifter and prospector. One of the Platte River sheriffs, Malcolm Campbell, had arrested Packer at the Fetterman Hog Ranch. Packer was charged with killing and cannibalizing five other prospectors with whom he had been snowbound in Colorado back in 1874. Manny Slaymaker was stunned at this news.

Gently snapping the reins, Manny said, "My gawd, old Al was in Fetterman every month or so. Picked up a little grub, had supper in our place, and was back off to the hills. Stayed up in that cabin that Crazy Horse used to hole up in before the war."

Shaking his head in disbelief, Slaymaker then wheezed. "Whooee, wait until Mary hears this! She served him supper, she did. Thought he was a lonely old harmless cuss. By gawd, he turns out to be a regular doodlebug. Why, this is downright gruesome!"

"Yes, a gruesome story," agreed Burlingame. He leaned over and looked at Slaymaker. "Whatever is a doodlebug, Manny?"

"A doodlebug? Well now, it's one of them little critters that makes a sandy hole in the ground, sorta like a funnel. Y' see, an ant comes along and falls into the hole. Scratches like hell to get out. Well, the doodlebug hears this racket going on, and he just comes up and grabs the ant. Yep, takes him down below and eats him. That's a doodlebug."

Henry Burlingame knew of this insect, but he had never heard it called a doodlebug. He said, "They call those bugs ant lions, Manny, ant lions."

"Ant lions? Well, that's one on me. When I was a tadpole, I used to yell down their holes. I'd holler 'doodlebug, doodlebug come up where you are.' Damned if the bug didn't stick his head out! Downright crazy, eh?"

Burlingame chuckled, then offered an explanation. "Vibration, probably. Your doodlebug is very sensitive and clever. Its little trap is nothing more than an innocent-looking dimple in the dust. But under that dimple, Manny, is an opportunistic little creature capable of claiming anything of value that comes its way. What it doesn't devour, it stores away . . . for a rainy day, more or less."

"A cannibal," replied Manny. "Oh, that's not all, Henry. Y' could fetch the critter out and put him in the palm of your hand. Play dead, he would. Flop right over on his back.

Yell at him, 'Turn over Jack!' By gawd, he'd flip right over, he would!" Manny Slaymaker jiggled the reins. He glanced over at Burlingame. "So, you had a parley with old Al. Did he 'fess up to eating those fellows?"

"I had a long chat with Alfred," replied Burlingame. "He claims it was all a big misunderstanding, a quarrel. A very defensive man, Alfred. He didn't deny picking a few of their bones, though. Survival."

"By gawd, I've never been that hungry!"

Burlingame went on. "Two deputies took him away in handcuffs. He's going on trial in Colorado, maybe in two weeks. It's an intriguing story, Manny, so I'm going to report the trial. I suppose you can read all about the details of his arrest in a day or so. Some reporter from the *Democratic Leader* was up there. He left on the night stage with Packer and the deputies. If they made connections down in North Platte, they probably went through here on the train yesterday. I stayed over at Fetterman, spent the night in your old place." Burlingame hesitated and sighed. "The service has deteriorated, particularly the food."

Manny Slaymaker smiled. "Well, you'll be eating some of Mary's biscuits and blackberry jam this afternoon. You can tell her yourself."

Katherine was happy to see Henry Burlingame again. They had met several times since the Crook campaign, twice in Cheyenne, and Henry had visited at the ranch shortly after she had built it. Katherine respected Henry; she enjoyed his conversation, particularly his observations about the burgeoning frontier, a word Burlingame detested. He was a knowledgeable man. Though she never discussed her life with the Oglala or her shady days in Deadwood, she knew he had some knowledge of her past. He had many sources of information in the far-flung corners of the West. Porter Webb said Henry was like a fox on the scent—the man could smell out the meat of a yarn anywhere.

Whatever, as far as Katherine was concerned, Henry Burlingame was a gentleman. He had never written a line about the dark side of her life. Katherine was silently amused when she introduced Susan Frawley, a vivacious, pretty woman in her early thirties. Here Katherine was, lodging a woman whose husband had helped her in her once-nefarious livelihood, a man whom she had even bedded. Of course, there was no way Burlingame could have known about this by-gone intimacy or that her trysts with Frawley ended when the Red Bird burned. Katherine was no home-wrecker. Upon Susan's arrival in Deadwood, she would have severed the intimate relationship anyhow. Those days were past, and Katherine didn't like to talk about the past. Burlingame knew this. As the conversation developed, Henry's face was expressionless.

However, Susan Frawley *was* aware that Katherine had first met her husband in Deadwood while Katherine was searching for Julia. Katherine had stayed in one of the hotels. She solicited Timothy to settle some property deeds. And two years ago, her husband had handled the Quinlan estate. They were all smiles when Susan said Katherine was one of her dearest friends and a generous contributor to Timothy's recent political campaign.

And Katherine Coltrane said, "Tim has been a big help to me, too. He can take a lot of credit for all of those hay fields in the bottom."

Henry Burlingame was very diplomatic and complimentary. He smiled at both of these charming women. "I believe if Mister Frawley had you two fair ladies at his side, he could be elected governor of the territory."

"You are too kind," Susan replied.

However, Katherine, with a tiny smile, said, "One step at a time, Henry. One step at a time. But you make a notation about that."

Everyone feasted at the K-Bar-C barbecue. Compliments were passed to Alva Tompkins, Gert Slaughter, and Mary Slaymaker, all cooks for the day. By dusk, Jeb Slaughter's crew had departed down the river road. Katherine insisted that Henry Burlingame stay the night. She said it would be too much bother for Manny to drive him back to the Star Hotel for a room. Besides, she had an extra room upstairs. Tim and Susan were using one bedroom, and four-year-old, Sally, another. Young Tim was bedding down in the bunkhouse with his friends, Porter and Joseph Brings Yellow, and the rest of the "cowboys"—another misnomer, and a word that Burlingame also hated. As Henry once had explained to Katherine, he had observed these so-called cowboys at their work several times. Indeed, some of them were barely men, but it was a man's work they were doing, and most often it was dangerous and dirty work. Burlingame told

Katherine he saw nothing romantic in living in the saddle ten to twelve hours a day, frequently sleeping on the hard ground, getting gored or pummeled by some longhorn, or trampled to death in a stampede. Thus, Henry Burlingame never used the word cowboy in his stories. Katherine saw some humor in this. She wanted to tell Henry that the women at the House of Mirrors always used the term for their rancher clients. She hadn't told him, though.

Katherine's hospitality was accepted. While Henry Burlingame was engaged in a conversation with Porter and Alva, Manny Slaymaker took the writer's suitcase upstairs to the spare bedroom. Preparing to leave for the line cabin, Alva had slipped into his sheepskin coat. Jack Cuthbert already was at the back porch with their horses. Under the light of a lantern, Katherine exchanged a few parting words with the two men, and they rode away.

When Katherine came back into the kitchen, Porter had young Tim in tow; they were headed for the bunkhouse. She poured coffee for Burlingame and sat down at the big table opposite him. She had taken quiet amusement in his assessment of her friendly relationship with Susan Frawley, but Henry's pointed interest in Alva Tompkins caused her to laugh outright. Burlingame asked in a rush, was this the drifter, Alva Tompkins, who along with another companion had such a bad reputation for rascality? Was he one of the two beggars who had ridden back with General Crook's wounded from Goose Creek back in '76?

"Yes," Katherine laughed. "That's Alva, the one and the same."

Burlingame set his cup aside and exclaimed, "Good God, Kate, what a remarkable transformation! What's come over the bounder? How did he manage to latch up with your operation?"

Katherine explained that Alva and Buford owned property up above her on Bluegrass Creek, rangeland where her cattle grazed during late spring and summer. Since they had struck up a friendship with her and had given her some assistance during the early days of the ranch, she thought it only appropriate to put them on the payroll.

"Alva is invaluable around here," Katherine said. "He's a dear person when you get to know him." She wasn't about to elaborate just how dear he really was.

"Why, I can't imagine!"

"I gave him some responsibility, something to do. It worked."

"Yes, I should say it did." Henry Burlingame took a sip of his coffee, then asked, "The other one, this Buford chap, is he up at the line cabin, too? I don't recall meeting him this afternoon."

"Buford is dead," Katherine replied. "That ruckus we had here with the Slaughters a few years back."

"Ah, yes, the killing," Burlingame said reflectively. "I'd almost forgotten all about that. I see. As I recall, this Buford was shot from ambush."

"I try to forget it, too."

"I'm sorry."

Katherine returned quietly, "The past is past, Henry. Past, but the mistakes, the blunders, they always seem to come back to haunt me."

"Ah, but through it all, you've fared well, Kate. You do have blessings to count, your ranch, all of these wonderful friends here today."

"I'm happy you came."

After a moment, Henry Burlingame said, "What of Julia? Have you seen her, lately?"

Katherine smiled wanly. "She's happy. I'm an absentee mother. But of course, Julia can't miss what she never had, can she?"

"Yes, I understand."

Katherine wondered if Henry Burlingame understood, if anyone understood.

Henry reached out and gave her a sound pat on the arm. He chuckled, then said, "Do you know what a doodlebug is, Kate? Do you know the story?"

"Doodlebug?"

"Yes, let me tell you."

Manny Slaymaker threw a big log in one of the fireplaces to keep the night chill out of the house. He snuffed the lanterns in the parlor and said good night to Henry Burlingame, who had just come down from his room. Burlingame, resplendent in a brocaded night jacket, had his pipe. He intended to have a quiet smoke on the porch before retiring, yet once on the porch, he discovered he had company. Joseph Brings Yellow, draped with a blanket, was sitting in the darkness staring across the river bottom toward the eastern foothills. The moon was up, the October air crisp, and a million stars studded the purple sky. The night scene from Katherine's big porch was spectacular.

Henry lit his pipe. He puffed several times. "A beautiful land, Joseph," he observed. "By day, by night, a land cloaked in beauty, eh? A camouflage. Sometimes, it can be so frightening."

Joseph Brings Yellow was motionless, almost in a trance. "Frightening?" he asked. "Yes, my friend, to some, but this land cannot frighten anyone who is born of it."

"The changing times. Oh, what it must have been like before the deluge."

"Deluge?"

"The migration, Joseph, the incursions of the white man."

Joseph Brings Yellow said, "I never knew it, either, Mister Burlingame. I was too young. The old ones talked about it. They used to come here to this very place, Indian Wells. The Lakota, the Cheyenne, they came here and spread their blankets. They moved on. No one owned the land."

"Progress," Burlingame commented dryly. "My God, Joseph, look at that sky!"

"Thievery," Joseph replied. "Our people thought they were the best. The white man was better."

"It was inevitable, destined to happen."

Joseph Brings Yellow contemplated for a moment. "A wise old man once told me a story about how a white man came to warm his hands on the Indian's fire. The white man was cold. It was a night like this, the air cold, the land beautiful, and the fire was warm. The Indian welcomed the white man. He came and warmed his hands. The Indian went away in the darkness to take a piss, eh. When he came back, the white man was gone. So was the fire."

Henry Burlingame chuckled. "That's a good story, Joseph."

"Yes, the old man who told it to me thought so, too. He laughed. He thought it was a big joke, but his laugh was bitter."

"Are you bitter?"

"No, why should I be? I know so little about the old days, only the legends. My life with Porter, the man the Lakota call White Hawk, has been good. I barely know my people anymore. I couldn't be happy on a reservation." For the first time, his head turned. He looked over at Burlingame in the shadows. "Maybe my French blood is thicker that Lakota. Do you suppose?"

"Did you know your father?"

"Marat? I don't remember him," replied Joseph. "He disappeared, maybe killed. If I saw him today, I wouldn't know him."

Henry Burlingame blew a stream of smoke. It quickly dissolved in the cold night air. "Ironic, isn't it?" he mused. "Julia. Kate told me Julia didn't know *her*, either. Julia is a breed, and she loves the reservation."

"She doesn't know anything else," Joseph said. "It's the only life she has. She's Lakota."

"I understand Kate doesn't go up to Pine Ridge anymore."

"You talked to her?"

"I tried to," Burlingame answered. "I had to change the subject."

"She can't go up there. She gets sick when she comes home."

"Depressed?"

"Sick, Mister Burlingame. Physically sick."

"Ye Gods!"

"Porter told her to quit going. It wasn't worth it to her or Julia. Now, I go. I make the trip twice a year. I take gifts from Kate . . . clothing, money." Joseph Brings Yellow stopped and sighed. "Julia has everything she needs. *Eyah*, everything but a mother."

All of Katherine's guests left the next morning. Porter Webb and Joseph Brings Yellow were away shortly after sunup. Later, Manny Slaymaker took Burlingame and the Frawleys to the little depot in Chugwater where they boarded the southbound for Cheyenne. Henry was going on to Denver for a few days, then Lake City, Colorado where the deputies were taking Alfred Packer to stand trial for murder.

It was almost one o'clock when Manny returned from Chugwater. He had mail, a letter for Katherine, and the latest Cheyenne *Democratic Leader*. Manny already had read the dispatch from Fetterman about Packer's capture. The old prospector had surrendered to Sheriff Campbell without firing a shot: Another story, however, had caught Manny's eye, one that he knew Katherine Coltrane would find interesting—Sitting Bull had been released from imprisonment at Fort Randall. The Hunkpapa chief was going to Standing Rock to be with his people.

Katherine and Mary Slaymaker were sitting at the kitchen table peeling apples. When Manny told her about Sitting Bull's release, she had only one comment. "The lying bastards held him as long as they could without going to court. He's the biggest chief in the Lakota tribe. He hates the *wasichu*. It'll be just like Crazy Horse. If they can't silence him, they'll find some way to kill him."

Manny looked up from the pipe. "Aw, come on, Kate, why in the hell would they want to do something like that? On the reservation?"

"Because he speaks for his people," Katherine replied. "And anyone who speaks out for justice, for better treatment or upholding the treaties, they call a troublemaker. That's why."

Katherine took her paring knife and slit open the letter in the brown envelope, the one with Jason Armitage's flourishing penmanship on it. It was brief, only a few lines. After a moment, she looked at Mary and then at Manny. "General Armitage has resigned his commission. His father passed away. He's going back to Philadelphia to take over the Penn Central Railroad."

"My heavens!" Mary Slaymaker said.

"My heavens is right," echoed Katherine. "The man hates the railroad business."

Manny put in, "Well, as I recall he didn't have much use for the army, either. He wasn't your regular cut, anyhow."

"No, that's not exactly true," said Katherine. "Burlingame once told me Bird Dog was one of the best officers in the West. And Porter backs that up. Porter says Bird Dog is one of the few men who understands the Indians, he and Ben Bradford. Neither one of them likes General Crook, that's true." Katherine plunged her knife into an apple. "Those men in Omaha and back in Washington are a bunch of assholes."

Mary recoiled and huffed, "Kate, my gracious!"

Manny Slaymaker slapped the table with the flat of his hand and guffawed.

Laramie Valley, 1884.

It rained that night in the Chugwater Valley. By morning, the rain was spotty, but in the higher elevations there was a skiff of snow, the first of the season. Kate had work to do. She put on winter clothing and donned her rain slicker. She wrapped a wool scarf around her neck and pulled her broad-brim hat to her brow. Jimmy Reynolds came with the horses, and the two of them rode off in an intermittent drizzle toward Jeb Slaughter's upper hay shed and corrals. During the recent cow hunt, the men had herded almost thirty heifers and cows with K-Bar-C brands into the pens. Katherine was going to move them up to her bottom land where she had some of her best shorthorn bulls pastured. She allowed the little drive would take no more than several hours. Mary Slaymaker promised stew and hot biscuits by the time she and Reynolds returned.

Near the south end of the hay shed, Katherine and young Reynolds met Jeb Slaughter's son, Matt. Mounted on a big bay, Matt was leading a mare toward the upper corral. A six-month-old colt was trotting alongside. Matt waved, then stopped at a gate, removed the lead rope from the mare, and ran her and the colt inside.

Reining to the side, Katherine pulled up and stared over the pole fence. The mare had a Circle-W brand on her rump. Surprised, Katherine asked, "Where did you pick up these two?"

Matt Slaughter pointed. "Over there across the river. Some of Porter's stock."

"I can see that," Katherine replied. "I wonder how they got way over here. It's thirty miles to his place."

Stepping into a stirrup, Matt said over his shoulder, "Be danged if I know, Kate. Strayed, maybe."

"Well, don't you think this is a bit unusual for this time of the year? Porter usually has his mares and colts bunched."

Matt grinned. "Unusual? Yes and no. She could have been out in the coulees all summer. I don't think Porter is gonna miss two horses, not when he has his nags running all over the range. I didn't cut any other tracks over there. I thought I'd run them down to our place this afternoon. Porter can pick them up the next time he or one of his men gets over this way." Nodding toward the corral where Katherine's cows were milling about, he said, "You want a hand with those?"

"You can help us get them moving up the road." Puzzled, Katherine stared at the mare and colt. Looking back at Jimmy Reynolds, she asked, "You think they're strays?"

Reynolds tucked once at his coat collar, then shrugged. "Like you say, Miss Kate, it's a far piece over to Webb's spread." Reynolds was wearing a new hat. Its curled brim was pebbled with raindrops. He removed it, whacked it against his thigh, and said, "Wouldn't take but a few minutes to ride over there and backtrack 'em. Reckon their prints will stand out right good in all of this mud."

Slaughter said, "They came down across that little rise yonder. All by themselves, far as I could see." He gave Katherine Coltrane a curious look. "You have some notion about 'em?"

"I don't know. It just seems damned funny to me, that's all." She reined around. "Go take a look Jimmy. Matt and I can get these cows headed in the right direction."

Kicking his horse into a brisk trot, Jimmy Reynolds headed for the distant knoll. Five minutes later, he was out of sight. By the time he reappeared in the flat, Katherine and Matt had moved the cattle about a quarter of a mile up the road.

Jimmy Reynolds had left in a trot, but he came back in a gallop. Motioning toward the rolling hills, he shouted, "There's a whole slew of tracks over there. By God, the other side of that ridge, there's sign all over the place! Moving north, must be twenty or so horses in the herd."

Katherine Coltrane shot Matt a quick look. "I told you it was funny, didn't I? Damnit, Porter was at my place a couple of days ago. He didn't say a word about selling horses. North? He never moves horses that direction. You know what I think?"

"Oh, shit!" moaned Matt Slaughter. "Rustlers?"

"I'd bet on it."

Jimmy Reynolds said, "That mare broke off, got under 'em sometime during the night. She trotted right down that little coulee to the bottom. Those tracks over the hill ain't no more than four or five hours old, either, barely water-logged."

Slaughter glanced down at Katherine. "Well, what do you

think? What can we do about it? They could be all the way to Fish Creek by now."

"Maybe," replied Katherine. She was trying to collect her thoughts. What could they do? One thing she did know—these men were stupid trying to pull a stunt like this on Porter Webb. By the word of Joseph Brings Yellow, Porter had been one of the best rustlers in the West during his younger days. Joseph said his brother-in-law knew every trick in the book, could steal a horse from right under a man's saddle.

As if reading her mind, Matt said, "Well, we oughtta let Porter know about it. I hate like hell to ride all the way over there, but I'll do it. One of you can let my pa know what's happened."

Katherine shook her head. "It would be a waste of time, Matt. By the time you're over and back, six hours are gone. Those men aren't going to waste much time getting out of this valley, but they'll have to rest somewhere along the line. They're not going to run their horses lame."

Jimmy Reynolds spoke up. "I'll bet Porter already knows those horses are missing. Joe's the outrider over there, and that Injun just don't miss anything."

"Well, that's the gospel," Matt replied, reflecting upon another time, that horrible day Katherine Coltrane had shot Black Mordecai. It had all come out later, how Joseph uncovered the damning evidence.

"Where could they be taking the horses?" Katherine asked.

Matt Slaughter smoothed the sides of his thin mustache and stared away thoughtfully. "They might hole up somewhere south of the big river, a hideout, even a ranch. They could do some blotting on the brands and rest up. They'd have to find a market out of the area, say like Lusk or even Chadron. Jesus, who knows? They could even go up the river."

"Deadwood? Sundance? The Black Hills market?" Katherine asked.

"Most likely where they'd end up," replied Matt with a nod. "Those miners up there buy any goddamned thing walks on four legs."

Katherine looked at Jimmy Reynolds. "I want you to ride on back and tell Manny. Tell him to ride to Chugwater. Have Luther get on that telegraph and put out some messages. Maybe he can reach Sheriff Campbell through Fort

Laramie or Douglas. Send another wire to Lusk, that marshal there ... Archibald ... Arch ..."

"Arch Langley," Matt said.

"Langley, yes," nodded Katherine. "He's a fire-eating bastard, isn't he? Tell him there's a five-hundred-dollar reward out. That should keep him on the lookout."

Matt Slaughter grinned. "Porter ain't gonna pay any five-hundred bucks, Miss Kate. You know that. If he gets his hand in this, those men won't be seeing any jail. More likely the short end of a rope."

Young Reynolds looked at Katherine. "What you aimin' to do?"

"Matt and I'll stop by and tell Jeb. We'll take a ride down the road, see if these fellows cross over to the mountains or make for the North Platte. I just can't believe they'll ride into some town with a herd of stolen horses. They may be stupid, but not that stupid."

"What about these critters?"

"To hell with them. They have the whole bottom. We can round them up tomorrow."

Jeb Slaughter's conversation with his son and Katherine Coltrane was brief and blunt—he didn't want either of them following rustlers. This was a posse's job. Katherine assured him they were only interested in checking the road to see if the thieves crossed over to the west side of the valley. What then? asked Jeb. Katherine said she and Matt would return; she would be happy to see someone get a posse together. Some of the men in Hartsville might be willing to participate in a chase. She suggested that to make it legal, Sheriff Campbell could lead the posse. Agreed.

Jeb Slaughter managed a wrinkled grin. "Just in case Porter don't know he's been rustled, I'll send a man over to his place. The shoe's on the other foot, eh? Let's see how he's gonna wear it."

Katherine didn't see much to laugh about. She rode along for several miles without saying a word. About four miles north of the Slaughter ranch, she pulled up. "Look there," she said. A rider was approaching. His hat was low, and he wore a yellow rain slicker somewhat like the one Katherine had on. About ten yards away, he stopped and held up a hand. However, Katherine noticed his other hand was on a rifle that rested across the front of his black saddle. Another thing she noticed with some surprise—he was a Negro.

Matt tipped his fingers to the brim of his hat. "Good morning," he said.

The stranger acknowledged them with a smile, a smile that was gleaming white, the widest smile Katherine had ever seen. In a startlingly deep and mellow voice, he said, "Not much of a good morning, my friends." His horse shied and danced to the side. "It's tolerable, though."

"Where you headed, mister?" Katherine asked.

The man tipped his droopy hat with a forefinger. "Ah, a lady," he said with his continuing smile. "South for the winter. Yes, ma'am, I'm moving south, and you people are going north. Not a good morning for a pleasure ride."

Matt Slaughter said, "We're looking for some horses . . . stolen horses."

"Yes, suh, I thought so," the man said. "I can't see no other reason you'd be riding this way." He nodded at Katherine. "My name is Jack Darby, ma'am. Some call me Blackjack. I reckon you can see why."

Jack Darby was still smiling. It was infectious. Katherine smiled, too, and said, "I thought maybe it was because you were a gambler, a cardplayer."

"Yes, that's my misfortune. Not that I'm colored but because I play the devil's game." After a short pause, he said, "Oh, those horses you're looking for. They're up the Laramie bottom about five or six miles."

"You saw them!" exclaimed Matt.

"Twice, in fact," replied Darby. "The first time early this morning. I got this for seeing too much." He parted his slicker and exposed his left leg. A big rag dark-red with blood was wrapped around his thigh.

Matt Slaughter blurted, "For crisesakes, man, you've been shot! Those sons of bitches shot you!"

"Oh, mercy!" cried Katherine, preparing to dismount. "Can you get down? Let me see what I can do . . ."

Jack Darby gently protested. "No, ma'am, you just sit. It ain't bleeding much no more. I figure I can make it down the road. Spread ahead somewhere. That's what I figure."

"My pa's place," Slaughter said. "We can be there in ten or fifteen minutes."

Aghast, Katherine reined about. "My God, Mister Darby,

how can you be grinning? You could have bled to death! Come on, let's move out of here right now!"

"I always grin," Darby returned. "My pappy told me it's the best way of staying out of trouble."

Matt Slaughter huffed, "Well, you damn well weren't smiling this morning, were you?"

"What about your horses?"

"Said they were upon the Laramie River, didn't you?" Matt said. "That's all we wanted to know, just the direction those rustlers were headed."

"I reckon I didn't know they were rustlers the first time I saw them," Darby sighed. "They came right around a bend crossing this trail, three of them. I figured they must have thought I was in their way, or they just plain hated coloreds. One of 'em started shooting."

"The dirty bastards," Kate said bitterly.

"I played possum right there in the mud," grinned Darby. "They kept right on moving, went right up the Laramie canyon trail."

Katherine stared at him in disbelief. "You said that was the first time you saw them. You mean you went riding up the Laramie after them? All shot up, and you went following them? Oh, mercy, Mister Darby, you were asking for trouble!"

"Are they camped up there?" Matt asked.

"No, they were making coffee, taking a little rest."

"Well, we know where they're headed," Matt sighed. "Posse won't have much trouble with it, 'less those men get over the top and make it into the Shirley Basin country. Rocky as hell in places over that way."

With his big smile, Jack Darby said, "They ain't likely going nowhere, 'cept to hell. They're dead as doornails. I killed 'em."

Chapter Eighteen

Life and Death

After Katherine Coltrane and Gert Slaughter put a clean bandage and compress on Jack Darby's leg, they moved him up to the K-Bar-C. When the southbound train stopped at the Coltrane water tower later that day, Katherine was waiting. She had a small overnight bag. She took Blackjack Darby to the hospital in Cheyenne where a doctor removed the .44 caliber slug from his thigh. As usual, Katherine stayed the night in her suite at the House of Mirrors, and Ruby Danforth joined her. She told Ruby that she had met a handsome, young colored man who would be at the hospital for several days recuperating from a gunshot wound—he might appreciate a friendly visit.

Three days later, Blackjack Darby limped from the train at the Chugwater depot. Manny Slaymaker met him, and the young man returned to the Coltrane ranch as Katherine had wanted. Blackjack was a handsome man, and he *was* young. He told Katherine he was twenty-seven. He wasn't a southern Negro; he was from New York, and had come west when he was seventeen. He knew horses. His father had been a farrier with the Federal Army during the Civil War, later a smithy in New York.

Katherine was surprised to learn that Blackjack had been the hired hand at Pete Quinlan's mule ranch outside Spearfish, until Katherine had inherited and sold the homestead.

During his recovery, Blackjack told Katherine that he was only a part-time cardplayer; he was a ranch hand, a broncobustster. Katherine Coltrane liked him; she enjoyed the way he talked, the mellow sound of his deep voice; she liked his easy mannerisms and his wonderful smile. Before Blackjack could mount a horse again, she hired him and put him in charge of the K-Bar-C horse herd. She told Blackjack to give Manny Slaymaker a list of anything he needed to set up shop in the big log barn, including a forge. By early December, the smell of smoke and cherry-hot iron, the sizzle of steam, often permeated the chilly air around the barn. Blackjack Darby was in business; he had found new friends; he had found a new home; he was happy.

Of course, Katherine could never tell if Blackjack was unhappy. Neither could anyone else at the K-Bar-C. He never complained, not even during those first days upon his return from the hospital. Katherine had to change the dressing on his thigh and disinfect the wound. She knew it was painful; even walking was painful. But Blackjack had smiled through it all. Katherine Coltrane thought he was a remarkable man.

Several others thought Blackjack was quite remarkable, too, Jimmy Reynolds among them. Jimmy had been in awe of him every since he had gone with Porter Webb and Joseph Brings Yellow to retrieve the stolen horses up on the Laramie. This had been one day after the shootings. Reynolds thought Blackjack's feat was a cunning and bold display of courage. Undoubtedly in pain, and weakened by loss of blood, Darby had managed to sneak up on the rustlers and dispatch them. What's more, none of the men had been shot in the back. Two were hit in the chest, the third took a slug in the middle of his forehead. More remarkable—after Porter had examined the bodies, he told Jimmy and Joseph the rustlers weren't killed by rifle fire. Lead from a revolver had done the fatal damage. Blackjack Darby, Porter said, was a gunfighter and a damn good one.

One of the first to benefit from the skills of the new hand was Joseph. He was at the K-Bar-C resting easy, enjoying a cup of hot coffee after a cold ride over.

Jack Darby took Joseph's big red gelding to the barn and put new shoes on it. When the work was done, Katherine, dressed in a long sheepskin coat and a fur-lined pullover hat, came and told Joseph she was going into Chugwater to see Maybelle Hatch and do a few chores. Maybelle had been ailing. He could tie his horse on behind the wagon and ride in with her. Katherine nestled herself in between Joseph and Jack Darby. Blackjack took up the reins, and they were away. It was almost noon when they arrived at the Star Hotel.

Katherine told Blackjack to drive around in back to the kitchen. Maybelle wasn't there. One of the nester's wives, Lucretia Swanson, who had been helping in the hotel told

Katherine that Maybelle was at her house next door. Katherine left to make a short visit while Joseph and Jack Darby went inside to have some coffee. Lucretia quickly poured two cups. She had never seen either of the men, but she thought anyone traveling with Kate Coltrane must be a good friend. She smiled once and darted away to the front to tell Luther that Miss Kate was about. No more than five minutes later, Katherine returned. Maybelle was resting; Katherine hadn't wanted to disturb her, but she did want to talk to Luther. She knew he had taken his wife to a doctor in Cheyenne several days past for diagnosis. After pouring herself a cup of coffee, she went through the doorway into the saloon with Joseph and Jack Darby directly behind her.

There were four men in the room, two at the bar talking with Luther Hatch, and two at a table near the door. When Luther saw Katherine, he hurried to the end of the bar, held her hand, and kissed it. He shook hands with Joseph, then Blackjack Darby. When Katherine asked about Maybelle's condition, he shook his head sadly. "Doctor says she has a liver ailment. Gave her some medicine to take, make her feel a bit better, but her liver's all big and hard. She gets tired."

"She needs the rest," Katherine said.

"Makes her mad as a wet hen nodding off all the time."

The brief conversation ended. One of the men near the door yelled at Luther Hatch. "Hey, what you doing letting Injuns in here? You can't be doing that, Luther. It's agin the law. Agin my principles, too."

Katherine Coltrane stared at the man, then back at Luther Hatch. "Who is that loudmouth? What wallow did he crawl out of, anyhow?"

"Poindexter hand," Luther said. "Maybe both of them. A bit soused."

The man shouted again. "What's this place coming to? You letting 'em sneak in by the back, eh?"

Katherine lit up like a firecracker. She shoved her chin out and yelled, "You mind your manners, mister. I don't know who in the hell you are and I don't much care, but if you don't like it in here, get the hell out."

"Wal, now, miss, I don't know you neither, but I sure ain't moving for no woman. Never did and never will."

"Her name is Coltrane," Luther Hatch said. "She just happens to own this saloon. Like she says, if you don't like it, you can move. Go on down the street to the Globe and have your drinks."

"Coltrane?" The man snickered. "What the hell am I supposed to do, tuck my tail and run?"

Blackjack Darby had a big grin on his dark face. He held his arms out wide, protectively wide, and said in a deep rumble, "You should leave, boys. Go out in the cold air and thin your blood. It has too much red-eye in it. Never quarrel with a lady, never. Not when she's the boss."

For a moment, the Poindexter cowhand lost his tongue. He took a long look at the tall man with the big smile. "Wal, for crisesakes," he finally blurted, "you ain't no Injun. If y' are, your the blackest one I ever seen. And what the hell you grinning at. You think this is funny?"

"I'm no 'Injun' as you say," Darby replied. "I'm a nigger man, and I'm not grinning at you. My teeth are just big, that's all, big and white. Are you too drunk to move? Shall I help you?"

The other man shoved back his chair and stood. "I'm not drunk, nigger, and if you want to step outside I'll show you."

"Wait ... wait," Katherine implored. "This has gone far enough." She turned to Luther Hatch. "Give them a bottle on the house, one for the road, and let's be done with it. Get them out of here."

A low deep-throated laugh came from Blackjack Darby. "You see, she's a lady. Besides, I don't like it outside. It's cold out there."

"Hogwash!" the first man said. "If you don't like it up here, you oughtta go back home and pick cotton."

"Please leave," Katherine asked again. "Here, take the bottle and leave."

"All right," the one seated answered. "That's a fair shake, I reckon, Injun or not."

But the other young man standing didn't move. He shoved his partner back into his chair. "I don't like niggers telling me what to do, Jake. You don't like Injuns. Well, by gawd, I don't like uppity niggers."

The two men at the bar sensed trouble coming. They moved to the side.

"Well, that makes it easy, then," smiled Blackjack Darby. "Like the lady says, if you don't like our company, take your free bottle and walk out."

"Not before I wipe that grin off your face," the man shouted. He jerked at his hip. Nothing was there but air. There was a resounding explosion. His hand was adrift, floating away from his body. Hit in the chest, he flew backward and collapsed on his back. Near the bar, a little wisp of smoke curled away from the shiny muzzle of Blackjack's revolver.

The man called Jake was horrified. Staring down at his fallen partner, he cried, "Why, you crazy son of a bitch! What the hell did you do that for? We had the bottle, didn't we? We had it! We had everything cozy, didn't we? Now, look at what you've gone and done! Got yourself killed. Oh, Lord, Lord!" His hands to his head, Jake rested his head on the table and began sobbing.

The young man's name was David Coombs. He wasn't more than twenty-five. One of the men said he was a nephew of Ivan Poindexter. Poindexter's brother-in-law, Orson Coombs, had a big sheep ranch to the west near Bosler. They draped Coombs's body over his horse, and Jake, after a sad look back at the small crowd, rode off to the south.

Katherine Coltrane wasted no time in getting out of Chugwater. The day had become a nightmare. She gave Joseph Brings Yellow a parting hug. He mounted up and rode east. Directly, Jack Darby swung the wagon around from the back of the hotel. Holding the bottom of her long coat, Katherine grabbed the iron rail and stepped up to the blanket-covered seat. She waved to Luther Hatch. To Blackjack Darby, she said, "Let's get the hell out of here."

She and Darby were almost a half mile down the road before Blackjack spoke. "I'm sorry for you, Miss Kate. Not myself. I shouldn't have killed that fellow. It don't bode well, not a bit. I messed up. No one likes a messer."

The air was nippy. Pulling her hat lower, Katherine replied, "If you hadn't shot him, the damn fool might have shot one of us." She cursed. "Jesus, I can't believe how vain, how stupid some men are! False pride, prejudice, it's a bunch of crap."

Jack Darby, a man who already had seen the worst of it in his young life, had no comment on this. After another long stretch of silence, he said, "That boy was ol' man Coombs' kin. The law will probably come looking for me, again, asking me to move on."

"The law won't do anything of the kind," Katherine said hotly. "I own the law up here, Mister Darby. Most of those boys would kiss my ass if I asked them."

Blackjack emitted a low rumbling chuckle. "For a lady, Miss Kate, you've got a helluva way of talking. Got yourself a short wick, too."

Another quiet moment passed. Katherine peered over at Blackjack curiously. "Just what did you mean about the law asking you to move on, again? What have you been up to, anyway?"

Jack Darby snapped the reins once. He turned and gave Katherine a wider grin. "You must own the law up in Deadwood, too. Leastways, you did."

"I have friends up there, important friends."

"Threw me in jail, they did," Darby said. "Some jackass didn't like the color I was showing . . ."

"Oh, Jesus, not that again!"

"No, mam, not the color of my skin. Hell, I had me some friends in Deadwood, too. No, the color of my cards. Said I was cheating."

"Well, were you?"

"Hell, Miss Kate, I play cards. I don't gamble. I play the game, and I don't have to cheat to win a few bucks now and then. No, I don't mind being called a nigger. Back home we're all niggers, but I don't cotton to being called a cheat. Well, one thing and another, this turkey neck calls me out."

"You killed him? Over a damn card game?"

"No, I busted his wing, a hand too." Blackjack Darby chuckled again. "That boy is gonna have a helluva time shuffling a deck now, I'll tell you that."

"So, they put you in jail."

"For safekeeping, they said. Seems like some of that ol' boy's friends wanted to string me up on one of those big cottonwoods."

"It happened before in Deadwood, I can tell you that," Katherine said. "More than once, too."

"Yes, ma'am, I know," nodded Darby. "Well, that night, Mister Givens came down to the jail. He had a talk with the sheriff . . ."

"Bullock? Seth Bullock?"

"Yes, mam. Another one of your friends?"

"I met him a few times."

Blackjack Darby's big teeth gleamed. "When Mister Givens told him I'd been watching out for your mule ranch for a year or so and was coming down here to work for you, well, Mister Bullock opened the front door and let me ramble."

"That damn Henry!" huffed Katherine. "He's a liar. I didn't know anything about you coming down here to work. He never wrote a line about it."

Jack Darby chuckled deeply again. "Mister Bullock swallowed the story, and I didn't have to see no judge about that shooting."

"Well, you won't have to see any judge around here, either," Katherine said. "If someone put a charge on you, it wouldn't get past the district attorney's office."

"You know him, too, Miss Kate?"

"Very well. I own a big piece of him, Mister Darby."

Even behind the clatters of hooves on the frozen road it was very resonant: "Heh, heh, heh."

Shortly before Katherine and Blackjack reached the K-Bar-C gate, a sharp whistle cut the cold air. It came from the south, back toward Chugwater. Puzzled, Katherine glanced at Darby. The northbound had passed early in the morning. No cattle cars were moving at this time of the year, so Katherine was mystified. She looked back and saw the black engine belching smoke and steam. When the train finally came into sight she saw a long string of flatcars, and at intervals men were rolling off logs next to the track bed.

Shortly, the engine puffed up to the Coltrane spur where the brakeman leaped off. He ran up, and with a long iron bar, threw the switch into the siding. The train huffed again, slowly moved forward and came to a stop directly in front of Katherine and Blackjack. The brakeman shouted, "Have to sit here until Number Ten goes by. Couple of hours."

"What's your freight, mister?" Katherine called.

"Telephone poles," he answered. He trotted over to the wagon. "Bringing a line through here come spring." He doffed his hat. He had a red scarf under it covering his ears. "By any chance are you Kate Coltrane?"

"Yes, I'm Kate Coltrane." She turned and introduced Jack Darby. "This is Mister Darby, one of my men."

The brakeman's name was Charlie O'Doul. He allowed it

would take four or five more hauls before all of the poles were dropped, but come spring, the telephone line would be in all the way to the settlements on the North Platte.

Katherine Coltrane's mind began to work. She needed a telephone. She wanted a line up to the Bluegrass cabin, too, but she could manage this later. With a smile, she asked, "How many in your crew, Charlie?"

"Seven."

"Well, I can't see any reason you boys should be sitting down here waiting two hours for the southbound. Why don't you come up to the house? We might be able to rustle up some coffee and a little grub."

Charlie O'Doul rubbed his gloved hands together. "By damn, Miss Coltrane, that's the best offer I've had all day."

"Yes, Charlie, and probably the only one you're going to get between here and the North Platte."

The men soon came. They warmed themselves by the big fireplace, drank coffee, and ate roast-beef sandwiches. About two hours later, Number Ten pulled in and took on water from the tank. The freight moved north a short time later. Next to the Coltrane siding were seven telephone poles. Charlie O'Doul thought six would reach her house, but he left one extra for good measure.

Chapter Nineteen

A Grave in the Snow

Excerpts from an interview with Henry Burlingame.

Jack Darby? Was he a gunfighter? In my opinion, no.
From what Porter Webb told me later, I suppose he
could have been a gunfighter had he wanted to be.
There wasn't any doubt he knew how to handle a
handgun. Webb said Darby taught himself how to
shoot. The young man had time to burn when he was
working for the freighter, Quinlan. He practiced every
few days out by one of the sheds. I knew a few gunfighters, saw several in action, and talked to others. I
only met Jack Darby once, and that was several years
after the shootings in the Chugwater Valley. Unfortu-
nately, I returned to New York after the Alfred Packer
trial. I don't think I mentioned this, but Alfred escaped
the gallows. Circumstantial evidence. Yes, and he
claimed self defense! He got forty years in prison,
though.

If someone could have interviewed Darby, those
Chugwater shootings would have made a splendid
yarn. I believe Kate shielded the man. She was very
protective of her employees. That worked both ways.
True, Kate knew how to take care of herself, but there
always seemed to be someone around in her family of
friends to look out for her welfare. For instance, this
Darby chap. He was a frequent companion of Kate's
when she made trips into Chugwater or Cheyenne. Oh,
there was some gossip about this. A few claimed
Darby was her hired gunslinger. He was an imposing
man in stature and in his manner of dress. His revolver
had one of those pearl handles, and he wore it so it
could be easily seen. The one time I did have an opportunity to talk with him, he certainly didn't strike me

as one who looked for trouble. I don't think he had a mean streak in him. He was a defensive man. Most of the shooters I knew never asked questions. They shot first. Porter Webb fit *that* mold.

It was late in the afternoon when Katherine Coltrane and Jack Darby stepped from the train in Cheyenne. Someone had put a Christmas tree in the station. It was decorated with a few silver ornaments and strings of popcorn. Outside, the street was bare, free of snow, and beyond one empty lot, Katherine saw a few leafless cottonwoods. They looked like skeletons against the drab countryside. She was always nostalgic about this particular location; her house had once been where the railroad equipment sheds now stood.

Katherine had come to attend to several business matters; she also planned to do some holiday shopping. She went directly to the House of Mirrors where she and Blackjack entered from the back and walked up to the second floor. They met Ida Hamilton, who gave Darby a key to the room next to Katherine's suite. Katherine pressed two hundred dollars into Blackjack's hand and told him to buy some clothes before the stores closed. The money, she explained, wasn't a gift; it was a Christmas bonus, something he had earned. But with a smile, she also told him she wanted him properly dressed; she didn't want him mistaken for some "poor colored" down on his luck.

Jack Darby's gentle rumble echoed down the hall. Ida laughed with him. Blackjack was very gracious. He would dress to kill. Yes, and in Katherine's graceful presence, he doubted anyone would mistake him for a poor nigger.

She opened her door and Blackjack took in her two suitcases. Katherine's quarters were grand and spacious, richly furnished in colors of gold and burgundy. She saw that young Darby was impressed; his eyes widened, his smile broadened. Katherine was delighted, and she opened the door to her bedroom. Except for the gilded tub partially hidden by a folding partition, it was decorated in shades of blue. A huge canopy bed was placed next to a large bay window. Katherine joked that this was her blue room. She always came here when she was feeling blue.

"This is my secret place, Mister Darby," Katherine said. "No one is supposed to know about it. Damn few do, and you're now one of the few. It's very private. Do you understand?"

Blackjack Darby pressed a big finger to his lips.

After Jack Darby left, Ida and one of the girls, Kitty Dunston, returned with several kettles of hot water. Katherine had already shed her traveling suit and underclothes. She wore a black silk gown trimmed in lace at the neck and sleeves. The water was poured, and Kitty left. Katherine went to a small oak cabinet and took out wine and two thin-stemmed tumblers. The two women took several sips before Katherine disappeared behind the boudoir partition to bathe.

Ida Hamilton had aged since those early days at the Red Bird, but she was still attractive. Her hair was auburn; she was almost as tall as Katherine. Now in her mid-thirties, she had nonetheless retained the beauty of her body. In her face, only a few lines had begun to appear, these at the corners of her eyes and across her forehead. Unlike Katherine, her face was rouged and powdered.

Ida seldom took a trick, and when she did, it was with one of her favorite gentlemen, usually a wealthy businessman or a politician. There was little need for Ida to work—she had eight girls employed in the House of Mirrors.

Sitting in a chair adjacent to the partition, a tall screen with Oriental designs on it, Ida puffed from a cigarette in a gold holder. She occasionally took a sip of wine. She was very candid because she and Katherine had come a long way together. Jack Darby, she said, was an intriguing young man. "What do you have in mind for him?" she asked.

Katherine had immersed. She was sponging herself, the delicate scent of lilac water mingling with the bubbles hugging her body. "For the present, keeping him employed and out of trouble. He's a big help at the ranch, a damn good blacksmith, too. I'd hate to lose him."

From behind the screen Katherine heard Ida again. "You said 'for the present.' "

"I never look ahead too far," returned Katherine. "It doesn't pay, I found that out with Julia."

"He's a good-looking buck."

Katherine smiled and sank lower in the tub. She flicked a few drops of water over the screen. "And, no, I haven't been bedding him."

"You've thought about it, though."

Holding her sponge high, Katherine squeezed it and let the water trickle down her face. She smiled to herself. Yes, she had thought about it, and visions of changing Jack's bandages suddenly danced before her eyes. If she had been embarrassed, he had been more so. Once, he had hardened; the blanket draped over his middle hadn't disguised it. She had been ashamed, not amused. She had wanted to touch, to peek! Oh, mercy, her wicked mind!

"It crossed my mind. That's not so unusual, is it?" Katherine said.

"With you, no, but I don't think it would be wise to start manipulating the young man."

"Nonsense, my sweet."

"Nonsense? You've done it before. You're a manipulator."

"All right, but always for the best, I hope."

Ida said, "What's best this time?"

Katherine sighed. "I'm not a fool, Ida. It would be a horrible disaster to get involved with him, even for a quick piece. It might be disastrous for him as well, consorting with the boss, a white woman. I don't even want to think about what the consequences could be. No, I know better. I have enough problems. And there's always Alva. I wouldn't disappoint him for the world, not after everything we've been through."

"Why don't you marry Alva and be done with it?"

"Me? Get married?" Katherine abruptly stood and grabbed her towel. "Alva and I have it the way we want it, very private. He couldn't stand being married to anyone. He's too damned independent. Besides, I don't love him. I adore him. I respect him."

"He cools your hot blood."

Snaking the towel around her body, Katherine stepped from the big tub. She stuck out a wet foot at Ida. "Kiss my big foot, sweetie."

Ida blew a kiss.

Katherine presented her backside. "How about this?"

"It's lovely honey," and Ida promptly pinched it. "Besides, I never have been able to understand why you two keep your affair so secret. Who gives a damn? You've been around. Sure as hell it's not your reputation, is it?"

"Reputation? Mercy, no," replied Katherine. "You can't gild a tarnished lily." She sat on the thick rug and began shaking out her hair. "No, it's more spicy this way, sneaking around like a child stealing cookies. Besides, Alva doesn't want to embarrass me. He thinks I'm a goddess."

Ida Hamilton almost dropped her glass. "Oh, my God! You're a soiled dove, for crisesakes!"

Staring up between her wet locks, Katherine said, "He's old enough to be my father . . . almost, anyhow. He says people won't understand. He doesn't like the notion of someone laughing at me, joking behind my back. Something like that."

"Hah! You're no spring chicken, anymore, either," Ida replied. "And let me tell you, age doesn't mean a thing. Some of the best men in my life have been the old ones. The only thing wrong with latching onto one of them is, he's sure as hell going to leave you a widow a lot sooner."

Katherine smiled. "Well, if he's rich, that's not so bad."

Ida got up and went over to the vanity. Picking up a brush, she gave it a toss and Katherine caught it. She started brushing her long hair. Admiring her, Ida said, "Well, you may not be a spring chicken, Kate, but you're still beautiful. Yes, I suppose a few people would snicker, wonder what the hell you see in Alva."

"Yes, and if I got involved with Jack, they'd wonder the same thing . . . a colored, a Negro, and without a dollar to his name."

Ida grinned. "Well, you could keep that secret, too, couldn't you?"

"It wouldn't be worth the chance. No, not on your life. Let sleeping dogs lie."

"Has he given you the big eye, yet?"

"Mercy, no! At least, I don't think so."

Refilling their glasses, Ida laughed lightly. "Be hard to tell, anyhow, wouldn't it? All he ever does it grin like a big black possum." In afterthought, she asked, "Do you think he grins like that when he's on a woman?"

"Mercy, how would I know?" She took the glass from Ida and took a sip, then giggled. "Maybe after he's been on one?"

"Oh, my!"

Shortly after dark, Jack Darby emerged from his room and presented himself to Katherine. Indeed, he had bought new clothes. He wore a gray derby; his suit was gray; his cane and boots were black, as he explained, to match the color of his skin. Katherine told him he was a handsome gentleman. He politely acknowledged this by doffing his derby and bowing. "At your service, madam," he said in his mellow voice.

Katherine laughed. "Madam? Oh, Mister Darby, you couldn't have said it any better!"

Though it was relatively quiet on the second floor, business in the saloon was brisk. The gambling tables were busy; musicians fiddled and picked, and holiday drinks were served at the bar: hot toddies and Tom and Jerry's. Through it all, Katherine was spending a quiet evening in her room. However, Ruby Danforth came for a short visit. Katherine suggested Ruby might want to make a longer visit sometime later in the adjacent room. Ruby Danforth smiled. Her sweet Kate was always making suggestions.

Shortly after Ruby left, Katherine's supper arrived. She ate alone, but around midnight Ida Hamilton jointed her. Ida brought a bottle of champagne. The two women reminisced, drank, and laughed until the early hours of the morning.

The next day, Katherine rented a buggy at Bollinger's Cartage. She made a stop at the bank to deposit two thousand dollars (portion of the profit from the House of Mirrors) before shopping for gifts at the stores. She also made a brief stop at Tim Frawley's office where she left presents for his two children. By noon, she had finished her chores; the buggy was packed with gifts. Instead of taking them back to the hotel, she had Blackjack drive to the Colorado and Southern depot where she met her old friend, Rolly Anderson. Anderson was no longer assistant station manager; he was now the manager, and he was very happy to see Katherine Coltrane. She thought it would be nice if he joined her and Darby for a noon meal at the Palace Hotel.

Surprised and flattered to be in the company of such a charming and famous lady, one who was such a good friend of Stanley Howard, now a vice president of the railroad, Anderson happily accepted.

It was a splendid occasion. Back at the station, Katherine explained to Rolly Anderson that since she had transacted all of her business in Cheyenne, she hated to spend another afternoon and night in the city. Her time was valuable; she wanted to get back to her ranch, and since the northbound didn't leave until nine-thirty the next morning, well, this was very inconvenient.

Anderson agreed saying, "Yes, it's regrettable, Miss Coltrane. I'm sorry."

Katherine struck a small pout, but then lifted her brow in surprise and said, "Say, Rolly, isn't there a freight that goes up to the North Platte every Monday and Thursday afternoon? This is Thursday, too. Do you ..."

"Yes, yes, but there's no coach, only two or three boxcars, North Platte freight."

"A caboose?"

"Well, yes, but that's for the workmen, the crew."

"Has a stove in it, doesn't it?"

"Yes."

"We're only going as far as Chugwater. That surely isn't much of an imposition, is it? I'll bet you can arrange something, Rolly, I just bet you can."

The small freight left at five o'clock. It didn't stop at Chugwater, but about seven o'clock it screeched to a stop at the Coltrane ranch siding. Katherine Coltrane and Black-jack Darby, loaded down with luggage and yuletide gifts, stepped off into the frosty air. There were happy good-byes from the brakeman and his assistant.

By Christmas, most of the K-Bar-C cattle had been moved from the upper ranges. Several of Katherine's men rounded up a few strays in the higher creek drainage and had them headed toward the Chugwater Valley bottom by midday. At the home ranch, the aroma of roast turkey and mincemeat pie wafted from Mary Slaymaker's big kitchen. In the parlor next to the big windows, Katherine had set a six-foot fir. She and Mary decorated it with several strings of red beads and paper ornaments. Katherine wanted this to be a cheerful and festive occasion for all of her friends, though most of them knew only about the symbolism of the Feast of Nativity. They were only Christians in the sense that they knew about the word of God, his prophet son, Jesus, and the Good Book. In the vanishing wilderness, priests and parsons seldom had been a part of their lives. Their altar was anywhere and when they chose; a glen of pines, a sage-covered bluff, or some rocky ledge overlooking the great prairie. Katherine Coltrane and her friends were survivors, the small evergreen bundle tacked above her door was symbolic of it.

The dinner was at mid-afternoon. Two tables were joined together and covered with a white cloth, a large candle placed in the middle of each one. Katherine had crystal tumblers, white china plates, and silverware. She thought everything was beautiful. All of the K-Bar-C hands were present, and Porter Longstreet Webb and Jospeh Brings Yellow had come over for the afternoon festivities. They were to stay the night.

Amid gentle laughter and a few awed expressions at the sumptuous portions of steaming food, they gathered around; Alva Tompkins graciously seated Katherine, Porter and Joseph to each side of her. Katherine glowed—this was one of the happiest moments of her life.

Momentarily, there was an awkward silence, a trading of looks. Who among them would offer thanks and pray for a blessing? Blackjack Darby, dressed in his new suit, white shirt, and black string tie, finally stood. His big smile brought smiles. Arms outstretched, he spoke in a low but melodious basso, "Let us pray and give thanks to God . . . to God and the Great Spirit . . ." He rumbled like distant thunder. Oh, how he rumbled, but it was more like a beautiful, rolling song, a heartfelt song of gratitude, an ode for blessing, a plea for forgiveness. Katherine's heart filled with joy.

When Blackjack finally said, "Amen," she repeated it softly, and husky amens sounded all around the two tables. Katherine smiled at Jack Darby. Her eyes were filled with tears. Yes, God was good.

If God were good, he was also merciful. Two days after Christmas, Maybelle Hatch died in her sleep. Though sorely grieved, Luther told Katherine he was thankful his wife's illness had been brief and her death had been painless.

Maybelle's burial plot was only about ten yards from Buford Reasons's. As with Buford's, her service was brief. There was no attending preacher, but Blackjack Darby, who had come along with Katherine, Alva, and the Slaymakers, said a prayer for Maybelle. The rest of the small crowd joined in when he recited the Lord's Prayer.

Afterward, Katherine and Mary Slaymaker helped with a small repast in the hotel dining room. By late afternoon, most of the people had departed. Alva elected to stay at the hotel. He could manage the saloon, and besides, Luther needed some company for a day or two. Katherine Coltrane agreed, and in afterthought suggested that since no cattle remained on the upper ranges, Alva and Jack Cuthbert close the line cabin for the winter and move into the Star. After all, it was closer to the home ranch than the Bluegrass cabin. Business at the hotel was slack. In their spare time, the men could help with a building project she had been contemplating.

Both Luther Hatch and Alva gave her a look of surprise. "And what might that be?" Alva asked hesitantly.

"Well, we have a little school," Katherine said. "What this community needs now is a church. I'm going to give them one."

Luther Hatch smiled and shook her hand. "That's wonderful, Kate, wonderful!"

Alva Tompkins turned aside and mumbled, "Oh, shit."

Chapter Twenty

Nesters

Excerpts from an interview with Henry Burlingame.

Was Katherine involved in politics? Yes and no. Involved, yes, but not directly. Kate was more interested in playing her hand behind the scenes. She never appeared in public. I can't remember anyone telling me a story about her participating in a rally or directing some aspect of a campaign. But she had tremendous influence. She was charming, and she had plenty of money.

I think I mentioned the power of the stock growers' association. Kate had a hand in this. By the time Tim Frawley was appointed chief circuit judge, a federal job, the cattlemen practically controlled the territory. Oh, there were skirmishes here and there with the nesters, as they were called, but seldom did any of these squabbles result in a court case. Most often, the farmer was frightened off or his complaint was forgotten by a law officer who always had more important things to do. The cattlemen controlled the law, most of the local judges, included.

I had numerous conversations with the ranchers about this conflict with the farmers. Certainly, there was rascality involved. I talked with Porter Webb, and I had to agree with him in one respect. A great deal of this land wasn't suited for farm crops. It was wild grass, tumbleweed, rock, and sage. At times, water was scarce, too. Only a few farmers managed to survive. In most cases, it was a precarious adventure to begin with. Oh, but men have dreams, don't they? One hundred and sixty acres of free land was a powerful incentive. The U.S. Government was hell-bent to create a farm empire in the West. Why, I can't even calculate

how many abandoned cabins and tar-paper shacks I
saw between the South Platte and the Milk River up in
the Montana Territory. Did I say dreams? Lost dreams.

Chugwater, April, 1885.

About two miles south of the K-Bar-C hay fields, the river
coursed through a cottonwood grove bordered by a wide flat
of bunchgrass and sage. The bottom provided good shelter
and feed for cattle, and quite often during late spring, some
of Katherine Coltrane's cows and calves wandered into the
area. Occasionally, a few of Jeb Slaughter's cattle foraged
there. Jimmy Reynolds, riding the river bottom this warm
spring morning was surprised when he came upon several
men felling trees. Across the river a hundred yards away he
saw four big wagons, cows and horses, and a large wall tent.
There were several people over there, too.

Curious, Reynolds rode over to the woodcutters and had a
brief conversation. It was as he surmised—they were farmers, an older man, George Crippen, and his son, John. They
had filed adjoining homesteads on the east side of the river,
a total of three hundred and twenty acres. They intended to
put in crops of corn, potatoes, and hay. With their sixteen
milk cows, they also considered themselves dairymen.
George said he understood that another man from Missouri
had taken a homestead nearby. However, he didn't know the
name of the farmer.

Jimmy Reynolds, with a tip to his hat, wished them luck.
He turned and rode back down the river trail. He didn't think
his boss, Katherine Coltrane, would appreciate sodbusters
settling on her upper valley range.

Katherine didn't appreciate it, but there wasn't anything
she could do about it, at least for the present. The Crippens
had deeded property; they were entitled to it; they were her
new neighbors to the south. So, the next day she paid them
a visit. Blackjack Darby accompanied her.

Even though the call was cordial, Katherine detected a
touch of animosity. The Crippens already had encountered
K-Bar-C cattle on their new property, including several cantankerous cows protective of their calves. Moving them out
had been a task. Katherine was sympathetic, but she suggested that George Crippen consider fencing the homesteads
with barbed wire. Crippen agreed this was one solution, but

at the present, very impractical. The cost of wire was prohibitive; he didn't have that much money. He thought perhaps her cowhands should keep the critters from moving too far south.

Katherine Coltrane said she would see what she could do. Her cattle would be in the hills in another week or two. Before she left, she paid her respects to the women, George's wife, Sarah, and the young wife of John, Ruth Ann. They were working around a big rock fireplace, preparing a meal in a black kettle. Flies fought for space around the cooking area; a film of smoke hovered over the campsite; the women's eyes were reddened. Katherine wanted to cry. Except for their long cotton dresses and homely short boots, the two women reminded her of her days with the Oglala. Ruth Ann, her legs awkwardly splayed to each side, was trying to find comfort on a wooden box. She was heavy with child. Sarah, armed with a long wooden ladle, had a soiled bandanna wrapped over her hair, and the bottom of her long dress had collected an assortment of beggar's lice and cockleburs. The conversation was brief because the two women didn't have much to say. Their eyes were on Jack Darby most of the time, and he was aware of it. When Katherine and Blackjack rode away, she said it was because of his continuing smile—they probably thought he found humor in their present plight. No, it hadn't been funny—it was pathetic—they looked like poor coloreds.

Several days later when Porter Webb and Joseph Brings Yellow brought Katherine four mustangs she had bought, she told them about her new neighbors. Porter said she was headed for trouble.

Because of the mild winter and assistance from some of the Chugwater men, Alva Tompkins and Jack Cuthbert had been able to get the new church enclosed and roofed by early March. Work came to a halt at calving time, so Katherine contracted the Tarkalson brothers again. They brought up their carpenter crew from Cheyenne and took free lodging in the Star Hotel. Within two weeks the church windows were installed and the interior finished. The little church had no steeple, but Katherine thought its location among the cottonwoods and elms next to the tiny cemetery made it look like a cathedral.

The congregation at the first service totaled nineteen, including a few from the K-Bar-C spread. Katherine came; so did Manny and Mary Slaymaker and Jimmy Reynolds. Jack Darby brought his majestic voice and sang one hymn. Also in attendance were the Crippens. Sarah and Ruth Ann were wearing colorful cotton dresses and bonnets. Katherine nodded and smiled to them. Since no minister was available, the stationmaster-barkeep, Luther Hatch, led the service. He read passages from the Bible, and his benediction was forthright and simple. He told the people they now had a house of worship. It was now up to them to go out and gather a flock. He was certain the Lord would bless them in their endeavors. Give thanks to the Lord, and blessings to Katherine Coltrane, who had given the church in His name.

After several thunderstorms in June, the weather turned hot. Most of the K-Bar-C cattle were on the upper ranges in the Sybille and Bluegrass drainages. Katherine also had several hundred steers and a small herd of horses ranging in the eastern foothills over toward Hawk Springs. Alva, who knew everything there was to know about contrary weather, told her it was going to be a hot, dry summer. Her critters weren't likely to put on as much fat as they usually did. He thought it might be prudent to conserve some grass by moving three or four hundred head over the western ridge to feed in the upper Laramie River country. It would take a few extra days in the fall to round them up, but it would be worth it. Katherine agreed.

Two days later, Katherine and five of her men packed bedrolls and grub; they cut out almost three hundred cows and moved them over the ridge in back of Bluegrass Creek. Amid the bawling of a few cows and lost calves and the distant yelps of coyotes, the party made camp for the night by the Laramie River.

The next morning, Alva Tompkins, Jimmy Reynolds, and Curly Bledsoe, a young Texan Katherine had hired in March, rode down the valley a few miles. Alva wanted to check the condition of the range and to see if any of Jeb Slaughter's cattle had wandered up the valley. In some places, the grass was already maturing. It was thick along the river bottom. Alva and his men saw no signs of Slash-S stock. He figured Katherine's cows would graze down to the Chugwater Valley by late summer. If they mingled with Slaughter's stock

then, it really wouldn't make any difference. They could be
cut out during the combined fall roundup.

Katherine, Darby, and Jack Cuthbert, making a circuit of
the country up the river, eventually topped a small rise overlooking most of the valley ahead. Cuthbert had ridden this
way several times. He said sheep from the Bosler and Rock
River areas sometimes grazed this far up. As Blackjack
Darby motioned to turn back to rendezvous with Alva's
crew, a shot rang out from somewhere above them. Blackjack, yelling, "Look out!" tumbled from his horse. Katherine
leaped clear and fell in the weeds a few feet below him.
Cuthbert, about ten yards away, jerked out his rifle and
scrambled into a thicket of buck brush.

For a few moments, there was an eerie silence. The call of
a quail floated across the valley, and Katherine heard one of the
horses already cropping grass. She also heard the beat of her
heart. In between thistles and cheat grass, she looked over at
Jack Darby. "Are you all right?"

"Stay down. Don't move," Darby replied. Then, with his
usual broad smile, he said, "I ain't hit, Miss Kate, but something is. Rattled me right good in my saddle."

"Where in the hell did the shot come from?"

Blackjack peeked between the brush. "Up there, those
bull pines, I reckon."

Rifle in hand, Jack Cuthbert began crawling around the
horses toward Katherine and Darby. "Must be a loner, huh?
Only one shot. What do you wanna do about the bastard?"

Darby lowered his hand in a settling motion. "Stay low. I
ain't fixing to stick my head up like some fool turkey."

"The son of a bitch!" Katherine cursed lowly. "A lousy
bushwhacker."

"Yes, mam," agreed Darby, "but why?"

Cuthbert said, "Maybe someone don't want us poking
around up here. Once I saw a sheepherder's wagon about
two or three miles up the river. Maybe one of them drover's
from Bosler is up here."

"Ain't no sheep 'round," Blackjack Darby said. " 'Cept
one. A big ol' black sheep. Me."

"Oh, mercy!" Katherine gave Darby a horrified look.
"Good God, you don't think . . . ?"

"That's right, Miss Kate. Someone in those trees don't
like Blackjack."

Though the bushwhacker's luck had been bad, his marksmanship was good. His shot had been from about one hundred and fifty yards. The slug had ripped off the top of Blackjack Darby's saddle horn.

Darby wanted to follow the lone set of tracks. Katherine, however, said it was pointless. First, the culprit had gone to the top of the ridge. There were rocks and shale slides up there and damn few tracks. Second, there were three spreads in the direction the bushwhacker had fled—Poindexter's, Coombs's, and Ernest Graves's. Coombs and Graves both ran sheep along with their small cow operation. Katherine discounted Graves. She didn't believe his men had anything to do with this. Ah, but Poindexter and Coombs both had good reason—Blackjack had killed their nephew and son, David in the saloon that miserable day last winter.

Katherine Coltrane suddenly recalled what Porter Webb had told her at Christmas after she related the story about the shooting. Orson Coombs, David's father, at one time was suspected of dealing in rustled livestock. No one had been able to prove it. Coombs always claimed he only took unbranded cattle on open range. Porter said Coombs was an expert in blotting brands and that once a cowhand with too much red-eye in his belly boasted of making a long drive west to Rawlins to sell Coombs's cattle. Porter said this didn't make sense unless the critters were stolen in the first place. The only livestock brokers in the area were at Cheyenne, no more than sixty miles from Coombs's spread.

Yet what Katherine Coltrane now suspected, she would never be able to prove. She was thinking about the three rustlers killed by Jack Darby down on the lower Laramie. Coincidence? Had the men been able to move the horses up the valley, they would have dropped down at Orson Coombs's corrals, only a few miles from Bosler. Maybe the rustlers had been Coombs's hired hands or had intended to sell him Porter's stolen horses. If so, no one was ever going to know it. The men were dead. Darby had killed them, and Porter Webb had trailed their bodies to Hartsville for burial. If this were Orson Coombs's game, Blackjack had spoiled it. Blackjack had killed his son, too. Coombs had good reason to want Jack Darby six feet under. Of course, so did Ivan Poindexter. Revenge.

Katherine Coltrane had revenge on her mind, too. She took this personally—an attack on one of her men was an attack on her. But she didn't want to get involved in a range war that would lead to more killings. She had to plan her retribution carefully, and if at all possible, it had to be done legally. She had some hard thinking to do.

Alva's weather prediction for the summer was true. It was unseasonably hot and dry. By late June, Katherine's men had already finished haying her irrigated fields—three weeks earlier than usual. In one respect, this was fortunate. The river was low. Her intake ditch two miles south of the ranch gate was now above the water level. Irrigation was finished.

If this were a minor problem for Katherine, it was a catastrophe for the Crippen homesteaders. They had worked from dawn to dusk all spring and early into the summer to build a one-room cabin with a sod roof. They had a crude log barn. Ruth Ann delivered a baby girl. She named it Charity. They had a few chickens laying eggs, and a small vegetable garden that Sarah had planted. They had everything but the most precious possession of all—adequate water.

Katherine's riders had watched George and John Crippen lay a long clay pipe into the river earlier in the summer. Katherine's men observed every move the Crippens made. Because of her own irrigation needs, she didn't want her neighbors drawing any more water from the river than they needed. Corn and potatoes needed plenty of moisture. It wasn't coming from the skies. It was barely coming to the Crippens' fields, and at high watermark they drew only enough to dampen the ground. By mid-June, their clay pipe was drawing nothing but air—it was a foot above the river. The Crippens' field went dry. As Jack Darby observed, "Water just won't run uphill." George and John Crippen watched their corn crop fail when it was two-feet high. The potatoes planted in a lower field close to the river were questionable. The dairy cows had cropped all of the nearby bunchgrass and were now foraging several miles from the barn. Only Sarah's small vegetable garden was producing, this because she and Ruth Ann toted up pails of water from the river every morning.

Katherine and Mary Slaymaker paid Sarah and Ruth Ann a visit in July to deliver a crib and clothing for the baby. Mary came away with tears in her eyes. She told Katherine the baby had been appropriately named—Charity. By winter, the Crippens were going to need charity to survive.

* * *

July melted into August. Alva Tompkins and Jack Cuthbert, armed to the teeth, made a cautious ride over the Laramie River range. At least twenty cows were missing, either strayed or rustled. They couldn't be sure about it until the fall roundup. But they were suspicious, and Katherine was incensed. Two days later, she was in Cheyenne at Timothy Frawley's new office in the Federal Building.

Sitting inside a small enclosure in front of his door was a prim woman attired in a black dress with a white collar. The large chignon resting on the back of her head looked like a black ball of yarn. She politely told Katherine that Judge Frawley would be busy most of the morning. He had appointments with several gentlemen, but, if she cared to leave her name, she would inform the judge and set an appointment.

Katherine Coltrane wanted to get out of Cheyenne the next morning. She didn't have time to wait. Drawing up fully to her five-foot-ten stature, Katherine said, "Please tell Mister Frawley a woman is outside. Her name is Katherine Coltrane. She wants an appointment, not tomorrow, but now."

Katherine was a very imposing woman. The prim little woman nodded once and said, "Yes, Miss Coltrane. I'll tell him."

Moments later, a man left the office followed by Tim Frawley, who took Katherine's extended hand and kissed it. He told the woman in the little cubicle he was not to be disturbed.

Katherine quickly told Frawley about her troubles. The weather was terrible. The hills were burning. No rain. The grass was short, and the river was in danger of going dry. Tim Frawley grinned. "Well, what the hell can I do about that?" he asked. "You're in the wrong place, Kate. You should have gone up to Pine Ridge and talked to one of your old medicine men friends. They know how to make rain. You have your dander up."

"You're damn right I have!" she huffed. "I know you're no holy man, far from it, but there is something you can do."

Frawley grinned again. "At your service, my sweet. Let's hear it."

In a rush, Katherine said, "I've got nesters above me. Sure as hell I'm going to have trouble with them over water. I have rustlers behind me. I have neighbors who want to kill one of my best hands because some fool kid made the mistake of drawing a pistol on him. I can't go into Chugwater without a pistol on my own hip. Yes, I have my dander up, and I want you to do something about it."

"For instance?"

"Get me a little jail and a U.S. marshal to go with it."

"What? In Chugwater?"

"You heard me, buster."

Tim Frawley rubbed a hand through his dark hair, hair that was beginning to show little shades of gray at the temples. After a moment, he said, "Chugwater is in the Cheyenne district. It's under Cheyenne's jurisdiction. You get your law out of Cheyenne, Kate. That's the way it's set up."

"It doesn't work," she replied. "It's thirty miles away, damn it. If there's trouble, it takes three hours to get up there. Four hours to my place. Another hour to Slaughter's. What the hell good is that?" She shook a finger at him. "And don't tell me the marshal can take the train, either. It only runs north once a day."

"Well, I suppose you people could hire a constable," Frawley offered lamely.

"Bullshit! A constable to chase drunks out of the saloons? I want a lawman who can ride. A man who can shoot if he has to. Someone who can do some investigating and scare the shit out of the troublemakers."

"Whoof!"

"Whoof is right!"

Frawley gave her a hapless look. "Something like this would take ... well, we would have to redistrict, set new boundaries, that sort of thing. Even get a judge for the district. Time-consuming, costly, for what it's worth."

"It's worth plenty," Katherine replied. "And look here, sweetie, don't forget who helped put you in that big chair."

"I always loved the way you operated."

"How long will it take?"

Judge Frawley shrugged. "I don't know. Maybe a few months. Maybe six months."

"Will you do it?"

"I'll see what I can do, Kate."

"Good." Katherine stood and smoothed her dress. "I'm going to stop by and see Susan and the children." She turned. Frawley got up and went to the door with her. "Listen," she said, taking him by the arm, "I have someone in mind for the marshal's job. He has a very good head on him. Smart. He's also very good with a revolver. I respect him and so do a lot of other people."

"Oh, you have someone in mind, eh? Well, now, I just thought you might." Frustrated but amused, Frawley shook his head. "Well, who is this would-be lawman?"

"His name is Jack Darby," Katherine replied. "He worked for Pete Quinlan up at Deadwood. Sheriff Bullock thought rather highly of him, too."

"Not one of your suitors?"

"You know better, Judge. I have no suitors."

Frawley said, "Leave his name with Miss McCarthy. She'll make out the appointment form when I get this completed."

Shortly after midnight, Katherine was startled from her sleep in the House of Mirrors by a resounding clap of thunder. She sat up in bed. Through a part in her blue drapes, she saw a jagged streak of lightning. The tops of the nearby buildings were briefly illuminated in brilliant white. The light faded, but Katherine continued to hear the low rumbling of distant thunder until she fell asleep again.

The next morning, the skies over Cheyenne were leaden. Katherine's first thought was that the summer-long drought had been broken, yet there wasn't a sign of a puddle in the streets, only a few dimples in the dust. The storm, what there was of it, was moving away.

Katherine had coffee and pastry next door to the Colorado and Southern station, chatted briefly with Rolly Anderson, and shortly after ten o'clock, boarded the northbound with a dozen other passengers.

About a half hour later, the conductor came down the aisle. Several passengers were curious about the bluish haze drifting below the gray clouds. Range fire up ahead, the conductor told them. A big one, burning most of the night. Katherine, who had been dozing, suddenly stiffened and peered out the window. She caught the conductor by his arm. Did he know the location of the fire? Somewhere around Chugwater, he told her. That was all he knew. Katherine slumped back in her seat. Oh, mercy!

When she stepped down on the station cobbles at Chugwater, Luther Hatch's long face revealed it—it was her range that was afire. With a grim look, Luther motioned to the western hills toward Bluegrass and Sybille Creeks. They were almost obscured by smoke.

Manny Slaymaker hurried up and took Katherine's suitcase. As he helped her into the buggy, she asked, "How bad is it?"

"Damn bad," he replied. "Boys rode out before dawn. Half of the mountain went up in flames. Wind. Blew like hell and nary a speck of rain." He shook his head and clucked at the horse. "Dry lightning, I suspect. Probably struck a tree or two somewhere. Damn place was a tinder-box, anyhow."

"How about the cattle?"

"Don't exactly know. Scattered from hell to breakfast. Curly came down just before I left. There's a few dead critters, all right. Curly figured the smoke got 'em, not the fire."

"The line cabin?"

Manny Slaymaker shrugged. "Curly never said. He filled some water jugs and rode out."

"Jesus!"

Several miles from the main gate, lightning split the dirty sky, this followed by a tremendous blast of thunder. The horse bolted, and Manny jerked reins for a moment. Several big drops of rain pelted the canvas top of the buggy. Then a gray sheet of rain came sweeping up the road. Moments later, Katherine and Manny were in the middle of a cloudburst.

Looking up at the sagging roof, Manny shouted, "You're too late, Lord, way too late."

Once inside the house, Katherine prepared to ride, but Manny told her there wasn't anything she could do. All of her men were up there; they were capable cowhands and under the circumstances, they were doing all they could. So, a worried Katherine sat with Mary Slaymaker in the kitchen, their chairs near the side window facing the sodden hills. Occasionally, Katherine leaned from the window and scanned the nearest slopes with her binoculars. Fortunately, these hills were untouched by the fire.

As the rain dissipated and the mists thinned, she could see patches of black and faint outlines of a few charred pines on the horizon. She heard Mary speaking. "They'll be hungry and tired." Several pans rattled. Now water was running, coming through the faucet, cold water from the pipeline up to Indian Wells. The big coffeepot was on.

Near mid-afternoon, Katherine finally saw four riders coming down the winding road, in back of them a wagon drawn by two mules. Jack Darby was handling the reins. Up at the big barn, Manny Slaymaker had seen the riders, too, and by the time Katherine was out the door, he was already talking to the man in front, Jack Cuthbert. Cuthbert's face was streaked with grime, and his bandanna hung under his chin like a dirty dishrag. There was a body in the wagon. The silent men dismounted and exchanged a few sad looks.

Jack Cuthbert finally said to Katherine, "Alva's dead. We saved the cabin but I reckon his heart just plumb gave out."

Two days after the fire, Alva Tompkins was laid to rest in a beautiful copper casket Katherine had ordered out of Cheyenne. He was buried next to his friend, Buford Reasons. Though deeply grieved, Katherine shed only a few tears, these when she had first seen Alva lying in the wagon. His mouth had been creased at the corners. Katherine thought she detected an almost imperceptible little grin on his leathery face.

It took four days to round up the spooked cattle. Most of them were moved to the hills north of Bluegrass Creek. A dozen motherless calves were turned out with several old cows in the stubbles of the hay fields adjacent the river. Jimmy Reynolds made a rough accounting—Katherine had lost eighty-nine head in the fire. Another fifty-plus cows were missing, probably had topped the ridge and fled into the Laramie River basin. Six thousand acres of range had been ravaged and wouldn't produce good feed for two springs.

It rained intermittently the rest of August. The drought of the long hot summer was over. Katherine Coltrane's troubles were not. Curly Bledsoe, the young Texas cowboy, told her he had been riding the bottom land. Next to the riverbank above the Crippen homesteads he saw a pile of boulders taller than his horse. It appeared to him the Crippens were preparing to build some kind of a weir or a dam.

Chapter Twenty-one

Marshal Darby

Coltrane Siding, Wyoming Territory, 1886.

At dawn on this warm May morning, Blackjack Darby saddled up and prepared to ride down to the hayfields to pull the ditch planks on the irrigation ditches. Blackjack had barely turned the ranch house when he saw a railroad coach sitting on the distant siding, a big coach, green and shiny. Birds were flitting about in the trees behind it. Staring, he danced his horse sideways for a moment, then trotted easily the rest of the way to investigate.

Sitting on a step of the coach was a man dressed in white, and even before Blackjack arrived at the siding, he had heard the plaintive notes of a flute. Here in front of him was the source. It was this black man who was stirring up the magpies, the jays, and robins from the riverside thickets.

Blackjack leaned forward in his saddle, and said, "Good morning. What the hell you doing here?"

The young man with the wooden flute looked up. For a moment, he stared up at Blackjack Darby. Finally, he smiled and replied, "Playing my flute, nigger. Yes, sir, playing my little ol' flute."

Blackjack's big smile broadened. "That's the skillet calling the pot black, mister. 'Sides, that don't sound much like music to me. Where did you get that thing?"

"Injun flute. My boss gave it to me."

"Boss? Where's your boss?"

The man jerked a thumb backward. "In there, getting himself dressed."

"This one of them palace cars?"

"Yes, sir, that's what they're calling them, all right." The man stared up at Blackjack again. "What you doing on that horse?"

"Sitting on it, boy," Blackjack grinned. "Ain't you ever been on a horse?"

"Nope, and I ain't likely to, either. 'Fraid I'd fall off and bust my ass." He cackled.

"What's your name?" Blackjack asked.

"Abraham."

"Abraham. That's one from the Good Book. Abraham what?"

"Abraham. That's all."

"You got no last name?"

"Sometimes, I do," the young man answered. "Sometimes it's Jefferson. Sometimes it's Washington. I even call myself Abraham Davis. For sure, I don't call myself Abraham Lincoln. Folks don't like that." He laughed again and slapped his knee.

Blackjack took measure of the palace car. He had heard about such coaches, but he had never seen one. "How'd you get here? Where you coming from, anyway?"

Abraham replied, "Freight train shucked us off here in the middle of the night." Pointing to the side, he said, "See that name painted on there? That's where we's coming from."

"I see it. What does it say?"

Abraham cackled. "Boy, you can sit on a horse but you can't read!"

"Never had time to learn," Blackjack smiled. "Been riding this horse for fifteen years. What's that writing say?"

"Says Pennsylvania. Says Penn Central Railroad, that's what it says."

"Pennsylvania. That's a far piece. I used to live in New York when I was a runt."

"Well, I'll be!" Pointing at Blackjack's revolver, Abraham asked, "What you carrying that gun for? You one of them cowboys?"

Blackjack grinned wider. "Have to protect myself. Injuns always sneaking 'round here looking to get a scalp." He took off his big hat and rubbed the top of his head.

Abraham cackled and said, "You ain't got much to get, boy."

After a moment, Blackjack asked, "What's that boss of yours on this siding for, anyways? Why you sitting here?"

"I s'pose he's aiming to go up there." Abraham nodded toward the ranch. "Has a lady friend." Abraham grinned and spoke lowly, "General Jason has lots of lady friends. Says this one is special-like."

"Special-like, huh? Your boss say her name?"

"I s'pose. Can't recollect her name."

Blackjack Darby pointed to the sign over the ranch gate. "See that yonder, boy? That's the name of my lady boss. She's special-like."

Abraham squinted. He grinned, too, somewhat sheepishly. "What's that sign say?"

"Heh, heh, heh," rumbled Blackjack. "You can't read, either, nigger. Can't read a lick, can you?"

"Never had time to learn," Abraham returned smartly. "Man, I been riding on this ol' car for fifteen years."

Shaking his head, Blackjack dismounted and led his horse across the two sets of rails. He called back, "Name's Coltrane, boy. Miss Kate Coltrane. You hear me?"

"Sure 'nuff, that's it. Miss Kate. I recollect that. The general says when the sun gets on that roof up there to start rattling my pans. I have to fetch that Miss Kate for breakfast. That's what the general says."

"Sun's coming up, all right."

"You got any mean dogs up there?"

"Heh, heh, heh. Big ones."

The man coming up the road was dressed in linen as white as snow. He had a long stave over his shoulder, and to Mary Slaymaker, who saw this apparition from the front door, she momentarily thought it was the grim reaper. She took a second look. No, it was a man with a black face. Gathering her skirt, Mary hurried to the kitchen to tell Katherine Coltrane.

Katherine, dressed in her nightgown and robe, met Abraham on the porch. Simultaneously, she saw the dark green palace car sitting on the siding far below. She was curious, but only for a moment. She was stunned when Abraham told her that General Jason was expecting her for breakfast.

"Bird Dog! Oh, mercy!" she cried, "Bird Dog!"

Startled, Abraham quickly took a glance to each side. "Bird Dog? That nigger cowboy said you had big ones up here." He took a firm hold on his stick. "If you ain't coming, I'll be going, Miss Kate."

Katherine whirled about. "No, wait. I'll go with you . . . just a moment." She hurried inside and slipped into some shoes, and returned excited and breathless. She bounded away like a whitetail, and Abraham had trouble keeping up with her.

Katherine saw Jason standing in front of the coach stairs. He wore a leather vest and a white shirt; his tan trousers were tucked into black military boots. She leaped into his arms. He twirled her around and placed her above him on the first step.

Wiping at the sides of her eyes, she said, "You devil! At least you could have written, told me about this. A telegraph ... even a telephone call. I have one up there, now. Oh, you crazy fool; it's so good to see you."

"I'm full of surprises," Jason smiled.

"Oh, yes, you always were, my sweet."

They sat opposite each other at the small dining table. Abraham came and refilled their coffee cups. Breakfast would soon be served, he said. Katherine was aglow. Jason Armitage told her his trip west was intended to be one of in-doctrination. The board of directors had suggested it. Jason was a railroad man now, and he knew absolutely nothing about railroads. He was on an extended journey meeting with other rail officials across the country, getting a first-hand look at their operations, discussing mutual problems about the burgeoning network of trackage.

Katherine smiled. "This is cattle-car country," she reminded him. "You don't move stock in Pennsylvania, Jason. There's more critters out here than people. I have nearly three thousand head on my spread right now. Porter has just as many, maybe more." She nudged him under the table with her foot. "You came up here to see me, that's what."

"A bit of a side trip," Jason grinned. "I had thought of getting switched into the line going to Chadron, stopping off to see Ben at Robinson."

"He's been transferred to Fort Lincoln," Katherine said.

"Yes, I found that out when I went through Omaha."

"So, I was second-best?"

Jason Armitage chuckled. "No. As a matter of fact, I had to change plans. I was going to Chadron first. I had it in mind, to send you a wire from there, advise you I was coming through. Sort of prepare you ahead of time."

She grinned and touched his leg again. "Prepare me for what?"

Abraham appeared carrying a large tray. He put a white plate filled with scrambled eggs and ham in front of Katherine, then another in front of Jason. In a silver platter covered with a white cloth were hot biscuits. Honey and jelly were in two silver-trimmed condiment jars. Abraham nodded when Katherine thanked him, then disappeared into a rear compartment.

Jason continued. "I thought you might want to take a little vacation . . . get away from your cows for a while. I plan to tie into the Union Pacific line down below. I'm going to San Francisco. I want you to go with me."

"Oh, mercy! San Francisco!"

"Yes, I think you would enjoy the city, the shops. We could be back here in . . . depending on connections, time in California . . . say, in three or four weeks." Jason forked into his eggs and took a bite.

Katherine was at a loss for words. She had never heard such an intriguing proposition in her life. And she was absolutely unprepared for what followed.

Jason touched a napkin below his black mustache. He smiled and said, "If things work out, we could extend the trip, go back to Philadelphia. I think you would like Philadelphia."

"Good heavens, Jason; you're a madman!"

"I'd like to be your husband."

Katherine's fork dangled, and her breath hung. She was astounded and utterly speechless.

"Does it sound crazy? Too sudden?"

Katherine finally blurted, "Yes . . . yes, it's crazy. Crazy, every bit of it!"

With a little gleam in his eyes, Jason said, "I'd give you this car for a wedding present. You could ride back and forth across the country. This is better than the fifty bucks I gave you the first time we met."

"Oh, you . . . you beautiful, wonderful, crazy coot!"

"Well, you once said something about it not being the right time, the place, circumstances . . ."

"We were sitting in the middle of an Indian war, damn it! And you said it, I didn't."

"Something about my career then?"

"Has anything changed?" Katherine looked at her plate. Her stomach was weak and queasy, her head spinning. "You don't really love me, Bird Dog. You can't be serious about this. Good Lord, we only have a few things in common."

Jason pulled up defensively. "Well, I love you a helluva lot more than I did my first wife."

Katherine had to laugh. "Oh, I adore you. You know it. A marriage proposal. I've had so few, but this is impossible." She finally took a sip of coffee to cut the dryness in her mouth. "Good heavens, you're the president of a railroad! Philadelphia isn't Cheyenne . . . the frontier. It would be a disaster, scandalous for you."

"Who knows you in Philadelphia?"

"Don't you read?"

"Those *Harper*'s stories? Innocuous! That fellow Burlingame made you into a heroine, a Western Joan of Arc."

"Which I'm not, and you damn well know it. A few other people know it, too. Dirty linen doesn't always wash clean, you know. Sooner or later . . ."

"You're not eating your breakfast," Jason said. "Abe will be disappointed. He takes pride in his cooking."

"How in the hell can I eat? You hit me over the head. I'm dumbfounded." Katherine took a piece of biscuit and munched. A crumb hung on her lip. Plucking it off, she flipped it at Jason Armitage. "Jesus!"

"Whoa!" he exclaimed.

"I'm sorry," she replied. "Besides, I just can't ride away like some piece of royalty, a queen, a jaded one at that. Mercy, I have responsibilities of my own, Jason. I have livestock. People here depend upon me. I have a dozen more in Cheyenne to worry about, too."

"You should sell that fancy whorehouse," he said dryly. "You don't need it."

"I've been thinking about it." And she had. Ida and Ruby were considering leaving in late summer. Ten years of prostitution had jaded them. They had money in the bank. They told Katherine they planned on going into a fashion shop and millinery business in Denver. More old friends on the move. Katherine began to lose interest in the House of Mirrors. Jason was right—she didn't need it.

Jason sighed. "I know you have responsibilities. You have quite a place up there on that bench. I took a look earlier this morning from the platform." He reached across the table and held her hand. "All right, let it rest. We can talk about it later. I can stay for a day or two. Perhaps you can consider this . . . the trip, anyhow."

"I don't want you to leave in a day or two," Katherine replied. "You can't get out of here without seeing Porter and Joseph. I have a room for you at the ranch." She leaned forward and whispered, "And ... and I won't let you leave without spending a night or two in bed with me."

Jason Armitage contemplated for a moment. He rubbed his chin and said, "You mean for old time's sake? How much will it cost me this time?"

Katherine whispered, "Only your health, Bird Dog. I'll probably destroy you."

Katherine Coltrane had telephones. They had been installed the previous summer a week before the range fire. She was on the main trunk into Chugwater and Cheyenne, but she had been unable to finagle a line to Porter Webb's place. So, she put one in herself. Her persuasive efforts were partially successful—the telephone company gave her almost thirty miles of wire at half cost.

Jason Armitage took advantage of the hookup to the Circle-W. He had a brief conversation with Porter, who said because of branding he and Joseph wouldn't be able to ride over to Katherine's house for another day or two, probably Wednesday at the earliest. Katherine immediately began preparations for a party, as she said to Jason, for "old time's sake."

For this evening, however, she would have Jason and Abraham for guests. While Jason talked with Manny and Mary Slaymaker in the kitchen, Katherine sent Blackjack Darby to get Abraham. Blackjack had a few other chores to finish, so he saddled up an extra horse for his new friend. Down at the palace car, he had to shout several times before Abraham poked his head out from one of the windows. Abraham was appalled when Blackjack told him the extra horse was for him.

Blackjack said, "You're gonna be 'round for a couple of days. That's what Miss Kate says. You can't be hanging 'round this coach doing nothing. You come on, now. You can help me shut some ditch gates."

"Man, you're plumb crazy! I ain't no cowboy. I'm a cook, and that's all I want to be."

"Miss Kate says you come up to the house for supper."

"Miss Kate didn't say nothing 'bout me riding that big-eyed devil, did she?"

"Heh, heh, heh. No, but if you want some fried chicken,

biscuits, and gravy, you better get your black ass out here and get mounted. That's not what Miss Kate says. It's what I say."

"He might bite me."

"It's no he," Blackjack replied. "A she, she is, a mare. She's gentle. She's no meat eater. She's old. She's so old she whinnys backwards. Now, you come on long. I ain't got all day."

"I don't like riding horses."

"How in the hell do you know that, Abraham? You never been on one."

The coercion stopped. Abraham, clad in his white coat and pants, a red bandanna over his head, came out of the coach. He approached the mare cautiously. To test Blackjack's word—she didn't bite—he stuck out his hand to her muzzle; he promptly received a slobbery lick.

Blackjack said, "Y'see, there. She likes you."

Abraham put a foot in the stirrup and pulled himself up by the pommel. He had seen Jack Darby do this earlier that day. He wasn't going to make a fool out of himself any more than he had to. Blackjack turned and rode along the railroad bed. Abraham's elbows stuck out like a chicken. The mare moved out slowly on her own accord and followed Blackjack's horse. By the time they reached a trestle about a mile to the south, Abraham told Blackjack he just might like horseback riding, after all. Darby chuckled. They rode under the trestle across the river. Darby headed up the bottom toward the Crippen homestead.

At least once a week, Katherine had one of her hands check the bank where the two farmers had hauled in boulders and a few logs. She had already warned George Crippen she wouldn't tolerate any damn above her property. She had over six hundred acres of hay under irrigation, and she needed every bit of hay she could grow for supplemental winter feeding. Katherine didn't object to Crippen's pipe intake; it didn't draw that much water. The clay pipe only functioned when the river was running high. Crippen told Katherine that he would take any measures necessary to grow his crops; a weir or dam was his only solution. Animosity built, this despite the fact that Katherine had enabled the Crippens to survive their first winter by giving them several tons of hay for their milkers, plus two butchered steers for their own bellies.

Blackjack Darby eyed the riverbank from below. The pile of boulders appeared to be larger, but nothing had been moved into the river. He turned away. It took about an hour to shut the gates on the irrigation ditches. He and Abraham had a good conversation on their way back to the railroad siding, part of it a surprise to Darby. The fact that General Jason had asked Miss Kate to take a train ride with him wasn't so surprising. She might do that. Sometimes she liked to get away from the ranch and go shopping. She was always buying gifts for people, even her hired hands. But his Miss Kate wasn't going off with General Jason to get married. No, sir, he told Abraham. That woman wouldn't let any man put a bridle on her. Blackjack Darby said that he heard plenty of men had tried, though. Miss Kate just shucked them off like peas. No man was a match for Miss Kate, and that was the truth of it. What's more, Abraham had no business listening to the general and Miss Kate talk at breakfast. Abraham objected. What did Blackjack expect him to do, sit in his kitchen and stick fingers in his ears?

A few minutes later, the two men came to the double set of tracks. Blackjack, after explaining that most horses were wary of rails and ties, dismounted. Abraham closely observed, then swung his right leg over the rear of the mare and stepped down. As they led the horses across the tracks, a wagon with two men perched on top came rattling down the adjacent road. Blackjack, recognizing Matt Slaughter and Zeke Murfitt, gave them a friendly wave and moved his horse to the side to let them pass. They didn't pass; Matt pulled back on the reins and came to a dusty stop. He and Zeke had their eyes on the man dressed all in white, a dark man wearing a red bandanna who was hoisting himself into his saddle.

Then Matt gave Zeke a little nudge. With a wink and touch of whimsy, he said, "Afternoon, Jack. Who's your new partner? Right fancy dresser, he is."

Remounting, Blackjack said, "Oh, him? Well, boys, he's one of them prophet fellers, sort of like a swami. Sees the future. That's his palace car, there. Miss Kate got this notion he might do some preaching at the church next Sunday. Fetched him out all the way from Pennsylvania, she did."

Matt Slaughter's jaw went slack. "The hell you say!"

"That's the gospel," Blackjack said. "I got a notion you boys might have a lot to talk about, too."

"Yes, sir?" Zeke said, staring at a puzzled Abraham.

Blackjack, smiling up at General Jason's cook, majestically swept an arm out to each of the men. "Matthew, Ezekiel, I know you been looking to meet this man. This is Abraham."

Toward noon the next day, Katherine Coltrane received a telephone call from Luther Hatch. Something startling was happening. The day before, two Colorado and Southern men got off of the northbound. They staked out a lot north of the station, had dinner in the hotel, and departed on the southbound later in the day. All they told him was that the lot had been purchased by the Wyoming Territorial Land Office, for what purpose, they had no idea. What was more curious, today's noon train switched a flatcar on the siding, a car laden with lumber and building materials. Luther said he had inspected the cargo. One of the boxes had a large sign painted on it—"u.s. marshal's office, chugwater, territory of wyoming." It was unbelievable, Luther said, but it appeared that a federal marshal's office was going to be built in Chugwater. Katherine Coltrane said, yes, from what he told her, it certainly seemed so. Luther also said a packet with both her name and Jack Darby's on it was in the mail pouch. He thought it must be important—it was from the U. S. Office of the Federal Court. Katherine thought this was interesting, too. Manny Slaymaker would pick it up later in the afternoon. She told Luther to give Manny five bottles of the best wine from the stock in the hotel. She was planning a small party for General Armitage and a few other guests.

When Manny arrived with the supplies and mail, Katherine put aside one bottle of wine and took the packet from Tim Frawley's office into her bedroom. She quickly opened it. Inside were several documents. One attested to the formation of a new territorial judicial district encompassing the area ten miles north of Cheyenne to ten miles south of Hartsville. The east boundary extended to Hawk Springs, the west to Rock River. Katherine Coltrane glowed. Mercy, by virtue of one office call, she had captured law authority over a dozen spreads, including those of Ivan Poindexter, Orson Coombs, Jeb Slaughter, the Crippens, and her dear friend, Porter Longstreet Webb.

Another letter attested to the appointment of Jack Darby as U.S. marshal, Chugwater. An attachment said Darby would be officially sworn in when a circuit judge was appointed for the new district. The marshal's salary was to be forty dollars per month, living quarters furnished in a four-room building to be completed by July 1, 1886. There was a duplicate of the attachment. Jack Darby had to return the copy with his signature within fifteen days. One line stuck out and caught Katherine's eye—his duties were to begin on receipt of the letter if he agreed to the specified conditions.

Katherine thoughtfully stared across her room. Oh, mercy, how wonderful! Yet, again, how deceitful. She hadn't said a word to Blackjack about this. In fact, in nine months she had almost forgotten it. But, how could he be anything but happy and proud? It was a prestigious and honorable job, wasn't it? Dangerous? No, she remembered dwelling on this at length. She hadn't lied to Judge Frawley when she said Blackjack was respected. Those few who didn't respect him were bigots and cowards. They were afraid of him, and this would make his job less dangerous. No one would dare confront a U.S. marshal, not without serious consequences or fatal retribution, either a bullet or the hangman's noose. She certainly respected Blackjack. She knew he respected her—too much to refuse this appointment. Yet, Katherine was nagged by guilt, the troubled thought that she had done this for herself as much as she had for Jack Darby.

The last of the items in the packet was a leather pouch. She untied the knot and peeked in, then emptied the contents into her lap. There were four shiny star-shaped badges, one with "U. S. MARSHAL" imprinted on it. The other three were deputy badges, one of which she held to her breast. She thought she had earned it.

About five o'clock, Katherine and General Armitage saddled up and took off for the Bluegrass cabin. Katherine had packed fried chicken, a can of peaches, biscuits, and the bottle of wine. She wanted to show Jason what everyone now called "the burn." She wanted to show him the cabin, too, and what Buford Reasons and Alva Tompkins had done for her at the very beginning. It was nostalgic. It was very sentimental, and until this late, sunny afternoon, she had never shared it with anyone.

Up through the burned hillsides, patches of fireweed and lupine were beginning to flower in brilliant reds, pinks, and blues. Shoots of new grass poked their shiny blades up from the charred soil, and a few buds sprouted below the withered sage. There were no cattle on this part of her range. Porter Webb told her it might take another year before it was suitable for cattle again. The only sign of cattle here now was an occasional carcass, or what had been a carcass. The mountain scavengers had left nothing but bones.

The cabin was unchanged. Except for a few fallen trees where Alva and some of the men had set a backfire to save it, it appeared as lovely as ever. It did look lonely. Since there was no livestock to tend, Jack Cuthbert had moved down to the home ranch.

Katherine opened the door. It was stuffy inside, but it was clean and tidy. She and Mary Slaymaker had come up in April. They spent a half day mopping, dusting, and cleaning out cobwebs. On the fireplace mantel were three coffee mugs. "Alva, Buford, and Kate." Katherine smiled wistfully at Jason. "I put them up there," she said. "I thought the boys would appreciate it."

Jason Armitage smiled back at her. And as if Alva and Buford were still about the premises, he said, "I'm sure they do."

She took him through the kitchen to the heavy plank door leading to her bedroom. "This is where it all started. They built this room for me. They wanted me to have the best. When I came down from Deadwood, I didn't have any idea about living here. It was the furthest thing from my mind. Alva bought the Star. He gave it to me. I spent my time up here and down there. Those were some of the best days of my life." She knocked on the door and said, "Anyone there?" In a higher voice, she said, "Please come in."

The door swung open and Jason peeked in. "Very nice, Kate," he said. "They were carpenters, too."

"Yes, carpenters, thieves, drifters, robbers, two lovable rascals no one gave a damn about."

"Except you."

"Just one little bit of attention," replied Katherine. "Just one little gesture of friendship, that's all it was, just a touch of kindness on that goddamned trail back from Goose Creek. I had no idea about the love that was in the lonely hearts of those two men. Oh, mercy, mercy." She momentarily teared up and turned away.

"They must have been clever fellows to cover their tracks

so well all those years," Jason commented. "The money . . . buying the hotel, helping you get started with the ranch."

"You can't believe how clever they were," Katherine returned. She wiped at the corners of her eyes. Turning to the door into the washroom, she said, "Look in here, Bird Dog. See what you can sniff out in this little place."

"A tin tub? A washstand? A towel rack?" He grinned at Katherine.

"I used to take my baths in that tub," Katherine said. "The water comes down here from a pipe up above in the creek. One day I was talking about getting some more money to go along with what I'd gotten from the sale of the house in Cheyenne. I had this idea about building a house down on the bluff by Indian Wells. Alva told me to look under the tub. I did." Shoving the tub aside, Katherine leaned down and pried two boards away. A canvas bag and several tin boxes were still cached in the hole. "I opened several of these," she said, looking up at Jason. "They were filled with pokes and greenbacks. Those two codgers had stashed thousands of dollars in this hole, thousands."

Jason Armitage puckered. His brow arched. "Where . . . ?"

"I don't know where they got it, not all of it," Kate replied. "I didn't ask, but most of it came from somewhere up near where they joined the ambulance train on the way back to Fetterman. The Lost Cabin diggings."

Jason exclaimed, "The Lost Cabin mine! Ye gods, Kate, that goes back to sixty-six! Six or seven Swedes were ambushed up there."

"Well, Alva and Buford found the place and took a helluva lot of gold out of a sluice." She hoisted the heavy canvas bag. "They didn't even count how much money they had. They didn't give a hoot about money. They collected it."

"Misers?"

"No, they gave it to me." She lowered the bag. "There's still three or four thousand dollars worth of gold here. Alva said save it for a rainy day. It rained like hell the day he died up here, but I don't think I'll ever touch this money, not unless I'm starving to death."

Jason grinned. "It may well be there a long time, then."

Katherine led Jason outside. The creek was bubbling through the rocks above them. She pointed to a shed. "See that shed, Bird Dog? You know what was in there the first time I came up here?"

"It looks like a chicken house."

Katherine laughed. "There weren't any chickens roosting in there, I can tell you that. There was a piece of hardware sitting in there, big hardware, an army howitzer."

"Oh, come on, Kate!"

"So help me, I'm not lying. You know me better than that."

General Armitage waved his arms around, then stared down toward the rolling hills below. "How in the hell did they get it up here?"

"Mules, a covered wagon." Katherine giggled. "All the way from one of your old stations . . . Fort Laramie. They stole it. They went back a few months later, and stole the ordnance to go with it."

"Ye gods, whatever for? What did they want with a howitzer?"

"Just the pleasure of making the army brass look like a bunch of assholes . . . which some of them were . . . and still are."

Jason Armitage heaved a great sigh. "This is unbelievable! It must have embarrassed the hell out of someone. I don't remember any report being filed on a stolen howitzer." He looked at Katherine curiously. "Whatever happened to it?"

Katherine Coltrane sat down on a boulder and clasped hands across her knees. She leaned back and stifled a laugh. "General, you asked me to marry you. In a way, I love you dearly, too. You tempt me, you surely do. I've been about everything there is to be in this lonely land, Indian, destitute mother, soiled dove, madam, killer, and rancher. You probably know me better than anyone alive, Bird Dog. I couldn't possibly burden you with another profession. Bandit."

"I don't understand," Jason said.

"That howitzer," she grinned. "All these years I've been dying to tell someone the story about that damn cannon. Oh, I suppose I could have told Porter or Joseph, but for some reason, I just couldn't bring myself around to it. Shame, embarrassment, I don't know."

"And now, a secret unveiled. The guilty confessing?"

"In a way, perhaps," replied Katherine. "I thought you might find the story amusing." She looked at him for a moment and said, "One fine morning we pulled that howitzer down to the road and robbed the Deadwood stage. We took more than fifty thousand dollars from the Black Hills squatters. Thieves, robbing thieves."

Shocked, Jason shouted, "Ye gods, that was you! Why I remember reading about it, but ... but it was a gang ... a regular gang of stage robbers."

"Three robbers, a young woman and two older men."

"Judas priest!" Jason Armitage started to grin. His grin widened, and he began laughing. Reaching, he took Katherine by both hands, pulled her up, and catching her under her shoulders, swung her high. Katherine was laughing, too. Jason embraced her and patted her back. "Kate Coltrane, you're the damndest woman I've ever met."

"Yes, General, I know."

She thought it had been a lovely afternoon and evening. She and Jason sat on the cabin porch; they had their little meal; they sipped wine and talked until dusk. Under a pale moon, they rode the trail back to the home ranch. This was pleasant to Katherine. The burn was out of sight. Like a velvet mantle, the cloak of darkness covered the wounded hillside.

Out of the night they heard the beautiful but lonely sound of a flute. It came from somewhere below, a melodious lament floating across the shadowy slopes. Jason Armitage told Katherine he had never heard Abraham play so well. It wasn't Abraham, Katherine answered. This was music from the heart and soul of a French-Indian. It was Lakota music. This was her brother, Joseph Brings Yellow, playing the flute. Joseph and the White Hawk, Porter Webb, had arrived early; she hadn't expected them for another day.

It was so. Soon, Porter and Jason greeted each other in the dim light of the back porch, two veteran warriors of the plains. They firmly shook hands, briefly embraced. They shared mutual admiration and respect for each other, for their friendship went all the way back to the Indian wars of the mid-Sixties. Soon they were seated at Mary Slaymaker's big round table, talking, laughing, and drinking coffee. Katherine left to find Joseph.

Joseph Brings Yellow was sitting on the top step of the front porch. Katherine often found him here when he and Porter visited. It was his place of meditation. Tonight, Jo-

seph was sharing the porch with two other men. Jack Darby
and Abraham had pulled up two chairs behind him. They
were talking quietly when Katherine appeared, but politely
stood until she told them she had only come to welcome Joseph and compliment him on his music. It wasn't her intention to intrude on their conversation. Blackjack Darby's
small laugh was low and throaty. He invited Katherine to
join them. He thought it was a rare occasion when two
blacks, a red, and a white could sit down together and have
a peaceful palaver.

Everyone smiled in agreement. But then in reflection, Joseph said somberly, "Ei, you are right, my friend. The last
time at the hotel it was one red, one black, and *two* whites.
It was not peaceful."

Katherine Coltrane shuddered. David Coombs had been
killed that horrible afternoon.

"Troublemakers," she said. "I don't think it will happen
again."

Joseph gave her a doubtful look. "Ei, they always have
friends. Have their friends been around lately?"

"Heh, heh, heh," rumbled Blackjack. "They're always
'round in those hills, Joseph. Never see their faces. Sometimes, see where they've been. I don't get to town much.
Most times, Miss Kate keeps me close to the barn."

"For a damn good reason," replied Katherine. She looked
at Joseph. "Poindexter's hands still come occasionally. They
don't hang out at the Star, but they're at the Globe, always
three or four of them."

"Bunched up like chickens," smiled Blackjack Darby.

"Looking for trouble?"

"Who knows what the hell they're up to?" Katherine said.
"I don't want to get involved in another shooting in town
but so help me, if I catch them stealing my stock, there's going to be some shooting or hanging out on the range, one or
the other."

Joseph asked, "You missing cows again?"

"I don't know yet," Katherine answered. "We never did
account for those sixteen last fall. No one can tell me they
strayed, either. Slaughter came up twenty or so short, too.
Probably all turned into beef by now." She looked at Blackjack. "It's like Jack says, the boys see a few tracks now and
then out there. Someone's poking around."

Joseph Brings Yellow grinned. "Maybe someone thinks Tall Woman is stealing cows."

"You know better, my brother. I've done a lot of things in my time, but rustling isn't one of them."

After a moment, Joseph said, "We stopped in town to stretch our legs. We talked to Luther." He stopped short, and even in the dark shadows Katherine could see the curl of a little smile on his handsome face. She knew exactly what he was thinking and what he was going to say.

Katherine said, "Yes, he called me on the telephone . . . after the train left. He told me about the flatcar on the siding . . . the building materials."

"A U.S. marshal's building materials."

"Yes," nodded Katherine. "I think it's wonderful."

"Tall Woman was very surprised, eh?"

"Well . . . well, yes, I surely was."

Joseph Brings Yellow grunted. After another moment, Joseph said, "Porter said you wouldn't be surprised. He said if the Lakota had you talking for them at the peace conference twenty-five years ago, they would own all the land as far as the eye can see. You wouldn't own this ranch, and Indian Wells would not slake your thirst. Ei, Tall Woman, I believe this. We wouldn't be sitting on this porch making talk. We would be spreading our blankets under the trees."

"Mercy! Why, twenty-five years ago, I was only . . . only ten years old. How can you believe such a thing?"

"I believe it." Joseph picked up the flute and began to play.

Katherine was in a quandary. The building materials were sitting on the siding; they hadn't even been moved to the lot, and Porter and Joseph already knew her game. Oh, they were much too clever not to figure out this one. And Judge Frawley was a close friend of Porter's, too. This was the worst problem about her close little family of friends—if one of the clan knew something, sooner or later everyone knew. No, she didn't feel guilty about this redistricting maneuver. In fact, she knew Porter would commend her for it. After all, it was beneficial to his operation, too. Her troublesome thought now was that she should have said something to Jack Darby about the marshal's appointment. True, she had already rationalized this problem away, but it wasn't enough. She wanted the appointment to be a pleasant surprise, not one he would abhor and politely decline. Blackjack might not look upon the job as honorable at all; he could very well think otherwise, that it was a deplorable job without adequate compensation for the risks entailed.

Katherine saw only one solution—she had to sound him out. She would this very night. But before she did, she went to the telephone. Another idea had suddenly struck her. She called Luther Hatch. It was a very brief conversation, but by the time she placed the receiver back on the wall, it was settled—she had traded the Star Hotel and Saloon to Luther for his livery, including six horses, four mules, the wagons and buggies.

About a half hour later, she sent Manny Slaymaker to the bunkhouse to get Jack Darby. She turned up the lamp by her desk in the front room, pulled up an extra chair, and waited. Blackjack came. He was wearing his usual smile, but his head was cocked. He was curious.

"Something important has come up, Jack," Katherine began. "It concerns you, something I should have told you about long before now. I apologize for it . . ."

"You don't have to apologize, Miss Kate," Darby said. "This is my home. You gave it to me. You just go ahead and lay the kindling on me. What is it?"

"You know about the new marshal's office going in at Chugwater . . ."

"I do."

"Well, I knew about it . . . a long time ago. I have a few friends in Cheyenne."

"I know that, too."

". . . So, I talked to one of them." She hesitated. "You're one of the best men I've ever had here . . . so I asked my friend if he could get you appointed as U.S. marshal for the new district."

Jack Darby's eyes widened, startlingly white against his black skin. "Heh, heh, heh, Miss Kate, why did you do that?"

"Because you're the best damn hand around these parts, that's why. Because I believe there's better things ahead for you than just being a cowhand the rest of your life. Do you understand?"

Jack Darby fell silent, and for one brief moment his great smile diminished; his white teeth disappeared. He finally said, "Miss Kate, I'd sure hate to leave this place . . . this place and you. You always make that ol' sun shine, even when it's raining. 'Nother thing, Miss Kate, do you think ol' Blackjack would make a good, honest lawman, and not go making a jackass out of himself?"

Katherine smiled and placed a hand on his arm. "I'd hate to see you leave, too, but you'd be your own man, have your own place, and anytime you needed help of any kind, it would be only a telephone call away. You'd have my backing and all the support you needed from my friends. I can promise you this."

"It sounds like a lonely job, Miss Kate."

"Where in the hell isn't it lonely out here?" she asked. "Everyone I know is lonely."

Jack Darby shrugged, and his smile came back. "I reckon that depends on who you are and your color. You always make me feel like family here. Sometimes I don't even know I'm colored till I see myself in the bunkhouse mirror." He sighed. "I can't believe I can be a U.S. marshal. I'm a Negro. It's just not regular, that's all." His grin widened. "'Sides, ain't that many boogermen to round up in these hills."

"No, but there's a helluva lot of livery work and smithy work to do," Katherine replied. "You can make forty dollars a month in the marshal's office. All you have to do is walk across the street and double your salary in Luther's livery."

"Heh, heh, heh, now just what are you telling me, Miss Kate? Mister Hatch ain't gonna pay me a big wage. Likely he'd go belly-up paying a hired hand."

"Luther doesn't own the livery, Jack. I do."

"Well, mam, I sure didn't know that."

Katherine grinned. "I should say, I did own it. I just gave it to *you* . . . a bonus for everything you've done around here for the past year."

Blackjack Darby was stunned, and this was the first time Katherine had ever read any emotion in his face. Huge tears welled in his eyes. Katherine's heart wept for him. She quickly reached over and turned the lamp wick lower.

It took several moments for Jack Darby to regain his composure. He drew a big sigh; he tried to smile. "Miss Kate," he finally said, "you know that some of the folks hereabout call you? Oh, they don't mean nothing bad about it, but they call you Kate the Great."

Katherine smiled, "I've heard they call me that."

"Fact is, they don't know how great you are," Blackjack said. "I do. I had a good mama, Miss Kate. I loved that woman with all my heart. Next to my mama, you're the greatest woman I've ever known. I reckon I got love for you, too. I'm all talked out, all talked out."

It was Katherine Coltrane's turn to fight tears.

The following morning Katherine worked in the kitchen with Mary Slaymaker and since it was a warm, balmy day, she elected to have the dinner for her guests on the front porch. The men brought tables and placed them together the same way Katherine always arranged them at Christmas. A few minutes after one o'clock, Katherine and her men sat down to a big roast beef dinner. Porter Webb and Joseph Brings Yellow were seated to her left. General Armitage, her guest of honor, to the right.

It wasn't necessary to introduce Jason or Abraham. After several days around the ranch, everyone knew them. They admired Armitage. No armchair general, he was an accomplished horseman; he talked and joked with them. Abraham? A greenhorn, but they liked him. He rode swaybacked Nellie and wore a red bandanna over his head. After the first day, Jimmy Reynolds had tied the bandanna under Abraham's neck; he presented the general's cook with a straw hat with a broad brim. The bunkhouse men made Abraham a cowboy.

The meal, the wine, and the conversation lasted almost an hour. Katherine finally stood and complimented Jason, then briefly related her first meeting with him at Fort Fetterman years past. He had been the interrogator for General Crook, and she told the men she had detested him.

"I'm afraid I behaved badly," she said. "I didn't tell him much of anything, at least not what he wanted to hear."

Jason Armitage spoke up. "You told me General Crook was going to get his ass kicked."

The men laughed.

Katherine responded, "Porter said that, too. You didn't believe us."

"I believed. General Crook didn't."

"He was a stupid man."

"As I recall, you called him an insensitive old fart."

Everyone roared.

"Well, he was."

"I believed that, too."

Katherine patted his head. "I'm happy you're here, General. We all are. You're a survivor."

"I'm happy to be here and have such good friends around me."

Everyone applauded.

Then, Katherine took a small leather pouch from her lap. Holding the bag out, she told the men that what was in it represented a new era for the Chugwater country. She briefly commented on the construction of the U.S. marshal's office in town. Katherine paused and looked around the two tables.

"The Federals haven't appointed a circuit judge for the Chugwater district yet, so what I'm about to do isn't official. We do have a U.S. marshal, though, and his appointment is official. His acceptance will be in the post tomorrow." Katherine looked happily at Jack Darby, and said, "Marshal Darby, please come up and let me pin this badge on you."

For a moment, there wasn't a sound on the porch. Then a piece of silverware rattled against a plate. Someone whispered, "Holy smokes!" When Blackjack Darby stood, everyone stood. Moments later, the K-Bar-C hands were wildly cheering.

Joseph Brings Yellow was smiling, not at Jack Darby, but at the woman the Sioux called Tall Woman. Tall Woman winked at him.

Chapter Twenty-two

Darby's Law

Coltrane Crossing, July 1886.

Katherine Coltrane held hands with loneliness, but she refused to succumb to depression. She had wandered in the dark canyons of the past before—when she never knew from one year to the next if Julia were dead or alive. For Katherine, happiness had been like a fleeting shadow or a wind-blown leaf lodging in some dark crevice, hopefully waiting to be set free by the next capricious breeze. She was beleaguered by sad memories—Julia, Standing Bear, Lieutenant Clybourn, Maybelle Hatch, Buford Reasons, and her dear Alva. Alva. She continued to grieve inwardly over his sudden death. It never showed outwardly, but she missed him. Those wonderful days long ago with him and Buford at the Bluegrass cabin were over, gone forever. This was difficult to reconcile.

Katherine also missed her big lovable Bird Dog. The day his palace car left, he waved from the back platform. He would return, he shouted. But she knew she might never see him again.

Katherine Coltrane fought to dispel these thoughts. She went to work beside her men as she had never done before. She helped with the branding; she drove a bull rake during haying; she helped move stock; she stretched wire. She checked on the upper Laramie River range with Jack Cuthbert and Jimmy Reynolds. No cows were missing, but one day in mid-July, she and Cuthbert topped the rise and stared down in disbelief. Hundreds of sheep were grazing in the green grasses below them. Not a K-Bar-C cow was in sight. However, far above them near the banks of the Laramie, something was in sight—a sheepherder's outfit, the wagon, horses, and the thin shapes of two men moving about.

Katherine Coltrane groaned. Jack Cuthbert reminded her that he had once told her about sheep in the upper valley. He also reminded her this was open range, public grazing land, and there wasn't anything she could do about it. Katherine thought otherwise, but didn't say anything to Cuthbert. She just stuck out her chin and told him to check his rifle and follow her. She kicked off down the slope.

They finally located K-Bar-C cattle along the river about three miles below the big band of sheep. Then Katherine began to backtrack, crisscrossing, occasionally leaning over and examining the ground. After a half hour of this, she told Cuthbert it was now time to have a few words with the sheepherders. Cuthbert wasn't surprised. He could also read sign—the K-Bar-C cows had been chased by the herders and their dogs.

It took Katherine and Cuthbert another ten minutes to reach the herders' wagon. Two young men were awaiting them; they had seen them coming, and they were alert. One stood beside the wagon, his Winchester leaning against the spokes of a wheel behind him. The other man was drinking coffee, but next to a wooden box close by was his rifle. Two mongrel dogs, one with a white eye, were sprawled out in the shade of the wagon. The men nodded, and one said, "Mornin'."

Katherine Coltrane didn't waste any time. "My name is Coltrane," she said. "Those are my cows down below, and I don't like you boys running the beef off of them. If I come over here again and catch you doing it, I'll dust your butts with a shotgun and shoot your damn dogs."

One of the men shrugged and gave his partner an innocent look. He said, "It's clear, Miss Coltrane, but y' see, Mister Coombs has a say in this, too. He don't want your critters up this far. That's his orders, so every time they feed this way, we just move 'em out."

Katherine retorted, "I don't give a shit what old man Orson wants. You stop hazing my stock, or I'll get the marshal coming over here right regular. I don't intend to sit on my bottom the other side of the mountain and have my cattle chased, rustled, or my men shot at by some lousy bushwhacker."

The young man holding the tin cup, replied, "Rustled? Bushwhacked? Now wait a minute, mam, herding cows is one thing, but . . ."

Katherine cut him short. "Bullshit! You boys mind what you're doing. And you tell Orson he'd better keep his goddamned sheep closer to home, up the valley five or ten miles farther, or I'm going to string wire and shut his ass out of here."

The man with the cup scoffed. "You . . . you can't do that, Miss Coltrane. Ain't legal. You'll have the law on your ass 'stedda ours."

"We'll see about that," Katherine said. She gave her hat an angry jerk, reined about, and said over her shoulder, "You tell Mister Coombs what I said."

As she nudged her horse into a trot, Jack Cuthbert leaned over and said, "He's right, you know. You just can't go fencing off this land that way. Sure enough, it'll get us nothing but a peck of trouble."

"There's nothing illegal in stringing wire across land if you own it, is there?"

"No, I reckon not, but you don't own it, Miss Kate."

Katherine smiled over at Cuthbert. "By this winter I will."

Jack Cuthbert momentarily stared at her, not in disbelief but in awe. True, Miss Kate was a woman of her word, but there were thousands of acres in this upper valley. He finally wheezed. "Phew, that's a mighty big chaw. Why, getting a chunk of this valley up here would cost a fortune, Miss Kate, even if you could buy it. And you were just saying the other day you're already cutting it close to the nubbin, the price of beef and all."

"You're right, Jack," agreed Katherine. "We'll be lucky to break even this year, even with some good fall shipments. But that's management's fault. It doesn't have anything to do with all the work you boys have been doing."

"Just what the hell you planning to do then?"

"I don't know," Katherine answered. She grinned at him, almost catlike. "But so goes the saying, where there's a will there's a way."

The next afternoon, Katherine rode into Chugwater in the buggy with Manny Slaymaker. She had several chores; she also wanted to see Jack Darby. While Manny visited the mercantile, Katherine went searching for the new marshal. She found him sitting on a plank bench under the overhang at the livery. He was watching a painter put whitewash on the new marshal's office across the street. When Blackjack saw Katherine approaching, he got up, pulled out his bandanna, and dusted a portion of the bench. Politely offering her a seat, he told her it was the best he could do unless she wanted to chance getting paint on her; his inner office had been painted that morning. Katherine suggested they go to the hotel and get some coffee.

Blackjack talked. Katherine listened attentively. The preceding day, the new circuit judge, Frank Hupp, had arrived. He administered the oath of office to Darby. Later, they had dinner, and the judge departed for Cheyenne on the southbound. Blackjack opined that Katherine's little ceremony at the ranch had been more enjoyable.

Katherine said that she had heard from Luther that the Poindexter hands no longer frequented the Globe Saloon regularly. She wondered if Blackjack's appointment had anything to do with it.

Darby grinned wider. "Lost interest in me. If they ever did have interest in me. Maybe it was because I went out to Poindexter's place and paid him a visit."

"Mercy! You didn't go out there alone, did you?"

"Oh, I had company, Miss Kate. Fact is, the man is an ol' friend of yours. Jake Cardwell."

Surprised, Katherine said, "Good heavens, Jake! He's the sheriff in Cheyenne, now. He's no marshal, anymore. Whatever possessed him to come up here? Why?"

"I asked Marshal Teague to give me a hand. He had a broken leg, and I reckon he didn't want to send some deputy. He got Jake to come. Says Jake knows everyone 'round these parts. For a fact, he does. Knew me, too. Says he saw me driving you 'round the city in a buggy."

Katherine nodded and reflected. This was a coincidence. The first time she had met Jake, he was sitting across from her in the very same chair in which Blackjack was now sitting. It had been a miserable, rainy day. He was searching for stage robbers. "Did Jake introduce you to Ivan Poindexter?" she asked.

"Didn't have to. The man knew me right off, wondered why in the hell I was riding with Jake. I says Jake's riding with me, and I'm on a social call. Well, Mister Poindexter says he don't want me on his property. Says I should get the hell off. All he has to say to me is good-bye."

"Oh, mercy!"

"So, I says I got something to say to him. I shows him my badge. I told him it was Darby's law in these parts, now.

Told him I didn't want him trifling with the law in any way. His boys go makin' trouble in town, and I'm gonna put 'em in my new jail and feed 'em bread and water till the judge comes up. Jake thought that was funny."

"Poindexter didn't."

"I don't know, ma'am. He just sat down on his steps and held his head. That's when I says good-bye."

"You're off to a good start."

"I like it peaceful, Miss Kate, an that ol' boy looked like a lazy ol' hound when I left. He don't cotton to me, but he's no spoiler, either."

"Orson Coombs may be," Katherine said. "You haven't talked to him yet, have you?"

"Maybe next week. It's a long ride over to Bosler. Have to pack my hot roll to make that friendly call."

"And take a couple of deputies with you."

"Don't you go worrying about Blackjack, Miss Kate. I may be green but I ain't no fool."

Katherine laughed, then sobered, and told Jack Darby about the confrontation she and Jack Cuthbert had the previous day on the upper Laramie. She wanted Blackjack to tell Orson to keep his sheep on the upper half of the range. She didn't want his woolies taking over the lower pasture. She also objected to having her stock chased.

Darby was sympathetic, but he knew the law. He finally said, "Miss Kate, those boys got no right pushing your cows, but if they squatted on that range first, they got first call on the grass. You can't move 'em."

"Damn it, Jack, you know when our stock went in there. You were on the drive, and there weren't any sheep in there, not a one."

"I recollect that."

"Well, can't you put a boundary or some kind of a marker to keep Coombs from coming down too far?"

"I reckon I could do that, but it ain't legal. 'Sides, your cows would pay no mind to it, would they? Heh, heh, heh."

In frustration, Katherine Coltrane stuck her nose across the table and screamed. "Well, what the hell can you do to protect me from that thief? One of his men even tried to bushwhack you. What *are* you going to do for crisesakes?"

Jack Darby's big smile diminished a tad. He said softly, "Talk to him . . . wait till I get some proof."

"Proof! Damn it, we might have had some proof last year.

You went and destroyed it. You killed three rustlers headed right for his place."

"Yes, ma'am, I'm sorry about that, too. But I sure as hell didn't know they were rustlers. I figured they just hated niggers."

Katherine Coltrane sagged in her seat. "I'm sorry," she mumbled. "I'm behaving like a spoiled child. I need a good kick in the ass, don't I?"

"Miss Kate, you know I wouldn't do that. I'm just trying to uphold the law, keeping the peace. Jake says it ain't no easy job. A man just has to do his best, that's all."

"I appreciate that," Kate said. "You're a good man. Please forgive me."

"No need to forgive a woman with spirit," Blackjack replied. "Woman without spirit is nothing but a hunk of hair and a shank of bone."

Katherine went back to the kitchen to get more coffee. When she returned, Blackjack Darby had his smile back. He said to her, "You remember that partner that Alva had, the ol' boy that got shot? He used to work for you. You remember if he wore one of those rings in his ear?"

Katherine took a sip from her cup and looked at him curiously. "Buford? Buford Reasons? Yes. Why, yes, he had an earring, a gold one."

Blackjack chuckled. "Well, Miss Kate, Jake told me a funny story when we were riding along back from Poindexter's spread. He says he was up here a long time ago looking for some stage robbers. I reckon they got away with fifty thousand dollars or so. Jake never did find a thing, 'cept a fool cannon they left behind ..."

Katherine suddenly felt a chill. "Yes ... yes, I recall that robbery."

"Seems like one of them drivers told Jake later he recollected seeing a ring in the ear of one of those fellows when they went around the cannon. Well, Jake had no recollection about a man with a ring, not until 'most a year later. He's always keeping his eye out and his ears open, y' know, and he hears about this Buford ..."

Katherine stiffened and said, "My God, Buford was no robber!"

"That's the funny part of the story," Blackjack went on. "Jake never got a chance to find out. Time he got onto it, some bushwhacker got Buford, and they already planted him."

"And I killed the man who bushwhacked him," Katherine said flatly.

"Yes, ma'am, I heard that story a few times." Jack Darby shook his head and laughed. "I reckon because Buford was an old buddy of Alva's, Jake thought he should have a talk with Alva."

"Jake never knew Alva. He never talked with him as far as I know."

"No, ma'am, but he says he saw him once. Alva was making fence for you. Well, he just figured any ol' man with fifty thousand dollars ain't gonna be making fence for a dollar a day. He sorta gave up his notion. Next thing he knows, those big shots down in Cheyenne offered him the sheriff's job at double what he was making as marshal. He thought that was funny ... said maybe if I hang on long enough, something like that might happen to ol' Blackjack."

Katherine wilted in her chair, but she managed a weak smile. "Who knows what can happen out here? Who knows?"

After Manny Slaymaker returned, Katherine said goodbye to Marshal Darby, who in parting promised he would do what he could to resolve her dispute with Orson Coombs. While Manny waited in the buggy, Katherine went over to the depot. Luther Hatch was busy moving a few parcels that had come in on the noon train. Katherine handed him a message she wanted sent to Henry Givens in Deadwood, and Luther, briefly scanning her writing, disappeared in the little office with the iron grillwork around it. He dutifully began dispatching the message, a rather cryptic one, which simply read: "Will sell Cheyenne house to you for $40,000. Need cash immediately. Please advise me in three days. Love. Kate Coltrane."

Luther finished the dispatch in short order and slipped the note back to her under the bars. In the past, he sometimes had been involved (involuntarily most times) in Katherine's affairs, both business and personal, but this message mystified him.

Katherine noticed his puzzled look. She simply said, "Like it says, I need money. I've been putting too much out and not taking enough in."

Luther replied, "We all need money. It's the age-old curse of civilization, money. I didn't know you still owned a house in Cheyenne. I thought you sold your property down there years ago."

Stuffing the paper back in her shirt, Katherine said, "I did." She pressed a finger to her lips. "Shh. That's all I can say."

Two days later, Katherine received a telephone call from Luther Hatch. An answer to her message to Henry Givens had just come over the wire. Givens had accepted her offer; she could pick up the draft for the money at the Cheyenne Wells Fargo Bank the next day. Additionally, Givens wanted to meet Katherine in Cheyenne on the first of August to sign the necessary documents. Katherine told Luther to send a reply stating she would meet Henry at the Palace Hotel, and that Tim Frawley's law firm would prepare the documents. Katherine was delighted. Everything was falling into place nicely.

The next day, she boarded the afternoon train and was in Cheyenne before Frawley's downtown offices closed. She made an appointment for early the next morning to enable her to catch the ten-o'clock northbound back to Chugwater.

Her second and last stop for the day was at the House of Mirrors. It was shortly after five o'clock when she met Ida Hamilton in the parlor upstairs. They briefly embraced, then Katherine retired to her private suite for the last time. This was the tenth anniversary of her close friendship with Ida, a friendship that had first begun in the dimly lit parlors and rooms of the old Red Bird Hotel and Saloon in Deadwood. Katherine knew it, and Ida knew it—their long relationship was coming to an end.

Katherine poured a glass of wine; she took her usual leisurely bath, scented herself with rosewater, and dressed in a matching pale blue negligee and nightgown. At the House of Mirrors she had no reason to disguise her long, slender feet—she went barefoot. Habit, she thought. In her long-ago night work, she discovered men weren't interested in her feet, and only one man had ever kissed them—Alva.

Katherine napped briefly, and near seven, Ida and Ruby Danforth arrived carrying a small basket of fruit and a napkin-covered platter of biscuits and fried chicken. Instead of using the small dining table, Katherine spread a cloth on the rug, and the three women sat cross-legged facing each other. Katherine pretended this was a picnic. They were no longer young women. When they were together like this, they felt like girls; this was pretense, too.

Katherine's news that Henry Givens had bought the House of Mirrors delighted her two dearest friends. They liked Givens and were anxious to see him again, even though they would work for him only several weeks. They had made one trip to Denver to rent their shop and a four-room apartment above it, and they planned to have the store stocked with dry goods and stylish women's apparel by the middle of September.

Katherine asked if there were a private entrance to the apartment from the back. Ruby told her there was, but its only purpose was to bring groceries into the kitchen, not gentlemen into the parlor. Smiles. Additionally, she never wanted to see another penis in her life. Never? Not even a peek. Maybe a little peek once in a while, but that was all.

Katherine and Ida laughed. Katherine finally said, "But what if a good man comes along, one you really like, maybe even love?"

Ruby Danforth replied, "I've seen a lot of good men, most all of 'em white. Still do. They love me up here. I love their money, but when I meet them on the street, they step by right smartly, like as they don't want to be seen consorting with coloreds. A good man is hard to find."

Katherine shook a chicken bone at her. "Well, when you get to Denver, you just can't quit keeping your eye out for one. Luther says Denver's a big city, lots of opportunity. He has a brother down there."

"Oh, me 'n' Ida, we got a good look, all right. Yes, and some of those men gave us the big-eye, tipping their hats and all. I saw a few high yellers like myself, too, but if one of those bucks goes falling for little Ruby, he better have a big jingle in his pockets. I'm not getting tied up with some no-account I have to make a living for. When I step off that train in Denver, I'm no whore anymore. I'm gonna be a lady just like you, Kate."

Katherine laughed. "I'm no lady, and you know it."

"Oh, maybe Ida 'n' me know it, but most folks don't. You go Sunday promenading down Denver town all fancied up, and who knows what you are or what you been. No one."

Ida grinned and said, "Unless you meet some old trick from way back when."

"Honey," Ruby said, "you just put your nose right high and keep on moving, that's what."

Katherine said, "Maybe when I come to visit, we can all go promenading, not for the men, but for ourselves, just the fun and joy of it."

"Yeah," Ida said dryly. "Three old soiled doves from Deadwood out there showing off their stuff."

The evening sped by. The women laughed together, and they cried together. The lamp wicks were burning low when they finally went to bed.

A young woman brought coffee in a small decanter; she poured, smiled once, and left. Attorney Frederick Dinsmore, his spectacles low on his nose, scratched a pen across a small sheet of paper. After a few notations, he looked across at Katherine Coltrane.

Dinsmore said, "Do you realize the grazing fees on this land over twenty years are considerably less than a purchase price? That is, even if the government agrees to sell?"

"Yes," Katherine replied. "But under grazing rights, I can't fence across the valley, and I'd have to have someone up there all summer outriding."

"Well, you said you want two homesteads to each side of the river."

"I thought if we can establish some kind of a base, it might make it easier to buy or lease the adjacent land. But, damn it, the territory can make just as much in taxes as they can in grazing fees, and I want ownership."

"You want a fence, Katherine," Dinsmore smiled. "That's what you want. You're an exception. Most ranchers dislike fences. They want all the open range they can get, and one of these days we're going to land in court because of it."

"Yes," agreed Katherine. "I want all the range I can get, too. I have no trouble sharing grass with Porter or Jeb Slaughter to the east and north. They don't run sheep or harass my stock."

Resting back in his chair, Frederick Dinsmore slowly sipped his coffee. He stared over the rim of the cup and said, "This may turn out to be a monumental task. I assume, or I should say, I hope the land office has plats on that range. If so, we'll have to lay out what you want, then get a survey crew to mark the boundaries. All of this, of course, has to be predicated on whether our land office friends will even consider a sale."

Katherine said testily, "Frederick, I don't want the whole damn valley. A couple of thousand acres will suit my needs nicely." She stared out the window and added, "I suppose a little bonus to the proper 'friends' might help. Porter once told me the court records are such a mess, no one can understand them."

"Yes, and we've had litigation because of it."

After a moment, Katherine asked, "What's this going to cost me? Oh, not precisely. Just a rough figure."

Dinsmore answered, "I haven't the slightest idea. But we'll start with the two homesteads. They won't cost you a dime."

Katherine Coltrane produced a sheet of paper from her leather-bound folder, and slid it across the desk.

Frederick Dinsmore perused the sheet, then looked up. He recognized one name, Manny Slaymaker. One of the homestead deeds would be filed for him. All of the particulars were listed—his age, place of birth. He was a bona fide citizen. Dinsmore asked curiously, "Who is this Joseph Marat?"

"Joseph Marat is Porter's brother-in-law."

Puzzled, Frederick Dinsmore studied Katherine for a moment. "Joseph? Joseph, the young Indian chap? But he can't homestead. He can't claim land, you know that."

"Ironic, isn't it?" Katherine said. "He can't get one little scrap of land that his people lived on for centuries."

Dinsmore shrugged offhandedly. "The government settled with them, gave them four or five reservations. I didn't make the law, but I have to abide by it."

"Or bend it," Katherine smiled.

"What do you mean?"

"Joseph is more white than Indian." She pointed a finger at the paper in front of Frederick Dinsmore "Look at the names, damn it. His father was Henri Marat. His mother was a breed named Nana. By my way of thinking, that makes Joseph more white than red. He was born at Fort Pierre."

"Do we have proof? . . . just in case."

"That's why I retain you people, Frederick," Katherine replied. "Tim fixed up all of those Chugwater deeds. My name is on one of them, and I can't claim either one of these. As you say, it isn't legal. Porter can attest to Joseph's parents.

Their daughter was his wife. Joseph has a birthright. You make it so. Rig it anyway you can, but make it so."

Frederick Dinsmore chuckled. "Katherine, you're in the wrong profession. You should have become a solicitor."

"In a way, I once was." She drank the last of her coffee, then stood. Katherine offered her gloved hand, and Frederick Dinsmore kissed it. From her folder, she pulled out another piece of paper. "Henry Givens bought the House of Mirrors. He'll be down here the first of August. Would you please make out a transfer of ownership. Ida Hamilton is no longer the owner."

Dinsmore gave a thin smile. "Yes, indeed."

Several weeks before Christmas, Joseph Brings Yellow rode in from the Circle-W spread. He was bundled in a sheepskin coat, had on a pair of mittens, and wore a wool scarf under his hat. He had a small leather bundle for Katherine. Mary Slaymaker brought Joseph a mug of coffee, and he and Katherine sat crosslegged in front of the fireplace. She gave him a curious look and asked, "A gift for me?"

"Yes, Tall Woman, a gift for you."

"Christmas comes early."

"You are worthy," Joseph smiled. "If I were your man, I would give you a gift every day."

"Oh, Joseph!" She kissed his cheek. "I do love you."

"Yes, I know . . . like a brother."

As she unwound the leather binding, Katherine said, "You do remember the old ways, don't you? A gift bound in leather, how nice, Joseph."

"Not from me," he said. "From your daughter, Blue Star."

Katherine's eyes came up. Pressing the bundle to her breast, she said, "Oh, you already went to Pine Ridge! You took the clothing, the little things? Oh, mercy, how is she? What's the news?"

"I did everything you wished," Joseph replied. "She is well. So is Grandmother White Bone, but her bones ache. They have plenty of robes. The lodge is secure. Men bring firewood. The Blue Elk watches over them. The agent, McKittrick, watches over them, too." He grinned. "I told her about the white man's Christmas last spring, about the prophet, Jesus, his birthday. She thought it was a good legend. She has a keen mind. She forgets nothing. This is her Christmas present to you."

Katherine unfolded the leather. "Moccasins! How beautiful!" Smiling through her tears, she said, "Yes, she forgets nothing, Joseph. She remembered how big my feet are." Katherine pulled off one of her boots and slipped her slender foot into the moccasin. "Perfect, Joseph, just perfect."

"To see you smile, Kate, is worth the train ride. I don't like the train. It's for white men, not Indians, but in the winter, I like it a little better." He grinned again.

"If you were with your old people," Katherine said, "you would be a chief, maybe a holy one of wisdom."

"A chief, yes. A holy one, no." Joseph pointed to the piece of leather. "There is a second gift, Kate. Julia made you a picture."

Katherine held the leather up to the light of the fire. A picture, indeed! It was beautifully colored, the drawing of a young woman in a white elk skin dress trimmed with fur and fancy beadwork. "Oh, mercy," gasped Katherine. "How wonderful! I'll hang this on a wall. It's much too nice to put away."

"Julia drew it. She says it's a picture of her in her new dress."

"The dress. Bleached elk hide?" Katherine stared at Joseph. "Grandmother White Bone? She doesn't have skins, anymore. How did she do this?"

"It was Porter's idea," Joseph replied. "The elk we shot last winter. Porter had two of the hides tanned and bleached in Cheyenne. I took them up with the rest of the gifts this spring."

"Oh, my dear Porter . . . and you. I love you both."

"Look closely. What else do you see?" Joseph asked.

After a moment, Katherine sighed, and her eyes glazed again. "Yes, my necklace. She's wearing my necklace. She's smiling, too."

"Ei, she's happy. You see, she wanted you to know this is the way she looked last summer. She became a woman."

Katherine blinked at Joseph. "She . . . she went through the ritual of womanhood? My little girl, Julia, a woman?"

"Yes, Tall Woman. Wicapi Hinto is fourteen winters."

Katherine leaned her head against Joseph's shoulder and softly wept.

Chapter Twenty-three

Gunfighters

Chugwater, September, 1886.

Katherine Coltrane's sharp eyes hadn't deceived her. She ordered Manny Slaymaker to stop the buckboard so she could take a better look. At a shallow bend in the distance, George and John Crippen were sloshing around in the Chugwater River. The men had a team hitched to a big wagon, and in the bed of it, she saw rocks and logs. She also saw a wall several feet high extending into the river. The Crippens were building their dam. Katherine gritted her teeth; she thrust her firm jaw out, and after one final glare at George and John Crippen, she told Manny to get the hell into Chugwater.

Katherine seldom read any emotion in the dark face of Marshal Jack Darby. The man's perpetual smile, his foggy chuckle, and his lackadaisical mannerism all contributed to his mask of indifference. He had been smiling when young David Coombs fell dead from a bullet in the chest. That same grin was on his face when someone tried to bushwhack him, and he even smiled when she complained about sheepherders chasing her stock. Mercy, he was impossible!

Marshal Darby was smiling now. After she had spilled out her story about the dam construction, he said easily, "Miss Kate, it must be hotter than the hubs of hell down in that river bottom this afternoon. Hot enough right here under the shed. You look all hot, too. What we need is a cool drink. I ain't seen your pretty face 'round here for three or four days." He took her by the arm. "Come on, I'll buy you a sassafras tea over at Luther's."

"My ass, sassafras!"

"A beer?"

"I didn't stop by to discuss the weather, damn it," Katherine said. "I know how hot it is. What are you going to do about that dam?"

"You want to join me in the hotel?" he asked.

"Oh, what the hell!"

"You're a nice lady, Miss Kate."

"Don't sweet-talk me, buster."

They walked to the Star Hotel, Katherine angrily kicking a few dried horse biscuits along the way. Marshal Darby's stride was more of a graceful glide. He never hurried.

One of Luther's sodbuster women employees brought two bottles of ale and glasses, and after pouring, Jack Darby touched his glass to Katherine's and asked, "To the weather or to your health?"

"How about to business? The business of water rights."

After a long draft, Darby smacked his big lips and said, "You ain't irrigating, are you? You need a head of water coming into your place right now?"

"Of course not."

"Well, I sure don't see a problem then."

Katherine set her glass aside and said, "There's going to be one helluva problem, Mister Darby . . . with me if you don't get your butt down the river and explain the law to those nesters."

"Did you take a look at their corn crop? You see the size of those roast 'n ears? Ain't no bigger than a cuke. Had good water all summer and they ain't no bigger than cukes."

"It's the topsoil, not the water," Katherine said. "They're wasting the water, that's what."

"They got some rights, too."

"A damn small share, not the whole river, not as much as they want, for God's sake." Her green eyes sparked. "Are you going to tell them, or am I going to get some of my boys busy with a stick of dynamite?"

"Heh, heh, heh. Now, Miss Kate, don't go talking foolish-like."

"All right, what then?"

Marshal Darby leaned back. He stretched out his long legs and clasped his hands behind his head. After a moment, he said, "I was thinking, why not just let those ol' boys make their dam. Now you ain't needing that much water, anyhow. Toting them rocks, that's hot work, regular swamp work. Probably take 'em another two weeks to finish. Say, 'long about then I'll mosey on down and tell 'em to tear half of it out."

Katherine's jaw went slack. "Why, that's terrible, Jack. That's a damn dirty trick. Why don't you just go down there now and get it over with ... tell them to stop their nonsense?"

"Cause I told 'em when they first started piling those rocks. I told 'em it was a'gin the law, and they told me to get my black ass off of their property." Jack Darby chuckled. "Let the damn fools work their white asses off. Those Miss'ous ain't got a lick of sense, anyhow. Come spring, high water's gonna roll the rest of the rocks outta there like a bunch of marbles."

Three days later, Katherine Coltrane took the train to Cheyenne to finalize the upper Laramie Valley transaction. She was elated. Frederick Dinsmore was very casual and businesslike, but she knew he shared her feeling. Within two months, Tim Frawley's best attorney had completed a business coup that Katherine thought would take five or six months. Additionally, he had the two homestead deeds.

Dinsmore unfolded a copy of the plat. Lined in red ink was a large area extending from below the eastern foothills to the slope on the west side of the valley. Two small squares also were marked in red, these along the curved line representing the river. Including the homesteads, Katherine's new land totaled 1,820 acres.

Katherine signed several papers. Dinsmore handed her two more. One was a small parchment with an official seal imprint on it attesting to the birth of one Joseph Marat. The other was a statement from the firm of Frawley, Dinsmore, and Williams. Total cost—$22,500. Katherine never asked for an itemized accounting; she wasn't interested in the legality or illegality of Dinsmore's expeditious work. He had done the job. She wrote a check and signed it with a flourish. She kissed Frederick Dinsmore on the cheek and left.

That evening, Dinsmore, Henry Givens, the new proprietor of the House of Mirrors, and Katherine Coltrane had a champagne dinner at the Palace Hotel.

In mid-September, six huge rolls of barbed wire arrived at the Coltrane siding. Katherine was determined to get the wire stretched before late fall. Winter was out of the question, and by spring it would be too late, her men too busy with calving and moving stock. Worse, Orson Coombs might have sheep on the Laramie again. Katherine also had another problem—the roundup for fall shipments to markets in Omaha and Abilene. She arrived at a partial solution. She decided to fence part of the Laramie Valley property. It would take a week or so. Her men could push the Laramie herd ahead of them on the way out.

Two days after the wire arrived, Katherine had four rolls lashed onto her wagons. She had two tents, hoodlum and cook wagons, and six men: four from the K-Bar-C and two from the Circle-W. Porter Webb and Joseph Brings Yellow had come over to help. On September 17, the party headed down the Chugwater River to where it merged with the Laramie. They made camp at dusk about five miles up the canyon. Several hundred cows were grazing the area, a few K-Bar-C brands among them, but most belonged to Jeb Slaughter.

The next morning as Katherine and her crew moved up the river, they encountered isolated bands of her stock. Most were working their way down the grassy canyon slopes toward the Chugwater Valley. By later afternoon when the wagons rolled across the great flat below Katherine's new range, there wasn't a cow in sight. There wasn't much grass, either. Sheep droppings were everywhere—Coombs's woolies had grazed the mountain meadows almost bare, but the sheep and their herders were gone.

Before dark, Jimmy Reynolds and Curly Bledsoe located one survey boundary marker on the east side of the range. Katherine said she would begin the fence line at this point. Joseph Brings Yellow found eight markers near the river, these indicating the two homestead parcels. The next morning after breakfast, the west boundary was discovered. Katherine's men had their line; they went to the hills and started cutting posts.

Through heritage and experience, Joseph Brings Yellow was very observant. In his search along the west side for pole wood, he discovered an unusual phenomenon. Along the edge of the range close to fringes of pine and juniper, he crossed a trail of cattle tracks. It appeared that thirty or forty cows and calves had moved along this fringe of cover. This in itself wasn't so unusual. What puzzled Joseph was that these cattle were headed south up the valley, not downriver like the rest of the herd. This was contrary. It took him only a few minutes to discover why—three pony riders were driving them.

Several other tracks intrigued him, too. They were not the padded prints of coyotes—they had been made by dogs—two dogs, he determined—moving back and forth ahead of the ponies. It was very clear—in several places the dog tracks had been partially covered by the prints of shod ponies. Joseph calculated the trail was three or four days old, but he continued to follow it for several miles. When he turned back for camp, there was no doubt in his mind—rustlers were at work again. The only cows on this range belonged to the K-Bar-C and Slash-S spreads. These cows had been stolen; they were headed for sale somewhere to the south or southwest.

When Joseph related what he had discovered, Katherine Coltrane exploded. Dogs! Orson Coombs had dogs—sheepdogs! Infuriated, she was prepared to ride down to Bosler for a confrontation. Porter Webb intervened. He was upset, too, but he reminded Katherine that she hadn't come all the way up the Laramie to chase rustlers . . . rustlers who were now long gone. She was a ramrod; she had two or three weeks of hard work ahead of her; her hired hands depended upon her. If this were Coombs and his men at work, Porter, by experience, knew how they were most likely to operate. Porter had a beef sandwich and a cup of coffee. He lashed on his bedroll and rode for the little pass above Bluegrass Creek. Marshal Blackjack Darby was about to earn his salary.

Jack Darby wasn't surprised at Porter's news. In fact, he had been expecting it. He began saddling up. He told Porter that he had two reports on his spindle of rustling in the McFadden and Medicine Bow areas northwest of Laramie. It was just a matter of time before the Coltrane and Slaughter outfits were going to be hit. However, unlike Katherine Coltrane, Darby wasn't convinced Orson Coombs was behind the Laramie Valley rustling. Granted, the rancher had a shady past, but from what Blackjack had learned from Marshal Henry Teague and Sheriff Jack Cardwell, Coombs had been running a clean operation for the past six or seven years.

"Coombs ain't stupid," Jack Darby told Porter. "He ain't likely to be stealing stock so damn close to his backyard."

"One of his men took a shot at you, didn't he?" Porter countered. "The man has every reason to get back at you and Kate. Kate was with you at the Star when you killed his kid, and he doesn't much like her crowding his sheep on the upper Laramie."

"I got no proof, Porter. Got no proof it was Coombs's people who took that shot at me."

"Proof?" scoffed Porter. "Who in the hell else would try to bushwhack you?"

"I don't know, but my bones tell me not ol' man Coombs. Maybe friends of those three boys I shot up last year. I just don't know."

"They were drifters looking to make a few bucks."

Darby slipped a couple of half hitches around his bedroll, then looked at Porter. "Yes, suh, but I always wondered where they was going. Miss Kate got on my ass about that, too. Said if I hadn't killed them, they could have followed them right to Coombs's place. Heh, heh, heh."

Porter Webb remounted. "What are your plans?"

"Gonna take me a ride into Cheyenne town, first," Darby replied. "Catch on with Marshal Teague. We'll ride up to Bosler, find out where those cattle came down if we can . . ."

"Law, Jack, those tracks are four days old! That's what Joseph said. Once those men get to the big valley, likely they'll get themselves lost in a thousand tracks."

"Likely," agreed Darby. "But if those boys head to Laramie, they'll be in the soup. Since that thieving up Medicine Bow way, Marshal Teague has some men watching 'round Laramie. *Ree*-ward, Mister Porter, *ree*-ward. Everybody likes that green stuff."

"Coombs used to go the other way when he filched open range stock . . . Rawlins."

"Long time ago, Porter, long time ago." Darby hiked into his saddle. "Say, you care to ride along? . . . sorta look after Miss Kate's interest in this? I'd be obliged 'case ol' Teague says his broken leg still aches. We might have to take the choo-choo up to Rawlins. 'Less I have some company, they might take me for one of those colored porters. Heh, heh, heh. A porter, eh?"

Porter Webb grinned. "I'd be obliged, Blackjack."

Marshal Darby and Porter stabled their horses at Jed Bollinger's Cartage that night. They had a talk with Marshal Henry Teague, who agreed to accompany them. After a good-night's sleep at the Grant Hotel, Darby and Webb met Teague at Templeton's Café for breakfast. Shortly after nine o'clock, they went to the depot. They were carrying bedrolls, and slung over their shoulders were rifles sheathed in leather scabbards. Several people stared.

Rolly Anderson came from inside the ticket cage and gave them a jovial greeting. "Time off for a little hunting in the Medicine Bows, gentlemen? It's that time of year. The bulls are snorting."

Marshal Teague answered, "Yes, Rolly, I reckon you can say that, a little hunting."

Marshal Jack Darby tipped his hat to Rolly Anderson. "I'm with them," he grinned.

"Oh, pshaw, Marshal Darby! I know that. How's Miss Kate these days?"

Darby looked at Porter Webb. "Mister Porter, here, says she was ill of sorts yesterday . . . got those ol' rustlin' blues."

"Well . . . I hope . . ." Rolly Anderson stared at the three smiling men. "Oh, pshaw!" he laughed. "Hunting? Yes, I understand."

A few minutes later, the Union Pacific westbound chugged into the station. At nine-thirty it left. No one would mistake Jack Darby for a porter—he and his two companions sat in the first car behind the engine with the mail clerk, a free ride courtesy of Rolly Anderson.

The men didn't go to Rawlins. About eighty miles up the line, they got off at Rock River where they rented three horses at the livery. They rode northeast about ten miles, and shortly after two o'clock they were atop a ridge looking down into the Laramie Valley—Porter figured Katherine Coltrane and her men were fencing thirty miles away.

It took another half hour before they discovered cattle sign—sign that Porter Webb thought was somewhat confusing. Undoubtedly, these were the tracks Joseph Brings Yellow had followed farther down the ridge. But at a small draw to the left leading down to the headwaters of the Medicine Bow River, the riders had split. A lone rider and two dogs trailed off toward Bosler; the herd of cattle and the other two men had taken a trail to the Medicine Bow River.

Porter gave Marshal Teague a curious look. "Now, that's a strange one." He nodded toward Bosler. "We all know what's down there. What the hell is the other way?"

"Rawlins," Teague replied. "About a hundred and fifty miles."

"What about in between?"

"Just what you're looking at . . . coulees, grass, flats, and the mountains." Teague pointed. "Anvil spread below Medicine Bow. They lost some cows a month ago. Ed Riggs. Over there to the north, Flat Iron. Up on Little Sheep Creek, the Frying Pan, fella by name of Jake Willets. That's about it."

"I hate like hell the thought of following tracks west," Porter Webb finally said. "We could be on these shitters all the way to Rawlins."

"That's possible."

Marshal Jack Darby reined his horse to the right. "Come on, gentlemen. I think we're gonna have to ride down and have a word with ol' man Coombs. See if he has a cow-chasing dog with a white eye."

"White eye?"

"Yes, suh," replied Darby. He chuckled and shook his head. "Miss Kate says one of those hounds at the herder's wagon last spring had a white eye. Had it on her like a spell all the time she was chewing on those two boys. I said it was the ol' evil eye. She didn't think that was so funny, said something about her days with the Injuns. Superstitious, I reckon."

Orson Coombs had a faded-gray clapboard house. It sat on a flat bordered by ash and cottonwood trees. A large log barn was in the rear, and this was surrounded by an assortment of flat-board pens and several pole corrals. Big white chickens were pecking around the barn. Bleating sheep were everywhere else. Porter and the two marshals rode in from the back, not by design, but simply because Coombs's house faced east; the men were coming from the western foothills. Even so, they had been seen by one of Coombs's Basque herders.

Jack Darby now wondered if he had been mistaken about Orson Coombs involvement in the rustling. Perhaps Coombs had reverted to his reputed old tricks, yet from all appearances, he certainly wasn't raising cattle—not a cow in sight.

There were a few horses, though, and two of them in a rear corral immediately caught the sharp eye of Porter Webb. Reining up, he carefully scrutinized them, then turned to Darby. "I doubt if we'll find any rustled cows on this place, but he's got two of my horses." Porter pointed. "That mare . . . the young spotted colt. I helped foal that colt last spring, sired by one of my Appaloosa studs. Now, how does that strike you, Marshal Darby?"

"Right peculiar," returned Darby. "That ain't your mark on their flanks, is it?"

Porter took a second look. Then Marshal Teague spoke up. "Frying Pan brand. Just a big flat burn with a handle on it. Willets's mark, blotted right over your Circle-W."

Blackjack grinned at Porter. "Maybe Coombs stole 'em from the Frying Pan 'stedda you."

"We'll damn soon find out," replied Porter. He turned his horse and headed for the distant house. Darby and Teague followed.

Orson Coombs, resting in the shade of his front porch, was waiting for them. He had a shotgun beside him. His wife, Bertha, Ivan Poindexter's sister, was in a chair next to the door. A rifle was propped up against the wall behind her. Faith Coombs, a twenty-year-old daughter, framed herself in an open window. Their hostility was obvious. None of them had met Jack Darby but the moment he rode up to the hitching rack, they knew who he was. This was the man who had killed David. Lawman or not, he was their enemy.

Initially, only Marshal Teague spoke. He knew Orson Coombs. Porter Webb vaguely knew the sheep rancher but had never spoken with him. Teague said, "Afternoon, Orson."

Coombs didn't move, nor did he return the greeting. "Don't bother to step down," he said. "State your business and get out."

"This is Marshal Darby from Chugwater," Teague began.

"I know a colored man when I see one."

"And Porter Webb . . ."

"Get on with it," growled Coombs.

Marshal Jack Darby was the one who got on with it. In a slow, deliberate voice, he told Coombs about the trail of cattle coming off the distant ridge, how the tracks trailed to the west, and how one of the riders and two dogs had come down toward his property. And another matter had unexpectedly risen. Porter Webb claimed two horses in the back corrals belong to him, a mare and a mixed Appaloosa colt.

Coombs didn't bat an eye. Without turning his head, he yelled, "Elridge, get out here!"

Elridge Coombs had been inside listening. He shoved the screen door and walked onto the porch. Elridge was twenty-two, and except for his blond hair looked strikingly like his late brother, David. He had a .45 caliber Colt Peacemaker on his hip.

Orson Coombs's eyes were still on the three mounted men. "Tell these men where you got that mare and colt back there."

"Billy and Orville gave 'em to me."

Jack Darby asked, "And who's Billy and Orville?"

Orson Coombs answered. "Two of Willets's youngsters from the Frying Pan. Been herding for me off and on this summer in their spare time. Two of Jake's boys. That answer your question?"

Jack Darby smiled and nodded. "Yes, suh, I reckon it does. They been 'round lately working for you?"

"Work's been done a week," Coombs said. "They came back today for their tally." For the first time, Coombs turned his head. "Orville? Billy?"

One young man opened the screen door. He edged over and stood to the side of Elridge Coombs. Coombs looked to the side. "Where's Billy?"

Orville scratched nervously at his unruly jack-straw hair. "Billy left."

Jack Darby, shifting in his saddle, grinned at Orville. "You wanna tell me where you came by those horses?"

Orville shrugged. "Found 'em, we did. Strays I reckon."

"Yes, suh, and were did you find 'em?"

"Over the hill yonder."

"Chugwater country?"

"That's right."

"Long way for you to be riding, son," opined Jack Darby. "Sheep wander over there? What you been up to lately?"

Orville Willets shrugged again. He had no answer.

Orson Coombs stirred impatiently in his chair. He suddenly got up and gave it a furious kick to the side and shouted, "Goddamn it, what the hell you boys been up to? Answer this man! You told me those horses were Frying Pan stock. You didn't say a damn word to me about fetching 'em on open range. Not a word. You 'fuss up! You boys stole 'em, didn't you?"

"Aw, paw . . ."

Then Marshal Teague intervened. "Those cattle, Orville . . . did you and Billy move 'em over to the Frying Pan last week?"

Jack Darby finally ignored Orson Coombs's order to sit his saddle; he slowly dismounted. So did Porter Webb, but their boots had no sooner touched the ground when Bertha Coombs cried out, "Don't you touch my boy! You leave him be, hear?" She had her rifle raised. It was pointed at Marshal Darby. "You killed my David! You can't take my baby!"

"Kill him, Mama!" screamed Faith from the window. "Kill the black bastard."

Orson Coombs took a big leap and slammed Bertha against the wall. Suddenly, there were two explosions, one from her rifle, the other from the pistol of young Elridge Coombs. Orson, hit under the chin by the rifle slug, slumped to the floor. Blackjack Darby felt a hot flash in his shoulder. He spun around once and grabbed for his revolver. Before he could pull it, two more shots sounded. Porter Webb had fired. Elridge Coombs and Orville Willets, both with .45 caliber pistols in their hands, flew backward. Elridge fell on the porch; young Willets crashed through the screen into the parlor. Only his legs stuck out, doing a quivering death dance.

Marshal Henry Teague said it was the worst mess he had ever seen in his fifteen years on the frontier. Orson Coombs, his son, Elridge, and Orville Willets, age nineteen, were dead. Marshal Darby had been shot through the left shoulder and almost died before Porter Webb got him to the hospital in Laramie.

Two days after the shooting, Marshal Teague and four deputies from Laramie and Rock River rode to the Frying Pan Ranch. They took Billy and his father, Jake, into custody. Orville Willets was the second son Jake had lost within two years. Jake Willets told Teague that his oldest, Thad, was one of the three rustlers killed on the lower Laramie River by Blackjack Darby.

The lawmen spent a half day sorting out rustled cattle—a total of one-hundred-sixteen from four different ranches. Thirty-eight head belonged to Katherine Coltrane.

Chapter Twenty-four

The Hoop

Coltrane Crossing, May 1888.

It was the wettest spring Manny Slaymaker could ever recall, and Luther Hatch concurred. There was intermittent rain for almost a month, but it was only the prelude. A three-day deluge in early May swelled the creeks, sending an already swollen Chugwater River spilling over its banks. The water swept away the last remnants of George Crippen's dam; it rushed over the greasewood flats and furrowed fields leaving a brown muddy slick in its wake. The Crippens were engulfed by sludge, and their ford over to the Chugwater road was impassable for five days.

Some of the K-Bar-C men braved the Coltrane Crossing below the railroad trestle to deliver emergency supplies to the beleaguered farmers. However, on May 16, the George and John Crippen families gave up. They deserted their homesteads, loaded two wagons, herded their dairy cows ahead, and began the long journey to Oregon. George Crippen said he was going to be a fruit grower. He had no animosity toward Katherine Coltrane; he was just one of many beaten men, yet more fortunate than most—Katherine gave him $500 to help defray trail expenses.

Though the heavy rains played havoc in the bottom, they rejuvenated Katherine's Bluegrass range. Only a few black snags from the old range fire remained. The slopes were now covered with a rich mantle of green—the nutritious forage had been renewed. When Katherine's hands finished moving in the cattle, she sent Curly Bledsoe, Jimmy Reynolds, and Jack Cuthbert up the Laramie River Trail. They drove two wagons filled with supplies. They were going to build a log barn and lay the foundation for a two-room house, a house the Tarkalson brothers had been contracted to finish by late July.

Several days after Katherine's work crew departed, Porter Webb and Joseph Brings Yellow arrived trailing two beautiful horses Joseph had trained for cow cutting. Jeb Slaughter was the buyer. Porter was dismayed when Katherine told him she was building a small house on the Laramie, but it didn't surprise the veteran rancher. Nothing Katherine did surprised him; it just flat-out pained him.

They were sitting around the table on the front porch eating a small meal Mary Slaymaker had prepared. Katherine tried to explain that her new enterprise was entirely logical.

"I have a stake along that river," she said. "I aim to protect it. When I have stock over there, I want a man or two around. I can't be chasing over to the Medicine Bow or who knows where trying to get my cows back. It's too damn much trouble."

Joseph soberly commented, "Big trouble when men die."

"Stupid young men."

Porter, perhaps better than anyone, knew the tenacious and gritty ambitions of Katherine Coltrane, her penchant for seizing any opportunity. But there *was* a limit. And this Laramie Valley acquisition had been more out of spite than necessity. Porter said, "You're extending yourself too much, woman. You have more land than you can afford or use. You're running skinny on help, too."

"I'm not shorthanded."

Porter grunted. "Why in the hell are you always calling me on that damned telephone then?"

Katherine pushed her plate aside. With a defensive air, she retorted, "Well, there are circumstances sometimes, aren't there? I surely never refuse you a hand when you need it." And as if needing confirmation, Katherine looked at Joseph. "Do I?"

"What Tall Woman says is true."

Porter wasn't persuaded. "You have way more problems than I do ... too many. And you're asking for more. You just can't set aside summer range for a rainy day. You have to utilize it to make it pay."

Katherine watched Porter place a piece of cheese on his bread. He eyed it critically, then put a slice of pickle on top. Satisfied, he took a big bite.

After a moment, Katherine went on. "You could help me solve some of these so-called problems. I've had this notion for some time ... just a notion, but it could help." She hesitated.

Porter swallowed. Touching a finger to each side of his mouth, he gave her a suspicious look. "It'll be a cold day in hell when you don't get a notion, Kate. You've had 'em right regular ever since I've known you."

"Tall Woman is a thinker," Joseph said.

Spearing another piece of cheese with his fork, and without looking up, Porter said, "You're close, Joseph. More of a stinker, I'd say."

Katherine Coltrane puffed up like a prairie chicken. "Hah," she huffed, "you enjoy my little stink! You love me ... both of you, and you know it. You just can't ever bring yourself around to admitting it. You're afraid to."

"I admit it," Joseph said.

"Great! You see?"

"But Tall Woman is too old for me."

"Wagh!" cried Katherine. She kicked under the table with the toe of her boot.

With resignation, Porter said, "All right, let's hear it. Let's hear about this latest notion. What the hell is it this time?"

Katherine assumed an elfin look. She put her elbows on the table and cupped her chin. Almost talking through clenched teeth, she said, "Solve a lot of problems if we latched up the two outfits, wouldn't it?"

Porter wasn't too sure he heard her correctly. "What?"

"Latch up. Combine the ranches."

"Oh, law!" Porter moaned.

"Not so good?"

"It stinks, Kate, it stinks."

"I stink, you said, not my idea."

"Both, woman, both."

Katherine said, "You're not thinking, Porter. We join ranches, we join work forces. If we put the two spreads together, don't you realize what we would control? Mercy! Everything from the Laramie to Hawk Springs. Good heavens, it's more than sixty miles across there!"

Porter Webb emitted a forlorn sigh. "Kate, I do like you. You've done well, a helluva lot better than some of the men in the territory. Fact is, one time I had a notion, too ... thought I loved you."

Katherine raised her brows in surprise. "Really? Mercy,

after all these years, a confession?" She glanced over at Joseph Brings Yellow. "Did you hear what he said?"

"I don't believe all that I hear, only what I see."

Porter's eyes crinkled at the corners. "A notion, I said. You were a good-looker, and I reckon you still are. It could have been a notion somewhere besides my head."

Katherine tilted her head and put a palm to her cheek. She said saucily, "I just might have obliged your notion, honey."

Porter replied, "And that would have been more trouble." Holding up a hand, he added, "What I'm saying is you've put a harness on everyone that's ever gotten close to you. Now, hold on a minute. I'm not saying they've been the worse for it. I'm just saying it won't work on me or Joseph. We know you too damn well."

"I said I love you both."

"Damn it, I know it, but you know right well neither one of us would ever hold still for such a thing. You've always been your own person. You've got a big heart and a good mind, but Lord love you, you're just too damn independent and self-serving for anyone to handle. You're a calculating woman." Porter sighed again. "What's worse, when someone falls into one of your little traps, they don't seem to give a damn. They just go down with a shit-eating grin on their face. No, Kate, latching up the spreads just wouldn't work out for either one of us. I'm a stubborn, independent bastard myself. If I wasn't, I sure as hell wouldn't be here jawing at you like this."

Katherine Coltrane fell silent. Porter had never expressed himself this way before. He had chastised her. He had once given her a violent shake when she was sobbing uncontrollably after Thomas Clybourn's troopers had freed her from the Oglala. But he had never cut her to the quick this way. Seldom was she at a loss for words. She was now.

"I never realized I was such a bitch," she finally said.

"Oh, shit!" Porter cursed. "You're no bitch. You're a damn fine woman. That's the whole nut of it. You're too much of a woman."

Katherine managed a faint smile. "Too much for you to handle?"

"There's nothing I can't handle, and you know it."

"Why don't you marry me then?"

"You'd have me in the kitchen churning buttermilk in a week, that's why."

Katherine looked at Joseph Brings Yellow. Joseph said, "I would like to see that."

One afternoon in late July, a buggy came through the main gate. A man in a white straw hat and linen suit handled the reins. Katherine, fresh from a bath, was sitting on the porch combing out her damp hair. She had spent the better part of the day driving a mule that pulled the overshot stacker. Initially, she thought it was Frederick Dinsmore, but no, Dinsmore wasn't that stout; he never came without an appointment, either. Moments later, she heard a hearty "hello." Simultaneously, she recognized the voice and the gentleman—it was Henry Burlingame.

Katherine was delighted. She wanted to shout out "Burly," the way Jane Canarray once addressed him. She didn't. It was "Henry, come on up. It's good to see you again."

Henry Burlingame immediately apologized for his unexpected visit, explaining that he attempted to telephone her from Chugwater. No one had answered. Haying, Katherine told him. Everyone was out of the house, even Mary Slaymaker, who had men in the fields to feed.

Katherine, fussing at her hair, excused herself. She directly returned. A beautiful silver comb held her hair back, and she carried a tray with glasses and two bottles of beer. The beer, she said, came from the cellar. It probably wasn't as cold as the stout Henry had once hidden in Goose Creek. Burlingame had almost forgotten about that episode, the long-ago time that Calamity Jane had drunk his beer and ultimately invited him to her wagon for entertainment. In recall, he laughed heartily.

Burlingame told Katherine he only planned an afternoon visit; he was going to stay in Chugwater overnight. He was on his way to the old outposts of Fort Laramie and Fetterman. The latter fort had been abandoned, but a rowdy settlement had taken its place. With a chuckle, he said he had finally decided to write a story on the notorious hog ranches at Three-mile, Six-mile, and Fetterman before they disappeared entirely from the Western scene.

When Katherine looked surprised, Burlingame said, "Scandalous, yes, but an important part of the so-called 'Wild West.' People have stories to tell. I listen. When the stories have some substance to them, I write."

"Yes, I know," Katherine replied.

"Within the parameters of propriety, of course."

"Of course."

Henry Burlingame smiled. "Yours is a most intriguing story, Katherine. Fascinating."

"You've already touched upon it, Henry."

"Yes, I have," Burlingame admitted. "An incomplete story."

"General Armitage accused you of making me into some kind of Joan of Arc. That's what he said."

Burlingame scoffed. "Nonsense, Kate. Women who compete with men, particularly those few who manage to win the game, always interest our readers. I'm not a fabricator. The facts speak for themselves." He paused in reflection, then said, "I saw Jason Armitage not too long ago in New York."

"How wonderful!"

"Yes, we had a nice chat." His eyes twinkled. "Are you planning on a visit this fall? Philadelphia? New York perhaps?"

"Ah, he told you."

"Yes, I think such a visit would be appropriate, a great adventure for you."

"He invited me."

"A remarkable invitation, sending a palace car to pick you up, a steward and cook, to boot. My gracious, Kate!"

"I have obligations here."

"Dash the obligations! Free yourself from the drudgery of this place for a month or so. You've bloody well earned it. I daresay you've never had a holiday in your life."

Katherine sighed. It was true. Except for one short trip to Denver to see Ida and Ruby, she had never been anywhere. "I'll think about it." She then told him there wasn't any need for him to stay in Chugwater for the night. She wanted him to take supper at the ranch; there were three vacant bedrooms upstairs. In fact, there wasn't any necessity for him to return to Chugwater at all—she could flag the northbound at the Coltrane siding for him.

Burlingame expressed surprise. "The train will stop?"

"You bet your boots, it will," Katherine said. "It will for *me*."

Because of Burlingame's visit, Katherine took the next morning off. Breakfast was leisurely and late. Manny and

Mary Slaymaker, friends of the writer for more than ten years, joined Katherine and Henry in the dining room. Afterward, Katherine and Burlingame took their coffee out to the front porch. It was only several hundred yards to the rails and the river below. Beyond this, part of Katherine's hay fields were visible. Burlingame exulted. There were colorful patterns in the distant fields, ribbons of cut grass, verdant patches of ripe meadows, and a few huge mounds of newly stacked hay. It looked like a beautiful painting, something created from an artist's brush. He recalled that he had once overlooked this valley from the porch with Joseph Brings Yellow, with the fields dark purple, the sky ablaze with a million stars and a velvet moon. Day or night, Burlingame confessed to Katherine that when he visited, he always felt in harmony with the world.

Out of the trees along the river, they saw three horsemen in file. The riders came to the rails and dismounted, then led their horses across the two sets of tracks. Slowly, they began the ride up the slope to the house.

Henry Burlingame said, "A respite from the early-morning sun, perhaps? Some of your hired hands?"

Leaning forward, Katherine squinted. "No, I don't think so. That one in the front looks like Porter, that damn saddle slouch of his."

"Ah, a pleasant surprise," Burlingame enthused. "One of my gunfighters. I haven't seen the rascal in several years, you know."

"Don't ever let him hear you call him a gunfighter."

"Oh, my, no. Discretion, Kate, discretion."

Katherine put her coffee aside and stood. "It's Porter, all right. That's Joseph behind him. I don't know who the other fellow is." She looked back at Henry. "I wonder what the hell they're up to? Porter always calls me when he's headed this way."

Burlingame said, "So do I, but I've learned the telephone is not always the most reliable of instruments."

A few minutes later, the trio was near the hitching rail below the porch. Porter Longstreet Webb crooked his arm. The palm of his hand faced outward in Indian fashion. "Morning, Kate. Henry, good to see you again." As he swung a long leg over the saddle, he said, "Brought along a friend."

Both Katherine and Burlingame stared. The friend sitting behind Joseph was almost his counterpart in dress, denim shirt and leather vest, denim pants and boots, and a drover's hat. There was a broad smile on the youngster's tanned face.

Then Joseph Brings Yellow held up his hand. However, his greeting was entirely different from Porter's. It was Siouan. It was poetic and beautiful, but Henry Burlingame didn't understand a word of it. He did know it was something very significant.

"Hau kola. Memeya wan cicugon. Wanna puyakwakage-lo. Hechetu welo, winyan, hechetu welo." Joseph gestured to his companion, then motioned to Katherine Coltrane.

Katherine returned haltingly, *"Hau, hau, waon welo, pila miya."* Suddenly in a state of shock and near collapse, she seized Henry's arm and wailed, "Oh . . . oh, merciful God! Oh, mercy . . ."

Burlingame held her for a moment. "What is it? . . . what's he saying?"

The moment was over. With an anguished cry, Katherine bolted down the stairs.

Porter Webb looked up at Henry Burlingame. "Joseph told her that what was prophesied he has brought. The circle, the great hoop, hasn't been broken. It's finished. It's all over, Henry. He says he's brought Kate new life."

"The young chap?"

Porter smiled broadly. "Better take a hard look, Henry. That young chap is Joseph's beautiful woman. She's come over the mountain to live. Her name is Julia . . . Julia Marat. An Oglala. But there's a helluva lot of Coltrane in her, too."

Excerpts from an interview with Henry Burlingame.

Oh, I can't remember all of the places I've visited in that big country. I can tell you this, though ... that day when Julia came home with Joseph Brings Yellow was one of the most memorable, poignant experiences of my life out there. So long as I live, I'll never forget those precious moments in front of the porch that morning. The sight of those two lovely women embracing and crying is indelible in my mind. I think God blessed me to bear witness to it.

The grandmother? I think White Bone was her name. Certainly, I believe that had something to do with the girl's return. The grandmother had died that spring. But I had a talk with the agent, Rudy McKittrick, that fall before I returned to New York. He said Julia had her bonnet set for Joseph since the very first day she saw him. I thought, my God, she couldn't have been more than nine or ten years old. Then, McKittrick told me something I'd always known. But one tends to forget. Indians are very patient people.

You asked about Blackjack Darby. Well, that was an interesting story, too. Two years after the summer of eighty-seven, I met Jack Cardwell on the street in Cheyenne. This big Negro was with him. Jake made the introduction, but before he even began, I knew the man was Darby. Blackjack Darby was one of his deputies.

Yes, I went back to the ranch, several times in fact. The last time was in ninety-three. Things never seemed to change in that place. It was still beautiful. Joseph and Julia came over from their home on the Laramie. He was breeding cutting horses and running a few cattle. They had a daughter, Sunshine. Well, this occasion happened to be one of those feasts that Kate always seemed to enjoy hosting. Jason Armitage was there, too, visiting for a week, and we were the guests of honor at the dinner. Sunshine. She must have been four years old.

Well, I was a little tired that night, and I retired early. When I was on my way to my room, I chanced upon another little moment I'll never forget. I stopped by the door, the bedroom Kate had always called "Julia's room." There was this little girl dressed in a pretty nightgown. She and Kate were singing. Kate was on the floor, and Sunshine was in the little rocker. She had that big doll in her arms rocking her to sleep. Oh, I tell you, I didn't tarry. I didn't want to intrude.

No, that was my last visit. I never went back. I just couldn't manage it with my bad legs, this bit with the cane. I did hear from Kate. She and Porter went up to Jane Canarray's funeral in Deadwood. She wrote me about that.

Oh, what a land it was in those days! It was high, wide, and handsome, and at times, extremely ugly. Yes, it was always very big. Most of the time, very lonely, too.

You are invited to preview
the new historical novel
by acclaimed author
Paul A. Hawkins ...

TOLLIVER

available from Signet in October 1994.

Fort Conner, Dakota Territory, September, 1865.

"Where in the hell did this buck come from?" asked Sergeant Burns. Sergeant Edward Burns, a medical aide, glared at a dazed, young Oglala brave who was sitting near the door. The Indian was bleeding profusely from a bullet wound above his right knee.

"Two of the boys dumped him there," replied Delbert Carnes. Carnes was a corporal; he was also an aide assisting the two surgeons in the rough-hewn log infirmary at Fort Conner. Corporal Carnes said, "He got shot the other side of camp ... stealing horses, I reckon. Some of his buddies got away."

After another contemptuous stare, Sergeant Burns said, "Well, drag his ass outta here. We haven't got time to go fooling around with Injuns. It's against regulations. Why in the hell didn't they finish him off in the first place? Damn this place! We got a bunch of idiots 'round here."

With a hapless shrug, Corporal Carnes said, "All right, whatever you say. He'll be bleeding to death, anyway." Carnes moved toward the door.

One of the army doctors at a nearby table turned. As Corporal Carnes lifted under the young Sioux's shoulders, the officer spoke. "Let's take a look at his leg." Then to Sergeant Burns, the doctor said with a nod, "Sergeant, give Carnes a hand. Get the chap on the table."

From a second table, Major Calvin Mudd looked up. Wiping his bloodstained hands on a towel, he said, "Good Lord, Tolliver, whatever are you doing? The sergeant's right. That scoundrel shouldn't be in here, and he's no concern of ours." Major Mudd motioned to Sergeant Burns, then to a heavily bandaged soldier on the table in front of him, "Get this soldier to a bunk, first."

Captain James Tobias Tolliver moved from his table over beside the stricken Sioux brave, knelt and briefly examined the leg wound. To Carnes, he said, "Here, help me get him up." Together, they lifted the young man to his feet and laid him on Doctor Tolliver's table.

"You've gone daft, Tolliver," Major Mudd said, shaking his head. Mudd leaned over and also inspected the wound. "Bone may be shattered. No exit. The lead is still in there. Waste of your time, James . . . against regulations, too."

Sergeant Burns, moving away with Major Mudd's patient, muttered, "Fellows back there ain't gonna be liking a hostile bedding down beside them, Captain. Likely the buck might be responsible for some of 'em being here in the first place." Burns, with the wounded trooper in tow, disappeared to the back where the long room was lined with plank bunks and hay-covered stretchers. A dozen men were there, suffering from an assortment of ailments, ranging from arrow and gunshot wounds to scurvy and malnutrition. General Patrick Conner's Powder River expedition against the hostile Sioux and Cheyenne was nearing a miserable end. Except for raiding several Arapaho villages, the general's military adventure and his orders "to hunt the Indians down like wolves," had failed. During the long hot summer, the hostiles had managed to outmaneuver him at every turn. The new fort he had built and named for himself had Sioux, Cheyenne, and Arapaho on all sides of it. He was now preparing to abort his campaign and withdraw to the safety of the big walls at Fort Laramie, two hundred miles to the south.

Major Calvin Mudd shook his head despairingly again. "I don't know what's got into you, James. We'll have to make a report this afternoon. Whatever am I going to say?"

James Tolliver gave him a sad grin. "Put it down under humanitarian aid. First, I'm a doctor. Second, I'm a soldier. I'm committed to saving limbs, maybe lives, too."

"The enemy?"

"Oh, come on, Cal," sighed James Tolliver. "Are you forgetting how many rebs we treated at Shiloh? For God's sake, the color of a uniform didn't make any difference, did it?"

"They were white men," countered Calvin Mudd. "Not savages."

"The young man is a human being, a life, and life is a precious commodity anywhere. You only have one to give. Isn't that how the saying goes?"

Doctor Mudd took another look at the brave's wound. "Nasty. If you get it stabilized . . ."

"I'm not amputating," Tolliver said. He looked into the eyes of the young Oglala; they were fixed, unmoving. "He's either damn brave or scared to death."

Corporal Carnes said, "He's damn lucky, Captain, that is what he is. By rights, he should be dead, you know. He's no kid. He's over twelve, ain't he?"

Doctor Tolliver began cleaning the wound; the warrior flinched several times, then groaned and closed his eyes. Yes, the young man was over twelve, probably eighteen or nineteen, and indeed, he was lucky. Some soldier had forgotten to do his duty, had disobeyed General Conner's orders—"Kill every male Indian over twelve years of age." Of course, Tolliver himself was disobeying orders—treating a hostile, and within full view of two subordinates and his superior officer.

With the assistance of Corporal Carnes, Tolliver went ahead; he probed; he fished out a lead ball; he plucked out a few bone splinters; he sutured and closed. It took twenty-five minutes, but he didn't use a saw. He had severed too many limbs in his six years of surgical work; he was deeply satisfied; he had saved this young man's life. All Tolliver had to worry about now was infection. And Sergeant Burns was right—he couldn't leave his patient in the post infirmary alongside the trooper patients. So, James Tolliver had Sergeant Burns and Corporal Carnes carry away the Oglala brave on a stretcher. They housed him in a supply shed behind the cook's quarters. Tolliver got a disapproving glare from Sergeant Burns—aiding and abetting the enemy was contrary to all rules and regulations. Dr. James Tobias Tolliver sighed with resignation. So what? The campaign was over. Everyone but two companies of galvanized Yankees was leaving for Fort Laramie. So was he. He was tired.

Until the next campaign, he had seen enough young lives wasted.

James Tolliver was twenty-eight; he had served two years in the war between the states; he had reason to be weary. With only two years of his commission remaining, assignment to the Army of the West had not been of his choice. He had hoped for a post at one of the medical facilities closer to his home in Philadelphia. He went reluctantly to Fort Atkinson, then to Fort Laramie, eventually into the command of Patrick Conner, an ambitious general seeking to enhance his reputation as an Indian fighter. (General Conner had gained some fame for a battle against the Paiutes in Utah in 1863. His troops had surrounded a large camp on the Oregon Trail. A total of 278 men, women, and children were slain by Conner's soldiers.)

This night Tolliver was particularly tired and weary. He reclined on his cot and listened to his companion, Major Thomas Stubbs. A good cavalryman, Stubbs was one of several aides to General Conner. Admittedly, the Powder River campaign had done little to enhance the reputation of the general. His thrusts against the hostiles had been badly blunted by the cunning of the Hunkpapa chief, Sitting Bull, and Red Cloud, the leader of the Oglala. Not only had the chiefs outwitted him, in most cases they had out-fought him. Discouraged and suffering unexpected hardships, some of General Conner's troops had deserted. Others were in such poor physical shape, they were unable to fight effectively.

Major Stubbs, puffing a corncob pipe, told Tolliver that undoubtedly General Conner was in for a severe reprimand from headquarters in Omaha. Certainly he wasn't going to get a second star for his effort in the Powder River country.

"That's bad enough," Stubbs said. "Now you go putting salt in the wound by taking one of the enemy under your wing. You've turned out to be a bleeding heart, and the old man doesn't like bleeding hearts. Oh, it's most admirable of you, sure, James, saving the youngster's leg, but it's entirely unorthodox. Yes, and without any consideration of the consequences to your career."

"I've always been unorthodox," returned Tolliver.

"You're also one of the best surgeons out here."

"What consequences? Boot me out?" For a moment,

James Tolliver's dark eyes twinkled. "Say, Thomas, I wouldn't mind that."

"Demotion. Ridicule for insubordination. The old man taking out some of his outrage on you. That sort of thing. Unpleasant business, I'd say."

"A pity. Blame the poor doctor for misdirected deeds."

Major Stubbs purred. A blue stream of smoke floated across the dimness of the small room. "Yes, a misdirected deed of your own, too." He paused, then looked over at Tolliver. "By the way, how is your young patient? Does he know what's going on?"

"Hmph!" Tolliver snorted. "Who cares? He's on the mend, if that's what you mean. I told some of the boys to take him a meal this afternoon. They didn't. I did. He muttered something entirely unintelligible. Perhaps a thank you, I don't know. Some fool had bound his wrists with rope. I took the ropes off so he could eat. I left them off. I helped him outside to take a leak. I took him a blanket for the night."

"He's a prisoner of war," Stubbs reminded.

"He's not going anywhere on that leg."

"The old man doesn't take prisoners."

"If the boy's my obligation, then that's the way it will be, Thomas. He's not out of the woods yet."

"Yes, and he may not get out of the woods," Major Stubbs replied. "The general wants him off the post. He has no room for prisoners of war. He doesn't want to feed the boy, either. We're short on rations." Major Stubbs took another puff on his pipe. "Rather an either and or, I'd say."

"Either or what?"

"Get him out of here or watch him shot for stealing horses."

"Nonsense!"

"Not my words, James."

"By gadfrey, we'll be leaving here in another two or three days!" exclaimed Tolliver. "What difference does it make?"

"Do you want to talk to the man about it?"

James Tolliver gave Stubbs an incredulous stare. "An Englishman talking to a hotheaded Irishman? Not on your life, not when he has the upper hand, I don't," Tolliver groaned. "Why in the hell does everyone make so much of this? One damn Indian with a bum leg! Good grief, the old man must have more important things to think about the way the hostiles have been kicking his butt."

"That's just it," mused Major Stubbs. "His ass is sore enough already. The fact that he's harboring one of those redskins responsible for his condition just rubs him the wrong way." Stubbs pointed his pipe at the door. "We've got to get that Indian out of here, James."

Major Stubbs went to eat supper. Captain Tolliver didn't. Instead, he rested back in his bunk and dwelled on what Stubbs had told him: "We have to get that Indian out of here." Obviously, there was some credence in this, but Stubbs hadn't contributed any ideas of how to get the Indian out. The "we" was only a matter of expression, and Tolliver was resigned to the fact that it was solely up to him to get the deed done. Under normal circumstances, the young Oglala probably could escape on his own. Surveillance around the fort was shoddy; with six cannons and two hundred men positioned inside, there was no fear of the hostiles attacking. They only picked on the troopers when they ventured away from the fort, or attacked the supply trains and escorts. This had been their usual game, and they were very good at it. The problem was that Tolliver's Sioux patient couldn't walk. Even riding a horse would be excruciating. And Tolliver had some fear that any extended riding might bring about more bleeding from the young man's wound.

After a few more minutes of deliberation, James Tolliver got up from his bunk. He stretched and yawned. He searched around in his duffel and found an extra shirt and pants. He had no spare boots, but he pulled out a pair from under Major Stubbs's bunk. He bundled all of this into a ball and tucked it under his arm. At Major Calvin Mudd's quarters, he spied a cavalry hat; he took this, too. Someone had left a gun belt with holster and revolver suspended on a wall peg by the door. He quickly fastened this around his waist. Once outside, he cached the clothing at the rear of the cook's quarters. He strode boldly over to the hitching pole next to the teamsters' barn. There was no use in trying subterfuge; this had to appear very deliberate and official. He did have time on his side—it was near dusk and most of the officers and men were at mess.

At the barn, he was greeted with a casual salute from a young man in boots, baggy trousers, and a badly soiled undershirt. "Riding the perimeter for the officer of the day," Tolliver said. "I need two mounts ... taking a scout with me."

"Yes, sir," the man answered. He pointed down the line. "Take any of them, but begging your pardon, don't those Pawnee have their own horses?"

"Chap says his pony is lame," lied James Tolliver. Without looking back, Tolliver led the two horses away. He threaded their reins through the wooden handle of the shed, picked up the bundle of clothing, and quickly ducked inside. One small window illuminated the interior. Directly under the window sat the Sioux brave, an empty plate to the side of him. Tolliver smiled. Obviously, someone had fed the young man again.

Squatting in front of him, Tolliver placed the bundle of clothing on the floor, then examined his bandage. There wasn't a stain on it, and Tolliver smiled again and said, "Good."

"Good," the youngster repeated. *"Wašte."*

"Friend," Tolliver said. "I am your friend."

"Friend. *Kola.*"

James Tolliver nodded. "Yes, friend. You catch on fast. If you could stay around here a few weeks, you'd probably speak better English than most of the soldiers." Placing the clothes in the brave's lap, he added, "Here, get dressed. Ready or not, we're taking a little ride." Tolliver made a few motions—riding, winding, going away. He positioned his hands in the shape of a tipi. Home, going home. He touched the brave on the chest. "You go home."

However awkward the sign, the brave understood. He nodded once and momentarily stared at the clothes. He gave the hat a flip with a finger and frowned. "I know, my friend," Tolliver said. "I know just how you feel. It's a disgrace, but damn it, it's the only way." After a few more gestures, he helped the brave to his feet. He had to help dress him, too.

The brave's mouth drooped, and he shook his head. "Good *Wašte.* No good."

Once outside, James Tolliver gave the Sioux a boost into the saddle. In return, he received his first grin. Yes, it felt good to sit in the saddle, but smiles were deceiving. Tolliver knew it hurt like hell. He also knew this young Indian would never admit to pain. Tolliver said, *"Wašte,* eh?" With a motion, he reined away, and the brave followed. In the evening dusk, they rode out from behind the building toward the gate. Here, a salute, the gate wedged open, and Dr. James Tolliver and his scout moved briskly toward the river bottom.

The next morning, Captain Tolliver had breakfast with several of his fellow officers. It was to be his last. By nine o'clock he was escorted to General Conner's office where Major Thomas Stubbs, standing next to the general's small field desk, read off the charges—one, insubordination; two, theft of U.S. Government property, one horse and accoutrement; three, aiding and abetting a prisoner of war.

General Patrick Conner's face was florid. He was a master of brevity. "How does the captain answer the charges?" he asked.

"I helped the young man," admitted Tolliver. "I didn't think he deserved to be shot a second time for trying to steal a skinny horse."

"So you took it upon yourself to steal one for him?"

"Borrowed. I'm not a horse thief, General."

General Conner exploded. "It was an act of treason, goddamn it! You're a traitor. That horse you stole was mine!" He slapped his hand on the desk. "Confined to quarters. Court-martial proceedings to be held at Fort Laramie upon return of this command. Dismissed."